MURDER
ON THE
WHITE CLIFFS

A POSIE PARKER MYSTERY #8

L. B. HATHAWAY

WHITEHAVEN

WHITEHAVEN MAN PRESS

London

First published in Great Britain in 2020 by
Whitehaven Man Press, London

Copyright © L.B. Hathaway 2020
(http://www.lbhathaway.com, email: permissions@lbhathaway.com)

A CIP catalogue record for this book is
available from the British Library.

ISBN (e-book:) 978-0-9955694-9-2
ISBN (paperback:) 978-0-9929254-9-9

For those who love the White Cliffs

PROLOGUE

It was too dark, too dangerous, to be out on a night like this. Any fool knew that, and whatever else Elsie Moncrieff was, she was no fool.

But still, here she was.

It was past eleven o'clock, and the November rain lashed down unforgivingly. She was certain that no-one had seen her leave. She'd locked the door of her flat in the staff quarters and walked briskly along the unmade gravel road running parallel to the beach. The tide was out and yet the foaming sea-spray from the breakers was carried on the wind to her in heavy salty slaps across the face.

She'd hurried past the blackness of the 'village' on the beach: past the Bay Bungalow and the holiday cottages, past the Excelsior Tea-Rooms, all catering for fashionable summer visitors; everything now shuttered and sleeping in wintry darkness.

All except the exclusive Bay Hotel.

The Bay Hotel boasted of being open year-round, but it was an exaggeration really. Elsie knew it well: knew they operated only a skeleton staff during November, the most unpopular month. Tonight only a few lights blazed out as she passed. Right in front of the hotel some local lads had built up a great mass of driftwood ready for Bonfire

Night next week, and Elsie carefully stepped around it. Occasionally she turned her flash-light on, just to check where she was going, but she snapped it off again each time, within seconds.

Elsie hadn't bothered with an umbrella, the wind made it impossible. No handbag either. She was wearing head-to-toe black oilskins, and she moved like a shadow through the storm.

A dog barked in the nothingness. The pulsing rays from the South Foreland Lighthouse, located further on towards Dover, did little tonight to break through the darkness. A couple of times Elsie thought she heard something crack behind her, a twig maybe, but when she turned, abruptly each time, she was quite alone. She chided herself momentarily for her nerves.

She'd turned away from the old smugglers pub on the beach, The Green Man, which should have stopped serving at ten o'clock, this being a Sunday, but which was still open.

Elsie hadn't taken the steep road which would lead up to the safety of St Margaret's-at-Cliffe, the village. She turned instead up the sharp precipitous lane which was Beach Road, passing the boarded-up black silhouette of Maypole Manor, heavy in its isolation. She headed on to the very top of the cliff, to Ness Point. Elsie's face was stinging by now, dead-cold, but she barely felt the discomfort.

Her fingers brushed against a piece of paper in her pocket, picked up from her own door-mat as she had left tonight, with her boss's handwriting on it. But she immediately disregarded it. Anything from Petronella Douglas could wait. Could wait forever.

Elsie turned her torch on once she was on the cliff-top, keeping it trained on the ground. She'd arrived at the place.

Here.

A bench.

Placed fairly near the edge of the cliff for the fine views over the English Channel, the bench was set back among a scrabble of gorse and low, twisty trees which had woven a sort of dense canopy over and around the seat, providing a place of safety. But the bench didn't seem quite so safe tonight; the wind whistling, the rain even worse up here on this outcrop.

Elsie was obviously the first to arrive and she flung herself down on the seat, drawing breath, surprised at the effort the fifteen-minute walk had taken out of her.

Where was he?

Had she come to the right place?

Was he, even now, waiting for her elsewhere? The man with whom she had such a connection, to whom she was inextricably bound. The man she had yearned for and keened for these last few months.

The note hadn't mentioned the cliff-top specifically. Nothing about Ness Point at all. It had been short.

**The usual spot. Come alone.
Half-past eleven tonight.**

The note had come like a bolt out of the blue this morning, totally unexpected. But the timing was perfect. Things were changing here fast.

The darkness, the wind and the rain, the storm all around, this position atop a cliff right at the very edge of England might have unnerved some, caused them to turn and run. But Elsie Moncrieff was tough, tough as you like.

Elsie told herself this now; repeated it like a precious mantra.

Reminded herself how well she had done here: how working at White Shaw in St Margaret's Bay for the famous Fashion House, Douglas & Stone, was a dream job which most women could only ever hope for.

But dreams could become nightmares, couldn't they?

And now Elsie was ready to leave. She just had to hope that her way out remained open.

As she waited for him, she thought how much she had missed him. Her other half. Gracious, a few months ago she had even written to that fancy Private Detective, that woman, Miss Parker: whose knack at solving crimes was equally matched by a photogenic rapport with the British press; whose huge-eyed beauty was often to be found staring out from the pages of newspapers and penny magazines. But Elsie had heard nothing from her by return. Not a dicky bird. Probably for the best, looking back.

And then suddenly the bench seemed to shift underneath her, re-adjust to an added weight.

He was here.

He'd arrived out of the night with no torch, no warning. Just like her, a spirit on the wind.

She'd sensed his presence before she saw him; the lemon tang of him perceptible even through the sea-salt spray. But hang about: there was something else here, wasn't there? Something just tangible. A woman's scent which wasn't natural or subtle.

A *town* perfume. An expensive perfume which Elsie recognised. A few of the women she knew wore it.

So was there a woman here too?

And as she turned to her left in the driving rain she breathed a sigh of relief. He was quite alone. No woman.

She saw from his outline that he was wearing a black oilskin coat with a high, funnel-necked sweater below, like a fisherman. He had a sou'wester hat on his head and he was staring ahead, out to the blackness of the sea. Because she knew him of old, she saw the worry etched in every line of his being.

'Filthy night, isn't it?'

When he spoke she was reminded of her childhood, the language of that time, when she had been a small, pig-tailed girl. The familiarity of it made her feel achingly sad. She was reminded too of the glory days, when they'd worked together so well, before. Nearby. When there had been three of them.

'I didn't mean for us to meet up here in the middle of a storm. It's hardly ideal.'

'No matter. I'd have traipsed through hell and high water to meet you. You know you can trust me.'

He turned to face her at last. 'But can I really, Elise?'

Elise?

She couldn't see his eyes, the bright blue which she knew so well, but she could hear the ice in his voice. Elsie frowned, perched forward on the bench. 'You haven't called me that in years. No-one has. I'm Elsie. Just "Elsie". Shorter, simpler. Better. You know that.'

For a few seconds he didn't answer.

'You were our golden child, Elise. Do you remember your little dolls? Your singing, your dancing. Your opera! You were so talented. Before we were here. Before all of *this*. This mess…'

Something was wrong.

Elsie stared at him in a dawning horror. 'What are you talking about? *What* mess? I've done very well here these last three years, in difficult circumstances. Are you here to tell me I've done something wrong?'

The man didn't answer immediately. But then he made a show of getting to his feet, and he pulled Elsie up with him, their raincoats slipping and sliding as they held on to each other.

'Not you, Elise. But it's a mess all the same. Look, we're in danger. Let's walk, shall we? Somewhere more hospitable. I had the strange idea that I was followed up here; I hope my message to you wasn't intercepted. That pub looked like it was still open. Shall we head there? Who would stop us?'

'*What* danger?' Elsie spat out a hoot of laughter. 'I don't care anyhow. I'm leaving. But I suppose you know that?'

The man stopped, pulled up short, so she nearly bumped right into him. And then came the anger. She shone her torch at him and watched in surprise as his beautiful, sun-tanned, rain-spattered face was riven with fury.

'What's happened to you, Elise? I *know* you wrote to Posie Parker by the way. And missing the all-important event last night? What on earth are you up to?'

'Is that why you contacted me? To scold me?'

He took her by the shoulders, but gently, sadly. 'Of course I'm not here to scold you. You're in danger, Elise: real trouble. We all are. *That's* why I came. I've been close at hand, watching things unfurl. I needed to warn you, if it was the last thing I did.'

'Liar!'

Confusion and anger bubbled over and Elsie shone her torch in his eyes on purpose, blinding him. He grabbed at it and they struggled, grappling together. He won and it went rolling off into the undergrowth somewhere.

'Now look what you've done.' Elsie was on her knees, scrabbling frantically. The flash-light belonged to Tony Stone. Which meant it was expensive: the best of the best. Elsie had borrowed it without asking. And Tony would surely miss it if she didn't manage to retrieve it.

She called out to her companion: 'Help me, won't you?'

And it was just at this moment that Elsie Moncrieff sensed a furtive shadow darting out of the undergrowth, smelt the strong town perfume yet again, and felt a sharp sudden push at the back of her slippery oilskin coat.

A powerful hand.

She yelled out, pointlessly, and then she was rolling, over and over, like a child's rubber ball bouncing down steps. Except these were no steps, and she was no child's plaything.

Terror engulfed her in that split-second, but the urge to survive was stronger, forcing herself to *think*, to *calm down*. In a minute this would all stop.

Someone would save her.

'*Elise!*' she heard him scream from behind her. 'No!'

In a flash she saw him lit up by a beam from the South Foreland Lighthouse along the coast, and she saw he was no longer alone. A woman was beside him, shouting.

Sodden chalk and wet grass and stones and seeping water were slipping past her in a nightmarish blur as her hands clawed at the air, but found no purchase.

And then suddenly she was falling, falling through the air, through a symphony of shadows, hundreds and hundreds of feet downwards.

The White Cliffs she had come to love were rushing past her, and she was engulfed in the roar of the sea below.

And in that nightmarish arc of a disaster Elsie – or *Elise* – heard him screaming up above, and all she knew next was blackness.

****

PART ONE
Bonfire Night
(Tuesday 4th November
to Wednesday 5th
November, 1924)

One

Richard Lovelace, forty-something and handsome in a gingery way, was standing in his shirtsleeves in the hallway of his fiancée's top-floor Bloomsbury flat, supervising a team of men who were carting out box-loads of another man's possessions.

It was taking an age.

At his feet were several tins of Manders' Quick-Dry pink paint in differing shades, ranging from spun-sugar through to fiery salmon, which he suddenly felt like kicking at. The Decorator was having an extended cup of tea in the kitchen, having been directed smartly to get out of the way.

Lovelace groaned at the passing Foreman. 'Dash it all, Smith! Hurry the blazes up, won't you?'

He had tried to stop himself checking his wristwatch every couple of minutes, tried to stop himself looking irritated, but now he cracked. Richard Lovelace was the recently-promoted Chief Commissioner of New Scotland Yard, a sought-after Police Detective whose ready laugh and gentle humour hid a razor-sharp wit and first-class mind. He had an impressive history of catching the capital's most hardened criminals, and he was in the middle of a high-profile case involving a raid on a jewellery shop on Bond Street.

Lovelace really needed to be at his desk right now on this cold November morning, prepping for an important meeting on the Bond Street case, taking place in one hour's time. Not here.

But his fiancée was Posie Parker, London's premier female Private Detective, and he loved her more than life itself. He'd have done anything for her. Quite literally. They were getting married soon and all this hanging around was part of *that*: the plan to have a future together.

It had been obvious to Lovelace when he proposed marriage to Posie four months previously that she would never in a million years agree to move to his suburban home in Clapham where he and his toddler daughter, Phyllis, resided. Posie would have to be dragged kicking and screaming out of her beloved Museum Chambers flat first, and that was no way to begin a marriage, was it?

So he'd tentatively suggested that they all move in *here* with Posie. It had been the only thing he could think of. And Posie had agreed readily, happily. Probably out of sheer relief that she didn't have to move, Richard Lovelace now thought.

The Bloomsbury flat was definitely big enough: four bedrooms, a large lounge, a modern kitchen, a nice central location, right next to the British Museum, with the shops and schools of Holborn and Covent Garden on the doorstep. It *needed* to be big enough: not only was there himself and Phyllis to move in immediately after the wedding, but there was also the small matter of Richard's Russian Housekeeper, Masha, and a waif-and-stray orphan baby, born very small and sickly, named Katie, whom Lovelace had adopted during the summertime and who would also need to move in with them when she was eventually discharged from Great Ormond Street, the hospital which had been expertly looking after her.

The wedding had been roughly pencilled in for Christmas-time. And this place had to be made ready first.

Rooms cleared. Re-decorated. One room in particular.

In Posie's not-so-distant past she had been the high-profile partner of Alaric Boynton-Dale, the celebrated Explorer: a glamorous and aristocratic adventurer whose exploits and dashing good looks had captured the hearts and minds of the nation. Whose death a year ago while abroad had caused outpourings of grief and filled column after column in the British newspapers.

Alaric had 'lodged' with Posie for more than a year, keeping a self-contained bedroom in her flat, rent-free, for using in between his expeditions. When he had died, Posie had locked his door, and the room hadn't been opened up again until this morning. And now crates of Alaric's clothes and rugs and maps were all being carried away, bound for the Royal Geographical Society in South Kensington, to whom Alaric had bequeathed all of his personal belongings on death.

This big job of clearing Alaric's messy room – which was essentially a beautiful and huge light-filled space with a stunning view over the London skyline – had been in Richard and Posie's diary for ages. The removal men had been booked and paid for, the Royal Geographical Society ready and waiting to start sorting through Alaric's treasures, the Decorator paid in advance.

Together they had decided that Alaric's old room would become the new nursery. A big room for Phyllis and Katie to share. There was even a small adjoining room which would perfectly suit Masha. A lick of pink paint and some sturdy child-proof iron bars at the window was all that was needed. And a trip to Gamages on High Holborn to buy some beautiful new toys to make it seem fresh and inviting: a compensation for Phyllis who was trading in her old home with its familiarity and its garden, neither of which she would have at Museum Chambers.

Simple.

Plain sailing.

Only of course it wasn't.

Lovelace glanced around at Posie's beautiful pale-green living room, with its expensive dark-wood drinks cabinet and framed hieroglyphs hung above the fireplace. He remembered that this was where they'd been when they'd discussed it all; planning things out, two months back. He frowned now at the memory.

It had been an August evening, but the air had already grown chilly and was smelling of autumn, the fire had been lit and was throwing flickers of shadows up the walls. Rare time alone for them, without Phyllis. The sofa which held them both like a strong ship seemed alone and rudderless on a candle-lit sea.

Posie had been on his lap, in his arms, the silk of her gown fluid against the roughness of his stubble, the scent of her Parma Violet perfume heavy in the air between them.

He'd been anxious about the move to Museum Chambers. And he'd said so.

'But Posie, are you sure it's not going to be too much of an intrusion? This place is beautiful. It's so very *you*.'

'And now it will be so very *us*. All of us. You; me; the girls; Masha. I'll even put the fancy glassware away if it worries you. We can re-do this room, make it special for *us*.'

'No, dearest one. No.'

'I insist, Richard. We'll choose the colour of the walls together. Anything other than pale green, eh? I'll put those hieroglyphs into storage and we'll buy new decorations in the new deco style. Or maybe we'll just have a great big wedding picture of us up there in its place instead? Darling love, please stop looking so worried about it all. That beautiful red hair of yours will all turn grey in an instant and then I'll feel terribly guilty.'

But before she could reach her mouth to his and cover his dear, familiar face with a hundred kisses, he said it:

'And Alaric's room? Will you open it up or will I? It's obviously something of a Pandora's Box for you, darling, and no wonder. But it seems to me the sooner it's dealt with, the better.'

Posie had nodded slowly. 'Absolutely. It's been laziness, really. It's quite time. You book the men and I'll just let them take everything in one go. I'll oversee it. We might as well paint the walls at the same time. Don't you think? We'll be nice and efficient.'

And then had come that tide of longed-for kisses and he'd given himself up to her at last – couldn't resist, just this once – and then he'd booked the removal men and the Decorator, forgetting about it all until late yesterday afternoon.

And then – yesterday – the plans for today's flat clearance had been abruptly changed.

They'd met in his office at New Scotland Yard – a new office, bigger, as befitted his new status, with a view out across the street-lights of the Embankment and the Thames – with Posie turning up unexpectedly at four o'clock, bounding in, clutching at a newspaper, looking wildly excited. Feverish almost, under the unbecoming pea-green shades of the institutional glass lamps.

Lovelace had groaned inwardly, because he knew whatever news was coming, it wouldn't be about to make his life easier.

Posie had flung herself in the chair opposite his own, sending a cascade of his important photographs of the Bond Street scene-of-crime spilling onto the floor. She had jabbed at an inside page of *The Times*.

'Richard, darling, it's just the perfectly oddest thing. Look at this.'

She slid the newspaper across the desk to him and he took it half-heartedly, like a man being handed a poisoned chalice. The front page showed the news of that day's General Election results: the landslide re-election of the conservative Stanley Baldwin as Prime Minister. There was a large photograph of Baldwin without a hat on, looking dishevelled somehow, despite wearing obviously expensive clothes, an eyebrow raised – as if in surprise at his good fortune – with his pipe clamped in the side of his mouth, in his trademark style.

'No, no, darling. The next page.'

Page two was busier, the stories cramped together. Most of the space seemed to be given up to Italian news, with stories of riots and anti-fascist protests taking place in Rome against Benito Mussolini's government. Posie reached over the desk impatiently and jabbed right down at the bottom, on the far right: a tiny thumb-nail box which almost vanished in the crease of the paper's centrefold.

'There. See?'

'Blink and you'd miss it, darling.' But he had frowned as he read the tiny news-report, tugging his fingers backwards through his thick hair as he did so.

Posie sat waiting, all a-jitter on the edge of her chair.

The story was short.

GIRL FALLS OFF CLIFF: ST MARGARET'S BAY, KENT

THE INQUEST WILL BE HEARD AT DOVER TOWN HALL TOMORROW (WED. 5TH NOVEMBER, 12 NOON) INTO THE TRAGIC DEATH OF MISS ELSIE MONCRIEFF, OF WHITE SHAW, ST MARGARET'S BAY. HER BODY WAS DISCOVERED VERY EARLY YESTERDAY MORNING (MONDAY 3RD NOVEMBER) BY A DOG WALKER.

MISS MONCRIEFF, HOUSEKEEPER TO THE FAMOUS FASHION DESIGN DUO, DOUGLAS & STONE, DIED ON SUNDAY NIGHT, 2nd NOVEMBER, IN INEXPLICABLE CIRCUMSTANCES. IT IS CURRENTLY BELIEVED THAT MISS MONCRIEFF ACCIDENTALLY FELL

OFF THE TREACHEROUS CLIFF KNOWN AS NESS POINT DURING A BAD STORM LATE AT NIGHT, BUT THE CORONER HAS (UNUSUALLY) RECORDED AN OPEN VERDICT.

IT SEEMS THERE MAY BE MORE TO THIS ACCIDENT AT THE CHIC RIVIERA RESORT OF ST MARGARET'S BAY THAN MEETS THE EYE. WE WILL BE REPORTING ON ANY DEVELOPMENTS.

Lovelace had looked up and raised an eyebrow. In truth he had had simply no idea why Posie should find this news so fascinating.

'Mnnn? What about it?' He was suddenly distracted by his pile of fallen photographs and also by his two secretaries who were gossiping too close outside his open door; friendly voices talking about stupid things. He needed to crack on.

'What is it, darling? Is it the Fashion House connection? That married couple who are never out of the press? Douglas & Stone? Don't tell me you know them? A slippery pair; something to do with the Prince of Wales, aren't they? Very unsuitable pals for him. They hardly seem *your* usual calibre of celebrity friends and acquaintances, I must say...'

Posie had huffed and puffed. She had got up and closed the door sharply.

'No, I don't know them and I've never met them. I don't go around collecting celebrity friends, by the way. My interest here is nothing to do with *them*. But don't you remember? I *told* you a few months back that I had received a very odd letter from a woman at St Margaret's Bay, in Kent. It was very late July, I think. I mentioned it specifically to you as we had worked on a case down there together some years back, remember?'

Lovelace frowned. 'Maypole Manor? That great house on top of the cliffs?'

'That's right. Although Maypole Manor has been bought and sold and bought and sold again since we were there three years ago. It's now unoccupied and I think there are plans afoot to demolish it entirely.'

Lovelace shrugged, unbothered. 'Good. Wretched place! But what's the connection to this newspaper story?'

Posie indicated towards *The Times* again. 'The funny thing is that it was *this* Elsie Moncrieff who wrote the strange letter to me. This poor dead woman, who has now fallen off a cliff.'

Lovelace hadn't been impressed. 'Well, it's a horrible way to die, my love, but these things *do* happen. What did the Moncrieff woman want of you, anyhow? What did her letter say?'

Posie bit at a burgundy fingernail. 'I'm going to go to the Grape Street Bureau and dig it out from the office filing now. I was just sitting waiting for my tea and crumpets to arrive at Lyons Cornerhouse on Trafalgar Square when I happened to chance upon this story. If I remember rightly, Elsie was very vague in the letter. She suggested there was something wrong at the place where she worked. *This* place, White Shaw, I presume…' Posie had wrinkled her brow, trying to recall the facts: she hated not having the information to hand.

'She never mentioned her famous employers, I'm sure of it. Miss Moncrieff wanted me to go down there and she would explain everything.'

Lovelace raised an eyebrow and kept it raised. 'Darling, have you considered that this poor woman was simply barmy? Maybe she took a voluntary running jump off that cliff on Sunday night? *That's* what was "wrong".'

'Suicide?'

Lovelace had shrugged. 'Well, perhaps she was off her head on something strong, eh? If she was exposed to the lifestyle of her employers, she'd have found it dashed easy to get her hands on any number of drugs; *if* the press are to be believed. Don't that couple have famously raucous parties at that beachside place of theirs?'

He picked up his Bond Street photographs carefully, stacking them together neatly, one by one. He checked his watch pointedly. Although he adored his future wife beyond all reasonable measure, he had a presentation to make within the hour.

He tried to wrap things up: 'Well, you didn't take Miss Moncrieff's case anyway, did you, my love? So you must have felt it was all fairly insignificant at the time.'

But Posie had shaken her head. 'I didn't take the case at the time as it didn't fit in with my travel plans. Elsie wrote to me at the end of July and I went to Italy for the whole of August – to San Gimignano – do you recall?'

Oh, yes. Richard Lovelace recalled.

It had been the longest month he'd ever got through, desperate for his new fiancée to come home. Desperate to know she hadn't changed her mind about him while out holidaying under the Tuscan sun.

Posie bit at her lip, defensive now. 'I wrote back to Elsie Moncrieff apologising that I couldn't come straight away, and I offered my services upon my return, in September; *if* that suited her. I was surprised not to receive a reply, but assumed things had all turned out for the best. But then a couple of days ago I found a pile of unsent, stamped mail – letters from *me* to my clients – all sitting stacked in Prudence's bottom drawer. She'd quite forgotten to post the wretched things. I had been looking for something else, something trivial – a packet of chocolate probably – and I came across the unsent letters quite by chance. Well, the awful thing is, my original reply to Elsie Moncrieff was among all the others; unsent, unread. So Elsie Moncrieff never knew that I did write back. That I wanted to help her…'

Lovelace had looked horrified. He hated sloppiness of any kind. It sent cold shivers down his spine. 'That's terrible! What on earth was Prudence's excuse?'

Posie half-grinned. 'Prudence has had her head in the clouds since this summer – ever since *your* Sergeant Rainbird jolly well went and proposed to her! I can only guess she forgot about them in a mad frenzy of wedding dress shopping.' She sighed. 'I was hopping mad, actually. I had it out with Prudence. Stern words. But now I've calmed down. What does it help if I'm angry at her? Most of the time she's a first-rate secretary and they're dashed difficult to find.'

And then Posie had rushed on, all the while wrapping herself back up in her expensive maroon woollen coat and matching beret, gathering up her newspaper and her beloved carpet bag. 'So, my love, you know me. I feel pretty awful about this whole thing. *Guilty*, somehow. As if I could have helped this poor woman in July, and I didn't.'

Posie had loitered at the door, Lovelace now rather frantically checking through some notes he had made for the speech he was about to give.

'I thought I'd just pop down to the Inquest, Richard darling.'

'Hmmm?'

'It's probably nothing, but I'd like to check it out. Satisfy myself everything was quite in order.'

'Hmmm.'

'It's *tomorrow*, Richard. So I'll be getting the early train from Victoria and heading on down to Dover. Are you listening to me? Actually, I'll stay in St Margaret's Bay, near where it all happened, at that very nice hotel, The Bay. I've already telephoned, and they were very happy to offer me a room, a suite actually, for a week or so.'

Lovelace suddenly snapped himself together. He had eyed Posie keenly, watchfully. He needed to be careful in his response, in his handling of her. Their marriage was supposed to be in six weeks' time. That meant there was still six weeks during which he could lose her. And they still hadn't agreed on a church. Or a venue. Nothing was booked, and no invitations sent, much to his chagrin.

This coltish girl.

'I see,' he said evenly. 'So you'll be away about a week, will you?'

'More or less. Not sure yet.'

'What about the fireworks and the bonfire on Clapham Common tomorrow night? It's Guy Fawkes Night. Phyllis will miss you terribly. And what about the wedding on Saturday? Surely you'll still come with me?'

It was Prudence, Posie's secretary's, wedding at the weekend. The long-awaited and mooned-over nuptials with Sergeant Rainbird.

Posie looked horrified. She'd forgotten. 'Oh, my golly! Of course, I'll attend with you. If needs be I can always come up specially for it and then hop on a train back down to Kent again afterwards, can't I? And I'm jolly sorry about the fireworks tomorrow with darling Phyllis. But it can't be helped I'm afraid.'

'And the appointment with the men to clear the flat tomorrow morning?'

'Oh!' She had shaken her head maddeningly. 'Oh my gosh! It had quite slipped my mind. But I absolutely must go to the Inquest. Is that all right, Richard? You look a bit glum. Can we simply cancel the men? Or can *you* attend and let them in? I *have* to go. You do understand, don't you?'

'It's fine, sweetheart. Of course, I understand.'

But if truth be told, it had seemed like the paper-thinnest of excuses for Posie to be upping sticks and rushing off to the South Coast like this.

No: he didn't understand. But Richard Lovelace loved Posie Parker and he'd get on with things as best he could.

Which was how he had found himself supervising

everything this morning, running out of time and humour.

Coming to his senses, he dashed to the window of Museum Chambers, pulled up the sash and hollered down into the street for his new man, Sergeant Fox, to come up to the flat as quickly as possible. The team of removal men were still carrying Alaric's things out at a snail's pace. The Decorator had also now finished his tea and was standing by, impatiently awaiting instructions, whistling in an intensely irritating way.

Once Sergeant Fox was inside Posie's flat, Lovelace was quick at dealing with things. He smartened himself up in just a few seconds, rolled down his shirtsleeves, patted down his unruly hair, all in the reflection of the glass frame of one of the hieroglyphs in Posie's lounge.

'Fox? You're going to stay here as long as it takes. I don't trust these removal fellas not to run away with the goods they're transporting. Supervise it all and do it efficiently. Oh, and get this chap to paint the room over there in pink. Several coats of the stuff. You hear me? I want a nice job done.'

'Pink, sir? Are you quite sure?'

'Absolutely.' The Inspector indicated the tins on the floor. '*You* take your pick of the colours, eh? Something relatively easy on the eye. If it's your choice then I can blame you when Posie hates it. Only joking!'

He passed across Posie's set of keys. 'You lock up when everyone's finished in here, won't you? I'm off. See how it feels to be a Sergeant? How well I'm using you now, Fox?'

'Sir?'

'I'm referring to your Sergeant's exams, lad. You did so well in passing them that I'm giving you all the best, most complicated jobs. Like choosing paint, and then watching it dry.'

'Very good, sir.'

Lovelace made to leave, wondering for the hundredth time how Posie was getting on right now, what she would find out at the Inquest, and what on earth she was really up to.

All the way back to his office he tried to tamp down his worry.

What was it about St Margaret's Bay which made him feel dreadfully on edge? In his mind's eye something dark and unpalatable seemed to rise up before him; the dregs of a memory, half-suppressed, half-forgotten. But what?

He remembered back to when Posie and he had worked the case at Maypole Manor. He had been happily, if staidly married back then, of course. Before the fire which had snatched his first wife, Molly, away from him forever. And Posie…well, she had had Alaric, who had been dashing around being dashing as usual.

Different times.

But the dead couldn't harm them now.

And the precise form of danger which had led them to St Margaret's Bay in the first place had been well and truly eradicated. So what uncertainty was clouding his mind? Whatever it was, he couldn't shake it from his thoughts during the entire drive back to Scotland Yard.

Good job then that he had taken measures; precautions as only he could.

Immediately after Posie had left his office yesterday he had made a telephone call to his previous Sergeant, Rainbird. Trusty, if unimaginative: a plodder who looked set to stay within the 'Sergeant' ranks for the rest of his life, but a reassuring policeman all the same.

Remembering the conversation gave Lovelace comfort now. He'd pulled rank. But he'd been acting on the orders of his heart – unusually – rather than his head.

'Rainbird?'

'Chief Commissioner?'

'The usual old "sir" will suffice. Just like before.'

'Sir?'

'Are you busy tomorrow, Rainbird?'

'I have leave booked, sir. I'll be taking a few days to prepare for my wedding this coming weekend.'

'All leave is cancelled. I need you to work tomorrow.'

'Oh?' The flatness in Rainbird's voice was not easily disguised.

'I need you on a train to Dover, to attend a Coroner's Inquest starting at noon. I'll send you the details.'

'I see, sir. Why is the Yard getting involved, sir? Something big, is it?'

'It could be. I don't yet know. Something or nothing, I suppose. You have my full authority to act as you see fit, Rainbird. A *carte blanche*, if you like. I need you to be my eyes and ears down there. Okay?'

'Oh, I see, sir.' Rainbird sounded hopeful all of a sudden. Scenting a sniff in the direction of promotion after having failed his Inspector's exams now twice in a row.

'Is there anything in particular I should be watching out for, sir?'

Lovelace had paused, and then coughed slightly apologetically. 'You can keep an eye out for my fiancée, Rainbird. But without making her suspicious, if you see what I mean.'

'You want me to follow Miss Parker, sir?'

'Not quite. No. That's too much. Just keep a friendly eye on the gal.'

There had been a slight pause. 'Do you believe her to be in danger, sir?'

'In truth I don't know, Sergeant. But I think that's what I am fearful of, yes.'

'Very good, sir.'

It wasn't good, but it was something, and this, Lovelace now thought to himself as his police driver swung through the iron gates of Scotland Yard, on the way to his meeting, was the best he could do in the circumstances.

* * * *

Two

'The Inquest into the death of Miss Elsie Moncrieff will commence in five minutes. There is a very slight delay, but please find your seats as quickly as possible!'

Posie Parker sat on a wooden seat in the ancient, high-beamed Dover Town Hall as the clock struck midday. A few tattered flags suspended high above swayed a little in the ice-cold air. Rain thrashed at the stained-glass windows which lined the right-hand side of the whole room.

She was glad of the delay as it gave her time to gather her thoughts. Glad too of her wool coat – fine quality, but from a couple of years back – which she'd had the good sense to leave on.

It was positively arctic in here.

All around her was a pulsing sea of black-suited movement, a noisy coming and going of journalists. Rows of mismatched chairs had been set out in the middle of the Hall, with the Coroner and his assistant and a stenographer perched above them on a small red-covered platform.

The whole affair had a very make-do, improvised feeling: there weren't enough seats for one thing, and clerks were running around in a panic dragging in stools, piano chairs – anything they could lay their hands on – for the men who were now crowding around the cold grey stone walls of this makeshift Coroner's Court.

The Coroner clearly hadn't been expecting such numbers, despite the fact that this was an 'Open Court'. The hum and laughter of the press pack was getting louder and louder, and the place had more a feel of a party than an investigation into a suspicious death. A junior policeman with ginger hair, his face heavy with concentration, was huddled conspiratorially near the platform, urgently whispering to the Coroner's assistant. He suddenly turned tail and darted off. Something was obviously up.

Posie was sitting near the front, in the second row. A couple of smartly-suited men, who seemed to be waiting to be called as witnesses, were sitting in the same row.

But Posie wasn't focusing on them. She was exactly where she wanted to be: right behind Petronella Douglas and Tony Stone, the married Fashion Designers, although Petronella Douglas had famously – and fashionably – retained her maiden name.

This couple were celebrities in their own right, and the former employers of Elsie Moncrieff.

A slippery pair.

From here Posie was close enough to see the backs of Miss Douglas' bright red plastic earrings, to observe her carefully shingled black hair and shaved neck, to smell her heavily expensive *Nuit d'Oranges* scent, to see how her hands quivered as she crossed and re-crossed her arms constantly, her many silver bamboo-shaped bangles clashing as she moved. Up close you could see her scarlet nail polish was ever so slightly chipped.

She's nervous as hell, Posie thought to herself. *But why?*

Posie's expert glance took in the immaculate back of the small, wiry blonde man in his early-forties at Petronella's side, registering the matching wedding bands on their left-hand ring fingers.

But she noticed too the yawning distance between them: the way they barely glanced at each other, their bodies held very much apart, their shoulders set rigid. *A couple who are not really a couple.*

Odd.

This couple were the reason the Court was full, of course. There were only two real British Fashion Houses who meant anything much these days. One was the traditionally elegant House of Harlow, and the other was Douglas & Stone.

Embarrassingly enough, for a girl who loved fashion, Posie hadn't known much about Douglas & Stone at all. She'd always thought they just did menswear. But like any Private Detective worth her salt, Posie had done her homework on the couple in front of her. She'd stopped off at Fleet Street the night before, at the *Associated Press* offices, where she knew a friendly journalist who always gave her access to their archive.

She'd searched through their press cuttings for an hour, keen to find out what had made darling Richard – who was normally rather non-judgemental – so very critical.

Posie had learnt that the married pair – the American wife, an East-Coast billionaire's daughter, Petronella Douglas, together with her Glaswegian husband, Anthony Stone – were famous for their very modern fashion designs. But the couple were still more famous for their high-society clients and the parties which they hosted.

The Prince of Wales was a client, and was often to be found in their company. There were lots of cuttings of him scowling moodily, his angel's eyes troubled, his hands shoved deep in a pair of Douglas & Stone high-waisters, the sea of St Margaret's Bay glittering behind him. And because the Prince of Wales, who was currently the most eligible bachelor anywhere on the planet, sold newspapers, it followed that anyone connected with him – such as this design duo – was of interest to the press, too.

Just before bed last night Posie had called her best friend, Dolly, the Countess of Cardigeon – wife of Posie's old family friend Rufus Cardigeon – to get the real gossip on the Fashion Designers.

If anyone knew anything about anyone, it was Dolly. Particularly if it involved clothes. Before she had married Rufus, Dolly had been running the costume department in a West End theatre, and it was a passion which had never left her.

Posie smiled now to remember Dolly's words last night, her cockney accent still very much in evidence, despite nearly three years of elocution lessons, all paid for from the fat Cardigeon purse:

'Douglas & Stone? It's a simple enough story really, innit, lovey? Opposites attract. *She's* the money behind the whole business, and *he's* the raw talent. Tony Stone is a funny little fella, but he's a magician when it comes to clothes. There's no-one better!'

'Really?' Posie had been genuinely surprised. 'Golly! So they really *are* good, then? I must confess I hadn't much been following them. If I'm feeling flush I'll have the House of Harlow whip something up for me.'

Dolly had coughed very hoarsely, and then she had sounded like she was lighting up a smoke. She had taken a drag of it deep into her lungs and exhaled in pure pleasure.

'Oh, darlin'! Mark my words, the House of Harlow are really *very* unfashionable now, particularly since Douglas & Stone got their Royal Appointment from the Prince of Wales. The House of Harlow will be out of business very soon. Sooner than your weddin' to Richard Lovelace. Which is *when*, by the way? I want to plan my outfit. And I'll be off to the South of France in January, for the sun. So make it snappy, darlin'!'

Posie had cleared her throat anxiously, caught off guard.

She'd looked down quickly at her left-hand ring finger, as if for reassurance, and seen the slender golden ring there, moulded like orange blossom, bearing a tiny but perfect diamond at its centre.

It had been purchased from an American Department Store in New York, where Traub, the makers, had a counter, as they did in most American cities. Mid-range, modern, not too showy: Traub rings could currently be seen gracing the finger of many a fashionable American girl who had just got engaged. But not on any English ones.

The American ring had, in fact, been Dolly's inspired idea. She'd seen an advert in American *Vogue*, and thought it would suit Posie and not break the bank. Richard Lovelace had then got a contact in the New York Police Department to buy it and send it over, with considerable effort. It was the third engagement ring Posie Parker had owned in her lifetime, and this one, probably the cheapest, was definitely the best.

It suited her the most.

'I think the wedding will be before Christmas. But we can't...' She had paused, awkwardly. 'We can't agree on a church, actually. That's all.'

Posie had imagined Dolly's raised eyebrows all the way over on the Pavilion Road in Chelsea, SW3.

'Oh? You're disagreein' over a *church*?' A sceptical pause. 'Well, you're cuttin' it fine, aren't you? There's only about six weeks left before Christmas, lovey. Never mind. Just as long as you're not gettin' cold feet. Richard Lovelace is a keeper, you mark my words.'

Dolly had paused before going on cautiously. 'You're not, are you? Gettin' cold feet?'

''Course not. So, Douglas & Stone. *That's* why I called, remember? Not to talk about *me*. They're the real deal?'

'Oh, yes. Rufus won't hear of goin' anywhere else now. Tony Stone makes him look positively *thin* in his suits. Which is a sort of miracle these days.'

Posie had frowned. 'And does Petronella do the women's side of things?'

A derisive snort had crackled down the line. 'Ha! You must be jokin', lovey. That woman wouldn't know one end of a pair of dressmaker's scissors from the other! She calls herself a Fashion Designer but that's all a lot of hot puff!

Like I said, she's just the money. Tony Stone does all the real work. They've been doin' menswear for years now, since the Great War, but this last year has been brilliant for women. Tony's really come into his own. There was a bridal collection. About a year ago now. Exclusive to Haresmythe's. Only about ten dresses shown, but it caused a sensation. Also a cruise collection. People were trippin' over themselves to be seen in those clothes at Menton and the Cap d'Antibes, I'm tellin' ya! People are eagerly awaiting the next collection. Should be fairly soon, I reckon. If I was you, lovey, I'd ask Tony to rustle you up a dress for your weddin'. Although six weeks *might* be cuttin' it a bit fine.'

Posie had ignored her friend's barb. 'What's the back-story on this pair?'

Dolly had been in her element. 'Back-story? Oh! It's legendary! Tony Stone was a very talented but completely overlooked trainee tailor from the poorest part of town when Petronella Douglas first met him in a Department Store in Glasgow, before the Great War.'

'Glasgow? What on earth was *she* doing there, anyhow? Isn't Petronella Douglas from New York?'

'Yes. But Petronella was always in and out of trouble in the States. Drugs, mainly. This time, she'd been sent over to Scotland as a punishment by her father, with him threatenin' to cut off her huge allowance if she didn't go. The Douglas family were originally from Glasgow, and Petronella was told to research her family tree or some such codswallop. I heard she hated it, and was always slippin' off down to London: it was as good as New York but without Daddy Dearest watchin' her every move. I think she saw a golden opportunity in Tony, snatched him up and married him at Gretna Green. She saw he could provide her with the talent behind her vision…'

Dolly had started coughing down the line, quite badly, but then carried on again in fits and starts: 'But the Great War was comin', so she took Tony back to the States to meet Daddy Dearest and try and get back in his good books. Petronella arranged for Tony to spend the Great War workin' with the best tailors in New York City, and all the while she was bidin' her time; makin' plans for their future Fashion House in London. Where she could be free to live how she wished…and that's how Douglas & Stone, the Fashion House, came about.'

'Gracious me. So Petronella is quite a schemer, then?'

'Yes. As I said, *she* doesn't know the first thing about makin' clothes. But she *does* know about celebrity clients. She's especially interested in famous people, like film stars. Or people with snappy ideas, inventors and the like. Not your boring old country aristocrat types like Rufus and me. We're too dull, darlin'. We spend hundreds of pounds on their clothes, but Petronella Douglas has never invited us to one of her parties. Not once.'

'And the Prince of Wales? Where does he fit into all of this?'

But then Dolly was coughing again, on and on, and Posie had winced and held off asking her friend if she was all right, because she knew the shirty response she would get. If truth were told, Posie was secretly very concerned for her friend's health, and she had been for a couple of years now. Posie was living in dread of hearing unutterably dreadful news about Dolly's fragile health, and the upcoming trip to France sounded just what was needed. Posie had waited silently for Dolly's coughing fit to subside.

'Sorry about that, lovey! This silly little tickly cough! It's nothin'! You were askin' about the Prince of Wales? Well, I can imagine he was practically *forced* into givin' that Royal Warrant to them. Petronella Douglas is *very* persuasive. She's just his type, too: older, American, bossy. Charming, when she wants to be. You can't wonder he and his father fell out about it.'

'Sorry?'

Another cough from Dolly. 'The King was totally against the granting of the Royal Warrant but the Prince went ahead with it anyway. The King apparently thinks Douglas & Stone are an unwise influence in his son's life.'

'Golly! Why does the King think that?' Posie had been thinking of Richard's similarly censorious attitude.

'Because of the parties. They look a riot! Douglas & Stone are part of the set who are makin' St Margaret's Bay ultra-fashionable, an English Riviera. Their house, White Shaw, is used for the parties most weekends, like a big film-set. They moved out of London to be based there. It makes them even more exclusive, apparently, although I wonder if they just couldn't afford town anymore, and closed up shop to save face.'

'Oh?'

'Yes. Very rum do. All I know is that whenever Rufus wants a new suit, Tony Stone has to come along here with his bag of tricks, like a little travellin' salesman! *Very* poor show for such a famous Fashion Designer, eh? They don't even have a London showroom anymore.'

Dolly had sounded dreamy. 'But the parties do look divine. *That* must be where the money goes. I lost count of the snaps I saw this summer in the newspapers: the Prince of Wales himself, once or twice; actresses and the younger Members of Parliament; golf stars and film stars. All trippin' onto the private beach and jumpin' into the sea clutchin' at champagne flutes! I even saw that dashin' Lord Boxwood in one photograph with a gaggle of women on his arm; all lollin' about eating sherbet water-ices.'

'I say! Lord Boxwood? You mean the inventor? The one they're calling a modern-day Da Vinci, because he can invent pretty much anything? Jeepers, I thought he was a bit of joke!'

Dolly had tutted disapprovingly, and assumed an air of conspiratorial authority: 'You're all wrong, Posie love. Actually, he's the government's secret weapon: it's all organised for him to get a government contract to make a run of British submarines for use in the—'

'Stop! Shhh!'

Posie had suddenly realised, horrified, that her less-than-discreet best friend was about to reveal – albeit without meaning to – potential government secrets down the telephone wires, these confidential secrets probably gained as a result of listening in on her husband, who was himself a member of the House of Lords. Posie almost panicked at the thought of *who* might be listening on the line, and she had changed the subject very quickly:

'Tell me, what's the problem with these parties exactly? Why does the King disapprove? Is there some suggestion of drugs?'

'I wouldn't know, lovey. But we all know the King is a real stick in the mud. Douglas & Stone are very *now*, very of the moment. But you'll see, like the House of Harlow, their time will pass.'

'Would you see them as "slippery", Dolly? What do you think it would be like to work for them?'

For surely this was what it was all about?

Elsie Moncrieff, who had reached out for help to Posie but not got it, had been employed by this couple who attracted controversy. What had it been like for Elsie to work for them?

Dolly had taken her time replying, smoking, enjoying the oddness of the question.

'Slippery? Yes, definitely. And what would it be like to work for them? Well…'

A pause.

'Tony Stone is completely focused on his work. Loves his job. He's famous for doing nearly everything alone, just hires in extra seamstresses for the big collections. But I'd say he pays well and he inspires the women, so I suppose he's a good boss. I've met a few of his part-time seamstresses. None of them have a bad word to say about him. And Petronella Douglas? I reckon she'd sell her soul – if she has one – to get on in life. If you were stuck working for her it would be like working for the devil. A She-Devil!'

And now Posie's thoughts were being dragged back to the present, to the Inquest, the reason *why* she had started this journey in the first place.

Back to the cold Dover Town Hall.

To Elsie Moncrieff.

The Coroner, whose hawkish, dark-featured face looked like it was permanently set in an angry scowl, had stood up and hit a gavel savagely, and the audience quietened down immediately.

'Order! I *will* have silence in my Court. Now!'

* * * *

Three

'This is an enquiry into the strange circumstances surrounding the death of Miss Elsie Moncrieff, Housekeeper at White Shaw, St Margaret's Bay. We are late starting because we had a procedural irregularity.'

The Coroner rustled some papers: 'We are here to find out *how* Miss Moncrieff may have died. The Pathologist who completed the Autopsy has recorded an "open" verdict, with no particular cause of death found, except for the obvious damage to the body caused by the severity of the cliff-top fall itself, and being in the water for a few hours.'

Posie had one of her usual silver notepads in front of her, but so far she hadn't written a thing. Her thoughts were still with Dolly, but what she heard next made her catch her breath.

'But things are not simple here,' continued the Coroner. 'We must investigate a suggestion from the Pathologist that a clear bruise in the shape of a distinct hand-print on Miss Moncrieff's upper back may be evidence that the deceased was, in fact, *pushed*. I should make clear at this stage that this strange bruise could, apparently, have been sustained at any time during the twelve hours *before* Miss Moncrieff's death. But we must consider that this *may* be evidence of murder.'

This terrible image immediately etched itself onto the minds of practically everyone in the place.

A murder? Well, it had been hinted at, hadn't it, in that strange notice in *The Times*? But hearing it here, officially, was different.

A clear bruise in the shape of a distinct hand-print.
The deceased was pushed.

All around her Posie sensed newspaper men suddenly sitting up straighter in their mismatched seats. Fingers were reaching urgently for pencils, hopeful of a gory story.

The Coroner hurried on: 'So did Miss Moncrieff jump? Was she pushed? Or was she just unlucky – falling in a terrible accident? In which case I will record a finding of "accidental death". *This* is what we have to try and find out here today, and to do so, I will call on a number of witnesses in order to form a picture of Miss Moncrieff and her state of mind, and of events leading up to her death. Please note that we have not been able to trace any of Miss Moncrieff's direct family, and therefore no relatives will be called today as witnesses. So, without any further ado, I call to the Witness Stand…'

But suddenly a door clanged noisily at the rear of the Hall, and the whole Court turned in unison.

'*Sergeant Rainbird?*' Posie half-hissed under her breath in surprise, fixing her gaze on the solid figure at the open doorway, the familiar florid ham-like face, the blonde hair greased down from the rain outside.

Rainbird hung about for a second, casting around ineffectually for a seat at the back, but the Coroner, growing angry, was on his feet.

'State your business, man! This is a Court in session here, albeit a public one which allows every Tom, Dick and Harry to sit in on it, like a circus! If I had my own way this would have been a private affair. You should have stayed outside rather than come in late like this. Newspaper fella, are you?' He gestured around the room dismissively. 'Like all these?'

'No. Scotland Yard, your Honour.'

A faraway flash of Rainbird's identity card danced in the thick damp air. 'Apologies for my late arrival, your Honour.'

'The Yard?' The Coroner frowned. 'I had no prior knowledge about *your* involvement in this case. Well... this is quite irregular. But I daresay you know your own business, what?'

His tone suddenly changed, relief creeping in. 'Do sit down, Inspector. Here, come down to the front. I'll just pick up where I left off, if you don't mind?'

'Very good, your Honour.'

There followed a dull-as-ditch-water testimony from the dogwalker who had discovered Elsie's body at the bottom of the cliff early on Monday morning. And during this, Posie was staring first at the back of Petronella Douglas' glossy raven-black head, then at Sergeant Rainbird, sitting in the very same front row.

Why was he here?

Posie simply couldn't understand it. What exactly was Scotland Yard's interest in Elsie Moncrieff's death? When Posie had mentioned it to Richard yesterday, he had hardly shown any concern over the case at all. So why was one of his Sergeants down here?

Was there some information regarding the death of Elsie Moncrieff which Richard hadn't been able to share, or hadn't *wanted* to share with Posie? But that was just ridiculous! Richard told her everything.

It was likely that Rainbird was covering this case for another of his bosses; that this Inquest was nothing to do with her fiancé, Lovelace, at all.

Since Rainbird had failed his Inspector's exams back in the autumn, he had been demoted and was now a jobbing Detective Sergeant taking orders from at least three Inspectors above him; one of whom was the irascible Inspector Oats.

It must be a difficult time for Rainbird just now, Posie thought to herself guiltily. He was about to embark on married life with a high degree of uncertainty hanging over his professional life. But then, surely this was a time of real opportunities, too? A time to look out for interesting cases in order to recover some pride. To act alone, perhaps?

Was *that* what Rainbird was doing down here in Kent at this Inquest? But Posie's thoughts were interrupted by the Coroner:

'I now call to the stand Mrs Tony Stone – whom I shall refer to hereafter as "Miss Petronella Douglas", as is her wont – in her capacity as one of the joint employers of the deceased.'

Photo flash-bulbs were suddenly popping and steaming chalkily, most of the audience now up on their feet, the dark stone room lit up garishly as the Fashion Designer shimmied her way to the Witness Stand.

As Miss Douglas turned, Posie realised she had been expecting something *more*. She hadn't yet seen the woman in the flesh, only in grainy newspaper photos. Immaculate as she was, Petronella Douglas was plain: her powder-caked face, round as a biscuit, had been layered up today with thick beige pan-stick, but all it did was highlight the lack of beauty. The severe black bob, black-and-white silk zebra-patterned dress and the blood-red accessories made the thin, very tall woman in her early forties seem like a caricature of a wicked stepmother in a fairy-tale.

Nevertheless, there was *something* about the woman which made her attractive; an easy power hung about her, seeming to promise a good time ahead.

'Please could you state the exact nature and duration of Miss Moncrieff's employment with you, Miss Douglas?'

A hesitant cough, then the glamorous silky reassurance of New York money purred into gear:

'I sure can, your Honour! Elsie was Housekeeper at our place here, White Shaw. She kinda came with the place.

We've owned it three years, and it sure is the bee's knees! These past couple of years White Shaw has become our Headquarters. Where we do *everything*. So Elsie needed to be organised, and she was: she ran the staff and the place like clockwork – there was never any trouble about anything – she was quite a woman: real hotsy-totsy if you know what I mean?'

'You mean Miss Moncrieff was a "Girl Friday", do you?'

'Sure. She'd look after our children, our twins Kit and Sammy, if we needed. And she helped me with the parties I hold, bringing in drinks herself sometimes. She was discreet, which is important in our business. Not to mention that Elsie was easy on the eye, a treat for some of our party guests: a doll. Elsie sure was a swell kind of girl. I couldn't have had a wet blanket working for me at White Shaw, could I? Not on your nelly!'

'And you'd say your employment relationship with Elsie was a happy one? *Both* sides were happy, I mean?'

'Oh, yes. Fine.'

'And apart from the fact of Miss Moncrieff's death on Sunday night, you otherwise intended her employment to continue with you on the same terms for the foreseeable future?'

'Sure thing, your Honour.'

'You said Miss Moncrieff came with the house. Did you advertise her position? In *The Lady* perhaps? Did you interview many such "swell girls"?'

'No. I can't say we did. We were living in London – a pretty fast life – at the time. It would have been quite impossible for me to interview loadsa girls!' A slightly regretful laugh. 'We had White Shaw built, you know, from scratch, in the new style. It's the Cat's Miaow! Right next to the Bay Hotel, on a glorious itty-bitty little beach. It was finished almost three years ago, about Christmas, 1921. Jolyon Peterson, the famous London architect, he did it all. He called me in the autumn, when he'd almost finished and said he'd heard of a young experienced woman looking for a Housekeeping job. Said she'd be perfect for us. And he was right.'

'I'm glad to hear it. And you obtained references for Miss Moncrieff? Or was the architect's recommendation enough?'

Petronella Douglas smirked as she looked about the Court. '*Of course* we obtained references! Swell references! You think I'm some kind of Dumb Dora? We sure have some *very* confidential clients, if you know who I mean. So it's vital anyone who comes near to the heart of our business has been thoroughly vetted.'

'So you checked out these references, then, did you?'

Petronella Douglas narrowed her small eyes. 'Oh yes.'

'Really?' A frown and a beat of silence followed before the Coroner smiled waspishly. 'Well, that's certainly good to hear, Miss Douglas. Now, coming to the personality of Miss Moncrieff herself, how would you have described her? I mean to say…was Miss Moncrieff a *happy* sort? Outgoing? Carefree? Full of the joys of spring? Or was she a dismal girl; withdrawn, secretive maybe?'

Posie frowned crossly. *He was hardly being subtle, was he?* In other words, the Coroner was asking if Elsie Moncrieff was the sort of girl who would throw herself off a cliff-top.

Or not.

'Secretive?' Petronella Douglas almost whispered the word. She had turned an unbecoming shade of red, almost a match for the blood-red of her outfit trimmings. She threw a look over at her husband and Posie saw the head and shoulders of the man in front of her stiffen. His wife recovered herself quickly.

'I wouldn't say Elsie was secretive, no. Nor depressed, if that's what you're getting at. I didn't know her as a friend, mind. She was just my employee.'

'Thank you. Did your Housekeeper have *any* female friends, Miss Douglas? Anyone who would call around and stay over maybe, at her self-contained apartment? Local girls?'

'Not that I know of, no. She kept herself to herself.' The Fashion Designer shrugged, and Posie felt the fickle interest of the press pack waning.

The Coroner was scoring through points efficiently – *done, done, done*. His assistant was chatting again urgently to the bobby from earlier, leaning down off the platform, receiving something in a brown paper 'EVIDENCE' envelope.

'Any men?' The Coroner scratched off another point on his list. 'Did your Housekeeper have any boyfriends? Any of the crowd from your so-called parties ever stay over with her, did they, Miss Douglas? If she was such a "doll"?'

Interest snapped back on in the room like a green-flashing beacon, and fury showed on Petronella's unremarkable face. 'You're kidding me, right, your Honour? *Of course* Elsie didn't mix with any of our clients in that way. What are you suggesting? That would be most improper.'

'No-one was suggesting anything *improper*, Miss Douglas.'

Posie heard the woman exhale. The *Nuits d'Oranges* smell was sickly now: a warm fug carried across to Posie on a wave of sweat and fear. Actually, it was starting to make Posie feel distinctly nauseous. Posie swallowed.

Still, at least it was something different from the perfume worn by virtually every other woman in the country just now – the heavily exotic *Phúl-Nana*, by Grossmith, which had a similarly inconvenient sick-inducing effect on her. In the run-up to her wedding these last couple of weeks Prudence, Posie's secretary, had obviously treated herself to a bottle of the stuff and the office at Grape Street was almost reeking of it. It was all Posie could do not to run for the tiny bathroom on the corridor every morning, and instead, she and her partner at the Detective Agency, Len Irving, had taken to opening all the office windows, never mind the cold.

Petronella Douglas stared at the Coroner, chin up, resolute, avoiding her husband and everyone else's gaze in the Hall. The armpits of her silk zebra dress were wringing wet and sticking to her unattractively.

'You asked about *men*, your Honour. Well, there was no-one. Not recently. But there *was* a man right at the start. Good-looking blonde guy, he was. They sure made a striking couple. I saw her go walking up on the cliffs with him. To Ness Point. The very same spot where she died. So, you see, the cliff-top path was *known* to Elsie. It's impossible to think she fell accidentally.' The American frowned. 'Or that she jumped off it.'

Posie had started to take her own notes, all in a hurry. Only in the last few minutes was the dead girl coming to life for her, becoming a *person*. The Coroner sat with his pen poised:

'So what was the name of this man, then, Miss Douglas? And what became of him? You said Miss Moncrieff knew him three years ago. I'm trying to find *anyone* connected with the deceased, you see. Am I to assume the relationship with this man finished?'

'I sure can't help you, your Honour. We didn't discuss him. Seemed to me he disappeared into thin air, just a couple of weeks into our time at White Shaw.'

'And there have been no other men, not recently? That's surprising, isn't it? A lovely girl like that? No other men at all?'

The American shook her head. Posie turned automatically to snatch a glance at Tony Stone, and saw how he was gripping the chair in front of him very hard, his knuckles white.

And then it made a sort of sense.

****

Four

It seemed pretty obvious to anyone with eyes and ears at this Inquest that the dead Housekeeper had been the paramour of Tony Stone. A temptress. Something dangerous.

This changed things perceptibly, and Posie was pretty sure that the eagle eyes of the Coroner hadn't missed a thing.

And while this was not a criminal court, and no-one was being accused of anything, Posie felt the hackles rising on her neck as she looked again with fresh eyes at Petronella Douglas on the Witness Stand. If Elsie Moncrieff had, in fact, been the love of her husband's life, everything Petronella Douglas had said so far was probably a pack of lies: Elsie certainly hadn't been a swell girl at all. She had been dangerous to Petronella. A danger at the heart of her fancy art-deco home.

But what did that make Petronella Douglas herself? Had she, in turn, been a danger to Elsie? Did she know more than she was letting on about how her Housekeeper had died on that cliff? Could she have been involved?

The Coroner seemed to be thinking along the same suspicious lines.

'Did anything unusual happen in the run-up to Miss Moncrieff's death, Miss Douglas? On Sunday 2nd November, or earlier, perhaps on the Saturday? Is there any light you can shed on whether Miss Moncrieff got into a fight during the twelve hours before her death?'

The hand-print.

'*I* didn't do it, if that's what you mean. Heaven forbid!' Petronella Douglas crossed her arms rather defensively. 'As it happens, yes: something unusual happened on the Saturday night. I was hosting a big important party, but Elsie didn't come and help me out. It was the first time ever. In three years. She said she had a dreadful headache, and stayed in her studio all Saturday night. It was a busy, important party. The rest of the staff had to work overtime to help me.'

'Do you know if Miss Moncrieff had any visitors that night?'

'Gee, I sure couldn't say, your Honour. I was too busy hosting my party to run around checking on the Housekeeper.'

The Coroner raised an eyebrow. 'You sound dismissive of Elsie's claims of ill health. Didn't you believe her?'

A shrug. 'No, as it happens. Elsie seemed fine to me all of Saturday, and then again on Sunday morning. No sign of a headache at all. It was all baloney!'

'You spoke to her on Sunday, then?'

'Yes, your Honour. Elsie helped to clear up the mess from the party. After a quick sandwich lunch she took the rest of the day off; it *was* a Sunday after all, and that was her usual day off work. I didn't see her again. I think she went to her studio-flat and stayed there for the rest of the day. I certainly heard music from her gramophone a couple of times. It was the devil of a day outside: rain was already pelting at the house. Elsie must have been crazy to go out later that night.'

'What did *you* do for the rest of the Sunday, Miss Douglas?'

'Me? That's easy, your Honour. I went to bed. I guess I was still slightly sozzled from the night before, and I was tired. Dead beat.'

'I see. Where were your twin boys on the Sunday? And your husband?'

'The boys stayed at school. At Dover College, where they stay over for the weekend if we throw a party. Tony left very early on Sunday morning, our driver Sidney took him to the station. Tony had to travel up to London. We have a big show about to take place, this Saturday, at Haresmythe's in Knightsbridge. It's hugely important. A pre-Christmas Bridal Show. Tony was organising all the details: the band, the models. He was going to return mid-week to collect the dresses, if things had run their normal course. Obviously, when Elsie's body was discovered on Monday I called him right back and he came home immediately.'

The Coroner changed tack, as if bored, and dismissed Petronella Douglas from the stand, asking instead for her husband to replace her.

Tony Stone was surprisingly short and fine-boned, with sad, droopy eyes and the thin frazzled face of a hungry wolf-hound.

His dapper emerald-and-white pinstriped suit with its exquisite tailoring added maybe a couple of extra illusory inches, but the fact remained that he was at least a full head and shoulders shorter than his wife.

He stared at the back of the Court without meeting anyone's gaze, drumming his fingers on the lectern as if he desperately wanted a smoke. He had a fascinatingly awful habit of sucking at his teeth, over and over, which Posie concluded quickly was probably just nerves.

'Mr Stone? Do you concur with everything your wife has just told this Inquest?'

'Aye, your Honour.' The voice was high and reedy, almost a girlish voice really, but raspy at the edges, the Glaswegian accent still strong, despite years spent away from that city.

'You even agree with your wife's answer when I asked if Elsie would have stayed on in your joint employment at

White Shaw going forward? When she answered in the affirmative?'

Tony Stone ran his fingers through his greasy sandy fringe of hair but remained silent.

'Mr Stone? Please answer the question.'

A sigh, the voice rising even higher. 'If it'd bin left tae me, yer Honour, then aye. Yes: Elsie would've stayed with us, ye know?'

'But? I sense a "but". Come on, man!'

But Tony Stone just shook his head. 'I didnae know anything.'

The Coroner cleared his throat at last, breaking the strange silence.

'This is *not* a Criminal Court, Mr Stone, and it is not our job to apportion blame. But it *is* a function of this Inquest to pass on our findings to the relevant authorities, including the police. And I can now tell this Inquest that when the Pathologist examined the body of Miss Elsie Moncrieff he found an unopened letter in her coat pocket, and on closer examination this letter was revealed to be from your wife, with Sunday's date on it, effectively sacking Miss Elsie Moncrieff with immediate effect.'

A gasp ran around the Courtroom. Posie chanced a look over at Petronella Douglas but the woman sat perfectly still.

'Does this information come as a surprise to you, Mr Stone?'

The Fashion Designer shook his head. 'Naw. It does not, yer Honour. My wife telephoned me on Sunday, late afternoon, in London, at ma wee club, where I stay in town. She told me she'd written this wee letter and was going to deliver it to Elsie that same evening.'

'And what was the reason for her ending Elsie's employment?'

'Ma wife didnae tell me, yer Honour. I am none the wiser on that point than ye are.'

The Coroner struck his gavel, attempting to hush the room. 'Well, we are lucky enough to have an Inspector from Scotland Yard here today, so I will show this letter directly to him. So Miss Petronella Douglas' words – and the perjury she has committed here in light of that letter – can be investigated by the right authority. It strikes me that your wife has some explaining to do.'

Posie gasped: the Coroner had all but pinned the blame for the death on Petronella Douglas. Almost accused the woman straight up of murdering her own employee.

Was that allowed? Looking about, she saw how journalists were eagerly putting away notebooks, pulling on scarves and jamming on hats, keen to be gone, keen to file their copy as early as possible. They had their story. They were leaving the room already.

The Coroner called for another witness, a manservant perhaps? A big, dark, handsome man in his mid-thirties with a rolling gait and a badly-set broken nose stood up.

Posie didn't catch the man's name, she was too busy watching the Fashion Designers: watching how Tony Stone sat with his head bowed, how Petronella held herself tightly, not moving an inch.

She saw that Sergeant Rainbird was now holding an EVIDENCE envelope – presumably the letter sacking Elsie – and he was looking singularly important. Posie noticed how he hadn't bothered to correct the Coroner's mistake. *Scotland Yard Inspector!* Posie smiled and wondered how long it would be until he bothered to correct anyone. If at all.

The dark manservant was at the Witness Stand. He was about to be addressed by the Coroner when the red-haired, wet-caped policeman from earlier stamped down the middle aisle, waving an eager fistful of papers. Posie watched in fascination as the Coroner beckoned up Sergeant Rainbird and then started to flip through the new papers, looking up from time to time as if seeking guidance. Rainbird had begun to look worried.

The last few journalists in the Hall now stood, glued to the spot, staring at the action unfolding. The manservant – quite forgotten about on the Witness Stand – looked as if he might grab at his overcoat and march out. He looked ill-tempered and nervy.

The delay went on for at least five minutes. Finally the Coroner stood up, ashen faced. *Something was undoubtedly very wrong.* Posie held her breath.

'I must adjourn, or rather *close* this Inquest. Fascinating though it has been to have a glimpse into the lives of these very well-known Fashion Designers, a massive irregularity has just been exposed. While we have been informed that Elsie Moncrieff had no family, and was a spinster with few friends, it seems she was also some sort of ghost who had no earthly records. No birth certificate, nor passport, nor bank accounts can be found for her, anywhere in the land. There is no Elsie Moncrieff recorded as being born in the last forty-five years within the British Isles. We have checked parish records, town records and the National Census. We have spent the last twenty-four hours checking tirelessly.'

Silence reigned heavily in the big room. Posie rubbed at her eyes in disbelief.

'In the last few minutes I have received confirmation from Somerset House in London who have coordinated these searches that they cannot assist us any further, and therefore I am forced to conclude that the woman who died by falling off Ness Point – currently in Dover town morgue – is to be pitied and her death investigated, but her real identity is presently unknown to us. Even tracing Elsie Moncrieff's previous references is difficult, as the architect who recommended her, the well-known Mr Jolyon Peterson, is currently holidaying in the Argentine. I will return an "open" verdict. The police will now take this matter forward, towards the Criminal Courts as they see fit.'

Lucky Rainbird!

But Posie was uneasy.

What had started out as a half-guilty attempt on her part to make amends for not answering Elsie's letter in July, now seemed infinitely more complicated.

The Inquest which Posie had expected to be fairly open-and-shut, although attended by an unusual froth of glamour and gossip, was now turning into a procedural nightmare, while the death itself was murky, with a background full of lies, intrigue and sub-plots.

And just who on earth *was* the dead Elsie Moncrieff, anyway?

Posie looked all about her as the room cleared. It was the fifth of November and tonight there would be a bonfire on Clapham Common which she could attend, making both her fiancé and her future little step-daughter very happy indeed. She could make the London train if she looked lively, and she muttered under her breath, cajoling herself along. 'I *should* jolly well go back up to London. Right this minute.'

Posie was picking up her carpet bag, and as she did so she heard the slight scrunch of a sheet of paper inside it. *Elsie's letter.* Her conscience twanged.

Elsie Moncrieff – or a woman calling herself by that name – hadn't received the dignity of a reply when she had asked for help. And now didn't she surely deserve the dignity of justice? Of a smidgen of Posie's time?

For something was wrong here.

And just like that, the decision was made.

Posie would stay on.

She felt a warm wave of relief flood over her.

Posie looked at Rainbird, who was standing awkwardly with the uniformed red-haired policeman from before. The bobby seemed to be waiting for direction from Rainbird. *He might be waiting for some time.*

Posie was on her feet in an instant, smart new burgundy suede heels with their tiny golden butterfly buttons snapping firmly on the stone floor. When Rainbird saw her approach, there was no surprise on his face at all. He must have seen her in the Hall when he came in, then.

Unless he'd been forewarned about her attendance?

'Good afternoon, Miss.' He made the introductions hastily. 'This is my, er, my associate, Miss Parker…and this is Constable Briggs, from the Dover Police Force. He was first on the scene on Monday morning.'

Briggs had a good goggle at Posie. 'I've heard of you, Miss Parker. A pleasure to meet you.'

The Constable grimaced as he turned back to Rainbird. 'But just to be correct here, sir. I were the *only* one on the scene on Monday mornin'.'

'Right…' Rainbird was flicking through a file Briggs had passed him, looking worried. He didn't seem to know what he was looking for at all.

Posie stepped in crisply. 'Are we taking this paperwork back to the local police station right now, sir? Or are we off for a look at White Shaw, the so-called Cat's Miaow?'

'The station, Miss Parker.' Rainbird frowned, and snapped the file shut. 'But *I'll* go in there alone. Then we can go on to this fancy house. Meet that strange couple. See what we can nose out there.'

'I see, sir. Right you are.' Posie tried to hide her frown at the idea of following Rainbird's orders. Presumably he had his own reasons for excluding her from entering the police station…

They started to move out of the Hall, Briggs buzzing along in front, leading the way. 'The station's just round the corner, Inspector, not half a minute's walk. It's the big red-brick building on Ladywell Road. I must warn you though that this little death has only been logged in our Record Book, not taken at all seriously. Well, we just assumed it was another suicide. You can't think what a relief it is for us, sir, to have you – a real-life Scotland Yard Inspector – in charge of all of this; what with how it's turning out now!'

Briggs was shaking his head in disbelief. 'What a time of it we're havin', sir! Our Chief Inspector sent word this morning that his wife has gone into labour with their first child, and he'll be away at least a couple of days. And there's a nasty bout of flu about; almost all of our lads at the station have been struck down with it. We're operating a skeleton staff here, sir, and all we needed was for this to blow up in our faces.'

Posie took all of this in, troubled slightly at her own unwillingness to correct the local policeman's assumption of Rainbird's rank.

What would Richard Lovelace say? But this qualm stayed very much at the back of her conscience, because quite frankly, who cared? She couldn't – and wouldn't – report Rainbird.

Of course not.

Because she *needed* Rainbird as her way in to all of this. Because she had simply no legal right to go sticking her nose into someone else's lovely home, looking for answers to questions about a Housekeeper.

A doll.

Because just like that, and all thanks to Rainbird, the case of Elsie Moncrieff was quite firmly in her hands.

Which was, Posie realised now with a dull sense of certainty, exactly what she had wanted all along.

* * * *

Five

Posie sat in the police motor-car, parked up against the kerb outside the Town Hall, as rain drummed heavily on the canvas roof. She was waiting for Sergeant Rainbird.

Outside, a brand-new memorial to the men of Dover who had died in the Great War was in the process of being finished: a suitably anguished bronze of a woman in the throes of grief had been polished within an inch of its life. Maybe there was a grand opening in the offing? Perhaps on the eleventh of November, in seven days' time?

Here in Dover their poor dead men were being honoured a full six years after the guns had finally stopped pounding in France and Belgium, but the delay was by no means unusual: up and down the country villages and towns had been scrimping in order to collect the money to properly honour their dead, and this often took years.

Posie had finished her thermos flask of black coffee, made early this morning at home, miraculously still quite warm, and now she took Elsie Moncrieff's letter out of her carpet bag. Again.

Posie started to read it for the umpteenth time that day, hunting for new meanings behind the words which had been typed more than four months before, in a summer which now seemed long, long ago.

WHITE SHAW, ST MARGARET'S BAY, KENT

28th July 1924

DEAR MISS PARKER,

FIRST, I HOPE YOU WILL NOT MIND THAT A DOMESTIC SERVANT (A HOUSEKEEPER, ACTUALLY), IS WRITING TO YOU. I HAVE MONEY THOUGH, AND PROMISE I CAN PAY YOU FOR YOUR HELP.

MY NAME IS ELSIE MONCRIEFF AND I HAVE WORKED IN MY CURRENT POSITION FOR THE LAST TWO AND A HALF YEARS. IT IS A VERY UNIQUE JOB AND MY EMPLOYERS HERE ARE A NICE MARRIED COUPLE.

BUT I WRITE BECAUSE I AM WORRIED, MISS PARKER. THERE IS SOMETHING WRONG HERE. I NEED YOUR HELP.

I CAN EXPLAIN BETTER WHEN WE MEET. IT WOULD BE BEST IF YOU VISITED ME DOWN HERE. I LOOK FORWARD TO HEARING FROM YOU.

YOURS, VERY SINCERELY,
ELSIE MONCRIEFF

Posie frowned. She'd overlooked the strangeness of the letter when she'd first received it; hadn't of course known just *who* Elsie's employers – the 'nice married couple' – had been. It was a real credit to the dead girl, and Posie couldn't help but admire her, that Elsie hadn't felt tempted to name them in a bid to get some sort of immediate reaction.

But now, on re-reading the letter, there were other peculiarities emerging: the shiftiness; Elsie's condition of only fully revealing the true situation to Posie in person; the insistence on Posie coming down to White Shaw.

Suddenly the door beside her was wrenched open and Sergeant Rainbird threw himself up onto the high leather seat beside her, with the front door jerked open in a similarly urgent fashion, followed by Briggs jumping into the front seat.

'Carry on, Driver!' ordered Briggs, relishing the bit of action. 'White Shaw, St Margaret's Bay, fast as you like!'

Posie looked over at Rainbird. Despite the all-pervading chill and the damp air, his pink face was looking decidedly sweaty. In his lap was the thin grey manila file which Briggs had handed him earlier, but it was slightly fatter now, and his fingers were fluttering against it. Rainbird was the very image of a man with everything heaped up messily on his plate, anxious not to be tripped lest he fell and lost the lot.

'Everything fine?' she whispered below the roar of the engine as they set off. She watched as Rainbird tugged at his tight white collar, trying to let in air. 'Yes, I had to make some telephone calls. Those Fashion Designers are expecting us.'

Posie moved forward quickly and closed the plate-glass window dividing the front from the back of the car, giving them some privacy.

'Have you, er, rectified their mistake?' Posie motioned subtly with her head towards Briggs and the driver. 'About your *position?*'

Rainbird didn't meet her gaze. 'No. You know how it is...'

She stayed quiet and watched Rainbird open the file and search through it, as their car sped through the river-like torrents of water dashing down Castle Street, the superb view of Dover Castle which towered above them obscured altogether by the solid sheets of rain.

Something odd suddenly occurred to Posie, and, feeling like she had quite the upper hand, she asked Sergeant Rainbird straight up:

'How come you haven't asked me what *I'm* doing here, anyhow? Who's paying *my* fees?'

Rainbird shrugged. 'I just assumed you were working on one of your cases, Miss. I figured if you wanted to tell me the *exact* angle of your interest you would, but in your own sweet time.'

Posie felt suddenly guilty at her sharpness of manner. 'Who is it you are working for at the Yard, Rainbird? It's not *my* Richard, is it? Or Inspector Oats? Oh, *please...*'

Rainbird made great play of shaking his head. 'I'm on my own, actually, Miss. But that's best kept strictly between ourselves.'

As she had thought. He was acting as a lone wolf. Like *she* always did. An opportunity which now looked like turning into quite a juicy case; a career-changer, wedding or no wedding at the weekend.

'So does Prudence know you're down here? Weren't you two meant to be doing some important things before your wedding on Saturday? *She's* taken the whole week off.'

Rainbird looked a bit put-out. 'Oh, it was nothing *that* important, Miss. You're still coming? With the Chief Commissioner, of course?'

'Of course. We wouldn't miss it for the world.'

Posie looked out as they reached the high ground above Dover and the cliff-tops and sodden fields spun past. The sky here was endless, even if it was full of rain. Posie kept thinking about Elsie's letter.

Why not show it to Rainbird? At least then he'd understand her interest. And maybe in exchange she could have a quick look at the manila file which he was hogging so greedily all to himself.

She handed Elsie Moncrieff's four-month-old letter over to Sergeant Rainbird all in a rush, before she could change her mind. She explained how it hadn't been answered by her office, without apportioning the blame onto Prudence – *his* fiancée – and thus saving them all a horrible embarrassment.

'See? So *this* is my exact angle, Rainbird. My "interest". Please read it and tell me what you think. Something's dashed odd, to my mind.'

She watched as the big, familiar man at her side took the paper and read it through. Then, as he had been trained to, he read it through again. He passed it back to her.

'Barmy,' he concluded, as if everything was already solved.

'What a load of guff! Maybe we're *all* barking up the wrong tree here, eh? We're all setting so much score by the Pathologist's findings of a hand-print on the body, that we're all now running about wondering whether the lass has been murdered. But it doesn't take much of a leap of the imagination from what's written in that letter to accepting the fact that the girl threw herself off the cliff on Sunday night, does it? Something "wrong"! More like something wrong in the head!'

He patted his grey folder now as if in relief: 'It all ties up with this lack of a proper identity, doesn't it? We'll probably find the dead lass was some crazy-in-the-head woman whose past wasn't very convenient for landing herself a plum job with famous people. So she re-invented herself and called herself Elsie Moncrieff. Maybe it all caught up with her and it proved too much? Poor lass.'

Posie stuffed the letter back into her carpet bag and looked at Sergeant Rainbird angrily, annoyed at herself for having let him read her client's precious words, for severing a trust which had been placed in her. Albeit a dead client's trust.

She was reminded suddenly, uncomfortably of her own fiancé's words about Elsie's barminess. How she ought to leave the thing well alone.

Well, what if both men were wrong?

There was a mystery here which went way beyond a false identity and falling off a cliff, Posie was sure of it.

But she needed to play ball: she needed Rainbird. However much he was annoying her with his slack methods and small-mindedness.

'So can I see the Pathologist's report?' she asked casually.

'Of course, Miss. Not much you didn't already know, though. Not sure you'll understand all the medical jargon either, Miss. But here you go.'

Posie, quietly enraged, flipped through the two orange pages of the post-mortem. Actually, it was true that the language was pretty indecipherable, not that she'd admit *that* to Rainbird. Instead, she nodded sagely. But the fact remained: in this report, Elsie was reduced to being a dead body on a slab in the Dover morgue. Posie tried not to look sick. Instead, she found what she was looking for and struck the page firmly.

'*This* is interesting. The hand-print itself.'

'What exactly, Miss?'

'The size of it. The Pathologist makes his point about it being obtained either on death or in the twelve hours before. But he refuses to be drawn on whether it's a female or male hand-print. The size is totally inconclusive.'

'Well, that's that then,' concluded Rainbird sourly.

Posie went back through the document. 'No, not quite, Sergeant. That's not the only anomaly. This report says that the Pathologist only examined the body when it was brought to the morgue, and he states his concern that the area at the top of the cliff where Elsie fell from hasn't been searched with a Forensic team on hand. He recommends that.'

Posie handed back the report. 'He recommends it even though there's been heavy rain since, and even though the evidence may be compromised, or erased. *I'd* follow it up if I were you, Sergeant. *If* you're taking over this investigation properly.'

Rainbird pulled back the glass. 'Hello! Briggs! I say! Did you fellas search Ness Point on Monday, after the body was found?'

Briggs shrugged, as if they were talking about a time long gone, not just two days previously. 'Er, in a manner of speaking, sir. As I said, it was just me. I walked over the whole of Ness Point, but there was nothing doing. It was soggy as a bog after that storm, and it were still raining. No hope of finding footprints, or anything like that, sir.'

'No signs of a struggle, Constable Briggs?' Posie cut in quickly, on the edge of her seat. 'It seems from what we know now that there may have been a fight on the cliff-top.'

Briggs caught Posie's eyes in the main mirror and she read the frustration in them, and the slight disbelief that he even had to answer her, combined with a fear of having messed up – it was all there in his glance.

'Nothing, Miss. Needle in a hay-stack territory, if you ask me. If you was thinking of going over there now, I doubt you'd find anything in the thick mud. A waste of time.'

'You're right, Briggs. Good man! That'll do.' Rainbird snapped the window shut firmly, as if to close the subject entirely.

Posie shook her head in disbelief.

Now they were speeding past the village of St Margaret's-at-Cliffe, past the church and the village hall, past the smart mid-range Cliffe Hotel, all boarded up for winter, on past other smaller guest-houses, all similarly shuttered.

The sea, grey and endless, sparkling like sodden diamonds, was on all sides now, like a thick woollen muffler. And then the road ahead led down, down to the sandy beach and the resort of St Margaret's Bay. They were at the level of the cliff-tops. Coming up, there was a layby on the right. Gates to a big, closed-up property. A property Posie still saw in her dreams.

Maypole Manor.

Between Posie and Sergeant Rainbird there hung an uncomfortable silence, a tacit acknowledgement that they had both been here before, to St Margaret's Bay, almost three years previously. *Another crime.* They had worked undercover then, in a tight, highly-effective team under the direction of Inspector Richard Lovelace, together with another excellent colleague who was now dead, Sergeant Binny.

Posie suddenly felt distinctly nauseous. She leant forward, rapped: 'I say! Driver, please pull up for a second, will you? Just here? In this layby?'

The motor slowed and pulled in. A huge iron gate was boarded up, with starkly painted 'KEEP OUT' and 'DANGER' and 'DUE FOR DEMOLITION' signs lashed up all over it. Wintery trees around the place hid from view the long drive and the house at the end of it, Maypole Manor, with its extensive cliff-top gardens.

Briggs turned around, surprised, but Rainbird gave a cheery thumbs-up, and Briggs, dismissed, chatted instead to the driver.

Rainbird rubbed at the condensation building up on the windowpane. 'Miss? Was there a reason you wanted to stop here? We should press on. Those fancy Fashion Designers are expecting us.'

Posie swallowed nervously. The case three years ago had been a deadly one, but it had been fascinating too. A New Year's house party gone wrong. In the snow. Perhaps the most dangerous of her career so far. And because of that particular case Posie was the person she was *now*. She had met people at that party who had made her *who* she was now.

She stared out at the gate, and whispered: 'You *do* remember the case, Sergeant?'

Rainbird cleared his throat. 'I won't forget it in a hurry, Miss. It went down as a bit of a legend at the Yard. All that snow, the murder, working deep undercover. But the Chief Commissioner – your, er, fiancé – he handled it marvellously.'

'Of course he did.'

At the time things had been different. Three years ago Richard Lovelace had been happily married to his wife, Molly. And Posie had been in the first exciting throes of her relationship with Alaric Boynton-Dale, the man she had later become engaged to.

But in the very midst of it all, totally unexpectedly, here, at St Margaret's Bay, she had met another man. A man she couldn't seem to shake from her thoughts, however much she tried.

'Look, Miss. Do you see that fancy golden sign which has fallen down on the ground? "CASA VENETO" it says. What's that all about, then?'

Posie, jolted from her thoughts so abruptly, stared at the sign, which looked like it would be more appropriate outside a London-based Italian brasserie or a nightclub, rather than atop a sea-front Manor House gate. 'At the end of the case Maypole Manor was sold, Sergeant. The new owners called it Casa Veneto.'

Rainbird snorted in a derisory manner. 'Silly sort of name, if you don't mind me saying so, Miss. Inappropriate.'

'I agree. I think the new owners only kept the place on for a year. They married and then divorced. I believe it's still known to the locals as Maypole Manor, and I think it always will be. The new owners tried to sell it, but to no avail. It's being demolished now. The place will be sold just for the land.'

Rainbird looked pleased. 'Too right. Who would want to live there, in the big house, with everything that happened? My heart fell when I was given – I mean when I decided to take – this Elsie Moncrieff case yesterday. This village seems to have a peculiar draw for strange things happening in it. I can't say I'll be unhappy to wrap everything up and leave here, pronto.' He flicked at the glass. 'Carry on, Driver.'

And then, as the car began its descent down the steep, winding road to the sea, Sergeant Rainbird passed across the entire grey manila file, and placed it between them in the middle of the seat.

'Only fair, isn't it, Miss? You've shown me your interest, now I'll show you everything they've got so far on this girl about whom we know so little. There's not much, I'm afraid. But there *is* the letter from Miss Douglas, firing the girl. See here?'

He pulled a separate 'EVIDENCE' envelope from the file, opened it and gave Posie a plain, white, neatly-opened envelope with 'ELSIE MONCRIEFF' written on the outside. Posie shook out the letter; one thin, small sheet with a bronze crest of the sea atop it, showing the intertwined names of 'DOUGLAS & STONE' as a header. The letter was scratchily written in black ink, as if it had been hurried over.

ELSIE,
FROM POINT OF OPENING THIS LETTER (WRITTEN SUNDAY 2ND NOVEMBER, 1924), CONSIDER YOURSELF DISMISSED FROM YOUR EMPLOYMENT AS HOUSEKEEPER AT WHITE SHAW.
YOU KNOW WHAT YOU HAVE DONE.
YOU HAVE ONE NIGHT (TONIGHT) TO CLEAR OUT YOUR THINGS AND GET OUT. I WANT YOU GONE TOMORROW.
PETRONELLA DOUGLAS.

Posie let out a disbelieving breath. 'Gracious. This is just downright *rude*. Thank goodness the poor girl never read it.'

Rainbird shrugged, tucking it away again. 'Depends, doesn't it, what it was all about. Maybe this Elsie really *had* done something awful? We can't tell from this letter, can we?'

'True enough. Well, Miss Douglas got her wish, didn't she? Elsie *was* gone the next day. No wonder the Coroner was so judgemental towards Mrs Douglas. What else is in that file, apart from the Pathologist's report?'

'Not much, really. Pretty thin pickings. There's a photo taken from the girl's studio-flat which Briggs here thought was important. We'll have to go through the studio-flat a second time, of course.'

'Of course,' Posie agreed. 'And why don't you call in Forensics: Dr Poots from London? They can check for fingerprints.'

'Fingerprints? Hold your horses, Miss. Forensics is a bit much, just for a suicide.'

Posie opened her mouth to protest that *surely this wasn't within a mere Sergeant's decision-making remit*, but then she looked down and saw the folder had bounced open as they went over a rut in the road, and on the very top, staring up at her, was a photograph, hole-punched and pinioned into place with official police green-string treasury tags.

A shiver passed down her spine.

Here was a snapshot of Elsie Moncrieff looking up at her. And for Posie it was like coming face-to-face with an old, impossibly long-lost friend.

'Stop the car again,' she demanded. 'Right now. Just here. I need some air.'

And she thought she might cry aloud with pain and a terrible recognition.

* * * *

Six

'Miss? What's the matter?'

Rainbird had dashed out after her. The rain had thankfully stopped but a mighty wind was slapping at them. And the thick privet hedge of the driveway they had swung into was doing nothing to protect them.

Posie had instinctively shielded the photograph under her coat lapel, but now she took it out again, tapped it nervously. 'It's just that no-one told me the dead girl was quite so beautiful.'

That much was true.

So far in all of this, Elsie Moncrieff had been a faceless, then nameless character who had been a useful Housekeeper. Now she had been revealed to Posie as having been strikingly beautiful.

Well, who could have blamed Tony Stone, really, if truth be told? If they *were* having an affair.

Obviously taken a few years back, the girl in the photograph with the finely-boned face had long fair hair, coiled about her head in a chignon, in the old-fashioned style. Elsie had been wearing a sharply-cut black coat, shielding her eyes from the sun.

'What a dreadful waste.'

Rainbird made a show of checking his wristwatch, but

when Posie gave no indication of hurrying up, Rainbird leant back against the car, folding his arms.

In fact, Posie was playing for time. Her thoughts were running away from her fast, inconveniently ahead of any solid facts. *I'm thinking with my heart here, and not my head.*

And her heart was beating very fast.

For in that split-second of recognition Posie had experienced a horrible feeling of *déjà vu.* A strange coming together of strands, previously left untied.

Was she just imagining things?

For she could have sworn that the girl in the photograph bore an uncanny resemblance to the man she had met in the very midst of the Maypole Manor case.

Max.

The mere mention of his name made her stomach churn and fill with butterflies.

Max had been German, trained as a medical doctor. And then in 1917, plucked from the livid horrors of a German medical tent in Messines, France, he had overnight, on pain of death, become a spy recruited by the most secretive level of the British Secret Intelligence Service, a highly-effective offshoot of MI5.

There had been no way back. After a spell of training he had been placed here at the front-line of England, next to its narrowest boundary of sea with France. He had been disguised by the Secret Services very convincingly as a Catholic priest; an elaborate subterfuge which had involved a complicated fictional private life, with a back-story about an illegitimate small son who lived locally. It had been so thorough it had taken Richard Lovelace in entirely.

Posie wanted to laugh now at the deception which had taken place.

Max had reappeared in Posie's life again after the death of Alaric, and although Max was wildly unsuitable, and had never offered Posie any promise of a future, he had been like a flame to which she, like a moth, had been irresistibly drawn.

A dangerous, delicious liaison, which every girl hopes for, and every girl fears. The end of the tale stung in the re-telling: Max had been lost in top-secret action in the summer just gone.

Dead.

Posie had never quite had the guts to tell Richard Lovelace all about Max, not properly. Although she was pretty certain he had guessed.

Posie had never loved Max. That much she knew. The affair had been nothing like the sort of love she felt now for Richard Lovelace: an all-consuming and almost hungry desire to share Richard's life and to share his joys and disappointments; to become his wife and to bring up his children, Phyllis and baby Katie who was still in hospital. To perhaps even bring new children into the world with him.

But still.

It was like picking at a scab. For surely, if she was truly honest with herself – *which she hadn't been up until now, had she?* – this trip to St Margaret's Bay was as much about Max as it was about her guilt over not dealing with Elsie Moncrieff's request for help.

Wasn't it?

Like a victim coming back to the scene of a crime, Posie recognised in herself a *need* to return here. Where, in her memory at least, Max still belonged.

It was ridiculous. And it was unfair; unfair on darling Richard. But the need was real.

Perhaps it was because she had not seen Max die? Had not mourned his body. Posie realised with a sudden sharp shock that she needed to lay Max's ghost to rest, to say goodbye, otherwise she would never be free of him.

Posie stared hard at the photograph of Elsie again. Was she seeing things which weren't there? Did this dead girl resemble Max at all?

Her heart was still hammering wildly but she felt a small sense of relief wash over her.

No: she must have been wrong.

It must just have been that the image of Max, very much in Posie's thoughts since her arrival in Kent earlier that morning, had been inconveniently superimposed by her brain onto the dead woman's face.

And how could there be a resemblance anyhow? Max had always told Posie he had left no-one behind in Germany. No-one to care whether he lived or died.

She passed the picture back to Rainbird, who was shivering in his thin trench-coat.

'I'm fine now, Rainbird. Let's go. Sorry to hold you up here.'

But then, unexpectedly, Posie saw a sign, rough black letters on a white board, half-hidden by the thick hedges.

It said 'NESS POINT' with an arrow indicating a sharp right, down an overgrown shingle track spinning off behind them, the trees and hedges along which were growing inwards, making the path seem as if it were one long, dark tunnel.

Posie must have been staring hard, at both the sign and the track, for Rainbird frowned and turned, following her gaze.

'Sergeant? What a stroke of luck! Don't you think we should go and have a look, just like the Pathologist recommended. Well?'

Rainbird looked as if he were chewing on a wasp, and looked at his watch again.

'Come on, Rainbird. It's now or never, you know that. Chances are that it will rain again later, and we only have a couple of hours' daylight left. Here we are, *now*. Those horribly self-centred Fashion Designers can just wait for us for ten minutes more, can't they?'

Rainbird huffed and puffed, but after a second or so he shuffled around the car to Briggs' passenger seat and motioned for the policeman to get out.

'What is it, sir? What we doin' along here anyhow?'

'This is the way to Ness Point, isn't it, Briggs?'

'Aye, that's right. The only way. About ten minutes down this track, all on foot, and don't I know it!'

'Well, you're going to be our tour guide, so look lively, man, and grab your torch and your regulation kit.'

'But I swear, guv, there wasn't anything to find out there!'

'No "ifs" and no "buts", Constable. We're all of us three making a return journey. Right now.'

* * * *

Seven

It was at least a ten-minute walk, and after about two minutes Posie began to feel every step.

Her smart burgundy heels pinched; they were not made for shingle, wet mud or chalky debris, but she couldn't exactly back out now, not after having virtually forced Sergeant Rainbird to make the trip. She marched on ahead, the two policemen walking behind her.

Posie thought longingly of the black waterproof boots she kept in the office at Grape Street for snow and rain, and how suitable they would be right now. She hadn't thought to bring them; hadn't imagined a trek out across cliffs like this.

When the track eventually opened up onto the green scrubland of the cliff itself she looked all about herself. Ahead was the actual cliff-edge, and she saw that 'Ness Point' was a real, *physical* point. Dotted about the place was gorse, and there was no fencing or protective device anywhere. A few feet back from the point was a dense group of scrubby bushes, all grown up around an almost completely obscured wooden seat. The grass all about was soaking and thick; wild almost.

Constable Briggs seemed to realise something was expected of him.

He indicated towards the bench: 'Where the body was found, below, on the rocks, indicates that *this* is where she fell from. Our nameless woman. It's a well-known suicide spot, actually. We get a fair few every year. But it's also a spot for sweethearts, too: seeking some privacy from pryin' eyes. Funny, that, isn't it, how people come up here for quite different reasons?'

Posie was about to remark that it wasn't funny at all, but just then a man emerged from the shelter of the covered bench; a man in his fifties with binoculars around his neck, and wearing head-to-toe black oilskins with very sensible waterproof boots. Posie envied him those boots, while simultaneously groaning to herself that the place hadn't been roped off and investigated.

Not only had the terrible weather had a chance to do its worst here, and wreck a possible scene-of-crime, but now there were possible sweethearts, and, from the looks of things, birdwatchers, thrown into the mix, too. All of them trampling heavily across the last place Elsie Moncrieff had ever stood upon this earth.

The man with the binoculars had something in his hands. He was turning it over, and squinting at it admiringly. Just then he looked up and his gaze alighted upon Constable Briggs. Relief seemed to wash over his heavily-set face.

'Officer?' the man called out, remaining where he was. The three of them hurried over and waited while Briggs flashed his formal papers.

The man extended his palm delicately. And for a few seconds Posie thought he might be going to show them all some rare dead bird, or an egg or something.

The article *was* egg-shaped, that much was true. But it was made of glass, and tiny, and it sparkled in the rays of a poor weak sun which was now trying to break through.

'See this?' said the birdwatcher, awe-struck. 'This is a real-life tungsten incandescent lightbulb! The very best, an "Ever-Ready", would you believe?'

Posie stared at the man like he had lost his mind. 'I'm sorry, sir. It's a *what?*'

The man had passed the small glass lightbulb to Briggs. 'It's from a flash-light, Miss. Probably the very best you can buy in the world right now. It hasn't smashed and it hasn't expired, either. Therefore, I think it must have sprung away from the main flash-light, if the whole torch was dropped. I dread to think how much the *whole* flash-light which this bulb became separated from would have cost. You see, Miss, this make – "Ever-Ready" – is only available to buy in the United States of America. I've been hankering after one myself for a couple of years now. Too dear though, by half.'

Posie smiled. 'American, you say?'

'That's right.' He turned to the two policemen. 'I wouldn't have kept it, Officers. I promise. I've been doing a bit of birding today up here and I've been using that there bench as a hide. Seen a lovely pair of ravens, and a cormorant, too.'

'*Where* was that bulb?' cut in Posie determinedly. '*Exactly?*'

The man motioned backwards. 'It was right under the bench, Miss.'

He indicated to a smart steel thermos-flask attached to his belt with a leather loop. 'I lost the lid of my flask of tea, see? It rolled right under. And when I got on my hands and knees, I found that little beauty there too. I wouldn't have found it otherwise.'

After taking the man's details and dismissing him, the policemen approached the bench. Posie was silent, but her thoughts were tearing away from her.

Rainbird, beside her, was giving Briggs a good dressing-down: 'Did you hear that, man? *Hands and knees?* That's what you should have been doing on Monday! You should have been looking up here *everywhere* for any pertinent evidence. I do realise we don't actually know if this 'ere lightbulb has anything to do with the dead woman, but it seems more than likely, doesn't it? Was a flash-light – of any make – reported as having been found up here or on the rocks below, or next to Elsie Moncrieff's body? Do we know if she had an Ever-Ready torch among her belongings? It sounds like it would have been a bally expensive purchase.'

'No, sir. No evidence of a flash-light among her known belongings. Nor was there any such torch found with the body. I'm sorry, sir. I really am.'

'Mnnn.'

They had approached the bench and now they were actually there, right at the cliff-edge almost, Posie could see just how perilous such a position might be on a stormy, dark night.

Of course Elsie had carried a torch. She must have. Only a fool would have come up here without one.

Posie took a few seconds to scan the view. It was magnificent, with its vista of the rough, choppy sea on all sides, extending to the horizon. To the left, you could clearly see St Margaret's Bay itself, and Posie noted that the tide was almost in, smashing in brown waves in high arcs over the shingle and sand beaches.

But Elsie wouldn't have been able to see anything other than the darkness itself when she came up here on Sunday night.

So what *had* brought her up here?

A sweetheart? An argument? An enemy?

Posie sat down on the bench, finding the soft shelter of the plants surprisingly calming around her.

For a second Posie fancied she was being watched, and a spine-tingling tickle ran down her neck and back.

But she shrugged it away as being ridiculous. For there really was no-one up here, spying on her.

Instead, Posie forced herself to look all about her, including right under the seat. Just as the birdwatcher had done not ten minutes before.

But the man had been thorough. There was absolutely nothing to be found. No cigarette butts, no food rubbish, no discarded handkerchiefs, no ripped-up letters conveniently explaining what might have happened up here.

Posie then walked right out to the grass at the edge of the cliff-top. She felt something drawing her on.

She took a deep breath, forced herself not to look out over the cliff and its immense drop down to the rollicking sea below. Above her, gulls circled, cawing.

'Careful, Miss,' called out Briggs in an old-fashioned chivalric way. 'It's slippery round about there. That might have been what happened to this Housekeeper lady. She slipped and fell, eh? We don't want to be adding *you* to that tally, Miss, now, do we?'

Posie ignored his patronising tone. Instead, she started to turn the ruined lumps of earth at the cliff-edge this way and that with the toe of her never-to-be-worn-again-in-London red shoes. The mulched-up earth could have been caused by the rain, or by the tramping to and fro of Briggs on the Monday morning, or by others coming past in the last two days.

But conceivably it *could* have been the location of a fight; a desperate scrabble by a desperate girl to hold on to earth which wouldn't hold her.

Posie felt a wave of sadness wash over her.

You didn't even know this girl, she tried to reason with herself. *What on earth is wrong with you?*

She dragged her mind back to think like a proper Private Detective.

Evidence wise, Briggs had been right that the grass and mud were offering up nothing, and that it would be extremely difficult – probably impossible even – for Dr Poots, the Scotland Yard Pathologist, to establish any certainty regarding clues. Rainbird and Briggs were turning back the way they had come.

One final kick of the turf in exasperation and something gold glistened.

Suddenly Posie was on her knees, not caring about the mud rubbing all over her coat and woollen stockings. She pulled at whatever was lodged in the wet earth. A necklace? A bracelet?

Up it came.

She had been wrong. She was holding a glasses chain, slim golden links in a long chain, with a neat tortoiseshell hook on the end for attaching to the spectacles themselves.

It was an expensive accessory, Posie knew without doubt. She had seen such things for sale in Paris, in Venice, in the Burlington Arcade in Piccadilly. Very far from here. And its classic, clever design was such that it could be worn by either a man or a woman.

But the chain was broken, the other end finished with one of the golden links ruptured and open, and the matching tortoiseshell hook was missing.

Posie fingered the thing gently, rubbing the mud away, not caring if it was all over her hands. *Broken.* Which could mean that it had been broken here.

And for such an expensive item to break would surely take some force? A tug, at least, if not a dangerous fight involving considerable strength?

But had Elsie Moncrieff worn glasses? Or a glasses chain? Posie sighed: there was only one way to find out, and that was by asking those who had worked with her.

Pocketing the delicate chain, her secret haul, and walking away quickly from Ness Point, Posie didn't bother to announce her find to Sergeant Rainbird when she joined him at the car, and they sat in an odd silence as they drove down the steep hill, passing the renowned smugglers pub, The Green Man, on the right, with its view straight out to the rough, rough sea.

Then they swung to the left, away from the direction of Ness Point, driving slowly past the 'village on the beach'. This consisted of a series of black-beamed villas and a shuttered building with 'TEA GARDENS' painted optimistically on the roof, all built right up against the majestic White Cliffs of England, and all straggling along behind a shingle road, against which the sea was lashing in vicious high waves.

But Posie was staring further on, beyond, to the last part of visible cliff of the bay. She was entranced.

For there stood an almost entirely glass-constructed house, new and sparkling, with a strange oval-like shape to it, like an abandoned false eye. It took the whole dramatic scene of St Margaret's Bay and stole it. It seemed to gather and absorb all the scarce November light somehow. A glittering monstrosity, a fake diamond.

White Shaw.

With a start, Posie realised that the car had come to a complete stop again and both Briggs and Rainbird were looking at her expectantly.

'Sorry?' Oh! Is *this* the Bay Hotel?'

'Yes, Miss,' answered Briggs solemnly. He nodded towards the brown-bricked, triple-gabled hotel with its smart white balconies and hopeful green-striped sun blinds, all now rolled up for winter. 'Quite the place, if you don't mind me sayin', Miss. There's normally no end of famous people larkin' about. Up to all sorts.' He tapped his freckled nose confidentially. 'Even royalty. But most of that's in summer, of course. Do you want to check in now, Miss?'

For a split-second Posie thought longingly of the suite she had booked with its central-heating and bathroom; it would be an opportunity to freshen up, to warm up from this damp November air. But she'd already wasted enough of their time.

'Golly, no. Let's press ahead.'

After the partition window had been closed, Posie turned to Rainbird. 'But *you* must stay at the Bay Hotel, too, Rainbird. Where else were you thinking of? The places up at St Margaret's-at-Cliffe all looked like they were closed up. And Dover is too far from here, surely? You need to be on hand. Close by.'

Rainbird looked embarrassed. 'I hadn't thought to spend more than the day down here, truth be told, Miss. I'm not sure if such a hotel would be allowed. You know, police expenses and all that…'

Posie clicked her tongue against the roof of her mouth impatiently. 'I'll make sure it's allowed. I think you should be near to everything. You can't get nearer than this. I'll speak to Richard if necessary.'

'If you think it's appropriate, Miss. I'd be grateful.'

'Good, that's sorted then.'

As they set off again, past the hotel and a closed-up holiday bungalow, they saw a sodden stuffed figure of Guy Fawkes sitting atop a mountain of wet wood in front of the Bay Hotel. It was receiving frantic last-minute attentions from a group of village men and boys.

A couple of likely lads had brought down metal bins which they were using to stuff full of sawdust, then packing them full of potatoes. Another enterprising lad was scrawling a sign saying 'BAKED TATTIES – SOLD HERE' and his pal was making a display of a heap of toffee apples in a none-too-clean-looking wheelbarrow.

To her horror, Posie's stomach rumbled. Apart from her lukewarm coffee in the stationary car, Posie hadn't eaten or drunk anything much since breakfast, which had been very, very early, and it was now coming up for two o'clock. She dug out the bar of Fry's milk chocolate which she always carried in case of an emergency.

'Looks like it will be quite a show tonight, Sergeant, doesn't it? *If* the rain holds off.' She split the foil of the chocolate and offered the bar to Rainbird, who took a clean half.

'We should be able to see the bonfire from the hotel, anyway. It looks like it will be a jolly big affair! Richard's going to the one in Clapham. On the Common.'

'I never held much sway with Guy Fawkes Night, if truth be told, Miss Parker.' Rainbird had bolted down the chocolate and now lit up a cigarette, inhaling deeply, looking slightly morose. 'Never could quite work out what it was we're supposed to be celebrating. And besides, all these bonfires, all these fireworks – worst was those Peace Day Celebrations in 1921– just adds to our workload, doesn't it? Always some accident to investigate here or there, eh?'

Posie was sorry she'd said anything, and fingered the bit of spectacle chain in her pocket and stared instead at White Shaw, as the car stopped right outside.

****

Eight

'My gosh! It looks like a giant armadillo.'

'Have you ever seen an armadillo, Miss? A real live one? I can't say I have.'

'Once, at London Zoo.'

'What was it like?'

'It seemed a sad, shy creature. As if it were lost. It barely raised its face from the ground, actually.'

'It was probably just hungry, Miss. Like me right now. What I wouldn't give for a round of potted-meat sandwiches.'

They got out, Rainbird stamping his feet against the chill, taking a last drag of his smoke before stamping on that, too. 'They're expecting us, Miss Parker. But you should know I don't have an official Search Warrant. We'll need their permission to do anything other than breathe here. So I need to play nicely, see? By the book.'

'I understand.' Posie smiled her widest smile. 'I'll be on my best behaviour, promise.'

Posie walked closer, leaving Rainbird behind, chatting to Briggs.

She stared at the mesmerising house: the private, shingly beach in front, so often photographed; the immense waves almost breaking over the glass front of the house; the white chalk cliffs right behind.

But then she realised it was all a mirage.

Up close the cliffs were shored up with ugly grey nets, to prevent chalk breaking away and falling on the house. Electric cables also swung wildly among the netting. This close it felt ominous.

It's dangerous, this house. From every angle.

A white-painted concrete wall with a gate in it ran in an ugly fashion right around the house, creating a vast courtyard in which some small outbuildings had been erected. Nearest Posie, near the gate, a car-port housed a navy-coloured van and some other beautiful, new cars. A tall, well-built, pimply man in his early twenties with a bald head but a very hairy neck, wearing a buff-coloured boiler-suit was slowly shifting boxes and suitcases into the open back of the navy van. He looked hot and bothered, despite the chill.

A black Lagonda was parked inside the wall, and a very easy-on-the-eye driver, immaculate in a navy-and-gold livery was standing beside it, looking wary. Posie followed his gaze and saw that the object of his worry was a bright red ball, moving at an erratic high speed.

As she watched, two little boys, quite alone, quite identical, both in peaked brown caps and matching brown gaberdine coats could be seen in the distance, within the courtyard, kicking the red ball with enthusiastic abandon.

All that glass.

Posie ran forward, leaving Rainbird behind. She crossed the courtyard, away from the front of the house and she suddenly appreciated the clever trick that Jolyon Peterson, the absent architect, had played; for the back of the house wasn't glass at all, but consisted of great rising walls of white-painted concrete, like the courtyard wall, heavy and cold and ugly. Only the front and roof of the place was glass. It really was a mirage. Posie shivered and pulled up her coat collar higher.

The two boys had stopped kicking their ball and had turned to stare instead at Posie.

They were standing at the back of a kitchen of some sort, sandwiched between the bulk of the cliffs and the great concrete back of the house. A couple of overflowing dustbins were placed unglamorously by a flimsy door with a patterned glass panel in it. Another bin in the same row was obviously used for small domestic fires, as ashes were strewn all about.

And now Posie saw she had been wrong about the twins being alone.

A big man, dark, handsome, in his late thirties, sheeny with sweat, was smoking a gasper and sitting hunched on the concrete step by the glass door, several feet behind the lads. He was also dressed in a dark-navy livery, and seemed lost in thought, completely absorbed. Looking again, Posie recognised him from the Inquest – he was the bulky, large manservant whose evidence had never been heard. His otherwise handsome face was disfigured by what was obviously a badly-set broken nose. What was he? A boxer? A bully-boy?

Posie turned to the twins. They were about five years old and they seemed mesmerised by her, kept whispering together.

Identical in almost every way, the lads had grey eyes the colour of the sea, perfectly tilted-up noses and waxy, rosy little faces under strawberry-blonde, reddish hair. When they opened their mouths, gappy, milk-tooth-less smiles were revealed. Both twins had no front teeth at all, but two more beautiful, delicate children you couldn't hope to meet. These must surely be the twins Petronella Douglas had spoken of at the Inquest. Kit and Sammy, wasn't it? The twins Elsie Moncrieff had sometimes looked after?

Posie almost felt like laughing: Petronella Douglas and Tony Stone, who were both distinctly plain people, verging on the ugly, even if they *were* fashionable, had managed to produce this breathtakingly perfect little pair of would-be angels.

Life was jolly odd sometimes.

You never knew what you might get: look at little Phyllis Lovelace with her sturdy little brown limbs and determined hazel eyes. There was very little of Richard in her to speak of, physically, but Posie loved her enormously, as her loyal, dependable character and willingness to see the best in anyone had come straight from her father.

Posie squatted down now on her heels, almost face-to-face with the boys. She realised she had absolutely no idea how they could help her, or how she could help them. *How much did little children really know about anything, actually?* She shouldn't even be here. Only a moment ago she'd promised Rainbird she would play nicely, according to the rules. She gulped.

'Hello, lads. Not at school today?'

The little boy nearest her shook his head mournfully. 'No, Miss. But we'd *far* rather be at school than be here. The tide's in and there's nowhere to play but back here in this horrid yard. It's like a prison!'

He bounced the red ball a couple of times, hard, as if to prove how confined the spot really was. 'We've been ordered out of the house; there's lots of shouting and banging of doors and packing of things going on. So we've got old Mickey here to watch us.'

Posie flashed a look over at the dark man, who was still miles away in his thoughts. She pressed on hurriedly: '*Why* exactly are you off school today, boys?'

The second twin stepped forward, not to be outdone. 'Mama says there could be trouble. Maybe people from the newspapers would wait at the school gates, trying to get to us. She thought it was best we stayed here all of this week. But it's *hateful*.'

'Why would people from the newspapers want to get *you*?' Posie frowned, genuinely uncomprehending.

The first twin raised an all-important eyebrow. '*We* don't know, Miss. Perhaps because Mama has fancy houseguests.

80

We're not supposed to know about them, of course. But we sometimes meet them, if they stay on. A real-life *prince*, sometimes. He was jolly fun, actually. Kept giving us chocolate and cigarette cards and wanting to teach us how to play golf.'

Posie was disconcerted. 'Ah, of course.' So the stories of royal houseguests were true. *Out of the mouths of babes.* Good job the twins *hadn't* been intercepted by any newspaper reporters, if extracting a story from them was so easy.

The second twin, less trusting, shushed his brother, giving him an elbow in the ribs, then looked embarrassed. '*You're* not from the newspapers, are you, Miss?'

'Oh, no. I'm here to see your parents, as it happens.' *Well, that much was true.*

The second twin looked hopeful. 'Are you here to replace Elsie, Miss? Because that's what we thought when we first saw you a few minutes ago. That you were coming to take her place.'

The first twin came closer to Posie and put his hand on her own burgundy leather-gloved one. '*Are* you? Will you take Elsie's job? Will *you* look after us from now on?'

Out of the corner of Posie's eye the huge dark man had finally seen her, was rising, quickly for such a big chap. She could see Rainbird too, hurrying over in a panic, leaving Briggs at the motor. She kept on: 'Do *you* boys know what happened to Elsie?'

The first boy shrugged. 'She just disappeared, Miss. Into thin air. One day she was here and the next she was gone. And "*good riddance to bad rubbish*", is what Mama says.'

'Oh. Does she now?'

'Yes. But we don't agree. Elsie was lovely.' The first boy turned to his brother. 'Wasn't she, Sammy? A diamond. That's what Papa said, and he was right.'

The other twin nodded, but he flashed slightly wary eyes at the big man now heading in their direction. 'She *was* lovely,' he whispered. 'We keep hoping she's coming back.' He looked like he might cry. A sudden pleading note entered his voice. 'We loved her, Miss. Although we never told her that. But *you'd* do, too, Miss.'

The first twin pressed Posie's hand tighter. 'We were just saying, Miss, when we saw you coming, that you look a bit like Elsie. You've got the same big blue eyes, and you look kind. But actually, Miss, you'd be a much better person to look after us.'

'Really?' Posie was amused, despite herself. 'Why's that?'

'Because you speak like we do, Miss. Clearly. Like the teachers at school, and Matron. You don't have a funny voice and use funny, odd words. That's what Elsie did.'

'Oh? Odd words?'

The dark man now loomed over the twins, arms crossed, a threat carved in every sinew, every line of his body.

The first twin looked up at him, and to Posie's surprise, the boy laughed disrespectfully. 'Like old Mickey here, Miss. Such a funny voice! We can't understand a thing he says either, and you can imagine what it was like when those two were together. Because Mickey was Elsie's boyfriend, weren't you, Mickey? And he's been crying ever since she left him.'

The small, beautiful boy laughed, and started to shout *boo-hoo*, *boo-hoo* sarcastically over and over again, making crying gestures as he ran off, followed by his more cautious brother.

The man, Mickey, raised an eyebrow, and rubbed the knuckles on his right hand in the palm of his left, as if limbering up for a fight: 'And who the sweet bee-jaysus might you be, Miss? You're trespassing: harrasin' these wee laddies. Tell me, are you from a newspaper? What exactly d'you think you're up to?'

But the Irishman's rancour was cut off abruptly by Rainbird, who had evidently waved some sort of identification in the air behind Posie's head.

'Scotland Yard?'

The man's frown disappeared into a polite, begrudgingly welcoming countenance. 'Oh, yes. I see.'

He nodded: 'We were expecting you both about half an hour ago. You could have come to the main front door though, eh? Not lurked around here. You were at Court earlier, weren't you? I'm Mickey. Mickey O'Dowd. I'm Tony Stone's right-hand man, just so you know.'

The big man called over to the twins. 'You'd better come into the main house, you pair of terrors! Cook can look after you.'

Their sudden high spirits quite gone, the twin boys trotted obediently over, and vanished through the back door. They all followed.

The house inside was like a strange dream. The rooms facing the yard and the cliff-face were a long run of workrooms with huge floor-to-ceiling panels of glass, so you could see everything inside. The rooms contained cutting tables and sewing machines, with cabinets full of spilling fabrics in whites and creams and silvers, some of which glittered in the dim light.

There were further rooms with mannequins, and a group of serious, aproned seamstresses were sitting together giving garments finishing touches, all in a rigid silence. Tony Stone, still in his emerald-and-white striped suit, was darting about the place, scissors and measuring-tape in his hands, completely engrossed.

'Business as usual here, I'm afraid,' explained Mickey O'Dowd in an apologetic manner, stopping and indicating to the women. 'Tony's literally just finishing things off for a big show at Haresmythe's on Saturday. I'll go in and tell him you're here now.'

Tony Stone appeared within a minute or so, on the heels of Mickey O'Dowd. He offered his hand politely and then, sucking his teeth, looked nervily about. Posie summoned up her cheeriest voice, covering the awkwardness: 'This looks a lot of work, sir.'

The man smiled. 'Och, aye. It is. It's normally just me. I dae everything. But the Bridal Shows, well, I cannae dae it all maself. We need extra hands tae help make the sheer number of garments we're showing, ye know? These ladies come doon fae London for two weeks and blast through the work. They stay in the cheapest rooms at the Bay Hotel. Today is their last day, as it happens.'

Posie looked at the women, at their fluid, expert movements, hands moving like graceful birds coming down to dip into water, over and over. She remembered that Dolly had met some of these ladies, all of whom had professed loyalty to this man. 'Did any of these women know Elsie Moncrieff, sir?'

'Och, no, Miss Parker. Mibbie they saw her go past once or twice in the corridor these last two weeks but the sewing rooms were never part of Elsie's responsibilities.'

There was a further string of kitchens, bathrooms, guestrooms. All without the huge windows, and less grand. Big Mickey swung behind them as if worried they might go off wandering in the house. Everything here was slick, very modern, with strip-lights everywhere and shiny chrome surfaces whose gloss still couldn't hide the fact that these other rooms were virtually windowless and meanly-proportioned.

Not to mention chilly: drafts seemed to whip through White Shaw like nobody's business. Posie felt cold, even in her coat.

As she passed the rooms, Posie was aware of snatches of movement: a cook in the kitchen, busily supervising the twin boys with mounds of pastry placed in front of each of them; a doe-eyed maid, immaculate in prim Victorian black-and-white, folding napkins, staring up with a barely-concealed interest.

A corridor in front of these smaller rooms had been created by the architect with a flimsy white partition wall and as they all headed through a perfectly circular white doorway in that wall, they were suddenly inside one huge glass bubble, one immense room, a cathedral of arching space.

'I say!'

And Posie stared around in genuine disbelief.

* * * *

Nine

The enormous room was set up like a London nightclub, with couches and coffee-tables and masses of unlit candles in sconces all about the edges – everything in white and red and black – and in the middle section of the room there was simply empty space.

The floor was made of clear crystal laminate in which millions of tiny pebbles had been set: the effect was of walking on a totally smooth, dream-like beach.

The illusion was completed by the architect's vision: the glass house was a miracle of proportions and light which meant that the Channel was visible from almost every side. The high tide's crashing waves seemed to lash against the very glass to the front, where the house had its own beach. There was not a boat in sight.

'Jeepers!' Posie was transfixed. 'It's like being on an ocean-liner!'

Tony Stone smiled, pleased at the analogy: 'Normally you would see ocean-liners passing by, Miss Parker, close enough to see the passengers' wee faces, ye know? And a whole load of other boats, too. But since Sunday with all this dreich, stormy weather, the Coastguard has banned sailing and there are all these patrols tae enforce the ban. This wee coast here is treacherous at the best of times. The whole fishing fleet is sitting pulled up at Dover, not able to go out. Hard times, Miss Parker, ye know? Now, why don't ye sit down here?'

Tony Stone was motioning for them to sit at a group of red leather sofas, and suddenly Mickey was serving them tea from a silver tea-pot and deftly offering up impossibly dainty *langue de chat* biscuits. Posie noticed that the man's hands were trembling throughout and she tried not to stare.

Tony Stone indicated to the manservant that he should sit down with them, as an equal, which he did, without questioning.

'We're just waiting on ma wee wifie. She knew you were coming, of course. In the meantime, please help yourselves.' Tony Stone indicated a walnut cigarette box on the table, filled with expensive Sullivan Powells. Posie watched in surprise as Sergeant Rainbird helped himself to the expensive smokes, taking several, and then proceeded to light one of them.

Posie took her tea and ate a single biscuit carefully but hungrily.

She scanned the place and reckoned that you could fit at least a hundred people inside comfortably, or, if people were dancing closely together, two hundred, maybe. A mezzanine balcony, all golden and decorated with garish Chinese dragons, circled half the room, and if you looked hard enough you could see that there were raised seats built specifically for a band. There were a couple of grand pianos, one white, one red, placed on zebra-skin rugs in different parts of the room. There were gramophones dotted about, too.

A party palace.

That was what this place was. It certainly wasn't a home.

The parties this room must have seen, Posie marvelled. *The parties Elsie Moncrieff had had to tidy up afterwards, in her job as Housekeeper.*

The guests she must have encountered.

But what danger had the Housekeeper walked into here? Why had she had to die? For Posie was certain that the answer lay here, in this very house. What had been wrong here? Apart from the dreadful décor, of course.

What had been so bad that Elsie Moncrieff had sought the help of a Private Detective?

Posie got out her silver notebook, just as Petronella Douglas flew through the circular door and dashed across the pebbled floor. She threw herself down on the sofa opposite Posie and Rainbird, next to her husband, whom she didn't greet, and lit up a custom-made red-and-black Sobranie cocktail cigarette, which she smoked in great urgent puffs through a long ebony holder.

Up this close, Petronella's kohl-rimmed eyes were smudged, as if she'd been crying and her nose looked red and sore.

Posie listened as Rainbird introduced her as an 'associate' of Scotland Yard, often brought in on cases of a sensitive or unusual nature.

Well, it was true, really.

But Petronella Douglas couldn't keep the smirk off her face:

'Oh, come off it! You think I'm a Dumb Dora? Gee, *we* sure know who you are, Miss Parker. You're one of them private eyes; diggin' out dirty secrets for a living. Mickey here recognised you all right. He told us so on the way back from Court.' Posie looked at the big Irishman, who looked pointedly away for a brief moment, somewhere out to sea.

So he had feigned not knowing who she was, out in that courtyard. *What else was he feigning?*

The American was enjoying herself now. 'But *I* knew I'd seen you before anyhow. In the news-sheets! Couple of years back, wasn't it? You were in your glad-rags, much thinner back then, and with that gorgeous Alaric

Boynton-Dale on your arm. Back in the day, huh? Poor man. Dyin' like that. You must feel *terrible*. Anyhow, it's all just fine and dandy with us, isn't it, Tony? If Miss Parker works here, with the police. Just so as we get to the bottom of who killed our itty-bitty little Housekeeper. *Poor* little Elsie.'

Posie was speechless with rage and hurt.

What a nerve! She hadn't been that much thinner when she'd been dating Alaric!

And was it possible to sound less sincere about the Housekeeper's death?

What a dreadful woman.

And Mickey O'Dowd was watching Posie too, carefully and intently from between long-lashed grey eyes, looking for a reaction. Well, he was dreadful, too.

But before Posie could say anything rash, or anything at all in fact, Rainbird rushed in: 'Did any of you know that the Housekeeper had no real identity papers?'

There was a brief silence, answered by shakes of the head all around.

Posie felt like rolling her eyes. *Talk about routine, ploddy police-work.*

She butted in, changing tack: 'At Court they said they'd been informed that Miss Moncrieff had no family. Seems strange. Everyone has someone, don't they?'

This was not quite true actually, Posie realised suddenly. After all, apart from Richard Lovelace – to whom she was not yet married – who on earth did *she* have in the world? She blustered on: 'So who told the Court this?'

Mickey O'Dowd crossed his long legs slowly, played with the little finger on his right hand, worrying at an imaginary ring. 'I believe it was me, Miss Parker, so I do. Elsie let it slip once that she was an orphan: no siblings. We were lookin' after the twins, as it happens, and she said how lucky those boys were to always have each other. Somethin' about twins, always having a connection. It stuck in my mind.'

Posie fixed him with a slightly incredulous look, although it sounded a believable enough story, actually. 'Well, we'll obviously be looking for evidence of family in her own room, among her belongings. And then checking her references thoroughly.'

Mickey O'Dowd smiled, and Posie saw with a flicker of surprise that he was actually exceedingly handsome. 'You have a Search Warrant for all of this, Miss Parker, do you now?'

Tony Stone cut in soothingly: 'Och, away with you, Mickey! That's all fine. It was Elsie herself who kept all the staff references – including her own – in her wee office next to the kitchen. Ye get on and help yerselves.'

Rainbird nodded gratefully, then got out an 'EVIDENCE' bag, and scrabbled around inside it. He produced the flash-light bulb found on the cliff-top; held it up in the immense room while everyone squinted, trying to work out what it was.

'An Ever-Ready flash-light – quite a new model apparently – must be missing this vital component just now. Can any of you tell me if you own an Ever-Ready torch, or if Miss Moncrieff did?'

Tony Stone looked flustered, tugged at his bright green lapel. 'Why, this is a wee bit awkward, because ah've got an Ever-Ready flash-light. It was a present from ma wifie here, last year, for my fortieth birthday, from America. A nice big yellow storm-light. I cannae say if Elsie owned one like it but I doubt it. You know how much these things cost? Hunners and hunners!'

'Where do you normally keep this yellow flash-light, sir?'

'In the wee hut ootside. But I havnae used it in months! We can check when we go ootside?'

'Thank you, sir. Now, can I establish each of your exact whereabouts on the night in question? Sunday night. The night Miss Moncrieff – let's call her that – died? Miss

Douglas, you told the Coroner that you went to bed. Correct?'

'Sure thing. I'd had a helluva day. I went to bed early and slept like a baby all through the night.'

The woman reclined lazily against the sofa, blowing a smoke ring ceiling-wards. She closed her eyes and Posie wondered if she had actually fallen asleep, or if she was pretending. Either way it was downright rude.

'And you, Mr Stone. You were staying in London? At The Oberoy?'

'Aye. The Porter there will remember me.'

'Thank you, sir. And you, Mr O'Dowd?'

Mickey came further forward on his chair, rubbed at both sides of his nose as if he'd recently taken off spectacles of which the bridge was too tight.

'Sunday afternoon and evening is my time off. I stay out usually, all of that time: I like to give Sidney the driver – he's my roommate – some space. Normally you'd find me in Dover, as I like to watch a fight or two. I keep a Brough motorbike in the car-port, I love riding it, but it was such awful weather I didn't go anywhere. I got myself nicely ensconced in my lodgings. Had some drinks, then fell asleep early.'

Posie looked again at Mickey, who had also taken a Sullivan Powell from the box and was smoking it casually, with a sense of entitlement.

She was horribly aware that he had barely taken his eyes off her since she had sat down, and she felt irritated by his unwelcome attention. She assumed he was the sort of man who preyed on single women in hotel bars. The man was obviously a first-class letch.

Posie addressed the Fashion Designers, turning her body away from him, deliberately excluding him. 'Please can either of you tell me why this manservant is sitting here, at this police interview, for no good reason at all that I can make out? It seems highly irregular.'

Petronella didn't move from her reclining position, still feigning sleep, and it was up to Tony Stone to answer, beetling forward on the sofa, his face anxious. A quick suck of the front teeth. '*I'll* explain, Miss Parker. I grant, it may look a wee bit unconventional. But Mickey looks after things here. We trust him with everything.'

'Why do you need such a man, Mr Stone? This isn't New York. Not last time I checked. Wasn't the Housekeeper enough?'

Rainbird clicked his teeth in irritation beside her. Tony Stone tugged at his immaculately-crafted lapels.

'Security, ah suppose, Miss Parker. A wee bit of peace of mind. We have fairly wild parties here sometimes. We have high-profile guests. Mickey gets rid of the chaff, ye know? He deals with those folks who hivnae got an invite, or those who cannae hold their drink, or cannae hold their wee tongues. Those who might make it dangerous for us.'

A bully-boy. *A guarder of doors. Of reputations. Of princes.*

Posie looked quickly at the Irishman, who grinned wolfishly back at her. He certainly looked like the sort of person it would be good to have around if things went badly for you. She turned again to Tony Stone, tiny next to his big henchman.

'Aren't these parties of yours frightfully expensive, sir?'

Tony Stone looked surprised, then laughed instead. He had a funny, tinkly laugh, not unpleasant.

'I'll say! But wifie here assures me they're worth it for publicity, for our image. She tells me they bring in clients. And she should know: she keeps an eye on our accounts. I must say, we have more orders coming in than we ever had before. So I guess it's a wee extravagance that pays off.'

'I'm glad.' Posie turned to Petronella Douglas, who was now sitting up again, eyes wide open, the pupils very large in her odd, small, dark eyes, and Posie saw a yawning hopelessness within; an addiction, a nothingness at all. Some sort of drugs were at play here, for sure.

Posie tried to tamp down the personal dislike she now felt towards the woman, to act as if she hadn't been insulted. 'So business is going well then, is it, Miss Douglas? Financially? If you look after the accounts?'

'Of course! Why wouldn't it? You know we have the Royal Warrant?'

'Ah yes.' Posie smiled broadly. 'And *was* the Prince of Wales himself at the party on Saturday, just gone? The one Elsie didn't attend?'

'No. He sure was not. The Prince is in Canada. On a big tour.' Petronella Douglas extinguished her cocktail cigarette angrily. 'I see *you* don't read the papers, Miss Parker.'

'Not if I can help it.'

And then Posie turned to Mickey, still watching her, catching him off guard.

'So tell me: *were* you Elsie Moncrieff's boyfriend? Is that what you were going to tell the Court today, if you had managed to give your statement?'

The Irishman laughed, but the smile didn't reach his eyes. 'Of course I wasn't Elsie's boyfriend. Although there were times I fair begged her to rectify that position. The Mistress was quite right to describe Elsie as a doll. But Elsie wouldn't hear of it, more's the pity. She wasn't the sort to conduct love affairs.'

So Petronella Douglas hadn't lied when she'd said Elsie hadn't had boyfriends. *Unless...*

Posie looked at all three of them, all sitting with their arms crossed, their cigarettes now extinguished. Rainbird seemed to have run out of questions and sat, dumbly, incredulously. So Posie charged on, into the abyss:

'I'd like to come to the reason why Elsie was being dismissed from her employment here. It needs answering. That unopened letter they found in her coat from you, Miss Douglas. It was very vague, just said: "YOU KNOW WHAT YOU HAVE DONE." *What* had Elsie done?'

A silence followed. Petronella Douglas looked angrily away, her mouth a hard, pursed-up artificial red line. Rainbird didn't make any attempt to push the question further.

'How illuminating. Thank you, all of you.'

Posie felt forced to go on, and turned to the diminutive Scotsman, asking the question which Rainbird obviously wouldn't dare to. A question which the Court hadn't asked aloud, either.

'Forgive my bluntness, Mr Stone. But I wondered, earlier on in Court, if perhaps *you* and Elsie were conducting an affair. Is that right? Is *that* what Elsie had "done" which so upset your wife?'

Beside her, Rainbird dropped both his grey manila file and his police notebook onto the floor with a clatter. Posie smiled tightly: 'Perhaps Miss Douglas had only just found out about it, on the Sunday? Am I correct, Mr Stone?'

At his lack of reply, Posie turned to his wife. 'Is that right?'

Tony Stone stared down at the floor, while his wife bristled up like a cat and almost spat at Posie, ferocious with an anger long pent-up, whatever drugs she had coursing through her veins now serving her with a wild energy:

'How *dare* you, Miss Parker! We welcome you – a scrap of nothingness, wearing a cheap little mass-produced Traub engagement ring – right into our home, even though you have no official standing in this enquiry at all, and you have the cheek to ask my husband this! *You!* Perhaps *you* would behave like that, huh? You with your line in dead fiancés! And I see you're engaged again now. You don't waste much time, do you? Your conduct here is outrageous. I'm sure tempted to throw you out right now. Not to mention making an official complaint to Scotland Yard.'

Her bluster and anger ebbed away, until there was nothing left, and the woman rubbed awkwardly at the heavy black kohl-liner around her eyes. Interestingly, it was Mickey O'Dowd, rather than her husband, who placed a great meaty hand on the woman's shoulder, surprisingly gently, the tremor still there.

And then Petronella was up, and running from the room without looking back, closely followed by the Irishman.

'*That's* playing nicely?' hissed Rainbird. 'We're about to be thrown out!'

But Tony Stone was looking straight at Posie and his gaze was sad. 'Och, forgive ma wife, Miss Parker. This whole matter has fair vexed her. But you know, you're all wrong: there was absolutely nothing romantic going on between me and the Housekeeper. As Mickey says, Elsie wasn't the kind. I swear it on ma wee boys' lives. I don't take it personally, these questions: I know you've got tae ask them, it's yer job.'

'So *why* was Elsie sacked, sir?'

Tony Stone looked outside to the darkening light which was massing over the endless sea, and more than a shadow passed over his face. 'I cannae tell ye the reason, Miss Parker.'

Can't, or won't, thought Posie as she pulled at the cheap little mass-produced engagement ring on her finger. *The man's lying*, Posie told herself. *Sure as bread is bread.*

She wanted to ask him whether everything was fine between him and his wife regarding their own marriage, and their fashion partnership, but Posie rather feared the consequences of angering the only person left who could allow them to remain here without a formal Search Warrant.

Posie pulled out the broken glasses chain, and put it in the flat of her hand. 'Just one more question, sir.'

'Ye go right ahead, lassie.'

She showed it to the Fashion Designer. 'Can you tell me, sir, did your Housekeeper wear spectacles, and was this *her* spectacles chain?'

Tony Stone fingered the links, the broken clasp, with his delicate, gentle fingers. 'Fine work, nice piece, eh?'

He gave it back. 'But nae: I never saw Elsie with glasses on, not once in three years. And I never saw her wear *this*. Ma wife, on the other hand, wears glasses sometimes, on a chain. But not like this. She normally wears red things, or black, or white. Or all three colours mashed up together, ye know?' He sighed. 'This here is right *classy*.'

And then the little man was on his feet, shaking a regretful head, checking a large, showy fob-watch.

'I'm right sorry, but it's almost three o'clock, and I've got to make sure our collection is packed up. I'll be heading up to London tomorrow myself.'

He threw a quick dubious look over at Posie, who had stood up, munching on another biscuit. 'I see you're wearing House of Harlow, Miss Parker, but ye would look much better in something less severe. Something less heavy, less frumpy. You're still quite young, aren't ye? And quite beautiful.'

Tony Stone was disconcertingly looking at her as if she might be a dressmaker's mannequin.

'Mnnn. I could get ye intae a wedding dress which would be quite flattering, shave pounds off, especially around the stomach area. Do consider it: I can offer good terms if ye promise tae name us in any wedding snaps in the newspapers. I'm sorry tae speak of business at a time like this, but we do have a wee crust tae earn. Think it over.'

The stomach area?

Posie coloured up red and didn't trust herself to speak. She felt a rush of anger and forced herself to count to five in case she stood up and hit the little man in the nose.

Gracious, she had thought him fairly harmless up until now, but now she was beginning to see how this noxious pair suited each other very well.

Beside her, Rainbird had the good grace to look thoroughly embarrassed. She even felt a slight pat on the arm.

Tony Stone fished in his inside jacket pocket for a key. 'You said ye needed tae pick through poor Elsie's studio? The staff all live in the outbuildings. I'll leave ye tae it. Take yer time. But be warned: I believe Elsie didn't keep her oon place too tidy, although I couldn't fault her running of the rest of this hoose. And it's best not tae trouble ma wife just noo. If ye need anything – or find anything – ye come and tell me. *She'll* be in bed with a Veronal.'

The Fashion Designer walked with them out into the yard from which they had come. It was now a scene of frantic activity. The last snatches of daylight were playing over White Shaw and a seeping sea-mist was closing in. The good-looking driver was backing up the drive in the large navy van where he parked and opened it up.

'Here! *This* way, lad!'

Tony Stone had bounded off and was energetically directing rails of tissue-wrapped clothing, each with large numbers attached, to be lifted and stacked carefully into the van, and the pimply boiler-suited lad from earlier was looking very down in the mouth about it all, trekking backwards and forwards at his Master's bidding, manoeuvring the rails about.

Mickey O'Dowd was also hard at work out here, checking items off a list. He looked impressive as he worked. Maybe the man really was indispensable? A jack of all trades. Maybe Posie had underestimated him.

Posie spied the flimsy, unlocked lean-to by the back door and cursed under her breath. 'We forgot to ask him to check about that fancy torch, Rainbird.'

'Well, we can't ferret about in the man's shed without his permission, can we? Besides, if it's gone, or been taken out and broken, we can't say with any certainty that it was Mr Stone who did that, can we? Could well have been Elsie herself who took the thing…'

'True enough.' But Posie was marching over to the lean-to anyhow. The door was slightly ajar and she pushed it open with the tip of her ruined shoe. Peering inside, what struck her was the emptiness. A small tool-box on a shelf; a broom, a rake, some wire-cutters. No torch or flash-light, of any kind.

'It's not there,' she announced triumphantly to a scowling Rainbird, who had been joined by Constable Briggs, hankering after a specific task.

'Briggs here is going to show us Elsie's flat, tell us if it looks the same today as when he checked it over on Monday morning. Here's the key. Open it up for us, man.'

'Right you are, Guv'nor.'

The studio-flat Elsie had lived in was part of the run of connected white-painted outbuildings, like Mews houses, with living-places for the staff on the floors above a set of storerooms below. The outbuildings were literally built right up against the cliff, and at the top of the steep white wooden steps which led to Elsie's apartment, there was a mini-balcony from which you viewed the back of the main house with its tarmacked yard, and then a sliver of sea beyond.

As Briggs fumbled with the key in the lock Posie saw trickles of water running down the shoddily-made front door. She shivered with the damp.

Rainbird, behind her, was trying to gain warmth from his thin coat collar, and seemed particularly out of sorts.

'We didn't get much in there, did we, Miss? From that dreadful pair. We got more from *you*. That bit of glasses chain. Where on earth did you get that?'

'Oh! *That?* Over at Ness Point, actually. It slipped my mind to mention it to you. Didn't seem important.'

'Didn't it, Miss Parker? And have you anything else up your sleeve right now?'

She didn't, as it happened. But she wasn't going to admit it.

****

Ten

With a flick of an electric switch, Elsie Moncrieff's studio was revealed to them.

It benefited from no natural light other than the one window facing onto the balcony, next to the bad-quality glass door they had entered by. The flat was sandwiched between two other such studios, up similar flights of stairs.

Inside, it was small but cosy. A single bed in the far, right-hand corner and a whitewashed table with a couple of matching chairs were the main furniture. A clothes-rack stood next to the bed, empty but for one old-fashioned black coat, shiny at the elbows with age.

A series of nicely-framed watercolours, in bright reds and blues, ran along the back wall, showing a mix of places: the view up Whitehall in London; the town-square in Dover; the beach here, looking towards Ness Point.

In the left-hand corner of the studio was a kitchenette, with a small Primus stove and a wooden counter with a tiny sink and a drying-rack.

Above the sink was a round mirror with a small shelf where cosmetic soap and a toothbrush in a glass with tooth powder were lined up neatly. *No bathroom*, Posie realised, taking everything in quickly. *So Elsie had shared a common bathroom*. But where was it?

And no fireplace here, or even a basic boiler for hot water. No way of getting or keeping warm.

Damp reeked in the place like a bad perfume, and a white slimy mould was rising up the walls. The place was bitingly, excoriatingly cold. This was a place which might be suitable for the summer months, maybe, but now it was absolutely dreadful. Talk about treating your employees well! But from the sounds of it, from Elsie's letter, she *had* considered herself treated well. Perhaps she had been used to worse?

Tony Stone had been right, though. The place was fantastically messy, impossibly so.

A small wicker table which held an expensive-looking gramophone was absolutely covered in papers and magazines. What seemed like at least a hundred gramophone records, a mix of classical and fairly recent jazz records, mostly out of their paper sleeves, were scattered everywhere.

A cheap chest of drawers to the right of the entrance door was pulled open at every drawer, and underclothes, hair-things and magazines all spilled out haphazardly. The cork tiles of the floor were barely visible under yet more newspapers and magazines. The bed was also covered in a litter of magazines, tissues, ribbons. Posie kicked at the papers by her feet and they crinkled, crisply.

'Golly!'

Posie stared at it all, Rainbird similarly taking it all in, in something akin to disbelief.

Constable Briggs tutted, disapprovingly. 'Aye, this is the same state as when I came in on Monday. Terrible, isn't it? That a girl who ran a house like White Shaw apparently so well, could live in a pig-sty like this. Still, it takes all sorts, I suppose.'

Posie stared at Briggs a moment too long, hoped her disgust showed clearly on her face. *How could some people employed in the police force be so completely and utterly stupid and unquestioning?* This man would get on well with Inspector Oats. They were of the same mould.

She turned to Briggs. 'What did you take from here exactly, Constable? And where did it come from?'

Briggs stiffened, as if under attack. 'I was told to take personal items, Miss, for identification purposes. You know: passport; identity papers; photographs. My orders were to look for a Will, and a purse of money or a bank savings book. But as you know, there was nothing.'

He indicated to the kitchenette area. 'I took that one photograph of the lass laughing, the one you saw. That was all there was! I asked Miss Douglas if it was Elsie and she said yes: but taken some years before, she thought. It was pinned to the mirror over there with parcel tape.'

Posie frowned: 'No purse? No handbag? Every woman has a bag of some sort.'

'Nothing at all, Miss. No money to speak of, either: just a few coppers about the place. Although the lass obviously wasn't short of money. She received a good salary as Housekeeper every month; she was paid cash in hand, apparently. And she obviously enjoyed her little luxuries: the records; that fancy gramophone.'

'Thank you, Briggs,' ordered Rainbird. 'That will be all for now. Go and see what's happening down in that yard, and keep your eyes and ears open, man.'

'Right you are, Guv'nor.'

Rainbird lit up another sneaked Sullivan Powell, leant against the damp wall of the flat. 'Not enough room to swing a cat in here, is there? Dreadful place, eh?'

Posie didn't like it. Not a jot.

She was yet to meet a woman who had no handbag. And this one had apparently had no clothes, or shoes, or make-up either. It didn't make sense.

Posie was about to open her mouth to say, '*Something is wrong here, Sergeant*' and '*This place has obviously been done-over*' when they heard a banging door, and a clatter of what sounded like a pan on a stove and cups clinking, then male voices next door. But it was as if the voices were in the same room as themselves.

Posie and Rainbird stared at each other, both motioning the other not to speak, Rainbird hastily grinding out his cigarette.

A shrill of a kettle's whistle sounded, then the splash of pouring water.

'Milk, Alf?' A cockney, London voice. Cheekily upbeat.

'Don't mind if I do, Sid. That's very kind of you. Nice little flat you fellows have got here, innit? Old Tony *did* say I could take ten minutes off the packing for my tea.'

The second voice was local, wheedling, and deferential to the first. Posie realised quickly that it was the bald pimply lad in the boiler-suit, with the navy-clad driver, whose flat, right next to Elsie's, they were having a cuppa in.

'Have some fudge as well, Alf. You go on. We've all got a long evenin' ahead, packin' up, then the bonfire. You goin' with Harriet? Well, goodness knows when you'll be gettin' off home for your supper.'

'Last orders, I expect!' A beleaguered groan. 'There's so much to do. An' I tell you something else. It's not just dresses he's taking up tomorrow morning in that van, either.'

'Oh?' The driver's voice was suddenly sharp, interested. 'What else?'

'Several suitcases belonging to old Tony, which he seems to have packed some time ago. Heavy as Hades. And trunks full of paperwork, blinking heavy, too. And big black flat cases full of drawings – they're special apparently and can't just be stuffed in any old how: they're for the clients to look through at this fancy show! I tell you! I nearly put my back out lifting that lot.'

There was a silence, broken by clinking cups, a sound of springs, someone sitting down heavily on a bed.

'What is it, Sid? You seem mighty quiet suddenly. Is

it this business with old Elsie? It's fair upset me too, you know. But I know you and she were real close. Must have come as a terrible shock for you, eh?'

'I still can't believe it, Alf. She was a fine gal, and it's a rum do, if you ask me. Fallin' off a cliff like that. But no. It's not *that* right now I'm thinkin' about.' He paused, as if judging whether or not to go on.

'I think, Alf, that our comfortable little shin-dig here is over. Tony's leavin' the Mistress. This place is *done*. It's time we all started lookin' for another job.'

Posie and Rainbird looked at each other, eyebrows raised.

'What d'you mean, Sid? Who told you this? Old Petronella herself, when she's been in here, with you? We all know you've been receiving extras of everything – money and food and perks – for all your carry-on with her since you arrived! And now look where it's got us all! So old Tony's found out, has he? We're all losing our jobs. You should be ashamed of yerself!'

Posie and Rainbird exchanged looks again.

'Easy, Alf. There's no need to get nasty about it. My carry-on with Petronella has got nothin' to do with Tony leaving her, I can assure you. She hasn't told me anythin'. And why shouldn't I have benefited from the affair? You've got to use what the Good Lord gives you in this life and I was blessed with a pretty face. I make no apologies for it.'

'So how *do* you know all this, then?'

There was a silence, as if Sidney was wondering quite how much to say to his not-as-smart companion. Then the sound of pacing footsteps.

'It was Elsie, actually. Last Sunday, after I'd left old Tony at Dover Priory for the fast train to London, I stayed on in Dover, as it was my mornin' off. I 'ad fish and chips on the Pier and played a few pin-wizard games in the arcade. But I came back here about one-thirty because I knew Petronella would probably be waitin' for me in here after lunch, and she keeps a master key to all these flats, so she'd just let herself in. Mickey makes himself scarce usually. Well, when I came up the steps, Elsie came out of her flat. She said she needed to tell me somethin'.'

'Oh?'

'It was Elsie's afternoon off. She was lookin' all about her to make sure no-one could overhear us. Then she said old Tony was leavin' the Mistress. Leavin' the house, the boys, the business, too. It would be very soon. Probably this week; same time as the new collection went up to London. And she said the moment he packed suitcases, and the big black trunks, and those portfolios full of sketches, it meant he wasn't comin' back. Well, that's *now*, isn't it?'

Sidney cleared his throat. 'Elsie said she wanted to warn me, as my boss. I asked her if *she'd* be all right, if *she* was lookin' for a new job, and she said she'd always been fine. She said she knew what she had to do.'

'Elsie?' Alf sounded more trusting now. '*She* said all of this? Well, then. I believe you. But *how* did Elsie Moncrieff know?'

'Dunno. I suppose Elsie overheard somethin' or other. A fight, maybe? But believe me, it's all over. It can't last five seconds without him, can it? This house, these parties, the guests. And *she* realised it, too.'

'Who?'

'Petronella.' Sidney sounded worried for the first time. 'The Mistress. Because she heard every blessed word, didn't she? She was lyin' in here, waitin' for me, like every Sunday. The walls are like paper. And then Elsie goes and drops this bombshell right outside. And I've never seen anythin' like what happened next.'

'*What* happened, Sid?'

'It was scary. Petronella just sat here, on the bed, where you are right now. Whiter than usual. I kept askin' her if she was all right, and she didn't answer. It was like the world had ended. We just sat listenin' to Elsie's gramophone records blarin' out next door, for what seemed like an age. Suddenly the music stopped and we heard Elsie lockin' up. She was obviously going out. It was almost two o'clock I'd guess. And then after a couple of minutes Petronella got up, raced next door, opened up Elsie's flat and then she started to howl and shout.'

'What was happening inside, Sid?'

'You tell me! I followed but Petronella had locked the door behind herself, hadn't she? So your guess is as good as mine. But what I *do* know is that she came out ten minutes later, all calm and collected. And Elsie must not have known anythin' was amiss, either, when she got back about an hour later: she just went into her flat and played her music again, so Petronella can't have messed anythin' up, can she?'

A sigh. 'I'd better get goin', Alf. Let's get this lot washed up, eh?'

There was the sound of cups being cleared. 'Tell me, Sid…' The lad sounded troubled. 'D'you think what happened to Elsie later that night had anything to do with what she told you on the steps? What Petronella overheard? You don't think…'

'I dunno what to think. Let's leave it to the professionals, shall we, Alf? And that tasty bit of stuff they call a Lady Detective! Did you see her? Coo-ee!'

But behind the bluster there was real worry in the man's voice. Undisguised.

And with that the door banged shut.

* * * *

Rainbird let out a long, low whistle.

'Can of worms, Sergeant, isn't it?'

'Too right. Inspector Oats would call it *a mare's nest*.'

'I know.'

Posie had kept her leather gloves on. She picked up an expensive French lipstick and a beautiful Mason Pearson hairbrush which were in a sponge-bag on Elsie's shelf by the mirror. Both costly, tasteful things. So where were all the other costly things that such a beautiful girl would have owned?

Who had moved them? Destroyed them? Stolen them?

She turned. 'I think it's time to bring someone else in here, Rainbird. Acknowledge we're out of our depth.'

She motioned around herself, at the tip. 'We really need this place fingerprinted, but to be honest I think we're too late. Goodness knows how many people have walked through here since Elsie left it. The local police have messed up: Briggs was out of his depth here alone. I think you and I both realise something is off here. This mess is completely fabricated, isn't it?'

Posie picked up magazines off the floor. 'Nobody has *this* many magazines, all on such varied subjects: fashion; cookery; knitting; foreign travel; gardening. All from last week! As if Elsie would have had the time to read them all. In fact, there are a couple of the self-same magazine! What use would someone like Elsie – living in a small bedsit with no real kitchen and no garden – have for magazines dedicated to those subjects? I bet Elsie never read a single one of these. Never *saw* one of these before she died.'

Posie took off her glove and felt the paper of the magazines with her fingertip.

'As I thought. The damp in here is dreadful. Everything is wet, or at least slightly so, but these magazines are still fairly crisp. Like they've only been here a couple of days.'

She looked about with a stab of fear. 'It's as if someone – or *some people* – organised the mess. Went and bought stack-loads of penny magazines just to throw about the place. It's clumsy, hurried. And have you noticed how there is simply *nothing* personal here – no letters, notes, photographs – in among this mess? *Something* here is wrong, and we don't have the full picture.'

She swallowed uncertainly. Posie had hoped to do this alone, but what they were facing here was too big, too evil, too *much*, without the right resources.

'I think you should call through to Richard – Richard Lovelace, yes – and get him to come down fast as he can. With the forensics chappies. Time for playing games is over, for both of us. We've had our fun but we need to check out what we've just heard from that driver next door. But we can't interview anyone, can we? We can't search the whole of White Shaw, or that van, can we, without Search Warrants?'

'No, Miss. We can't.'

Posie's thoughts were running on ahead of her.

'I wonder *what* Petronella Douglas found in here to make her go loopy? It must have been bad for her to then go and write a letter which would terminate Elsie's employment? Because these two things are linked, aren't they? Why did Petronella not reveal any of this part of the story to the Coroner today?'

Rainbird was over at the door. He looked beaten, boiling hot, despite the cold. He didn't look good at all. Maybe he was coming down with the flu, too?

He sighed: 'Do *you* reckon Petronella Douglas did the girl in, Miss Parker?'

Posie shrugged. 'I really don't know, Sergeant. Not at the minute. Practically everyone I'm meeting here seems odd, or else suspect in some way.'

'I'll go to the Bay Hotel, Miss. I feel shivery, if truth be told. I'm going to get a hot tea. I'll call the Chief Commissioner from there; less chance of being overheard, even if most of them *do* seem to be out in the courtyard just now. I'll start getting the Warrants we need. It's almost time for Briggs to go home, Miss, so I'll send him off duty.

I can't see any reason for keeping him on here. No actual *danger* seems imminent. Wouldn't you agree?'

'I very much hope so.'

But when he'd gone Posie found herself sinking down heavily on one of the white-painted chairs at the table, feeling utterly defeated.

Elsie Moncrieff – as Posie still called her – seemed to have been admired by her staff as a woman of integrity. She had felt duty bound to inform Sidney, the driver, about her concerns for his job. But she had said to him that she herself would be fine, that she knew *what she had to do*.

So *what* had she been planning to do in her immediate future? And what of the strange letter in the summer to Posie? Where did *that* fit in?

And what about her actions in the days and hours before her death? Had Elsie really had a headache the night of the party, on the Saturday, which meant she couldn't work? What had been in here which had so angered Petronella Douglas on the Sunday, just a few hours before Elsie died? Where had Elsie gone on the Sunday afternoon when Petronella had broken in with the master key? Where had she got that hand-print on her back from? Had Elsie angered someone?

It all seemed odd.

And Posie got up again, despite a wrenching tiredness, and walked around the room, searching madly for anything.

But there was nothing.

* * * *

Eleven

Posie stood in exasperation in front of a small rickety night-table next to the bed.

An uninspiring collection of items were gathered on top: a much-needed red rubber hot-water bottle, a blue-and-white saucer containing a few coins. The only drawer revealed a Penhaligon's travel candle, a couple of balls of very fine quality teal-coloured wool with a Central London shop name on the wrapper. There were also expensive bone knitting needles; a pin cushion, some embroidery threads.

So where was the real girl in all of this?

Elsie Moncrieff, reveal yourself to me, Posie felt like screaming aloud into the room. *Despite the fact that someone has obviously been in here and tried to obliterate any last traces of you.*

Covering you up with cheap penny magazines.

As if anyone would be fooled!

Well, Posie Parker wasn't fooled. And she'd make sure Richard got onto it himself, when he got here; however senior he was now, with all the might of Scotland Yard ranged firmly behind him.

Oh, Richard. I need you here.

Posie balled her fists into her eyeballs and sighed, thinking of her fiancé. It was quarter-past four. Hopefully

Rainbird would catch Richard before he left work. He was probably just tidying up the office for the day, giving last instructions to those two secretaries of his, but really thinking of his evening ahead, of taking Phyllis to the delights of the Clapham bonfire.

Posie closed her eyes, as if she could summon him, genie-like, to appear in front of her. *I'm out of my depth. What have I walked into here? This girl has not only died, but it's as if she never lived.*

How terrible.

Posie suddenly, unprofessionally, put her head down on Elsie Moncrieff's pillow. The damp chalky scent of the place came to her strongly, shot through with something else, a light gardenia, maybe? And something else. Peroxide, maybe? Hair dye? Dolly smelt like this after a visit to her hairdresser in Piccadilly.

The scent of the dead girl.

Funny how this mix of scents was about the only thing which was tangible so far about Elsie Moncrieff, and it was entirely ephemeral. It wouldn't last much beyond another day or two. Couldn't help anyone at all as evidence.

Posie stretched out on the bed, suddenly exhausted, the day catching up on her, the slight nausea which she had never got rid of in the car threatening to engulf her yet again. Was she coming down with the flu, like the staff at Briggs' police station? Like Rainbird?

Poor Rainbird.

With a jolt Posie remembered he was getting married in just a couple of days' time. Flu at your wedding was definitely not what you wanted.

And suddenly Posie felt something pushed down in the bed, about where her legs were. Hurriedly, she scrambled up, pulled back the quilt. But all that was revealed was another rubber hot-water bottle, blue this time. This one still filled up with water.

Posie chided herself for getting excited: whoever had

combed the room – *but looking for what? Hiding what?* – had checked Elsie's bed, too. It went without saying. Had Posie really expected to find clues about the dead girl tucked conveniently under the quilt?

She left the full hot-water bottle where it was and threw herself back again on the pillow, absent-mindedly picking up the empty red hot-water bottle from the night-table, twisting its screw-lid in and out, over and over.

But who has two hot-water bottles?

Posie hastily swung her legs over the bed and sat bolt-upright. Her heart beat a little faster. Could *this* have been the one hiding place Elsie had managed to keep safe and guarded to the end? Feeling the thick rubber body of the red flask, scrunching at it a little, Posie was rewarded by hearing something rustling inside. Pulling the metal top off, and using the knitting needles from the nearby drawer and a pair of tweezers extracted from her own carpet bag, Posie took the bottle over towards the main electric light, was about to turn the flask upside down on the table-top.

But before she did so, there was a knock at the door. Posie hastily placed the flask back on the floor, among the mess.

Posie stuffed away the knitting needles and tweezers. 'Come in, please.'

The flimsy door was pushed open, and a woman's petite silhouette was revealed for a second, emblazoned against the darkening sky outside. Thankful it wasn't Tony Stone or Petronella Douglas, Posie watched the visitor step lightly into the room, and then she recognised the woman – *the maid, was it?* – she had seen fleetingly before, earlier on, in the kitchen.

The girl was perhaps twenty, if that. Huge-eyed but plain, the ruffled black-and-white uniform doing nothing for her drab blonde hair or her waxy complexion.

An insignificant little mouse.

Posie smiled in real relief. 'Hello. Can I help you? I'm Posie Parker; I'm working with the police.'

'Yes. I know that, Miss Parker.' A sharp, local voice.

'I'm Harriet. Harriet Neame. I'm the Housemaid here, the *only* maid here, as it happens.'

She cocked her head to the side, and Posie was surprised by the sudden flash of cunning she saw there. 'Maybe I can help you, Miss? Help Miss Moncrieff, I mean.'

'I would say that Miss Moncrieff is past helping now, wouldn't you, Harriet?' Posie said tartly, thinking of the body in the cold morgue.

A strange light danced in the girl's eyes. 'Maybe we can help each other, then?'

Posie felt a surge of distaste. 'Maybe. Sit, won't you?'

Posie indicated one of the white wooden chairs at the messy table. She sat down herself, but didn't speak, just let the silence go on, folded her arms. Posie noticed how Harriet's eyes kept flickering to the closed door of the flat. Outside, men's voices could be heard shouting, doors banging. Some reassurance was needed, and Posie did her best:

'You have nothing to fear from speaking out, Harriet. Were you and Elsie Moncrieff friends? Did you know her well?'

'No, Miss. But I owed her. It was Miss Moncrieff who got me this job here, right at the start, almost three years ago. And she got the job for Alf, too, and for his aunt, Ruth, the cook. *Through* me. Alf's my man, see? We're saving to get married.'

'Ah.' Posie thought of the pimply lad in the car-port, who had drunk tea next door. Well, beggars couldn't be choosers, she supposed.

'My congratulations. And did Miss Moncrieff hire Mickey O'Dowd as well as you three?'

'Nah, the Master picked up Big Mickey from one of his nights out in Dover. I expect it was at the Two Kennels. The Master likes to watch a spot of fighting, and that's Mickey's world, through and through.'

But Harriet was anxious to return to the subject of herself, that much was obvious. 'Miss Moncrieff hired *me* specially, Miss. For a reason. That's what I came to tell you.'

'Oh?'

The girl nodded. 'I was soiled goods, Miss. I'd advertised all about town for a job. Nothing would have been too lowly for me, even though I'd learnt my letters well. I'd grown up in the Orphanage in Dover, see? And when I got my first job at seventeen, I got the sack after just a few weeks. Stealing. Silver spoons. I got hauled up in Court but the Magistrates let me off on account of my youth. So I got another job in a big grand hotel on the Dover sea-front, but they let me go six months later.'

'Stealing, again?' Posie said, in as non-judgemental a way as she could.

'Among other things, Miss. They didn't like my way of listening in on the guests and acting "slyly" with what I found out.'

'Ah.'

Blackmail, Posie presumed.

This insignificant little mouse was turning out to be not quite so insignificant after all. Unless Harriet Neame had later changed her ways?

'Miss Moncrieff contacted me through an advert I'd placed in the *Dover Herald* ages back. She said she needed a small, reliable staff very quickly for White Shaw. She asked me straight up if I knew anyone else who could come and work for good wages. So, I told her about Alf and his aunt and she fair bit my hand off for them.'

'Despite the fact you had no good references?'

A nod. 'Miss Moncrieff said she didn't care. I remember in that interview she said, "*Everyone has the right to rise again like a phoenix.*" And she laughed, like it was funny. She said she would make sure the owners of the property didn't know about my real past; they weren't the sort to check details. But Miss Moncrieff knew what I was good at, see? Turns out that was the reason she employed me.'

Posie stared in disbelief as the girl fished in her pocket for what turned out to be a very thin, black notebook. '*This*.'

Harriet patted it proudly. 'Listening at doors, at walls. Listening to the Master, and the Mistress. To anyone, and everyone. I was especially good at hovering next to men at parties who didn't look at me as I handed them drinks.'

'And then you wrote down what you heard? And passed it on to Miss Moncrieff?'

A simple nod.

Posie felt horrified. What on earth had been going on here? What had she stumbled into? She tried to keep a cool head.

'Did the Housekeeper ask you for *particular* information?'

'No, Miss. Sometimes there was nothing; weeks of nothing. But then there'd be lots of parties, a run of the things in the summertime. And then I'd report weekly.'

Posie tried hard to disguise her disgust. She was convinced now that this girl was probably very dangerous. 'Did Miss Moncrieff ever discuss your findings with you?'

'Not once. But often I'd find a half-sovereign left in the bottom of my toothbrush cup, as a thank you. So I assumed I'd done well on those occasions.'

Posie pointed at the black notepad.

'What is your intention now with *that*?' She knew instinctively that Harriet Neame was not about to give the thing to her; something which was both illegally-gained, and damning, and potentially explosive, all in one go.

'This was my current one, Miss.' Harriet tapped the notebook. 'I hadn't yet dropped this one off to Miss Moncrieff, although I *would* have, if she hadn't fallen off that cliff. She would have found this one interesting, especially as she missed the party on Saturday night. This one contains a few surprises. Particularly about Lord Boxwood. Are you interested, Miss Parker? It could be very *valuable* information. I might also have other information to whet your appetite.'

Ah. The old blackmail tricks.

Posie looked at the girl directly. 'I cannot enter into a negotiation for this information, Miss Neame. It is beyond my powers.' She took a deep breath. 'But I *do* have contacts. Perhaps there would be an opportunity for new employment? In exchange for this book?'

Harriet snatched at the book, and pushed it smartly into a capacious pocket in her white apron. She shrugged, not happy. 'I see, Miss. At least you're straight with me.'

'Where are the other notebooks you filled in? There must have been many over almost three years?'

'I gave them all to Miss Moncrieff. I suppose she read them and burnt them.'

Posie blew out her cheeks in exasperation. What she was uncovering was something completely unexpected. Harriet had been Elsie Moncrieff's eyes and ears in places she couldn't get to. But *why*?

Harriet Neame made Posie's skin crawl, but she knew too that this might be her only lead. Or leads…

'Is there anything you can tell me, Miss Neame, about Elsie Moncrieff? Anything at all?'

The Housemaid sat in silence for a few more seconds which felt like minutes passing.

But then she nodded assertively:

'Yes, I can tell you several things, Miss. Like how Miss Moncrieff was full of mysteries. I'm certain of it.'

* * * *

Twelve

'We shared a bathroom, see?'

Harriet explained that she and the cook, Ruth, lived in, and shared the small studio right next door, on the other side of Elsie. But the bathroom for all the women was in the downstairs of another of the buildings, a few doors along.

Posie looked sympathetic. 'That must be inconvenient, and chilly. Especially at night!'

'It is, Miss. But I'm lucky, it saves me a pretty penny. Ruth, too. Alf lives in town. That was part of the deal. Miss Moncrieff said "no hanky-panky on site", which is a bit rich, given how much of *that* there actually is.'

'You mean Petronella Douglas and Sidney the driver?'

The maid looked quite surprised. 'Oh! You know about that? Well, the sharing of our bathroom was good in a way; it made Miss Moncrieff paying me and my giving her back the notebooks much easier. But you learn a good deal about someone when you share a bathroom, whether they like it or not. And that was Miss Moncrieff's first mystery.'

'Go on.'

'It was odd but Miss Moncrieff never did her hair here. Her hair was that fashionable bright blonde, set in an immaculate wave, but she never once had a bath in our bathroom, and she never once dyed her hair here. It was a mystery to us! Miss Moncrieff must have gone to Dover and had it done every week, but I don't know how she fitted it all in. I never actually followed her, not properly. Not *meaning* to.'

Posie shivered inside her coat, suddenly desperate for a cup of tea, for anything at all which was warming. But she'd stay here now until she was frozen up with cold if it meant she might get something, *anything* from this awful creature who saw so much, noticed so much.

'What else was a mystery, Harriet?'

'I think she was married, Miss Parker. Although she always referred to herself as "Miss". As if she was a spinster.'

Posie looked keenly at the unusually sharp-witted girl. Elsie having a husband was not something which had so far occurred to her, or to anyone else.

'Do you have any evidence for this?'

A twitch of the small, snub, rabbit-like nose.

'No, but I could swear that when she interviewed me, Miss Moncrieff was wearing a wedding band. From the minute I came here, I never saw it again. Although maybe that was because there was a policy in place about wearing no jewellery. I only wear *my* real-ruby engagement ring in my time off, see? Maybe Miss Moncrieff didn't want to have one rule for us and one for herself?'

'Maybe. Harriet, did you have any sense what Miss Moncrieff had been doing *before* she was at White Shaw?'

'Not really. She told Ruth once that she had Dutch connections, a Dutch mother, maybe? That she spoke with a bit of an accent on account of her mother. But she'd grown up locally, I'm sure of it. She'd worked as the Housekeeper in some churchy place.'

Harriet knew this because Elsie Moncrieff had once told Ruth, the cook, when they were counting out candles in the kitchen together. And Elsie Moncrieff had joked that they got through more candles at White Shaw for parties than in her last employment, in a proper church.

Posie frowned, missing her notebook, making a mental note to follow up Elsie's references, with or without the help of the architect who was currently over in the Argentine.

Harriet nodded more certainly, back on firmer ground now: 'Before all that, I'm pretty sure, Miss, she was a nurse. Probably in the Great War, I reckon. She was a good one, too.'

'Oh? How do you know?'

'Once, a couple of years back, my Alf, he got battery acid all over his arms and face, in an accident out in the yard, and we thought he might lose an eye. But Miss Moncrieff knew exactly what to do. When he got to hospital, they said she'd saved his eyesight, maybe even his life. She wouldn't hear of being thanked though, or of telling us about the Great War.'

Interesting, Posie thought. But did it really add anything to the background she was forming of this strange dead Housekeeper? Women had flocked in their hundreds to volunteer as nurses in 1914, and four years later the government were taking pretty much any able young woman they could get their hands on. It wasn't exactly unusual as a background, nor was the reticence to speak of the experience. The sights and sounds most nurses had witnessed out on the front-line haunted many even now.

Posie changed tack. 'Were there any visitors to Miss Moncrieff here? I'm guessing you'd know about any, given the thinness of these walls?'

A regretful shake of Harriet's head. There'd been no visitors. The studio-flat had been a sanctuary for Elsie which no-one had dared to enter.

'Not Tony Stone?'

A shake of the head. 'But they got on pretty well. They laughed and joked with each other in the house. Nothing untoward, mind. Mostly they had contact because all the fabrics for the business would be ordered to the house and it would be Miss Moncrieff's job to check through it all. She did all that in her poky little office. It was up to her to pay the fabric suppliers too, and the seamstresses when they came. I think the Master appreciated it: he's terrible at office work; gets into a right flap. He's always happiest when he's cutting and sticking together his suits. I heard him saying often enough "*I don't know what we'd do without you, Elsie.*" Well, now he'll have to do without her, won't he?'

Posie frowned. Tony Stone had been *grateful*. The twin boys outside had said the same thing, saying their dad had called Elsie a 'diamond'. Someone he needed about, not somebody to push off a cliff.

'That all seems a bit outside the duties of a normal Housekeeper, surely?'

'Normal?' Harriet laughed. 'Well, this isn't a normal place, is it?'

'So nothing romantic with Tony Stone. And the big Irish fella? Nothing there, either?'

The girl's face clouded for a moment. 'Big Mickey O'Dowd? You must be joking. He's useful, I'll give him that, but when he's off duty he's in The Green Man along the beach here, or otherwise he's in all the pubs in Dover, getting drunk. In fights, too. Alf's seen him often enough. Says it's an embarrassing way for a man to carry on. There's no way Miss Moncrieff would have put up with any of *that*. She was real classy. They didn't have much to do with each other, and when they did there was no love lost. I heard her laying into him once, when we'd all just started working here: "*Take that thing off, will you?*" she was saying angrily. "*What will people think?*"'

'Oh? What was he wearing?'

Harriet motioned at her neck. 'Religious jewellery. He's Irish, see, isn't he? A Catholic. Big Mickey was wearing a St Christopher, I think. Well, he won that battle, because he wears it still. But they were forced together, sometimes. They would take those poor twins out for a walk at the weekend, if the boys were home. Miss Moncrieff would walk with them all the way along to Mrs Morse's tea-rooms at the end, and Big Mickey would jog along at the back, usually with a ball to play with. I expect the Master and Mistress felt that Big Mickey could handle the twins if they got out of hand, and Miss Moncrieff would add a sense of decorum. But it beats me why the twins don't just stay at school, 'cos they're under everyone's feet at the weekends. Parties or no parties. And Miss Douglas is a terrible mother. Never sees them. She can't cope with them at all.'

So far Petronella Douglas, the famous Fashion Designer, the thrower of famous parties, the gatherer of important guests and patrons, the actual money behind the Fashion House, seemed to have featured little in Harriet's story. She seemed conspicuous by her absence. Posie pointed it out.

'The Mistress?' Harriet made a big show of holding her nose and snorting, several times over.

'Cocaine?'

'Oh, yes. Lots of it, Miss.'

Posie was only hearing what she had already suspected.

It didn't surprise her at all. And Petronella being a drug addict made perfect sense, as did the lethargy, the unpredictability, the love of wild parties, the lack of real work. The Veronal taken now, mid-afternoon, among the chaos and stampede of a show being packed up, was most probably not Veronal at all, but a few pinches of the white stuff.

'Golly. But did Miss Moncrieff get on well with Petronella Douglas, would you say?'

'Oh yes, Miss. Had to, didn't they? It was a real shock when Alf told me today that the Inquest announced the Mistress had given Miss Moncrieff the sack.'

'Any idea *why*?'

But Harriet shook her head mournfully, as if she had missed a rare treat. 'Nah, I can't overhear everything, can I?

Mistress had me working most of Sunday with Ruth in the kitchen. Unfortunately.'

Posie was still thinking of Sidney, the driver: how it seemed he may have been close to Elsie Moncrieff. He seemed interesting, worth investigating.

'Did Miss Moncrieff have much to do with Sidney?'

A flash of some strong emotion coloured the maid's peaky little face and for once the girl seemed reluctant to speak. Drew herself up proudly.

Posie felt like laughing. *Was this jealousy?*

Harriet pursed her mouth up sulkily. 'He didn't arrive with us. He's new. Only been here a few months, actually.'

'Oh?'

'Yes. Only since late June this year. You asked if she had much to do with him. Well, I *do* know that Miss Moncrieff had him in *here* now and again, for a drink. He was the only one allowed. Special. You'd hear the glasses chink and some music playing and then about twenty minutes later he'd leave. I don't know what was going on there, Miss. But I do know it all took place in the dark. Or by candlelight…'

'Candlelight?'

'That's right. I was coming back from the bathroom once and I noticed her flat was all dark, but I could hear music and laughing; sounded like dancing. It seemed odd. So next time he popped over I made it my business to go outside and have a look at the windows of her flat. It was the same thing again. Candles. Same every time…'

Posie was thinking hard. But Sidney's position in all of this seemed unclear.

'I never understood, Miss. But I wondered if Sidney had been "got", like me, Miss. For his skills. Miss Moncrieff recruited him, I'm sure of it. There was a perfectly good driver here before; an old buffer from St Margaret's-at-Cliffe, actually. And then this old buffer suddenly retired and Sidney arrived from London almost overnight, ready to take his place. It seemed odd to me. Maybe Sidney was useful to Miss Moncrieff? He's very *handsome*, isn't he? Looks like that dark fella in *The Sheik*. You know, Rudolph Valentino.'

'You mean he was getting information for Miss Moncrieff too?'

'That's right. A honey-trap. Brought in specially. For Petronella Douglas to hang herself up in and to get caught out on…'

Posie was thinking nineteen to the dozen. Could this be true? Hadn't she heard the man say himself that he spent most of his Sunday afternoons in his bed with Petronella?

What kind of tangled mess *was* all of this?

It was like smoke and mirrors. One minute you felt you had a hold on the information, then everything changed and warped again. Posie tried to reason it out.

'You said Sidney replaced the old driver at the end of June?' she asked casually. 'Can you think why *then*, exactly?'

Harriet narrowed her eyes, weighing up the benefits of sharing her information. At last she nodded.

'I reported a telephone call I'd overheard to Miss Moncrieff. It was mid-June. By chance I'd heard Petronella almost sobbing into the telephone in her bedroom, on the line with her Bank Manager. I was listening at the door, pretending to dust out on the landing. Petronella was in a pickle of some sort: there were creditors of the company closing in, and nothing to pay them with. She wanted to completely re-mortgage this place. Petronella said to the Bank Manager that she'd be able to pay the loan back. Easily. All in one go. And in just a month or so.'

Posie stared at the eavesdropper. 'And Elsie was interested in this information?'

The girl shrugged. 'All I know is that Miss Moncrieff became very busy in the weeks after this: on the telephone a good deal herself, going up to St Margaret's-at-Cliffe to send telegrams at the Post Office, and to *collect* telegrams. Then along comes Sidney. End of June it was. Maybe Miss

Moncrieff reckoned Sidney could follow the story through to the end. Get in places she couldn't…'

Posie made a mental note to speak to Sidney as soon as possible. If he refused, he would be forced to speak to the police the next day.

Posie was thinking of secrets. Of the layers of secrets in this strange place. How they all centred around White Shaw and these hedonistic, wild parties. Around the drug-addled, party-throwing Petronella Douglas.

And now a girl had died because of secrets.

She changed tack. 'You said Elsie Moncrieff was full of mysteries, Harriet. I think you followed her, didn't you, to try and uncover one of those mysteries? What did you discover?'

The maid looked sulky at being caught out. 'Sunday afternoon was Miss Moncrieff's time off. Elsie usually disappeared around the same time, just before two o'clock, every Sunday. It seemed odd to me. After a few months I thought I'd see where she was going.'

'And?'

'It wasn't very interesting at all.'

A small moue of distaste. 'Sometimes she walked down to the tea-rooms, Mrs Morse's place, to use the telephone-booth inside. Always at two o'clock. But more often she'd go to the Bay Hotel, also for the telephone, also at two o'clock. But I never found out what Miss Moncrieff was doing. I always had to hurry back here. And I couldn't get close enough to listen. Well, not really.'

Goodness, Posie thought incredulously, *had Harriet Neame thought this could have been another opportunity for blackmail? To turn on the very person who had recruited her?*

Whatever had occurred, Harriet obviously hadn't obtained anything worthwhile, and for this Posie felt strangely vindicated on Elsie Moncrieff's part.

'She also painted a good deal of the time, Miss. On odd hours off, and sometimes on Sundays. Always on the beach. But not always alone.'

Posie narrowed her eyes: here at last could be a glimmer of light.

Had the painting been a front? For a love affair? With the blonde man Petronella Douglas had spoken of, from three years before?

'A man joined her? A good-looking man?'

'Nah, Miss. She was sometimes joined by a woman. *Not* good-looking. The woman had a canvas, and one of them big wooden triangular things.'

'An easel?'

'That's right.' Harriet looked impressed. 'A *proper* artist.'

'They knew each other well, Miss Moncrieff and this artist woman?'

'I dunno, Miss. They looked like they were talking, but not laughing and joking, how some women friends do.'

Posie stared at the watercolour paintings on the wall with renewed interest. They were amateur paintings but beautiful all the same. Rare and vivid colours.

Harriet followed her gaze.

'You know this isn't how Miss Moncrieff would have kept this place, don't you, Miss? That someone *did* this. She was a stickler for order, Miss Moncrieff.'

Outside, what sounded like a gong was ringing. Posie whispered, without quite knowing why: 'What's missing from here, Harriet?'

Harriet was reaching for a thin, cheap, black gaberdine trench-coat.

'I dunno, Miss. I was never allowed in. But where is all her make-up? Her paints? Her lovely clothes? She made them herself, you know. She'd have kept them neat as a pin. She made things beautifully, Miss. Talk about being in the wrong job! Shame she had to wear black all the time for work. If she went out on her own time she wore teal; bright turquoise. Everything matching. Looked like a movie star, she did. She even had a fancy turquoise leather bag.'

'She had a handbag?'

Harriet smiled carefully. 'Oh, yes. Italian leather. Miss Moncrieff took good care of it. Real lovely to the touch.'

Odd, Posie thought to herself. There had been no handbag mentioned in the Pathologist's list of items found with the body, and none had been found up on the cliff-top, nor on the beach. There was nothing like a teal-coloured bag here now, either.

And Posie cursed under her breath.

There was the sound of the gong again.

'I've got to go, Miss. There's early supper to be served to those twins and I've got to help Ruth in the kitchen. They'll all be heading over to the bonfire afterwards at six.'

Posie stood up, hoping her luck would hold. 'Do you know what happened to all of Miss Moncrieff's things? How the room got into this state? Because *this* is how the police found it, isn't it?'

'I dunno, Miss. I wasn't here. More's the pity.'

Harriet explained that Monday was always her day off and she'd gone early into Dover. So she'd missed the drama when Elsie Moncrieff's body was found. She'd missed all the subsequent panic that had gripped the house.

'I can't say what happened here on Monday, Miss Parker. Not truly. But I *do* know there was a fire still burning in that incinerator-bin in the yard when I came back in the evening. I had a bit of a poke around. There was a paint box in among the cinders. The metal casing hadn't burned away, only the paints themselves. And that's when I knew, Miss Parker. Knew that Miss Moncrieff hadn't died accidentally.'

Posie felt a shiver run right through her, although in her heart of hearts she had known this too, known this all along. Perhaps the prized teal-coloured handbag had been burned, along with everything else?

The girl stood at the door. 'You'll remember what you promised, Miss? A good word for me. A reward? I've got interesting information here. Something called the

"November Drop". Happened here on Saturday. It could be important for you. Other things too. Don't forget, eh?'

And with that the maid stepped out into the darkness, leaving Posie alone.

But then, only a couple of seconds later, the girl came back in again. 'There *is* something which was odd, Miss. I've just remembered. I should tell you; it can't hurt her now, can it?'

'Mnnn?'

'Those times I heard her on the telephone, Miss, those Sundays. Down at the tea-rooms or at the Bay Hotel. I swear she always said the same thing, Miss, at the start of the conversation. It was odd. She said – and I'm sure of it – "*Burning Dog*".'

'Sorry? "*Burning Dog?*" Why would she say that?'

'I dunno, Miss. I thought I was mistaken the first time. But no: she said it again all the other times, too. It made no sense.'

Like everything else here, thought Posie to herself, as this time she was left quite alone.

Posie counted on her fingertips the new information: honey-traps; mortgaged houses; companies in debt.

And what of Elsie being married? Her trips to the local hotel? Who was the artist friend? What was all this about burning dogs? Why did everything in Elsie's room have to be messed up or burned?

And could she even trust the little snitch who had reported all of this? A little snitch who had been hoping to trade information for money.

Posie shook her head, somehow shocked to the root of her core by what she had just heard.

Nothing makes sense. Nothing at all.

* * * *

Thirteen

Posie retrieved the hot-water bottle from the floor and sat with it on the bed.

She'd never felt so anxious, so tentative about the discovery of clues before. Posie put her gloves on.

After a few minutes of fruitless jemmying around, she took her nail scissors from her carpet bag and cut into the rubber. It took a while, but she managed to split the rubber seam open and pull the thing, which had obviously never been used for its proper purpose, apart. A few items fell out onto her own white handkerchief which Posie had spread out upon the bed.

'I say!'

The first thing was a ring. A woman's golden wedding ring. So the dreadful maid had been right!

Elsie had been married.

Heart hammering, Posie picked it up, hopefully, turned it a couple of times in the light. It looked almost new, the heavy gold band had not been worn away, and it was hardly scratched. A few years of usage at the most.

Posie stared at the inside carefully, and made out a very delicate engraving there.

It was completely incomprehensible.

Posie laughed at herself: what exactly had she been hoping for? She put the ring down, tamping down her irrational disappointment, and moved on to the next items which were old studio photographs.

They were tiny. Smaller than the inside of her palm, and tied together with a piece of grubby white satin ribbon.

The first was of a handsome boy, maybe six or seven years old, very blonde, with a page-boy haircut, sitting in a wicker chair. But he was wearing the dark, formal, expensive dress of many years before. It must have been taken a few years before Posie's own childhood began.

Sitting next to the lad was a big, very expensive-looking teddy bear, with madly staring glass eyes. The boy looked rather afraid of the bear. *As well you might*, thought Posie ruefully. Teddy bears were very strange toys, when you thought about it. She'd not be in a hurry to buy any for Phyllis, or for Katie. No way.

There was nothing written or marked on the back of the photograph, not even a studio stamp.

And then Posie picked up the second photograph. The second half of the pair. A girl this time. A similar age, maybe younger. Taken at the same studio, in the same wicker chair. Must have been exactly the same year, the same session.

The little girl stared defiantly forward at the photographer, chin raised, eyes giving nothing away. Her beautiful fair long hair was divided into two careful plaits with ribbons. The teddy bear had been thrust aside, and in her arms instead was a girl-doll, a beautiful thing, an expensive and treasured toy, obviously. It was dressed as if for a communion or a wedding with a fancy veil puffed about its head.

Elsie?

Posie flipped the photograph over, and was luckier this time around. Scrawled there in pencil was '*1890*'.

But nothing else.

That was two years before Posie's own birth, and Posie was currently thirty-two. And so if this was Elsie in the picture, she had been at least eight years older than Posie. Which made her roughly around forty years old when she had died on Sunday night.

With a heavy heart Posie put the photographs down, face-up. She fought off a wash of sadness at the sight of the small, hopeful faces. A brother and sister, probably. There was a definite likeness between the two. Mementos of an age gone by, lives scattered and lost, hopes and dreams all forgotten. The boy probably lost in the carnage of the Great War, along with so many others. Completely inexplicably, Posie thought she might cry.

What on earth is wrong with me today?

The last item was a very thin, waxy, bluish, inky piece of paper, rolled up tight like a sausage.

Unwrapping it carefully, which was difficult with her leather gloves on, Posie saw that it was the second layer from a carbonic paper block, and she saw at once how this sort of thing simply wasn't made for being stored rolled-up like this in a tight space, which Elsie might not have realised. Posie saw how the carbon ink had smudged the copied typewritten words irreparably.

There was a date, that much was legible. It was earlier that same year, January 1924. There was a heading, which looked like 'AGREEMENT', and then a mass of patchy half-sentences, almost none of which could be read. 'FEES' stood out, as did 'HOLIDAYS', but that was because these were underlined headings, and anyway, what help were these? Such headings could apply to many sorts of contract. Especially employment contracts.

Was this simply a copy of Elsie's contract here as a Housekeeper?

How dull.

Posie puffed in exasperation. So near, yet so far! Oh, for Elsie to have kept the first, top, clean original. The top copy would no doubt have survived the close compression of the hot-water bottle.

As she started to collect up the items together, hopes pretty much extinguished, Posie suddenly saw there was a tiny piece of card, no bigger than a postage stamp, lying upside-down on the handkerchief. She had completely missed it. It had been so small she hadn't seen it flutter out of the bottle.

Picking it up and squinting, Posie saw it had been ripped from what had obviously been a telegram; that unmistakeable pinky-cream rough card used by the Telegraph Office which was familiar to one and all.

There were a few words printed there, one below the other.

SCHNEIDER.
ABER ROT.
DER ENGEL

Posie's heart was racing. She had no idea what those words meant, or signified, or whether there had been other words, now lost forever, in that untraceable, undated telegram. But she felt the creeping, unaccountable closeness of Max here. Almost felt his breath upon her.

German words.

Could it be a coincidence? Neither Posie nor Richard liked, or believed in, coincidences, and had frequent discussions about it. But it *could* be, she supposed.

Why were these particular German words so important to Elsie? Had she understood them? Spoken German? What was her connection to Germany?

What on earth had Elsie been doing here? Had she known Max when he had been down here, in this area, posing as a priest? Or was that *too* much of a coincidence? This place had been built almost three years ago. And Max had still been here then, although he had stayed on only for another couple of months.

But still, there was a definite overlap.

Posie suddenly felt galvanised into action. She put Elsie's well-hidden treasures together inside her handkerchief and placed them in a pocket of her own carpet bag. She stared at the studio-flat for the last time and left, locking up quickly.

Descending the wooden steps, she crossed to the house and almost ran headlong into Tony Stone. He seemed in a genial enough mood. 'Ah, Miss Parker! Did ye find everything yer wanted in Elsie's wee place?'

Well, hardly, Posie thought bitterly to herself, but she simply smiled politely and returned the key to the Fashion Designer. They stood awkwardly for a moment on the back steps of White Shaw.

'So were ye looking fer me, Miss Parker? Or is it somethin' in the hoose itself?'

'The references, sir. I should have a look through them. You said I could?'

For a moment he looked blank. 'Oh! Yes. Of course. In Elsie's old office.'

'Do *you* read references, sir, when new staff are hired?'

'Ah, well. It happens rarely, you see, that we have new staff. I expect ma wifie reads them, and if nae, Elsie certainly will have done.'

Posie tried not to roll her eyes in exasperation. So nobody in this house read references. Elsie had judged her employers well enough to realise this about them.

Good old Elsie. Trusted so blindly by all.

Posie stayed forcibly upbeat, trying not to show any sort of judgement in her voice. 'How are your preparations going, sir? For the show?'

131

'Aye. Almost done, I'm pleased tae say. I've just locked the wee van up. The seamstresses are all gonnae leave now. There are two wee charabanc buses sat over there tae take them back tae the station in Dover.' He indicated towards where the lit headlamps of a pair of open-top vehicles could be seen, glowing yellow through the scattered sea-mist.

The Fashion Designer opened the back door to his home and indicated Posie should go in first and they passed the glass-fronted kitchen where the twins were sitting eating an early supper under bright lights. The cook, Ruth, sat comfortably beside them, eating too, and Harriet was standing with her back to them all at a scullery sink. Tony Stone stopped and stared, pressed a hand to the glass. A brief look of regret seemed to pass over his face, a resigned sense of sadness.

Posie risked an impertinence. 'You can't join your boys for supper, Mr Stone? I'm sure they'd enjoy that.'

Tony Stone frowned again and shook his head regretfully. 'Nah. The bairns won't mind. I cannae finish yet. So much work for these wee shows. Still, the payback comes with orders afterwards.'

'Of course.'

Payback.

'The office is up ahead, Miss Parker. But you may need to wait a couple of minutes.'

For ahead of them, snaking up the freezing cold corridor and into the very office she had come to poke around in, were the hired seamstresses. All were dressed ready for the unsuitable open-top buses; their felt cloche hats pulled well down over ears, their coat mufflers up. A small valise at each woman's feet was the only evidence of their two-week stay here at St Margaret's Bay.

Tony Stone must have seen the look of vague incomprehension on Posie's face. He laughed easily. 'They're gonnae get paid! Each girl is getting her two weeks' salary. I've got Mickey set up there in Elsie's old office doing it all himself, counting out the wee beans from the strong box, and typing up a payment slip for each girl. Och, though, I miss Elsie! This sort of thing was exactly what she was so good at!'

Posie nodded, only half-listening.

She was thinking of the van Tony Stone had just locked, with that prized Royal Warrant emblazoned upon it, so carefully packed up with dresses and goodness knew what else inside it. Perhaps, if Sidney was correct, the van would be leaving here forever on the morrow. As would Tony, who was now peering anxiously into his various big dimly-lit sewing rooms, as if he was desperate to get into them again and work, to get away from Posie.

Perhaps this would be his last night working in them, ever?

'I was just wondering, sir…' Posie smiled sweetly.

'Yes, Miss Parker? How cannae help you? Do just say the word.'

She played with her engagement ring in a noticeable way. 'You mentioned showing me a wedding gown? I'm actually getting married before Christmas, and I haven't had anything made yet. I'm willing to pay good money. I'm a woman of some means, actually. And I promise you quite some publicity; I know journalists on many of the London papers.'

This last bit wasn't *quite* true. Posie knew *one* journalist well, but she wasn't going to let worrying about a bit of over-embellishment spoil her approach now.

'So I was wondering, Mr Stone, if I could possibly have a look through your van, at your different styles of bridal gown? But I wouldn't want to get in the way of any of your, er, personal items, if you've got your own things stashed away in there, too?'

Tony Stone flicked through his sparse, greasy hair, sucked at his front teeth noisily. He looked like a man who had been put on the spot.

'Perhaps Mickey could open the van up again for me if you're too busy? Or someone else? Sidney, maybe?'

Panic, barely supressed, had flickered for a second or so in the Scotsman's eyes. 'Och, no. I'm afraid it's not gonnae be possible for ye tae take a wee lookie this evening, lassie. How about I have a think about it and bring the gown I think will best suit ye over to yer hotel? Later on this evening? The Bay, is it, yer at? We'll speak about terms only if and when it comes to it, eh? Now forgive me, but I really must go.'

Posie hoped she looked grateful. 'That sounds perfect, sir. Thank you.'

The seamstresses all seemed to have collected their envelopes of cash, and they were nodding at Tony Stone in a slightly awe-struck fashion as he disappeared into one of the big modern sewing rooms, closing the glass door behind him, visibly relieved to be alone at last. And now the seamstresses were making their way to the back door Posie had just come through.

On impulse, Posie spoke in a loud, carrying voice, calling out to them as one: 'I say! Hello! Ladies!'

The women all stopped in their tracks, faces tipped upwards; earnest sunflowers seeking light underneath the dark, mainly unflattering cloche hats, which were the height of fashion but which, in truth, suited so few.

'My name is Posie Parker.' She was digging in her bag. She found her business cards and started handing them out quickly. 'I'm with the police. I know you're all just off home, and you can't wait to leave, but I'm here investigating the death of Miss Elsie Moncrieff. The Housekeeper? You'll have heard all about it, I daresay? You'd have seen her too, I'm guessing, several times a day these last two weeks. This was her office and you were working in the rooms just next door.'

The stocky, middle-aged woman nearest Posie had drawn her mouth up unattractively in a hard line. 'What of it? What you accusin' us of, Miss?'

'Nothing! Nothing at all,' Posie answered reassuringly. 'I'm just after any information you might have. Or anything unusual. Or if you saw the Housekeeper acting strangely in your time here, or meeting anyone unusual? Anything at all, really.'

The same woman thrust Posie's card disdainfully into her oilcloth holdall. 'Nah. We don't know anythin'. We didn't have anythin' to do with that blonde gel, did we, gels? Nothin' at all!'

She looked around her fellow-workers for solidarity, obviously relishing her role as their self-appointed spokeswoman. 'That blonde lassie were too fancy for the likes of us, weren't she, gels? Didn't so much as say hello, or bring us tea, or anythin'. Talk about a Housekeeper! Sent that wishy-washy little maid in to us, that's all she ever did. Spoke real fancy and fake, she did. Grand, like an actress on the stage. She were real proud. And you know what they say…'

Posie frowned. 'No? What do they say?'

The same seamstress had indicated to the others to move on, as a group. 'They say pride comes before a fall, don't they? Well, she fell all right, didn't she?'

The stocky seamstress laughed harshly as some of the other women giggled with her, but others gasped at the wrongness of it all, the sick humour; frightened eyes flashing over at Posie beneath those dratted hats. Thumbs were being bitten in nervous gestures, bags clutched more tightly than necessary. An anxiousness to leave pervaded the place.

These women – or some of these women – know something, Posie thought to herself with a sudden, complete certainty. *But what was it they had seen?*

She called out, over and above the head of the unhelpful ring-leader. 'You have my business card, ladies. It gives my London address, but I'm staying here, at the Bay Hotel. At least for the next few days. If you would like to, and you have any information which may assist me, please call me at the hotel, or send a telegram to me, and I can arrange to telephone you back. I promise I will keep what you tell me confidential and your details will be protected. There may even be a reward in it for you.'

At the stupefied silence, Posie grabbed at anything. 'Ladies, for the sake of justice, I implore you to help me. Whatever you thought of Miss Moncrieff – grand, fancy, whatever – she too had come through the Great War. She'd been a nurse, seen terrible things, helped many. And for what? To survive that and fall off a cliff? Perhaps be *pushed* off a cliff? I need information. I'm looking for justice to be done here.'

There was much harrumphing and muttering, but Posie saw at least one girl of about her own age turn and throw a quick puzzled look backwards, as if in a sort of promise.

Well, it was better than nothing.

A case like this could turn on a few words heard at the wrong – or right – moment by witnesses brave enough to speak up. *If* they were brave enough to speak up.

After the last woman left, Posie strode to the end of the corridor, to the tiny, sparse, cupboard-like office of the dead Housekeeper, and saw that the big Irishman, Mickey O'Dowd, was still sitting at the tiny mahogany desk which faced the door. A smart black portable typewriter was placed in front of him, a carbonic paper pad and a neat pile of typed, loose-leaved top copies beside it. There was also an open black strong-box containing white paper notes. A glass desk-lamp pooled a yellow light over Mickey's work. He was engrossed, his glossy black head bent over, still typing away, and he didn't notice Posie standing in the open doorway.

Which was a good thing, as Posie was completely astounded.

What amazed Posie was his skill.

Mickey O'Dowd, such a big man, with such big hands,

was using the typewriter as if he did so every day of his life. In fact, he could teach Prudence, Posie's secretary, a thing or two. He was typing at lightning speed, and manoeuvred the carriage return mercilessly, belting through the page of typing as if someone was holding a gun to his head, before expertly ripping off the top copy and prising out the blue, inky copy beneath. Once finished, his hands, trembly once again, sought out a cigarette, a light, and he inhaled with relief, his head thrown back, his gaze somewhere on the ceiling.

Suddenly he twigged he wasn't alone, and he looked over at Posie, his eyes narrowing.

Caught.

He stood up, taking the last document he had been typing and placing it on top of the pile with all the others.

'Miss Parker? Oh, what a pleasure. What's all this about now?'

* * * *

Fourteen

Posie edged a little more into the tiny room. Mickey seemed even bigger and more intimidating now it was just the two of them alone, and his eyes glittered at Posie searchingly. The smell of whisky on the man was strong, although a clean scent of vetiver lay beneath it. And there was something else, too – something strong. Was it boot polish?

'How can I be helping you, now?' He pulled at his right-hand little finger in that nervous tick of his.

'I'm actually just after references for all the staff. Mr Stone said they were in here, and I should help myself.'

Mickey O'Dowd tapped the clever inbuilt shelving unit at the side of the desk. Several black files were placed there neatly. His eyes roamed the shelves and then he passed the file labelled 'STAFF' to Posie.

'If you give me a minute I'll clear out and you can have the space you need for your *vital* investigations.'

Posie ignored the sarcasm and watched as he covered up the typewriter – an expensive model of the Remington number 5, the very smallest kind – with its special black cover. He locked up the money box, too, as if Posie might be tempted to steal something. Posie watched him as he picked up all the receipts for the women's pay, the big hand grabbing up the typewritten information – and then Posie saw a snippet of the text – 'THREE POUNDS PAID'.

She gasped involuntarily.

'*Three pounds?*' Posie almost squeaked out the amount and she looked at Mickey O'Dowd in disbelief.

No wonder the seamstresses were happy to work here!

'*Three pounds?* For only two weeks' work? That's an astronomical amount, Mr O'Dowd! I pay my secretary not even twice that for a full year's work! What on earth were these ladies doing?'

Mickey scowled, folding the receipts over on themselves, out of Posie's sight. 'I dunno, Miss Parker. It's not my world, fancy high-end fashion, is it? It struck me as a wee bit over-generous, too, if you must know, but these were my instructions: three pounds to each and every seamstress, and that was that. I take orders, Miss Parker. That's all I do here.'

Posie cocked her head on one side disbelievingly. 'You type pretty well, too, though, don't you, Mr O'Dowd, for all your role here as a glorified tea-pourer and bodyguard?'

Mickey O'Dowd suddenly seemed to find what she said funny, and a grin – the first proper one Posie had ever seen – cracked across his face, and there it was again: that surprising charm, the ruined good-looks. A version of what a man might have been.

'Aye. You've hit the nail on the head there, Miss Parker. I *do* type pretty well, I can't deny it. Although I'm not used to wee girly little machines like this one. This belonged to Miss Moncrieff, Lord rest her soul.'

He reached out and gently tapped the black folder Posie was holding. 'I wasn't always like this, Miss Parker: full of tremors and a general lost cause. You'll find it all in there. In the Great War, before all of *this* nonsense, I was in the Royal Navy – best job in the world – and I was a lowly telegrapher below decks. But I was part of a wonderful team doing communications ops. I had to type a dashed sight faster than you saw me doing just now, I'll tell you! It was nice to have a practice again, just now.'

He moved to the doorway and looked back, eyebrow raised, 'Now, if there's nothing else you need from me, I'll be off. It's Bonfire Night, and I've got some serious drinking to get in before it starts.'

'Hang on a second, won't you?'

Posie sat down in the vacated wooden chair.

'Tell me, did Elsie Moncrieff warn *you* that Mr Stone was leaving here? For good, I mean? That you'd most probably have to look for another job? Because that's what he's doing, isn't it? Tomorrow. Elsie Moncrieff knew it. Tony Stone is leaving here; he's packed his bags. Which is why he won't let me look in that van!'

The big man held himself still in the door-frame, although his hands trembled continually. When he spoke his voice was calm, the Irish accent reassuring.

'Elsie Moncrieff was a very thorough sort of person, Miss Parker. I admired her more than you can know, so I did. But that doesn't mean she was always right. Maybe she misjudged people? Didn't see what was really happening?'

'And what *is* really happening?'

The man laughed easily. 'Beats me! I just packed a load of wee flimsy fabric items into a van, so I did! *You're* supposed to be the Detective, aren't you? And no, there was never any mention to me that I might need to look for a job. Perhaps if wee Tony *is* leaving, he'll take me with him? Maybe I can be his glorified tea-pourer wherever it is he's going, eh? Anyhow, I'll always be all right. Rise again like a phoenix, I do. Every time.'

Posie stared at the space left at the door as Mickey left without looking back.

Those words…

Hadn't Harriet, the maid, said those very same words tonight? But she had put them into the mouth of the now-dead Elsie, three years before, when Elsie had been

140

recruiting the girl. '*Everyone has the right to rise again like a phoenix.*'

Trying, and failing, to harness together what she had heard today, Posie gave up. Instead, she opened the black references file, ready to copy out information.

But something in her bag rustled, and she realised it was the folded carbonic paper found in Elsie's hot-water bottle.

Posie unfurled it, compared it to the full block on the desk and saw it was exactly the same size and make. So it seemed likely that whatever the Agreement had been, it had been typed up, and signed, here at this very desk, on this very typewriter, using this same pad.

But who had the Agreement been between? About what? And what did this empty block tell her, anyway?

Precisely nothing.

Another dead end.

Addressing the 'STAFF' file again with a heavy heart, Posie found herself automatically turning to the entry for Mickey O'Dowd. She'd heard he had met Tony Stone in a pub in Dover, and that he hadn't been part of Elsie Moncrieff's own specially-hired team, but what Posie read there about the man gave her a great thumping shock.

She read that Mickey O'Dowd had been awarded a Victoria Cross.

The highest medal in the land, always awarded for acts of extreme bravery in wartime.

It seemed Mickey had been on the doomed HMT *Aragon* – a Navy ship carrying troops – when it had been torpedoed off the Egyptian coast just after Christmas, 1916. Its sister ship, the *Attack*, came out to help it, but was torpedoed too, sinking within minutes. Sailors on both vessels had clambered aboard the sinking ships, singing 'Keep the Home Fires Burning', as loudly as they could as they awaited whatever fate dealt them out. That fate had been death for most.

Posie whistled under her breath.

The *Aragon*!

It didn't bear thinking about. The fate of that doomed ship, with nearly a thousand souls lost, including nurses, had made the British news for weeks. It had become – sadly – a household name, a symbol of war. An image too poignant and desperate to forget in a hurry. This was in the period before the German U-boats started to attack pretty much any enemy vessel at sea, civilian or military, and before the British had started to retaliate in exactly the same manner, and so what had happened to the *Aragon* had, in early 1917, seemed particularly horrific.

Posie put the file down, and exhaled heavily.

There were no details here in the reference about what Mickey O'Dowd had done exactly to deserve so high a distinction for bravery on that evening, but the act or acts must have been considerable, for the Victoria Cross was not handed out lightly.

There were simply dates of service recorded here, stating that Mickey had been in the navy from 1914 until early 1917. And then there were the telling words: 'RETIRED ON GROUNDS OF ILL HEALTH.'

Posie bit at her lip, cross at herself for pre-judging the man. So much for the lowly telegrapher below decks!

She noted down the dates of service and moved on, reading a typewritten reference supplied for Elsie Moncrieff herself, on an expensive, thick, cream-flocked paper.

It was surprising.

The reference was from the Archbishop of Canterbury's office, with the swirling shield and fancy mitre as the header, and it was dated three years previously.

It stated that Elsie Moncrieff had worked as the Housekeeper in charge at 35 Snargate Street, Dover, running a bed-and-breakfast hostel. It had been specially for the use of serving Anglican and Catholic priests, all on their way to or from the Continent in the course of their religious duties.

The hostel was described as containing some sort of small private chapel within it, for use by the clergymen, which Elsie had apparently kept in impeccable order, as she had the hostel itself. The place had apparently been paid for by the Archbishop's office, and the reference in front of Posie had been signed by the Archbishop himself, Randall Davidson.

Posie thought of the maid, Harriet. Of her knack of picking up on things. She had reported to Posie that Elsie had spoken of candles, of working in a church. Well: she had been wrong, hadn't she? But right in a way, too.

Clergymen.

Catholic priests.

Posie's heart thumped hard against her ribs as she noted down the address. Hadn't Max been down here posing as a clergyman? *A spy disguised as a clergyman.* Was that where these two had met? *If* they had met. So far she had nothing linking Elsie and Max together, apart from a few paltry German words and a growing sense of unease.

Posie flicked through to the next reference.

Posie saw that Harriet Neame and Alfred Walker, Harriet's fiancé, along with Ruth Walker, the cook, all had identical reference letters from 'THE BRISTOL HOTEL, DOVER'. Posie remembered that Harriet had said Elsie was going to forge her reference for the purposes of the job at White Shaw, and so it had presumably been made to look as if all three had previously shared an employer and moved together, *en masse*.

Elsie had been good, for these were truly wonderful-looking fakes.

Posie turned to the last reference letter.

It was for Sidney Sherringham. The driver. The honey-trap, who had only been working here since summertime.

The letter was from HM Pentonville Prison in North

London, where Sidney Sherringham had apparently been a first-class driver. He'd driven anything and everything at Pentonville: horses, carts, ambulances, the executioner's van, but in the last few years, since the Great War, he'd mainly driven the Prison Governor around.

Posie put the reference down, flummoxed. Was this real? Or was it another of Elsie's fabrications?

Somehow, despite the impeccable authenticity of the thing, it didn't ring true.

Posie looked up, up into the darkness of the small office with its flimsy walls and the cold corridor outside, and she was miles away, in a world of her own.

Except for Mickey, whom she hadn't recruited, Elsie had surrounded herself with employees who were odd. Hoaxers. Possibly criminals.

Why? What *had* Elsie been up to?

As more questions seemed to raise themselves, Posie realised with a chilling certainty that she wasn't alone anymore in the Housekeeper's office.

She felt the hairs rise on the back of her shingled neck.

For at the door, dark against the blackness of the corridor outside, a man stood.

And not only was he staring at her intently, but he was wielding a well-aimed gun.

* * * *

Fifteen

Posie forced herself to breathe normally. The knot of fear in her stomach felt as if it might snap at any moment, and yet she willed herself to remain calm.

She was looking down the barrel of a very smart 1906 Parabellum Luger. It gleamed. These small Lugers cost a fortune, and Posie had been threatened with one on her very first case, just like this. Not that *that* was particularly comforting, as things went.

She took a logical guess as to her visitor's identity: the man wasn't big enough to be Mickey, nor small enough to be Tony Stone.

The honey-trap.

'Mr Sherringham, I presume?'

In the darkness her voice was hard as steel, brittle as spun-sugar. 'And to what do I owe this particular honour?'

He shimmied across to her, pulled up a small wooden stool, and sat himself down opposite Posie. He stared hard at her, and she continued to stare back, despite the gun still trained on her.

In the continuing silence, Posie concluded that Elsie had chosen well, if one was in the market for a beautiful man as bait. Sherringham fitted the bill completely. This man, in his mid-thirties, was utterly gorgeous.

The Sheik.

Quite.

He did look like Rudolph Valentino, it was true. But leaner, with long, slender fingers and a measured, quick step. He was downright beautiful, with a face which was dark and sun-tanned, with rolling eyes and slightly flaring nostrils and a way of throwing his head back which called to mind a horse on the verge of throwing its rider.

Slowly Sidney lowered the gun. Posie kept her eyes on him, not the Luger. And she saw in her peripheral vision that he had placed the weapon on the desk.

She watched as the man crossed his arms over his navy driver's livery. *He doesn't know what to do next*, she thought to herself in surprise. And that was when Posie realised there was fear on his side, too.

'Are you "the Angel"?'

Posie couldn't help but widen her eyes in disbelief. 'Sorry? The *what*?'

Too late she realised her mistake. It sounded as if she were laughing at him. She watched as a flush of shame suffused the dark, beautiful face, and Sidney grabbed at the gun defensively.

The Angel?

She hastily backtracked: 'No, no. Hang on. No, I am not "the Angel". And I'm sorry if you expected me to be.'

She pushed across one of her business cards, and then, on impulse, she pulled Elsie's letter from her bag, pushed it into his line of sight.

'I'm Posie Parker, I'm a Private Detective. I'm working with the police to find out what happened to your boss. How she died.'

Posie stared at the man, still looking as if he might flee. She tapped the letter authoritatively. 'I'm here on personal business, Mr Sherringham. I might not be your "Angel", whoever he or she is, but Elsie Moncrieff *did* ask me to help her, late this summer, just gone. And I didn't manage to, and I regret that wholeheartedly. Which is why I'm here, really. Trying to understand what happened on Sunday. I'm too late, of course, but I believe I can avenge Elsie Moncrieff.'

She took the letter out of its envelope and placed it in front of him. 'You can read it, if you don't believe me.'

At last the man took the paper, scanning through the words before returning it to Posie.

'It certainly looks like Elsie's writin', Miss. And I'm awful sorry about the gun. I'm all on edge, see? I was watchin' you for ages. And then I suddenly thought you might be "the Angel", clearin' up. Elsie always told me that if things went wrong here, this Angel person would turn up and sort it all out: get rid of incriminatin' documents and so on.'

Posie flicked calmly to the blue Pentonville Prison notepaper. 'You mean incriminating like this? Because it's fake?'

The man held Posie's gaze. 'You seem to know a lot, Miss Parker.'

'Lucky guesses. But my lucky guess is that you never worked at Pentonville Prison, and that your name probably isn't even Sidney Sherringham. I think it's something much nicer and more exotic. Well?'

He narrowed his eyes, then nodded. 'You're right, but never you mind about my real name. And I'm a dancer, by the way. What's usually called "*a professional partner*" for ladies on their own. My normal employers are the Embassy Club on Bond Street, London.'

Posie tried not to look shocked. 'You mean,' she coughed delicately, 'a gigolo?'

Sidney laughed easily now, perhaps relieved at having shared his true identity. 'Well, I wouldn't go that far, Miss. But I'm certainly the best the Embassy Club has on its books. And I'll still be the best, when I return there next week. It's how Miss Moncrieff found me, see? She asked for the best, paid for the best, and cut my bosses at the Embassy Club a very good deal to hire me out on a month-by-month contract down here. Everyone was happy.'

'Including Miss Douglas, I presume? Because that's why you were brought here, wasn't it? To seduce her…'

Sidney raised an eyebrow. 'But do you know *why*?'

Posie answered carefully. 'I think Miss Moncrieff knew that Petronella Douglas was in financial trouble and that she had arranged to re-mortgage this place. I think Miss Moncrieff wanted *you* to tell her if and when the loan was repaid. Because, for some reason, she couldn't find this information out for herself. Is that how it went?'

Sidney nodded, then shook out a cigarette from an expensive-looking gold case emblazoned with a tantalizing 'CC', and took his time over lighting it up.

When he smoked he threw his head up at the ceiling and blew one smoke ring after another, watching them disappear into the darkness.

'Like you say, Elsie couldn't get near enough for the answers herself. *I* was needed because Petronella has a separate telephone, with its own line, up in her bedroom, which she stays in most of the time. She takes incoming calls on that number. And the bedroom is where Petronella keeps all of her business papers, too: firmly locked up.'

There was a glimmer of pride in Sidney's smile. 'I was quick in finding things out. I was here at the end of June, and by the beginning of July I'd already reported to Miss Moncrieff that the mortgage loan had been repaid.'

Posie moved further forward on her chair, impatient. '*Who* made the payment to cancel out the mortgage?'

Sidney shrugged slightly, inhaling again. 'I heard Petronella on the telephone to her Bank Manager while I pretended to sleep. First couple of days of July it was; ever so hot. She sounded so proud of herself. Petronella said: "*The payment is coming from Taylors. That's the reference you need.*"'

Posie grabbed up her notepad and was writing frantically now: '"Taylors?" So who was that, Sidney?'

'No idea. I don't think Petronella knew herself. She'd received the information about "Taylors" in an earlier call that same afternoon. It was weird. She said to that earlier caller: "*Taylors? That's the reference, is it? Well, frankly I don't care as long as they make it quick, and Daddy doesn't have to find out.*" Petronella just sounded relieved, kept thankin' the person on that first call.'

'And you have no idea who this first caller was?'

'I'm not certain.' Sidney grabbed up some carbonic paper and ground out his cigarette on it, causing an acid-sweet stink of smoke to engulf them both. 'But I'm pretty certain I heard Petronella refer to that earlier caller as "Mr Tell."'

Posie frowned. '"Mr Tell"?'

'Yep. I just supposed it was an accountant, or a broker. You know: probably chargin' terrible rates of interest for a second big loan to repay the first. But my job was just to report what I heard. I didn't care what Petronella was up to, did I?'

'Quite.' Posie ran her hands through her very short, shingled hair. So far what she was hearing about was fairly dull, simply a financial transaction – perhaps unwise or questionable – arranged for a slightly desperate woman. Was *this* what Elsie Moncrieff had gone to such lengthy, costly measures to hear all about?

'Was Elsie happy to hear about this?'

Sidney nodded eagerly. 'Oh yes, Miss. After that I had to report on every conversation with this Mr Tell. Although there weren't many. I reckon there's been a call a month. All called *in*. Recently there's been a few more, and most of them have been about the "November Drop".'

The November Drop. This was the second time Posie was hearing this now.

'What's that?'

Sidney shrugged carelessly. 'Dunno, Miss, I assumed it was another chunk of money comin' through in November. A chaser after the first? And heaven knows Petronella Douglas probably needs it now. The cost of these parties! I'm surprised she doesn't need a "drop" every single month.'

Foxed, Posie held onto something which seemed to make sense. 'And Petronella Douglas was scared her father would find out? She wasn't worried about Tony's reaction?'

The driver looked incredulously at her. 'Nah! I don't think Tony Stone knew what was goin' on. Never does! How she treats him is despicable.'

'How so?'

'Tony Stone does all the work, but he doesn't get so much as a small salary. Petronella spends whatever Tony makes, which this year is loads! I've been through the company paperwork when Petronella was asleep, or drugged up. She keeps it all on her desk in a red-and-gold Chinese lacquered box and I know where she keeps the key. Tony Stone is not even a Director of the company which uses his name! The two Directors are Petronella and her father, back in the States. Tony isn't mentioned once.'

Posie stared. 'Golly! That *is* terrible.'

'Isn't it? You know he sleeps in a small cupboard-sized room off one of the sewin' rooms along here? He's never been into Petronella's room since I got here. They barely tolerate each other.'

Posie thought about the twins, sitting in the kitchen. She felt dreadfully sorry for them and said as much.

Sidney laughed. 'Don't you worry, Miss! Those boys are survivors. Besides, you know they're not really their own flesh-and-blood sons, don't you?'

'Oh?' Posie was writing hurriedly, professionalism overcoming the desire to gossip, although it was sorely tempting.

'They're adopted. Out of the Orphanage in Dover. Petronella and Tony picked them up as a job lot when they had this place built. As you do! The twins must have been wee toddlers when they were brought here. Talk about rags to riches!'

'Or rags to rags, if Petronella's financial situation is so dire?'

'Yeah. Maybe. But I *do* know that it was Petronella who wanted the boys. I've sneaked through the papers in the red box. She's kept copies of her letter of application to the Orphanage to re-home the boys. She writes that it's her life's biggest regret that she and her husband couldn't have their own children; that her husband was unable to have children havin' had mumps in his early twenties.'

Sidney almost laughed. 'Readin' between the lines I'd say she blames Tony for the lack of a child, blamed him continuously. Maybe that was the root of all the trouble? Tony looks in on the twins when the fancy takes him, but once you know the back-story, it's pretty obvious he's not that interested; that they're not his kids. Isn't it?'

Posie shook her head as the puzzle of the twins started to come together. 'And does Tony know about you and Petronella? Being together?'

Another shrug. 'I'm sure he does. And I think he's relieved. There's a strange kind of unexplained hatred between those two. Somethin' simmering. I've been wonderin' when and how this hatred might explode.'

Sidney looked up at Posie from beneath those crazily-long lashes. He picked the gun up, blew on it theatrically and then put it into his inside breast pocket.

'And it happened this Sunday. The day Elsie died.'

* * * *

Sixteen

Sidney explained that he had joined Petronella in the early evening on Sunday, up in her red-tiled bedroom at White Shaw, by prior arrangement. But when he'd got there she was pacing about, off her head already on a mixture of champagne and cocaine.

She had been obsessively calling Tony at the Oberoy Club in London, every ten minutes or so, despite the receptionist having taken countless messages. Sidney had lounged on the great oriental-style bed, smoking and leafing through old *Photoplay* magazines and pretending to doze.

'It was awkward, Miss. Petronella didn't seem to care that I was there at all, which was unusual. I wondered how soon I could leave. But then, suddenly, Tony called her back. I remember there was some problem with the telephone connection.'

Posie bit at the pencil end. She felt like some odd intruder in an eavesdropping contest, and couldn't imagine how the man in front of her had felt at his part in all this.

'Petronella was acting like a lunatic. She kept saying, "*Is this a trunk-line call?*" And then she started screaming: "*I'll get rid of her one way or another.*" I assumed she was speakin' about Elsie.'

Posie felt a shiver clip its way down her spine, and then she stared intently up again at Petronella's lover.

'Tony obviously tried to retaliate with something of his own. But Petronella was scathing of him. She was laughing and sayin': "*You're not going anywhere!*"'

Posie wrote it down, frowning. 'It seems as if he was threatening to leave, doesn't it? Like we suspect Tony's actually doing now.'

Posie flicked her notebook shut. 'Did you think of those words, Mr Sherringham – "*I'll get rid of her one way or another*" – when you heard about Elsie's death the next day?'

Sidney exhaled slowly. For the first time Posie saw something like genuine emotion flicker across his face.

'I agree it sounds bad for Petronella. And I'm the last person who would want to defend her. But I swear to God, I shared Petronella's bed all Sunday night and Petronella never left it. *Not once.* That must rule Petronella out, surely? *I* am her unwilling alibi.'

'Maybe you fell asleep? Maybe Petronella drugged you?'

Sherringham shook his head, resolute. 'No. I was awake all night long. I'm scared of storms, see? Always have been, since a kid. I heard every thunder-clap; every pitter-patter of rain. Don't you think I've not played it all over in my mind to see if I've missed somethin'? But Petronella was nowhere near Elsie that night. Although I realised the next morning how very much Petronella hated her; how deep it all went.'

Posie jerked her head upright. Another puzzle piece coming together?

'Was Petronella responsible for defacing Elsie's room? For getting rid of her things? That's a criminal act, you know?'

'Yes. I know.'

He explained how on the Monday morning a waiter from the Bay Hotel had come pounding at the door of White Shaw, early, about seven-thirty, waking the household. It was still dark. The waiter brought news of the discovery of Elsie's body, and explained that the Hotel Manager was telephoning to the Dover Police Station.

Sidney held his curly black head in his hands for a few seconds before surfacing. He looked troubled. 'Petronella put a hysterical call through to Tony in London, and left a message tellin' him what had happened and to get back home. Then Petronella screamed at me to bring the car around, quick as I could, which I did. And then she started yellin' at Mickey O'Dowd, whose face was greyer and drunker than I've ever seen before, and she told him to light that incinerator they use in the backyard.'

Posie was incredulous: 'Surely the police would have been on their way over while this was all going on? It would all have looked mighty suspicious?'

Sidney shrugged. 'I dunno, Miss. But only one bobby arrived in the end, a good few hours later. In fact, it was the same red-haired bobby who was here today.'

'How fortunate. Or unfortunate. So where did you drive Miss Douglas to, so early?'

'The Post Office up the hill. We fair stripped that shop bare,' he remembered. 'Every magazine got scooped up. Newspapers too.'

'Did Miss Douglas ask you to help her any further? Go into Elsie's flat?'

'Nah. She ordered me and Mickey to go to our shared flat. We watched through the window, though. It was a sad show. She ran in and out of Elsie's flat, pullin' out all sorts.'

'It all went on that burning fire?'

'Yep. And then Petronella went inside with all those magazines and she must have scattered things about; made it look a real tip.'

'You didn't say anything to Mickey O'Dowd about how strange this all was?'

Another cigarette was taken from the gold tin and lit.

'No. The man's not much of a talker, but he was shakin'. Worse than usual, like. Poor lad: you know he was one of the survivors from the *Aragon*? Although it could have been the drink not yet worn off. He hits the bottle hard, that one. But he must have been in fairly good physical shape, because I turned my back shortly afterwards – I couldn't bear to watch any more – and he went out and started to help Petronella to bring big bulky things covered in sheets down the steps from Elsie's room.'

'What things? What happened to those?'

'I dunno, Miss. They took them off behind the house somewhere.' Sidney inhaled deeply. 'It doesn't look good for Petronella, does it, Miss Parker?'

Posie shook her head slowly. 'No, it does not. Did anyone other than you and Mickey see this little performance with Elsie's things?'

'Only Ruth, the cook. I saw her come out on the back step and just stare. Then, while Petronella and Mickey were luggin' the big items away, Ruth stepped forward with a big stick and dragged out a couple of things from the fire. Clothes, maybe? Elsie had some fine stuff.'

'I see.' Although Posie didn't see.

She didn't see at all, in fact.

'By the time Tony arrived back in a cab, the damage had been done. Everythin' burnt and ruined. It was about ten-thirty in the mornin' and Mickey was still standin' at the incinerator, stirrin' it all. Tony looked dazed, completely broken. Those two men just stared at each other, but there was nothin' to say, was there?'

Posie was confused. 'You mean that both of them thought Petronella had killed Elsie?'

'Exactly,' nodded Sidney, jabbing his cigarette in the air as if to prove a point. 'It was like they were both now in some pact to cover everythin' up. Why else would Petronella be burnin' all of Elsie's things?'

'And the policeman? What did he say about the burning bin?'

'I don't think he said anythin', Miss. He arrived just after Tony and seemed on the back-foot. He was especially on the back-foot after Petronella had offered him somethin' sweet and alcoholic to drink inside the house.'

'Dash it all!' Posie exclaimed in complete disbelief. How had this happened? Complete police incompetence from first to last.

She eyed the man in front of her keenly. He was fidgety, and seemed desperate to move, to get away. As if the chair could not contain him.

What a dancer he must make.

'Why haven't you left for London already, Mr Sherringham?'

The man looked a little shamefaced. 'I wanted to attend the Inquest today. I wanted to see what unfolded about Elsie; if Petronella gave herself enough rope to hang herself with. Actually, I thought "the Angel" might make himself or herself known to me. But I'll leave tomorrow. I've had enough of this place.'

Not if Scotland Yard turn up first, Posie thought to herself archly.

Suddenly Posie remembered the maid, Harriet, and her almost jealous reaction when she had spoken about Sidney; how he had been special to Elsie.

Special.

Perhaps he had been Elsie's closest confidant here? Or even more than that, if the candles had been anything to go by?

It was now or never. Posie spoke in a whisper, almost under her breath:

'Were you Elsie's lover?'

'Oh no, Miss. She wasn't the sort.'

Posie nodded, believing his sincerity. 'Tell me, what was Elsie up to here? *Really* up to, I mean? I think you might be the only one who knew.'

The nostrils flared, the wild-horse eyes darted, and for

a second Posie thought the man might run away. Then Sidney rubbed the balls of his hands into his eyes, blew out the last of his cigarette smoke.

'I dunno, Miss. Honestly, I don't. At first I thought Elsie might be workin' directly for Tony; plantin' *me* here to get evidence of Petronella's adultery so he could push for a divorce. Poor man deserves a break from her, doesn't he?'

Posie raised an eyebrow. This had never occurred to her.

'But pretty soon I got rid of that view. Tony's not organised enough, and how would he pay both Elsie and myself? With *what*? He has no money, poor beggar. I later came to think that Elsie was workin' for the government, for the big money men.'

'You mean the Revenue?'

'Yes. I wondered if she was really down here checkin' on whether the Fashion House was quite legit.'

'Golly!' Posie frowned.

'But somethin' was goin' wrong here for Elsie, Miss. You know that yourself, don't you? Look at this letter she wrote you a month after I came! Tryin' to bring you in here, although I've no idea why. And Elsie was runnin' low on funds, I know that. She was sometimes goin' in to Dover, sellin' her own things.'

Posie thought of Elsie Moncrieff, the centre of this puzzle, of how no-one had said anything about the person she had *been*.

As if he could read her thoughts, Sidney shook his head regretfully.

'She were lovely, Miss. Beautiful, snazzy. I missed London but Elsie made me feel like I was still *there*. We'd have a drink together, throw on a record, and she'd put on her bright red lipstick and then we'd dance in her flat with only a candle or two burning. Almost in the dark, see? That was always her choice. We met a few times a week. Just for a few minutes. Nothin' romantic ever happened, but cripes, how that girl could move! When we danced around her flat it was like we were dancin' as if it was the end of the world.'

He swallowed nervously. 'You know she wasn't from here originally?'

'Not from Dover?'

'Nah, not from *England*. She spoke in this proper, clipped English, but she told me once she'd been born abroad. South Africa, I think she said. Well, when she'd had a glass of wine and we'd collapsed in laughter after dancin', that's when you'd hear her accent. I'll miss her. I can't believe this has happened. You find whoever did this to her, Miss Parker. I believe you can.'

He stood up, and Posie followed.

'Will you miss it here? The parties?'

Sidney laughed bitterly. 'The parties? No, not if this last one on Saturday was anythin' to go by. I was servin' drinks and then I had to play the piano when the fella they'd booked didn't turn up on account of the worsening weather. It was all chaotic. Petronella had taken more cocaine than usual, and she was embarrassing; fawning over that famous blonde Inventor all evening. The one with the glasses.'

'Lord Boxwood?'

'That's right. Him and his strange wife. Mickey O'Dowd must have been drunk already at the start, because of all the hundred or so people at the party he managed to spill hot coffee all down that Inventor's wife's dress, and she fair screamed at him about it! And then we had Tony runnin' off every half an hour or so to check on his precious sewing, all jittery. And Elsie didn't come. Said she had a headache with the stormy weather. She was well out of it, if you ask me. Although when I went to bed in the early hours, I know she was still up, because the light was on in her flat, and I could hear her hummin' away, and she had a record playin' very low. She sounded happy.'

They stood together at the door onto the cold, dark corridor. Up this close the man smelt of peppermints, of coffee, of green forests. It was somehow intoxicating: no wonder he was in demand at the Embassy Club.

But Posie *had* to ask about the gun.

'And was that glitzy little Luger *Elsie's* gun, by any chance? Or did Elsie give it to you when you came to work here? For your own personal safety?'

Sidney Sherringham whispered very low: 'Nah, Miss. You're right: it was Elsie's. She kept it in the compartment beneath her gramophone. I saw my chance on Monday mornin' – when Mickey and Petronella had disappeared off with a big bulky item – and I fair dashed up Elsie's steps to retrieve it. I thought I might be needin' this gun, see? Danger suddenly seemed to be lurkin' everywhere. I haven't gone anywhere without it since.'

And as Posie crossed the yard outside, looking up at Elsie's dark flat, she could safely say she had simply no idea what the Housekeeper had been up to here, happy or not.

And why on earth she had been keeping a gun.

Everything about her seemed shrouded in the thickest sort of mystery.

* * * *

Seventeen

The Bay Hotel was the exact opposite of White Shaw.

In contrast to the thin walls and modern, chilly rooms, the hotel felt comfortingly solid. Everything was dark green, from the gold-and-olive striped wallpaper through to the emerald velvet of the public telephone-booth's little curtain. A fire roared merrily in a sturdy tiled fireplace and empty sage-coloured sofas formed a lounge-like nook at the window facing the sea.

It all seemed very cosy.

An orange light could be seen flickering from outside, where the huge bonfire was now brightly, dangerously ablaze.

Posie looked at the group of sofas and felt a sudden desire to lie down and sleep for a very long time, to hibernate and rest. To stop all this wretched *thinking*.

But she waited with her carpet bag and her holdall at the empty receptionists' desk, her heels now dashed uncomfortable after hours spent standing up in them.

She seemed to be quite alone, but somewhere nearby she heard glasses clinking.

Next to the sign marked 'WINTER VACANCIES – PLEASE ENQUIRE' was a price list of the hotel's services and a brand-new copy of a Macmillan's *Highways and Byways in Kent*, and Posie was just about to pick it up to leaf through it when a tubby little man appeared, apologising profusely. Apparently a good few of the staff were down with the flu, and it was all hands to the deck here, too.

'Frederick Potterton, Deputy Hotel Manager, at your service. You're Miss Parker, aren't you, Miss?'

The man, in his early forties, wearing immaculate green sateen, kept smoothing back a stray greasy forelock of long, dark hair, across an otherwise bald head.

'Down from *London*, Miss?' The Deputy Hotel Manager managed to make the capital city seem both exotic and very far-away, all at the same time, while conveying to Posie that by coming from London she was really in a preferred category of guest.

'That's right. And yes, I'm Posie Parker. But how did you know?' Posie laughed nervously. 'Surely I'm not your *only* guest?'

'Good Lord, no, Miss. We have a couple of other overnight guests booked in, and some of the local folks will be stopping in to dinner tonight, at our restaurant, after the bonfire finishes outside. We're the best restaurant you'll find around here by far.'

The man nodded proudly. 'Actually, we've just had a refurbishment of the hotel: full electricity; some rooms with hot water; a full-sized ballroom and a brand-new heated swimming pool! Outside, of course.'

He seemed to come to his senses, realised Posie wouldn't be using the outside pool any time soon. 'But as it happens, I was specifically told to look out for you, Miss. It was that Police Detective from Scotland Yard.'

He started scanning the Guests' Register frantically.

'Wetbird, was it? Waterbird?'

'*Rainbird*, Mr Potterton. Did he leave me a message? Am I to meet him here in the lounge?'

'Oh, no, Miss. The fella didn't look right at all, Miss. He

was sweating like he'd been running a long-distance race. Then shivering. Looked like the flu. I packed him off with some honey and lemon and a hot-water bottle. I reckon he'll be out for the count, all night probably.'

'Ah, I see. Thank you.'

'He told me to tell you he hadn't managed to place the call to London. He was very sorry about it, he said.'

Posie instantly stopped feeling tired. She quickly looked at her red wristwatch and saw it was now exactly six o'clock, time for the official Bonfire Night event outside to start.

It was usual time for Scotland Yard policemen to head home. But she desperately needed those Warrants to search White Shaw; to cut through the muddle and mess and inefficiency of Briggs and the local police. To get to the bottom of Petronella Douglas' deceit, which the woman had been allowed to get away with for quite long enough.

Richard Lovelace would certainly have left the office by now, but Sergeant Fox, a savagely-keen whippersnapper of a Detective, eager to bite at the heels of anyone else in the queue ahead of him for promotion, would surely still be in.

'Can I use the telephone? It's urgent,' Posie asked, already heading for the booth.

''Course you can, Miss. We've had some trouble with the line, on account of the storms, but it should be working again now. We do have another telephone line in an adjacent building, the holiday bungalow, also owned by us, if you have problems. It's not booked out right now.'

But, as it turned out, the line to the Operator and then through to Scotland Yard worked perfectly and Posie got connected easily to Fox, who sounded fresh as usual.

'I need help, Fox. It's a case the Chief Commissioner will have charge of. Can you get a message to him, urgently? Tell him to get down here, to St Margaret's Bay, quick as he can. Tomorrow morning.'

'I'll try, Miss, but I can't promise anything. He's been tied up all day, Miss Parker, in emergency meetings on a sudden case. I think he's been called to one now. I just saw him leave with a driver. Going to Whitehall.'

'Oh?' Posie frowned. 'What case is that?'

'Missing persons, Miss. Dunno anymore at the minute.'

'I see. Well, this is important too. I need you to help me, and to get me some information. I think you might have to work very late tonight, Fox, to get all this done, and I'm sorry. But I promise you you'll get merit where merit's due. I'd like you down here first thing tomorrow, Sergeant, too. I'm sure that the Chief Commissioner will be more than happy for you to help out. Trains leave from Victoria. The first one is at five a.m. Be on that one if you can.'

'Very good, Miss. What do you need?'

'I need comprehensive Search Warrants for tomorrow morning. Full authority to search where and whom we like at White Shaw.'

'Noted, Miss. Anything else?'

Posie got out her notebook, where she had been busily writing down details in Elsie's little office, and she read out what she had written there.

'Just check that these people actually exist, and if they have ever been in trouble with the law, will you? Criminal checks. Oh, and the Fashion House – Douglas & Stone – can you check its financial standing. Ring Rutherford's, their bank on the Strand, and find out how they are *really* doing. Check with Companies House, too: get any recent documents they may have filed. Check the Land Registry for details of the property, White Shaw. See if there are any outstanding mortgages on the place. Dig around and see what's been happening.'

'That's *it*, Miss?' A hopeful, slightly desperate note was in Fox's voice.

'No. I need you to try and find out if a marriage ever happened...'

Posie gave the details to a now-deathly silent Sergeant Fox.

'And lastly, can you do some official telephoning for me? Throw all the weight of the Yard behind you. One's a London number, and the other is abroad. The Argentine, actually.'

* * * *

A few minutes later, up on the first floor, standing on the plush carpet outside Posie's suite, Mr Potterton fumbled with the keys.

'It's our best suite, Miss. Hot and cold running water, and your own bathroom with a good-sized bath. Wonderful views. I hope you'll be very comfortable here. And that sick policeman is just next door.' He indicated to a door further down on the right. 'If you should need him.'

The suite was indeed lovely, and Posie said as much, to which Mr Potterton looked especially pleased, as if he personally owned the place.

Twin bedside lamps mounted in the wall had been switched on, but burned low, illuminating the gold-and-green covers of the inviting double bed. An assistance bell on the wall had a label marked 'RECEPTION' below it. The room was long and narrow, and taking up most of one side was a large triple-bay window overlooking the sea.

The lime silk curtains were pulled back, as were the white nets beneath. A telescope was placed at the centre of the window, and a narrow window-seat, upholstered in lime-coloured silk, surrounded the window. Between the window and the bed was a good-sized mahogany table, with two silk-upholstered chairs pulled up at it. Further down the room on the same side as the window was a set of French doors, which led onto a balcony. The room was pleasing. Comfy and grand all at the same time.

Posie placed her holdall and bag on the bed, and walked to the window. She now had a perfect, bird's-eye view over the massive roaring bonfire right below, and the dark, shadowy crowd of figures around it. Beyond the fire, beyond the people, beyond the beach, was endless blackness, endless sea. You couldn't hear the waves crashing from here, just the crackling of the fire.

'Quite a crowd.' She smiled back towards Potterton, who seemed eager to talk.

'Oh, it always is. One of the highlights of the year for St Margaret's Bay.' The tubby man padded keenly to stand beside Posie. 'Look, Miss, they're about to light the Guy! There'll be fireworks on the beach later. Nothing like you have up in London, of course.'

And here he looked at Posie hopefully, wistfully. 'I hear the Peace Day Fireworks in London three years back were something out of this world, eh? Were you there for them, Miss Parker?'

Posie shook her head, unable to add to the legend. She had been away in Oxfordshire, at a country house, working on a case. But she had listened with wonder to the descriptions of the big, cornflower-blue fireworks which had lit up the London night-skies, delighting so many.

Mr Potterton shrugged, not put off. 'Oh, well, good job we've got a dark, moonless night tonight for the fireworks, eh? Will you go down and see the display, Miss?'

'I'm not sure yet.' And she wasn't.

'You've got a good view of it all from here, anyhow. Best view in the hotel.' He pointed rather sadly at the telescope. 'You can see the Calais Town Hall clock from here on a clear day! Not to mention the Channel and the beach. The boats...'

He sighed heavily. 'Not that *you'll* see any boats, Miss. A real shame. We've not had any boats out here the last few days, nothing. Not even a little dinghy. It's too dangerous, they say.'

Posie remembered Tony Stone mentioning the same restrictions earlier, in the chilly lounge of White Shaw. She was about to wish Mr Potterton good-evening, and go and run a bath, when she realised he seemed to be lingering on purpose.

She noticed he had now moved and was standing plumb in the middle of a line of framed watercolour paintings hung on the wall by the doorway.

They were all of the view from this very room. One was even *of* this very room.

She gasped. 'I say!'

Potterton followed her gaze. 'That's right, Miss. I daresay you know who painted these?'

'Elsie Moncrieff?'

An excited nod, but wary eyes.

Posie stood stock-still, exactly where she was. She let the silence go on, and then the man's words gushed over.

'I daresay my boss, Mr Cluff – he's the *actual* Hotel Manager – wouldn't want me saying anything. But he's off with this blessed flu, and has been since Monday morning. So what he doesn't know can't hurt him, can it? I saw you goin' past earlier, all official-like. With the police. A proper Lady Police Officer!'

Posie didn't outright lie, she just smiled encouragingly, which she hoped didn't amount to an untruth.

'I figured you must be down here about poor Miss Moncrieff. And I thought I'd let you in on something.'

'Oh?' *Please do.*

'Aye. Miss Moncrieff booked this very room every Sunday, Miss. From two o'clock onwards, until midnight. Every single week; every single Sunday these past three years.'

'My gosh!' Posie tried not to gasp at this unexpected news. 'She paid in advance, did she?'

'Yes, Miss. She paid per quarter, see? But I think she was expecting the arrangement here to end.'

'Really?'

'She paid like usual from June to the end of September, but where normally she'd then pay right up to the end of the year, she only paid until the end of *this* present week. Nothing was paid for the rest of November or December at all. Like she wasn't planning on carrying on this arrangement.'

The information could mean something, and it could mean nothing. Hadn't Sidney Sherringham said that Elsie might have been running out of money? Maybe it was just that.

Or maybe – as seemed most likely – Elsie had been planning on leaving here in November. On the implosion of the Fashion House which she had known to be coming.

The Sunday afternoons made sense at last. The Bay Hotel, aside from being a place to telephone from, had been a near-at-hand refuge for Elsie. A chance to indulge in some luxury, to bathe, to wash her hair and to bleach it, well away from the ceaseless sullen surveillance of Harriet and Ruth.

Little luxuries.

But this wouldn't have come cheaply. And Elsie Moncrieff, who was revealing herself to be far from a routine Housekeeper, had probably had to pay top-drawer prices in order to guarantee a discretion which had lasted up until now.

It seemed that Elsie had been in receipt of another, solid income, which covered all these expenses. But what was it and where had it come from?

Posie asked casually: 'She paid well, did she, Mr Potterton?'

'Oh, aye. I'd guess at least twice the normal rate, triple maybe, for such an unconventional arrangement. Although...' he coughed and muttered darkly, 'Most of the proceeds of this arrangement went directly into *pockets*, if you catch my drift.'

'I quite see. But what did she do here, Mr Potterton? Because Miss Moncrieff lived so close by, didn't she?'

The man shrugged. 'We have quite a few locals who come and partake of our services, Miss. When they want to do *private* things.'

Posie almost laughed. 'You mean Elsie met men here?'

Mr Potterton tugged at his one greasy forelock again: 'I didn't say *that*, Miss. As it happens, I don't usually work on Sundays – Mr Cluff does – I've only worked a few Sundays in all these last three years.'

'And what *did* you observe on those occasions?'

The Deputy Manager shrugged with barely-suppressed disappointment. 'Not much, actually, Miss. The first time, you're right; she *was* with a man. This would have been more than three years ago, in autumn, 1921. When those Fashion Designers were just about to move into that great glass monstrosity. Disgraceful, I call it!'

'But what was he like, this man?' Posie's heart raced, hopeful for something concrete here. 'Was he German? A priest?'

Had this been Max? Was this the connection she had – in her heart – been looking for?

But the man shook his head. 'No, Miss. This fella was English. Very distinguished voice, he had. Posh as you like. Short blonde hair. Wore thick, round gold spectacles. Smoked a pipe. I remember it well because you don't see that much anymore, do you? The two of them seemed to know each other well.'

Posie felt her heart and her expectations fall flat. This didn't match Max's description at all, or anyone's description, come to think of it.

Unless it had been Sidney Sherringham's mysterious "Angel"? *If* he existed.

'I brought them tea in here, Miss. Darjeeling, I think it was. They were sitting here at this table with a lot of paperwork, which they tried to cover up as soon as I got near. As if I might spy!'

Mr Potterton sounded slightly offended at this memory, and then looked slightly gleeful. 'I did see *some* photographs, though. They were pinned to sheets of typewritten paper. There were a couple of the Prince of Wales, and a few of that Petronella Douglas with other folk. There were magazines, too. *Vogue*, is it? With photographs printed of Petronella Douglas again, and ringed in red ink. Lots of red ink.'

What on earth had Elsie been doing? Planning, by the sounds of it. But who had been the man she had been doing this with?

But Mr Potterton – who was turning out to be almost a good an observer as Harriet the maid – was rushing on:

'But it wasn't just *men*, Miss. I don't want you to get the wrong idea. Mr Cluff spoke of Miss Moncrieff having tea with a lady friend here; a fellow artist. It must have been summertime last year. Mr Cluff told me about it when I was given the task of hanging the pictures in here; they were a gift to the hotel, see? And the only other time *I* saw Miss Moncrieff here on a Sunday was this last one. Just gone.'

'The day she died,' Posie muttered, slightly under her breath. For some reason the news that Elsie Moncrieff had been *here*, in this very room, on the Sunday she had died, unnerved Posie.

But why?

It certainly made sense.

'What did she do this Sunday, Mr Potterton? I mean, after her telephoning from the booth downstairs at two o'clock sharp?'

Mr Potterton looked taken aback for the very first time. 'Oh! You know about that?'

'"*Burning dog?*" Yes, I do. As do you. Because you listened in, didn't you?'

The man flushed scarlet and it suddenly dawned on Posie that Elsie's doll-like allures had not been lost at all on Mr Potterton.

'What went on in that telephone call, Mr Potterton?'

The man was caught out. He splayed his hands apologetically. 'I couldn't help but overhearing, I was stacking leaflets at reception…but I didn't hear much, Miss. Only snippets. You're right: Miss Moncrieff said that weird thing about a dog, and then there was a long pause. I thought she'd been disconnected, but after a minute or so she raised her voice angrily. She was saying, "*What do you mean I can't get in touch?*" A few seconds later Miss Moncrieff slammed the telephone receiver down in its cradle. Went up to this room. And that was it, Miss.'

But had that been everything? Posie was quite sure that this funny little man had the potential to be quite stalkerish in his devotions.

She'd push her luck now.

'I think you were solicitous, Mr Potterton,' she nodded, tentatively. 'Maybe you came up here later, on the off-chance that Miss Moncrieff might need something? Even if she didn't ring that handy bell…'

Mr Potterton beamed at Posie's perfect understanding.

Yes: he had come up twice to the room. Once, right after the telephone call, at about quarter-to three. And then, much later, about eight o'clock.

He'd hung about the door.

Both times there had been a man in with Elsie. The first time, early in the afternoon, it had sounded like an argument was going on.

'Funny thing, Miss, but it sounded like Miss Moncrieff was arguing with the same fella I'd seen her with more than three years ago.'

Posie stared. 'Are you sure?'

Mr Potterton shrugged 'I'm not a betting man, Miss, but I'd lay a wager on it being the same fella. Same posh tone, an arrogance almost. He kept saying, "*You can't do this!*" But Miss Moncrieff was having none of it. She said: "*It's no surprise that I'm leaving. I've told you now for months.*

The time is now. I'm meeting the Angel tonight and I'll be telling him too. I'm out.'''

I'm out.

But out of *what*? And 'the Angel', again.

So this Angel was a man, after all. It was all so frustrating. Like sand falling through your hands.

'Go on, please. This is really wonderful information, thank you very much.'

Potterton looked childishly pleased. He frowned. 'The other stuff didn't make much sense to me, to be honest. They were whispering, but loudly. Miss Moncrieff sounded cross: she was saying something about the "November Drop", whatever that was. She said: "*I've called and no-one's talking.*" She said it was his mess now to sort out, the man, I suppose. He sounded angry. Kept saying: "*You weren't even there!*" I think he thumped the wall, or something, and all I heard of his rant was: "*I don't know what happened,*" and something about "*vanishing*". It sounded pretty heated.'

Posie chewed at her lip savagely. This man in the room, whoever he was, had been angry. What if it wasn't the wall he had been hitting, but Elsie herself? That hand-print. Was that how she had come by it?

Mr Potterton cleared his throat. 'Something odd happened next, Miss Parker. I actually knocked at the door. I'm not ashamed of meself. I was worried for her safety.'

Posie's heart began to race. Was this a positive identification of the man inside?

'But when she answered, almost straight away, she was as neat as a new pin, and the room was immaculate, although it stank, I must say – of bleach and pipe smoke – and she was quite alone.'

'Alone?' Posie's eyes widened.

'Aye. She assured me she didn't need anything at all. So I went back to my desk, and she left a few minutes later. I kept an eye out for the fella with the posh voice all afternoon. There's only one exit and you have to come past reception, but no-one came past. It was like the fella was a ghost.'

Hardly, thought Posie, not liking to dampen the man's enthusiasm for his tale. What seemed likely was that the man, with the aid of a ladder or well-placed dustbin, could have shimmied up and down to the room from outside, using the iron-work balcony.

'And the second time you, er, overheard Miss Moncrieff, at eight o'clock, was it this same chap? This posh fellow?'

'I don't know, Miss. I didn't hear the voice. But I'd say not. The first fella was angry, strong, a bully maybe. This second person was almost weeping.'

'Are you sure it was a man, then? Not a woman?'

'Well, now you mention it, I couldn't be sure. Yes, it could well have been a woman. But this time it was Miss Moncrieff who was being the bully. She was whispering angrily; something about *"an Agreement"*. There was definitely a rustling of papers. She said she thought the other person in the room was just nervous. It would all work out just fine. That's it.'

Posie thanked the man for his invaluable help, and told him he might have to repeat what he'd said to Scotland Yard officers the next day, at which he puffed himself up with pride. Posie also told him about the arrival of a team of Scotland Yard policemen the next day, all of whom would be needing rooms.

'So make a few ready, please. And I think they'll need a centre, an Incident Room, away from White Shaw. Do you have anywhere suitable?'

It turned out the Bay Bungalow, the self-contained little house sandwiched between the Bay Hotel and White Shaw, could be used at a moment's notice, complete with telephone equipment and lots of space. There was a connecting passage even, running between the hotel and the bungalow, so that hot food could be brought to-and-fro between the places in bad weather, for the guests' convenience.

'Sounds perfect.'

Posie's stomach rumbled loudly. It seemed a long time since she had eaten anything, apart from a couple of biscuits and that measly bit of chocolate.

A bath then. And something to eat. And then a good deal of thinking, and puzzling.

But first things first.

'Could you send up cheese on toast, please, Mr Potterton? Cheddar, if you've got it, and Worcester sauce on top. Lashings of it. At least six slices, with butter first. Don't skimp on it. And a pot of tea. Strong tea, not Darjeeling. You'd better send exactly the same through to Wetbird through there. Put it all on my tab, please.'

And then Posie went to the window, and watched the huge, captivating, unforgettable fire raging below.

* * * *

Eighteen

On cases like this, where there were more questions than answers, Posie had always found the best way to move ahead was to clear her mind.

Or else, eat.

The cheese on toast had arrived quickly, and was delicious. Posie stood munching it from the triple-bay window. Below, there were at least a hundred people gathered about, probably more. The tide was out, and down over the wooden railing and onto the sand, you could just make out lads gathering in the darkness, silhouetted black on black, setting up the firework station.

Small children waved sparklers, and were constantly getting dragged back from being too near the roaring bonfire by weary parents and baby-sitters. Posie saw the excited faces of the Douglas-Stone twins, rosy cheeks below warm school hats, the bulky figure of Ruth the cook looming closely behind them.

To Posie's surprise she saw the white, doughy face of Petronella Douglas, standing close to the little boys, her deep-set eyes lit up for a moment by the bright orange light, her all-black clothes making her seem discombobulated; a stray face without a body floating above the crowds.

Petronella was talking, trying to get the boys' attention,

but they were engrossed in the fire, and in each other, and seemed to ignore her. Posie watched as the woman marched over to the lad selling toffee apples, bought two of the sticky treats, and then returned to her sons.

Posie saw Petronella offer the apples to the boys; saw how the twins didn't bother to turn around to face her; didn't bother to take the sweets. Rejected, and looking stupid, after a couple of minutes Petronella threw the apples into the bonfire, and the boys laughed.

Posie felt a stab of pity for the American, and remembered Sidney Sherringham's tale of how much Petronella had wanted to have children.

Well, even if she was a drugged-up, barely-there mother, Petronella Douglas *had* tried just now. She wasn't terrible. The problem seemed to be that those children didn't want *her*. Maybe something about twins being so completely self-contained? Posie watched as Petronella disappeared into the entrance hall of the hotel below.

Snatches of action, of faces, caught the flickering orange light below.

Posie saw the bent, broken-nosed face of Mickey O'Dowd, circling the fire, loitering behind the twins for a moment, smoking a cigarette. After a few minutes of this he leapt athletically over the wooden railing which separated the small promenade from the beach, and headed down to where the fireworks were now being organised.

He's like a moth to a flame when there's danger, Posie thought, with not a little admiration. *Stupid, brave man.*

Then, perhaps fifteen minutes later, outside the hotel, away from the bonfire, a brightly-lit motor-car drew up and Posie saw that it was a taxi. Mr Potterton came out of the hotel, attending on the car personally, and two men got out.

One of these, peak-capped, looked as if he were the driver. He pulled out two large suitcases. The second man – shorter, fatter, wearing a big fur coat – simply stood by, staring at the bonfire with an incredulous, self-important stance.

Posie saw Petronella suddenly dart out from the hotel below, making for the fat man. She pecked at his cheeks and then they, together with Mr Potterton and the driver with the cases, disappeared, presumably into the hotel itself.

Forehead pressed against the cold glass, Posie looked back to the crowd, and she suddenly gasped as a flash of turquoise caught her eye among all the blackness.

Screwing her eyes up, she saw now that it was a handbag. Unusual. Distinctive.

Only a very beautiful, confident woman could have carried that bag off. Could have worn such a colour. And Harriet the maid had spoken earlier of one such bag, hadn't she? *'Italian leather … Real lovely to the touch.'*

It had been too good to be burned as rubbish.

Hadn't Sidney said that Ruth, the cook, had dragged out some things from the incinerator when no-one was looking? This must have been one of them. Posie opened the window, craned her head out as far as she could to get a better view.

In her rush to see what was happening she barely noticed the seeping cold, the smoky, charry air, the particles of black ash wafting everywhere.

Who was holding the bag? Surely only one…but had she got the nerve ?

The turquoise was flashing among the dark coats of the crowd, in and out. And then Posie saw the woman carrying it come into full view, on the very edge of the crowd. The headlamps of the retreating taxi, reversing, lit up the woman like a flare, and the pinched, exposed face of Harriet was fully revealed.

'My Gosh!'

Posie noted how Harriet was arm-in-arm with Alf, the fiancé, both eating toffee apples.

And now there was some other ruckus.

Another man had appeared, confronting Harriet, his poise one of intense anger. He was shouting right into Harriet's face. Alf had stepped back helplessly, and Posie saw Harriet, chin up, look ready to defend herself.

She's defended herself all her life, thought Posie. *She's not going to stop now, is she?*

The man was revealed as Sidney Sherringham.

He was grabbing at the turquoise bag, pulling it roughly by its strap from Harriet's shoulder. The crowd around the bonfire were beginning to turn, to pay attention. Posie leant right out but could barely make out any words above the crackle and hiss of the flames.

Maybe the odd word?

Despicable? Dreadful?

Not yours.

It seemed as if, short of tearing the thing off Harriet's arm, and causing a proper scene, Sidney could not win the battle over the handbag. He shook himself off and disappeared into the shadows below, as did Harriet.

What drama!

What a lot of emotions a good, plain bonfire could bring out in people.

Posie shut the window, finished her supper, licked her greasy fingers and decided to run the bath.

It was now eight o'clock.

As she was waiting for the big, lion-footed enamel bath to fill, she heard a knock at the door. Opening it just a crack, she saw it was Mr Potterton, looking harassed. He was holding a silver tray, with a bottle of unopened Harvey's Bristol Cream Sherry on it, with two sherry glasses. He almost bowed, and then headed to the table where he put down the tray.

'Sorry to disturb, Miss. This is courtesy of Miss Douglas,' he said, pulling at the greasy lock again. 'She's in the hotel bar downstairs. There's a note attached.' Then he stood back stiffly, as if waiting for an answer.

Posie took up the folded-in-half hotel notepaper which was fastened to the sherry bottle with a loop of string. The writing was square and legible, but looked hurried:

MISS PARKER,

SAY, I THINK WE GOT OFF ON THE WRONG FOOT. I'M SORRY.

I DIDN'T MEAN THAT ABOUT YOUR LITTLE TRAUB RING. IT WAS RUDE OF ME. IT'S KINDA SWEET IN AN ITTY-BITTY WAY, ISN'T IT?

PERHAPS WE CAN CHAT?

I'VE SENT YOU UP A NIGHTCAP BY WAY OF APOLOGY. IF YOU FANCY SOME COMPANY YOU JUST GO AHEAD AND TELL THIS PUFFED-UP COMB-OVER OF A HOTEL MANAGER AND I'LL COME UP AND JOIN YOU.

OTHERWISE I WILL SEE YOU TOMORROW OVER AT THE HOUSE.

YOURS, HOPING FOR THAT DRINK,

PETRONELLA DOUGLAS

Posie looked up, trying and failing to hide her disbelief.

'She's drunk, Mr Potterton?'

'She's *something*, Miss. She's been waiting for her father to come down from his suite for forty-five minutes now, so she's been knocking back liquor during that time at our hotel bar. With whoever will come and join her. Rather the worse for wear.'

Posie frowned. 'Her *father*, did you say?'

Potterton gave an excited little nod. 'Yes, Mr Bruce Douglas. Arrived this morning at Southampton, off the ship from New York. *Very* impressive hotel guest for us; most kind of him to bestow his patronage on us. But I gather from Miss Douglas' reaction downstairs that it was some sort of surprise, her father arriving like this.'

What a time for Petronella's father to arrive! The

Housekeeper dead and police crawling all about the place; Tony Stone about to leave and cause havoc. And Petronella herself with a complicated-sounding secret, involving a financial mess-up and risky loans which she didn't want her father to find out about.

In for a penny, in for a pound, Posie thought to herself bitterly.

'Send her up, please. Tell her I'm ready for her now. I'll delay my bath. I'm waiting.'

'Right you are, Miss. I've still got a bottle of sherry to deliver to Mr Bruce Douglas. I'll drop it off to him and then I'll go directly and give Miss Douglas your reply. *If* she is still conscious…'

Intrigued, Posie waited at the table, watching the fireworks as the display started up. Huge violet blooms spread across the night sky, reflected in the sea. Rockets and whizz-bangers went up. Golden Catherine Wheels nailed to driftwood whirled and glittered in their fiery, short-lived beauty.

And Posie waited.

Ten minutes passed. The fireworks ended. The bath was now stone cold.

Posie, crotchety with waiting, ran the water out, and overcome by tiredness, decided not to go downstairs to the hotel bar. Let Petronella Douglas seek *her* out, if that was what she wanted.

Posie decided instead that she would simply go to bed, even though it was impossibly early by London standards.

She closed the heavy curtains and moved one of the green silk-covered chairs from the table to the bedside as there wasn't enough room on the tiny wall-shelf for her night-things.

She set up her travel clock, her jewellery roll, her cold cream and her bottle of Parma Violet on the seat of the chair.

It was almost eight-fifteen and she threw off her House

of Harlow lounge-jacket, and was about to change into her night-things, when suddenly there was a soft knock at the door. How absolutely typical of the wretched woman to choose *now*!

'Miss Douglas? I'm just coming.'

But it wasn't the American.

It was her husband, Tony Stone, and he was holding a tissue-wrapped, papered-up something which was bigger than he was, and for a bizarre moment Posie had the strange impression that he had arrived on the tide of a catastrophe, holding a white, prone body cradled in his arms, like a dancing partner.

And then she saw the Douglas & Stone wooden hanger, the navy ribbon, the Haresmythe's label attached to the hanger with a handwritten number '40' scrawled across it, ready for the show.

Tony shook the white tissue out, and indicated into Posie's room. 'Cannae come in, pet? I've got yer wee dress here.'

Posie, caught off guard, merely stepped back and opened the door wider.

'Will you take a drink, Mr Stone? Can I offer you sherry? Or tea?'

'Nae. Nae. I willnae be stoppin', pet.' He hurriedly closed Posie's door, hanging the dress carefully from a hook on the back of it which she hadn't even realised was there, before opening the door again and hovering on the threshold.

'I promised ye a wee frock, and here it is. I dinnae like tae break promises. It's the one I think will suit ye best, pet. It's right lovely. Maybe try it on and leave it fer me at reception with a note if ye like it? I'll come and pick it up later on tonight and pack it again in the van. I have tae have it back fer the show, ye know? There's only one frock – a prototype, if you will – of each design. If customers like what they see they can order exactly the same thing, in their size, see? But this one here, it should fit ye just fine, and I'd get it returned tae ye right in time for yer wee weddin'.'

Fidgety, sucking his teeth again, pulling at his thin hair, the man seemed a bag of nerves. But maybe he had heard about the arrival of his father-in-law? Was he all ready for his trip – however permanent he wanted it to be – the next day? A trip which Posie knew wasn't going to happen.

Not if the Warrants, courtesy of New Scotland Yard, were in place, locking everything down.

'Thank you, Mr Stone. What kindness. What about payment?'

'Och, well. Let's see if it works first fer ye, eh? Mebbe ye willnae like it?'

And with that he was gone and the doorway and the corridor were both empty.

And then, completely to her surprise, Posie felt crazily excited. She'd barely thought about what she was going to wear for her wedding to Richard Lovelace; she had just thought she would pick something 'suitable' at the last minute, something warm enough for a winter wedding.

In truth, Posie had owned a wedding outfit before, a couture white tweed suit, but that had been arranged for a doomed wedding to another man, Alaric Boynton-Dale, and was now long gone.

She found herself pulling away the number '40' and all the tissue very carefully, despite her impatience. Wondering what Tony Stone had imagined would suit her best. What if, by some awful stroke of bad luck, the thing was dreadful? Not to her taste, or, more likely, not her size. Now, at age thirty-two, she was at the upper end of what could ever, even generously, be called 'slim'. 'Plump' would be much more apt, really.

In a nice, peaches-and-cream type way, of course, which a lot of men seemed to love.

But it meant Posie couldn't just easily throw on *anything*.

Certainly not the current fad for dresses which had been cut with the svelte, boy-like models of the moment in mind.

But as the paper came off, the gown was revealed to her like a dream.

'Jeepers! How divine.'

It was definitely beautiful, and definitely unusual. And it would, from the very first glance, fit easily. Perfectly, in fact.

Posie found herself kicking off her day clothes and pulling the bridal dress over her head in one easy movement.

The dress was a beautifully-executed trick; the thinnest cream velvet had been cut on the bias, lending the ankle-length gown a simplicity which was an illusion. You could tell a master of the craft had shaped and made the dress. Small panels of lace were inserted, window-like, into the low-waisted bodice in seemingly random vertical places, but when viewed in the mirror Posie saw their very placing had the effect of making the wearer look thinner, taller, more elegant.

A small skull-cap in matching cream velvet with a tiny, floaty veil had been wrapped around the hanger. And Posie stuck it on.

She laughed at herself in the mirror, at the way the outfit made her dark hair and blue eyes stand out, at the way she felt so comfortable, and gorgeous. Not like the last House of Harlow wedding outfit, whose seams had seemed to grow ever more restricting and uncomfortable as the wedding day had grown closer, whose warm but scratchy material had never offered comfort, only prim boundaries.

This was perfect. Unutterably lovely.

'Gracious!' Posie exclaimed to herself under her breath as she took the gown off and hung it up delicately. 'I'm quite prepared to allow that funny little man his peculiar ways, now that I've seen for myself the way he can work a piece of cloth into something almost magical. Dolly was quite right. The man is simply a wizard!'

Having called a maid to take the dress to reception, together with a grateful acceptance note to Tony Stone, Posie found her tiredness had been replaced by a buzzing, nervous energy.

In her silk pyjamas now, she snuck between the closed curtains again and saw that most of the crowd outside had now gone, but the bonfire was still roaring merrily. She reached over to the table, picked up the bottle of Petronella Douglas' gift of sherry, broke the paper ribbon and the fabric-seal and poured herself a glass.

It wasn't about celebration, it was more an aid to sleep, but Posie felt she should make a toast anyway.

She muttered an almost silent 'To Elsie Moncrieff' under her breath, and then wondered if Elsie Moncrieff had ever sat right here herself, just like this, in what had ostensibly been *her* room.

And as Posie fell, a little later, into a doze, she thought she heard a motorbike's distinctive *putter-putter* sound outside as it roared off. She felt dopey, like she had a cold coming: heavy and tired. At one point Posie thought she heard a girl scream somewhere nearby, but that must have been her imagination because the windows were shut and the walls seemed sturdy.

The luminous hands of the travel clock set on the chair beside her bed declared it to be past ten o'clock.

And then sleep came.

Welcome but not restful, sudden but not comforting.

* * * *

PART TWO
Ashes and Smoke
(Thursday 6th November, 1924)

Nineteen

She had been dreaming. One of those dreams which was so real you felt like you were in the place itself. The dream was of Tuscany.

In her dream Posie could almost smell the incense from the churches and the heat of the baking-hot stones of San Gimignano, that town of medieval skyscraper-style towers where she had been staying in August. Back when she had taken a holiday at the same time as Elsie Moncrieff had asked her to visit White Shaw.

In her dream Posie could hear the bells of the towers ringing, smell the sweet artificial strawberry flavours of the ice-cream at Lorenzo's, a gelateria she had frequented at least once a day on her holiday. Sunflowers were placed in cheap glasses on every table outside the gelateria in the square by the Duomo, and Posie was sitting at one of these tables in a thin, blue-striped seersucker summer dress. Someone was next to her, near her, but she couldn't quite see their face.

The light was heavenly, dappled yellow with the overripe afternoon sunshine, but the square already had pockets of shade, fast-growing in its corners.

Then the dream changed violently, and a cold wet wind got up, sending the tables and chairs skittering over, tablecloths blowing, sunflowers flying, tourists running. The summer square was suddenly grey and very cold.

Something was wrong.

And deep in her subconsciousness Posie recognised the truth of that. Something *had* been wrong, out there in Italy.

Posie had left San Gimignano and Tuscany itself with something troubling her, something barely acknowledged. But what? What had left such an impression, held down beneath the surface but important enough to re-emerge now in a dream?

That feeling of someone next to her…

The cold wind again. Posie tossed and turned frantically in her big, comfortable bed at the Bay Hotel.

But the wind was real.

And suddenly Posie was horribly awake.

She was sitting bolt-upright in bed, pulling the covers right up about her neck.

The dreams of late afternoon sunshine and heat in Tuscany fell away instantly, for her lovely room, here at the Bay Hotel, so cosy before, was cold and chilly. It was completely dark, too. The fire in the grate was out, and the electric lamp on the wall by the bed was now turned off.

The curtains at the large window had been pulled back, wide open. One of the windows was open and the night air, soaked and heavy with sea spray, had filled the room like a fog. It must have been open for a while.

'What on earth? But I didn't open anything!'

Posie looked almost automatically to her travel clock, but she saw with a fright that none of the things she had placed by her bed on the chair were there anymore. The chair was empty of everything, as if it had been cleared hurriedly. Had *she* done that, in her sleep? Knocked things over? But no: there they were, placed on the floor. By squinting Posie could just make out that it was past two o'clock in the morning.

But *who* had done this? Someone must have got in.

Why had someone come into her room as she slept? A thief? Someone perhaps looking for Elsie's hot-water bottle with its strange collection of precious items whose importance Posie couldn't yet ascertain? But Posie had hidden those things well. They were in her handkerchief, inside the cushion she herself was sleeping on.

Posie clutched at the bedclothes, squinting through the darkness to find out just what was happening. The service bell was too far away on the wall for her to ring. She must get out of bed, and *run*. Run to the sick Sergeant Rainbird in the next bedroom. Or to that foolish Deputy Manager downstairs at his desk. Anything was better than this. And then she saw him.

There was a man in her room.

Right now.

She thought she would scream.

She tried to move, but she couldn't. Frozen, it seemed, in the bed, unable to move or call out, Posie watched in a terror which seemed to paralyse her.

The man sat on a chair at the big table, beyond the end of her bed, his back to Posie. He was dressed in rain clothes, with a fisherman's hat. He sat with his back slightly hunched, bent over, concentrating completely on his task at the table. There was a very slight clicking sound, a screwing sound, a *tap-tap*.

But what was he doing? Posie didn't dare dwell on the possibility that he had a weapon with him, that he was adjusting it or mending it, that he *needed* it. Would he turn on her any second? Was he in a tight spot? Was he a criminal?

Whoever he was he seemed to be fumbling with something now, something up on the table beside him. Then sounds came of a zipper being undone, a popper.

And then, as Posie's eyes grew sharper in the darkness, she almost gasped, but instead she stuffed her fists into her mouth. The man had her very own beloved carpet bag next

189

to him on the table, and he seemed to be pulling things out of it.

Another click, another tap.

There was a blinding light. Shocking in its intensity. Bright as day, almost.

It must have been a beam of light from the South Foreland Lighthouse, and it cut through the room, sharp as a razor, catching on the cut-glass of the sherry glasses, refracted off the metallic tray on the table. Then it was dark again. A pulling, papery sound could be heard, and Posie saw in horror that the man at the table was going through her purse. He finished at last, presumably having found what he wanted.

Move, move, move.

But try as she might, Posie couldn't move. She watched as the man stood up, then walked away, without looking once at Posie.

He went to the French doors, seemed to hesitate for a couple of seconds there, pulling at the lace curtains, then opened the doors in a tearing hurry, pulling off his hat at the same time. The next beam from the lighthouse caught him there, outlined his profile, and Posie gasped, and her fear turned to shock, surprise.

No. To anger.

Or worse.

Unmistakeable now, she'd have known that tall, thin figure with the bright blonde hair anywhere.

'*Max?*'

It barely came out as a whisper. A whimper on the thick salty air.

She spoke more to herself than to him: 'What are you doing, love?'

You're supposed to be dead. I was told you had disappeared in action.

'Max? Look at me!'

But now the darkness and the salty air were coming up

190

at her even thicker than before, and Posie felt as if she were being pulled under a terrible wave, lost at sea. The wave went on and on, crashing over her. Posie tossed and turned under the bedsheet and the blanket, which now seemed inadequately warm.

Sleep, of some normal sort, must have come at last. Posie sensed the darkness outside lifting. There was a sound of feet stamping in the corridor. She heard snatches of words; hurried conversations which didn't make any sense.

'Terrible case, Poots. Helluva surprise on top of everything, eh? Get the girl out from under there and give me your verdict; anything useful at all. And what do you reckon here, eh, Doctor? With my Posie? Drugged? It's not like her, dash it all.'

A deep, querulous voice: 'You know I deal with the dead, Richard. Not the living.'

A resigned sniff from somewhere nearby. 'But it could be that she's drugged, certainly. She looks "off". Could be this wretched flu doing the rounds. Same as your Sergeant next door, poor lad; useless to everyone. I looked in on him and *he* seems to have lost the plot. He's talking about a bally intruder in his room, going through his things, taking stuff out. Delusional. I'd let her sleep, Richard. Let them both sleep. It feels deuced damp in here to me. Won't help her, will it? Order them to light a fire and keep it well stoked.'

'I'll do that, Doctor. *You're* telling *me* it's damp! Dashed thing is that when I got here the windows and doors were all open; the room was full of mist! I sat down on this here chair and got the shock of my life. The seat was soaking wet! Like someone had thrown ice-cold water all over it on purpose. Very rum do. Strange place this, and no mistake.'

'Mnnn. I'll get on…'

A slight breeze. More footsteps and more voices. The smell of woodsmoke. The sound of fire-belchers.

And then a voice calling her name, over and over. She tried to open her eyes. Closed them again.

'Posie?'

A familiar cough. 'Darling? Posie love? Tell me, darling girl. Are you quite all right?'

The room was flooded with daylight, grey but bright. And Richard Lovelace – *her* Richard – was sitting, head in hands, on the chair beside her bed. On seeing her look up at him he smiled quickly, joyfully, and the worried creases around his green eyes softened. He took her hand in both of his own.

'Thank the Lord,' he muttered. 'I was beginning to get worried there.'

'What time is it?' Posie sat up, feeling a horrible mix of nausea and absolute hunger rip through her insides.

'Just after ten o'clock.'

'What? *Ten?* What about the Warrants? I asked Sergeant Fox to obtain Search Warrants. To search White Shaw but also to stop people leaving early.' She felt like sobbing. 'Now it will be too late!'

Richard Lovelace shook his gingery head and lit a cigarette.

'Nah,' he said, inhaling deeply. 'Fox is a good lad. If he says he'll do something, he bally well does. He organised those Warrants and we duly closed White Shaw right down.'

He checked his watch. 'And we did that a good two hours back. We've been here – me, Fox, Dr Poots and his Forensics laddies, with a team of several good London bobbies – since dawn. We all came down on the mail train. We've set up in that little bungalow place next door; the sort of place you could run to ground in. Rest assured, darling, no-one has left White Shaw, except those fresh little twins, who I sent back to school sharpish.'

He grinned like a boy suddenly. 'You should have seen the excitement on their little faces to have a ride in a real police car! But everyone else here is confined to their rooms, fretting away, with some of my best lads guarding the place. Searches – searching for *anything* – are being conducted as we speak.'

'Including Tony Stone's van?'

'Including the van. It's already been done. There was nothing of any interest there, my love. Just dresses. Patterns. Designs. And his pathetic little suitcases. Fella was doing a bunk, would you believe? He had a couple of interesting documents with him.'

'Documents?'

'Nothing connected with here. Both to do with London. One was a lease he's already signed on a small set of rooms in Covent Garden, for working in. And the other was for a lease on a bedsit to live in, for himself. In the Oval. Hardly glamorous.'

Posie sank back into her pillows. So Elsie had been right that Tony Stone was leaving for good.

Richard Lovelace got up and rang the assistance bell. He came back to the chair, which Posie saw had been covered over with several towels, and he sat down with a slight grimace and then looked at Posie with concern.

'I'm going to ask the maid who answers that bell to draw you a good, hot bath, and to bring you whatever breakfast they can manage. Eat it in bed. You don't look good, darling. Let's see if a bit of food and a bath will help, eh? I'll be back here in forty-five minutes. And we'll go through things then, all right? I'm afraid there's something rather pressing waiting for my attention outside. I promise I'll sort it all out and then come back.'

And Posie, formerly so gung-ho about doing things by herself, and being here at the Bay Hotel all alone, was secretly relieved.

She watched as Richard Lovelace gave orders to the small, local girl who had answered the bell. She was aware of the maid in the bathroom, the water running, the fragrance of some expensive scented salts wafting out to her. She watched another maid arrive with hot buttered toast, and a pot of tea on a bed-tray. As she ate it she tried her best not to remember the dream, or anything of that long, dreadful night.

Pushed it all away.

She stood up woozily, and headed to the table, feeling delicate and sickly, as if she had been partying hard all night long.

And got the shock of her life.

* * * *

Twenty

On the table, plumb centre, was a very smart torch, in excellent condition apart from one large dent and scratch running all down one side. It was yellow and black, like an oversized wasp. On the side a large, neat black script read 'EVER-READY'.

This *must* be the torch belonging to Tony Douglas, the present from America. Probably used by Elsie Moncrieff; taken by her on the night she died.

Posie didn't pick the thing up. Instead, she put on her gloves, careful not to leave her own fingerprints, then reached for the torch, turning it over, expecting – or hoping? – to find it empty of its bulb.

Because of course, that super-duper bulb had been found by the bird-spotter up on the cliffs, where Elsie had fallen.

But Posie felt her heart sink.

For the bulb was here, and when Posie pressed the red button on the side, a glaring full-force beam shone out, bright even in the daylit room. Confused, she put it down, turned it off. It certainly hadn't been on the table last night. Who had put it there? And why?

And if this *wasn't* the flash-light connected to the bulb found up on the cliffs, why had it been placed here in such a way? As a red herring? As a warning of some kind?

Sighing, the small mystery unsolved, she walked to the bathroom, across its black-and-white floor tiles, undressed and stepped into her bath.

Posie lay back, sinking her head beneath the hot water, not caring that her short dark hair was now soaked and she didn't have a shingling iron or hot brush with her to set it again properly. She didn't give two hoots.

The hot water was blissful. To be alone, to feel away from everyone and anyone. Perhaps *this*, this luxury alone, had been the reason Elsie Moncrieff had come here every week?

She'd enjoyed the same room, the same bath.

Elsie Moncrieff.

Under the water Posie suddenly started up in surprise, opened her mouth and almost choked on a rush of water. She flung herself upwards, grabbing at the sides of the tub to steady herself, before rising quickly, sending water crashing out of the bath.

'That's it! I know what Elsie was up to!'

She felt an idiot for not seeing it before.

'Oh! My gosh, it all makes sense.'

Grabbing at a thick towel, not caring to look at herself or sort out her hair, she bounded into her room again and pulled out the first of her two soft woollen day-dresses which she had brought. This one was piped in cream, but the main cloth was cornflower-blue, the same colour as her eyes. It had mother-of-pearl buttons in two rows down the front, with a low waist, but its main attraction had always been that Posie could move – even run – freely in it. She dressed hurriedly, frantically.

Leaning over the table with her notepad open, she composed a very quick list of points, then dragged a comb through her hair.

She doused herself in Parma Violet perfume, and applied Maybelline coral pink lipstick to her mouth without checking for accuracy, dabbing a bit on her cheeks and rubbing it in furiously. Posie sat down to put her Mary-Jane heels on, gripping at the chair next to the bed for the extra force she required in place of the shoe-horn she hadn't packed.

Posie frowned and recoiled suddenly, sitting bolt-upright.

The seat of the chair was wet.

Wet-through. Freezing to the touch.

And instantly the snatches of the conversation Posie had overheard earlier between Richard Lovelace and Dr Poots, Scotland Yard's Pathologist, came back to her. Richard had said this seat was wet, hadn't he? That the room had been damp when he'd arrived at dawn; the windows open to the night.

The horrible dream of the night, the intruder in her room – *had it really been Max? But that would be impossible, surely?* – rushed to the forefront of her mind.

In that dream the windows had all been open. The French doors too.

Had it actually happened? Had Max got in, opened the windows? He had – in her dream – sat at the table, tapping at something and making clicking sounds.

'Oh!' Posie put her hand to her mouth. Had the bright light she had seen actually been the flash-light being flicked on? Lighting up the room?

It certainly seemed powerful enough.

Scales were falling from her eyes. Had the man at the table been fixing the torch? Putting it together again? Was *that* what the tapping had been? She remembered seeing him going through her carpet bag, but that was wrong, surely?

But there it was, over on the floor, by the table.

What had he been doing with her bag, for heaven's sake?

The whole thing was odd. Horrible, inexplicable.

The very opposite of her proud moment of clarity back in the bathroom.

And then Posie remembered something else. Something Dr Poots had said while she half-slept. He had mentioned that Rainbird was being delusional, speaking of an intruder in his room, going through his things.

Delusional. So were they *both* being delusional about the same thing?

Posie checked the time. Richard was a stickler when it came to time-keeping, and she knew, sure as bread was bread, that he would be back when he said he would be. That gave her just five minutes. But it was enough.

Taking Elsie's treasures in the handkerchief from under her pillow for safety's sake, she stuffed them in her carpet bag and left the room, turning the key in the lock behind her. Heart hammering, she raced along the corridor to the next door. She pounded on it like a woman possessed.

'Sergeant Rainbird? It's Posie. I need to come in.'

A grunt and a groan came from within. But on testing it, Posie found the door was open and it swung back easily, revealing a small, long room, about an eighth of the size of her own, with a single bed on the left-hand side, set against the wall, and French doors at the far wall, leading onto a balcony, with the same view of the sea as her own.

It was the room right next to her own, and Posie realised that the rooms shared the long open balcony running along the whole front of the hotel.

She marched to the French doors and tugged back the thick curtains and lace nets, identical to her own, flooding the room with light. She stood looking out at the choppy, white-crested sea, still devoid of any boats. Another groan came, louder this time, from the bed.

'Rainbird, this is important. Did someone – a man in black, with a hat – come into your room last night?'

A pause. 'I dunno, Miss. But I think so. I was woken by those blessed balcony doors banging, like someone had got in. I thought I'd dreamt it, but then I saw this fella over by the desk and he was going through my bag, and that grey folder. I would have got up and clobbered him one, but I couldn't move my body. I thought it was flu at the time, but now I just don't know.'

Posie, trying not to look at Rainbird too closely in his borrowed-from-the-hotel night-attire, hurried to the desk. The grey manila case file was there, open on the Pathologist's report, and the line about the hand-mark on Elsie Moncrieff's back seemed to stand out brighter than anything.

'Did *you* leave this folder open on your desk last night, Sergeant?'

'No. I did not.'

On closer inspection, although without touching it, the cardboard cover and the pages of the folder seemed to be damp, curling together as they dried.

'Did you spill water on the file, Sergeant?'

'No! Of course not, Miss. I'm always careful.'

On the floor was Rainbird's black leather police briefcase. Posie hauled it onto the desk.

'Can I?' she asked, observing how Rainbird was now sitting up in bed, following her every move.

'Be my guest. What are you looking for, Miss?'

Posie fished around, and then pulled out the 'EVIDENCE' bag from yesterday. 'This!' she exclaimed.

It was empty.

'The bulb we recovered from Ness Point is missing,' Posie said, matter-of-factly, but feeling a stab of terror. 'It was in here, when you went to bed?'

'Oh yes, Miss. Oh lawks, what are you saying? I've gone and lost a piece of evidence? The Chief will have my guts for garters. And I'm already in enough trouble.'

Posie replaced everything neatly, trying to pretend that her hands weren't trembling.

'No, you didn't lose it. You won't get in trouble, Rainbird. I promise. *I* have the bulb. It turned up elsewhere. I'll try and explain but not now. I *can't* explain things just yet. Rest if you need to.' She attempted a grin. 'Otherwise Prudence might just kill me if you go home looking like you did yesterday!'

Then, as she was leaving she saw, down on the floor, a silver tray with a bottle of Harvey's Bristol Cream Sherry on it, with one cut-glass goblet next to it, a sticky brown residue within.

The seal on the sherry had been ripped open. Next to it was the note, scrunched up, and a loop of string. Posie squatted down and read it.

INSPECTOR,
A TOKEN OF APPRECIATION FOR ALL YOUR INVALUABLE WORK HERE TODAY.
SINCERELY, PETRONELLA DOUGLAS.

'Sincerely! What a joke!' muttered Posie as she said goodbye and closed the door, remembering how Briggs had been similarly plied with drink on the morning of the discovery of Elsie's body.

She padded up the corridor again with more questions raised than answered, with more danger lurking than she cared to imagine.

She tried to recover the logical reasoning of her bath time. Posie sat down at the table in her room, made sure the two other seats were dry, and poured the coffee she had had the foresight to ring for. She started to eat a biscuit, and then another.

When, two minutes later, Richard Lovelace and Sergeant Fox arrived at her door, she had forced all thoughts of the night-time intruder, and of whether that had or hadn't been Max, right from her mind, together with thoughts of misplaced lightbulbs and flash-lights and open, wet folders.

Posie tried to appear calm as she sat the two men

down at the table, hiding her hands which refused to stop shaking. She took out her notebook and saw how Richard and the Sergeant did the same.

Richard was formal now, every inch the Chief Commissioner. He cracked the knuckles of every finger on his right hand, a singularly unappealing habit and one which Posie hated with a passion, but something he only indulged in at moments of real stress or worry. She ignored it with an effort.

'I'll tell you both about Elsie Moncrieff, shall I?'

'Please do, darling. This looks like it's going to be quite some story.'

* * * *

Twenty-One

'Elsie Moncrieff was a professional, gun-toting spy,' said Posie, matter-of-factly.

'Tip-top. I'm not sure *who* exactly she was working for. But the clues were all there at the Inquest. I should have realised it then. There was no "official documentation" to be found for her; it was as if she didn't exist. She'd covered her tracks well, and gave little of herself away. She couldn't afford to get close to anyone, despite being a beautiful and vivacious girl who loved music, and fashion, and dancing.'

Posie was sure of her story now:

'She'd surrounded herself with expertly-chosen people to spy for her; to hear things she might not be able to. Elsie was actively reporting to someone, and she checked in once a week, from here. She had a special call-name. It was "*Burning Dog*". This hotel, and this room, in fact – by some strange fluke – was her safe place. Every Sunday afternoon.'

She indicated to the paintings on the wall. 'These were painted by Elsie. Lovely, aren't they?'

Lovelace looked over at them briefly. 'Er, yes, darling. They look familiar though.' He shrugged. 'I'm sure I've seen something like them recently.'

Sergeant Fox was tirelessly eager, his policeman's

notebook open on his knee. 'What exactly was she spying on, Miss?'

Posie frowned. 'My feeling is that Elsie was placed at White Shaw to spy generally, mainly on the guests who would come to the lavish parties. But then, especially this year, she started to concentrate on Petronella herself. Almost exclusively. Elsie even went as far as to hire a suitable lover for the woman.'

Fox whistled beneath his breath. '*That* doesn't come cheap! Elsie Moncrieff must have been serious about wanting information.'

'Quite. She was especially fascinated by Petronella's financial affairs. Elsie evidently thought there was something fishy about it all.'

Posie explained about Petronella re-mortgaging White Shaw, about the Fashion House being in trouble. The repayment of the loan by 'Taylors'. The oddness about "Mr Tell".

'Do you have anything from the bank yet, Sergeant? Or from Companies House?' she asked hopefully, but Fox shook his head.

'I'm still waiting for pretty much everything you asked for, Miss. Sorry. It will come this morning, I'm sure of it.'

Posie looked directly at Richard, who so far hadn't said a word. He had lit up a cigarette and was smoking it now in careful, long, slow drags, like he had all the time in the world.

'There are still a few things I'm unclear about,' Posie said, anxiously, consulting her list.

'First, I feel there was a man involved in all of this, helping Elsie. Especially right at the start of the project, but I don't know what happened to him. Or who he might be. There is a suggestion this very same man met Elsie in here again, on Sunday afternoon. It's all jolly odd.'

She shook her head in puzzlement as Fox faithfully took notes.

'And second, I don't know *what* Petronella found in Elsie's flat on Sunday, but it sent the Fashion Designer over the edge: caused her to write the letter terminating Elsie's job as Housekeeper; caused her to go wild at her husband on the telephone that evening. Caused her to act very strangely after Elsie's death was reported the next day.'

'*How* did she act strangely, Posie?' asked Lovelace quickly.

And Posie told them about the desecration of Elsie's room, and then Petronella offering a drink to the local bobby when he eventually arrived, playing for time.

Posie was almost at the end of her list. 'It seems to me that things were concluding here, whatever the "Operation" was. Elsie was definitely leaving here soon; hadn't paid the bill on this place beyond this week, in fact. So, what was she up to?'

'Are you sure Elsie was leaving, Miss?' asked Fox, puzzled.

'Oh, yes. She was overheard saying she wanted "out". To the mysterious man in this room on Sunday, in fact.'

'I see.'

'And the last thing which puzzles me are the reports time and again of the "November Drop". Whatever *that* might be...'

She broke off, hopeful for a breakthrough: 'I say! Richard, do *you* know what the "November Drop" was, or *is?*'

But Lovelace just splayed his hands apologetically, shaking his head. 'Absolutely no idea.' And he was back to smoking again.

Fox leant forward excitedly. 'Look here! Do you think Petronella Douglas found *evidence* of Elsie's spying activities, maybe in Elsie's flat? And she killed her because of it?'

Posie nodded grimly. 'Quite possibly. That would make sense, wouldn't it? But Petronella Douglas is not our only suspect for Elsie's murder: there's no shortage of strange people at White Shaw. There are people who are horrid little blackmailers, like the maid, Harriet, and possibly her fiancé, Alf. There's also a whole heap of men who may have been in unrequited love with the beautiful Elsie: men like Tony Stone, or Mickey O'Dowd, or even – but at a push, I'd say – Sidney Sherringham. All possible suspects.'

Lovelace stalked over to the French doors, flung them back. He ground out his cigarette on the balcony then stared out moodily across the Channel, watching the tide begin to go out. He seemed preoccupied.

Posie felt there were still too many loose threads. She called out, a little louder, so Richard could hear her out on the balcony:

'I still don't know why Elsie Moncrieff wrote to *me*, back in July, asking me to come here. Surely that was crazy? Asking a Private Detective to barge into a carefully-controlled environment? I would have worked out an Operation of some kind was afoot, surely?'

'Maybe that was exactly what Elsie wanted, darling?' called back Richard Lovelace, fiddling with the catch on the balcony doors. 'Maybe she wanted to call time on things for some reason? Blow the thing out of the water? You said she was leaving soon? Maybe a "boo-sucks", if you like, to her employers?'

Posie stared hard at her fiancé. 'So *who* were her employers? Look here, Richard, I think Elsie may have been German, although she covered it well. She spoke excellent English by all accounts, but she couldn't quite lose the accent: the twins spoke of it, and she told one person she had been brought up in South Africa, while telling another that she had Dutch connections.'

Lovelace frowned. 'Clever girl, then, wasn't she, this Elsie? You're saying she avoided anyone making a German connection by explaining away her slight accent with just-about-likely other Germanic alternatives?'

'That's right. There *is* some link to Germany here, I know it.'

But Richard didn't reply anymore, for he was suddenly on his hands and knees right by the French doors, picking something up off the carpet.

Posie reached down to her carpet bag, drew out Elsie's treasures and carefully shook them out on the desk. She picked up the tiny smidgen of telegram, with its German words, and showed it to Richard as he crossed the room back to her.

'Look at this! These are the things Elsie hid and didn't want anyone to find. See? She was receiving messages in German.'

Richard read the snippet of telegram, all the while raking his hands through his thick auburn hair. Posie watched as his eyes ranged over the other things of Elsie's, and she saw how he looked angry, frightened, uncomfortable, all at the same time. In direct contrast to his Sergeant, who looked plain excited.

In particular, Richard's eyes seemed drawn to the small sepia studio photographs of the children. He bit at his thumbnail anxiously but stayed silent.

Posie had to finish. She had one more point.

'I don't know *why* Elsie died, see? Normally, Richard love, you tell me most murders are committed for love, and if it's not for love, it's about money. But not in the case of a spy, surely? There *must* be another set of rules for spies. Normal rules don't apply to them, do they?'

Posie realised she had, throughout, avoided any mention of Max. Well, she wasn't sure of his involvement yet, was she? *If* he was involved.

But this omission troubled her, as did Richard's actions now. For in his hand was a small piece of paper, business-card sized, and he laid it down now on the table, in front of Posie, silently and without explanation. The paper was soaking wet and the black ink had run badly.

She almost gasped.

She wanted to stand and protest, but she sat stock-still.

It was a scrap of paper in Max's cramped, scrawled handwriting.

* * * *

Twenty-Two

But it wasn't new. It belonged to Posie, in fact.

It was a number – WHITEHALL 8977 – together with a name.

Thea Elleridge.

Max had told Posie that if ever she was worried about him, she should call this number. Posie suddenly heard Max's voice again, echoing across the empty months: '*Only in an emergency, ja?*'

This woman had been Max's handler. His boss.

Thea Elleridge was an extremely senior MI5 officer whose responsibility was the handling of the very best of the spies which the service ran. A tight, secret web of men whose existence, pay, duties and orders were all tied tightly to her.

An offshoot of MI5, this elite sub-group were the best of the best.

Posie had met Thea at the end of the summer just gone, when Posie had been informed of Max's death in service. She had been struck by the tight, impressive woman whose cold, steely demeanour could be forgiven when considering her obvious dedication to King and Country, and her dedication to her team of spies, too.

Richard Lovelace knew Thea Elleridge of old, too. They

had attended some police intelligence training together, way before the Great War. And although it was only a slight acquaintance, the two of them sometimes traded mutually-beneficial information and contacts.

This paper with Thea's contact details on it had been carried about by Posie for a year now, folded carefully into a section of her purse. Not got rid of, as she had been instructed to do, by MI5.

Posie's heart was thumping hard.

She felt guilty, angry. As if she had let Richard down. But did Richard know that this was something Max had given her? There was no mention of Max's name on the card, was there? Richard had seen Max's handwriting before, just once, when working another case. And if he *did* recognise it, was he angry at Posie for keeping it?

'That was in my purse,' Posie said defensively, as if accusing her fiancé of rifling through her possessions. 'How come *you* have that?'

Fox looked from Posie to Lovelace without understanding, slightly uncomfortable.

Richard Lovelace, still standing, looked puzzled. He pointed towards the balcony. 'But I found it over there, love. By the French doors. Looks like it was pressed into the sill, but because it got so damp with the condensation on the glass, it fell to the floor. Who knows how it got there? I simply thought that you'd thought of Thea Elleridge as being a good person to telephone; to ask her some of the questions you've been very cleverly bandying around here. No? Oh, well, then. Not that telephoning to Thea would have done you a lot of good.'

'Why not?'

'I called her myself, first thing today. About another matter. But she's got the flu. Like half the bally country, it seems. So I tried again and got through to one of her colleagues instead.'

Just then there was a knock at the door.

Dr Poots, Scotland Yard's Pathologist, poked his head in. He nodded curtly in Richard's direction. 'As I suspected, Lovelace. There *was* something in the sherry; a heavy sleeping-drug. Probably Chloral or Veronal. I tested it in the back of the Forensics van and the toxicology proves it nicely; my cobalt acetate solution turned a bright blue. Same for both bottles.' He fussed with his black velvet dicky-bow-tie, his staple workwear.

'Now, I've got that wee lassie out from under there, Richard. Helluva mess. I daren't move her far. I'm going to conduct my initial analysis in the back of the refrigerated van. Not the usual thing at all. Hardly ideal.'

Lassie?

What 'lassie'? Posie looked from Dr Poots to her fiancé but nothing more was said.

'Right you are, Doctor. Let me know your findings.'

Lovelace sighed deeply, sinking into one of the chairs.

'What "lassie"?' Posie asked, softly.

'Later, darling.' Lovelace seemed to avoid Posie's gaze and then started giving orders to Fox.

'Sergeant, arrest Petronella Douglas. Right away. She's our main suspect in all of this.'

He checked his wristwatch. 'It's just after eleven o'clock. Right now Miss Douglas is under lock and key in her own bedroom. Throw the book at her, my lad. Make the arrest on suspicion of the premeditated murder of Miss Elsie Moncrieff. The evidence is all stacked up against her, and list it if you have to: the letter she wrote sacking the Housekeeper; her ransacking of the Housekeeper's room and burning things on the morning Elsie's body was discovered. By the sound of it she's guilty as hell. Guilty of *something*, eh? And it may well be murder.'

Posie was about to protest, say that on Sidney Sherringham's evidence Petronella Douglas had been nowhere near Ness Point on Sunday evening, but Lovelace was on a roll, ticking points off on his fingers:

'Also, charge her with wilfully hindering a murder inquiry, Fox. And for destroying evidence. And lastly, charge her with the non-consensual drugging of innocent civilians.'

Drugging? Posie stared hard at Lovelace but said nothing.

'Right you are, sir,' answered Fox eagerly.

'Take her to that bungalow we're using next door, put her in the least comfortable bedroom there. Get her some food and drink but then leave her alone. We'll go in later and see if she talks. We're working in a state of emergency so we don't need to take her to a proper police station just yet, not for another twelve hours. *If* we press charges. Once you've done that I want you to join Poots and see what you can do to help on this next issue.'

'On it, sir.'

After Fox had hurried out, Posie took another biscuit and nibbled at it. She stared at Richard, wanting to ask him about the orders he had just given, much of which she hadn't understood, and about his conversation with the Pathologist, but Lovelace seemed to have crumpled now that he was alone with her, sitting with his elbows on the table, his head in his hands. Not the pose of a Chief Commissioner at all.

'Darling?' She edged closer, touched him lightly on the dark-blue tweed of his jacket. 'The drugging you just mentioned. Was that *me*? Was *I* drugged?'

'Yes, Posie.'

She looked quickly over at the sherry bottle, which had looked like it was intact the evening before. Drugged, with a heavy sleeping draught. Which would explain – or partly explain – the mad dream about Max. Wouldn't it?

Somewhere inside she felt a deep sense of relief, of release.

'But why on earth would Petronella Douglas want to drug *me*? I have nothing to do with her! It doesn't make sense.'

Richard sat up, his eyes clear but sorrowful. 'It wasn't just you, Posie. It was Rainbird too. And *why* were you both drugged?'

He sighed. 'It's likely that the lovely Miss Douglas was playing for time. Maybe she needed time to dispose of some more evidence. Or maybe she was going to run away? Away from any investigation you and Rainbird were conducting, perhaps?'

It still didn't make any sense.

Richard half-laughed. 'But she didn't know you had arranged for Scotland Yard to come in this morning, did she? I suppose she thought that if she drugged you both, by the time you woke up, all the little birdies would have flown and the investigation would come to nothing. Quite a neat plan, actually.'

Richard Lovelace looked suddenly cross: 'Especially as neither you nor Rainbird were operating down here in any officially-sanctioned capacity.'

He huffed. 'Especially not Rainbird. Passing himself off as an Inspector! The fool! Did he think I wouldn't find out? The Coroner told me all about "Inspector Rainbird" in his report yesterday, as did that inept Constable Briggs, who I've managed to side-line for now. What the blazes did Rainbird think he was *doing*? He could lose his job – such as it is – for this. He risks being thrown out of the force. Not even the iniquity of being back in uniform!'

Posie felt her face flush with shame. *She* had known that Rainbird was down here without proper authority and she had colluded with him in it for her own ends. *She* was partly to blame for the mess.

'Oh Richard, I know it's not right, but he's supposed to be getting married on Saturday, and maybe nerves are getting the better of him? Can't you give him one last chance?'

Lovelace raised an eyebrow, and then laughed. 'Oh darling. You're too soft. Well, let me think on it.'

He seemed quite forgiving of the whole thing, surprisingly. More than was quite normal, actually.

'One thing's for certain, Posie. We won't be sending Rainbird and his lucky lady a bottle of cream sherry as a wedding present, will we?'

But Posie gasped aloud at his words: 'Oh! Dash it all! I forgot! Talking of sherry, Petronella's father arrived here last night. He was probably checking up on the company, and Petronella wasn't yet ready for that. I know that Potterton was taking Mr Douglas a bottle, too, as a nightcap. Chances are it was also drugged. Someone had better check on the old chap, surely?'

'Too right.' Lovelace silently watched Posie while she ate another biscuit. He grinned suddenly, but his eyes were sad.

'I'm so glad this hasn't affected you much, Posie. That you've still got an appetite. How I've missed you these last two days, darling. And I feel wretched, Posie. Wretched that I let you walk into all this. That you've been *drugged*! It's a deuced terrible mess to say the least.'

Posie grinned back. 'A mare's nest?'

'Oh sweetheart, worse than that. This place is properly dangerous, darling. You haven't heard the half of it yet.'

'What?'

He cleared his throat ominously. 'Actually, there's something you should know. There's been another murder.'

Posie stared, open-mouthed. She felt as if she had been slapped about the face, almost aware of a physical pain which stopped her from speaking.

'It was last night. I wanted to keep it from you until you felt better, Posie. But I can't hide it from you anymore. Most likely it was a murder in cold blood.'

'*WHAT?*'

Posie stood up, as did the man she had promised to marry. The floor was coming up at her, reeling, and she held onto the table for support.

'Tell me everything, Richard. Is this what was so pressing earlier? Dash it all. Another murder! Who on earth was it?'

* * * *

Twenty-Three

Richard Lovelace described it as he had seen it unravel earlier that morning.

It had been getting light. Seagulls were circling in the lightening grey sky overhead. The air was smoky, damp, salty.

The Scotland Yard team had just pulled up with several police cars and a Forensics van borrowed from the local force. The vehicles stopped on the tarmac of the promenade outside the Bay Hotel.

But they were unable to get any closer to their destination of White Shaw itself because the smouldering hulk of last night's huge bonfire lay across their path. It was being dismantled and attended to by a group of local men, who were in no particular hurry to get on with their day, it seemed.

The Scotland Yard policemen had started to get out of their vehicles when a shout had suddenly gone up.

'Help! Help! A *body*!'

It was a shout filled with panic, terror. A local man, scared witless: 'There's someone under here! On the ground! My Gawd! There's a hand sticking out from under the wood! Get 'er out! Mebbe she's still alive, eh? Help! Help!'

And then there were policemen running in every

direction, Lovelace included, issuing orders, getting the local men to stand back.

Dr Poots, spurred into professional action faster than he had anticipated, was on his hands and knees at the edge of the still-piled-high, smouldering bonfire. He was by the side of the woman. For it had been a woman.

Her arm, intact and unmarked, was indeed protruding from the bonfire, albeit at a strange angle.

'An itty little thing, she seemed,' explained Lovelace now, sadly, to Posie. 'Thin, like an under-nourished child. Tiny wrist. A small gold engagement ring could be seen with a chip of a red stone. She was clutching a bag in her hand, which was virtually intact. Very distinctive. Turquoise leather.'

Posie gasped. *But why the blazes was she so surprised?*

'Harriet Neame,' she whispered. 'The maid whom Elsie had set up as an informer here. Harriet was jolly good at her job. *Too* good I expect. Hence her murder. She must have crossed someone.'

Lovelace nodded.

He knew already that it was Harriet. Because within a couple of minutes of the discovery, at around five minutes past eight, a young tall bald lad who apparently worked at the big house, arriving for his day's work, had strolled over to have a gander at what all the fuss was about, everybody watching Dr Poots trying to gently dislodge ashes and wood from around the body. He'd got the shock of his life when he'd recognised the engagement ring, the hand it was on. He'd fainted. Had to be brought around by Dr Poots and his trusted bottle of 'Crown' lavender smelling salts.

'That was Alf,' said Posie, feeling breathless. 'How dreadful for him.'

'Poor lad. Helluva shock. But good job he didn't arrive a couple of minutes later. When Poots *did* manage to uncover the girl, it turned out that one arm and that bag were the only bits of Harriet which looked vaguely normal.

I reckon those poor corpses on display at Pompei which you're always going on about wanting to visit have got more life in them than this wee Harriet Neame. Tragic. Absolutely tragic. She was burnt up pretty badly.'

Posie *had* to ask. 'But was she…was she…?'

'Alive? When she was put in the fire, you mean?'

Lovelace shook his head grimly. 'Poots doesn't think so, which is a small mercy, I suppose. Thinks he can see some sort of stab-wound on the back. He's checking now. Seems likely she was murdered and then our killer wanted to dispose of the body quickly and effectively. Poots thinks she must have been shoved under the bonfire late last night.'

'Why bother with the bonfire?' asked Posie quizzically. 'The sea would have been easier, surely? It's right here!'

Lovelace shrugged. 'The sea is too bally rough at the moment to trust that a body thrown in will be taken conveniently away forever. The tides all around these White Cliffs are unpredictable. A corpse could well be washed in again.'

Lovelace cleared his throat. 'Maybe our killer knew this and thought he or she would try the bonfire as a suitably efficient method of elimination of evidence? Shame they messed up with that hand sticking out. Chances are without it, Harriet would have been swept away with an ash brush this morning and we would never have found out.'

Posie was silent for a few seconds, remembering Rainbird's prophetic words – was it only yesterday? – when they had spoken of the annual excitement surrounding Guy Fawkes Night. His dour pessimism:

'Always some accident to investigate here or there, eh?'

Well, this was more than an accident, wasn't it? And although Posie hadn't liked the girl, far from it, Harriet Neame hadn't deserved the sort of death she had had meted out to her last night.

Justice was important for everyone, snoops included.

'Harriet Neame was alive at about seven-thirty last night,' Posie explained. She spoke about Harriet's argument with Sidney Sherringham; explained about the turquoise bag.

'I couldn't hear the whole argument, unfortunately.'

Lovelace pulled his fingers through his hair, testily. 'This new murder isn't about a wretched bag, though, is it, Posie?'

'No. But it just shows you that Harriet was out of her depth. She was meddling in things which didn't concern her, which she didn't understand. She was an excellent snoop, and I bet she wanted to be an excellent blackmailer, too. But to make that step requires real intelligence, and I'm unsure if Harriet had that. She certainly underestimated her killer, didn't she?'

Lovelace lit up another smoke. 'What we don't know is whether Harriet was killed because she knew something about Elsie's death, or whether she was killed because of some incidental knowledge.' He took a deep drag. 'So what *did* Harriet know?'

Posie laughed, but bitterly. 'A lot. She certainly knew about a "November Drop" – told me she had information about it in a black notepad – but I think she had no clue what it actually meant. She also knew that Elsie Moncrieff came here to the hotel and called somebody every week, with the call-sign "Burning Dog". *That* must have been dangerous knowledge in itself; the most dangerous, I'd say, but again, I don't think Harriet would ever in a lifetime have guessed at Elsie's real profession.'

Lovelace stubbed out his cigarette in a green glass 'BAY HOTEL' ashtray, shaped like an anchor.

'I'll need to get this investigated. This Ruth woman needs to be quizzed about the turquoise bag; *how* Harriet got hold of it exactly. We'd better search the dead girl's room, too. Look for this missing black notebook. You can do that, can't you, darling? You know what you're looking for.'

'Of course.' Posie reached for her coat, hat and gloves. She wrapped a fine gold-and-burgundy leaf-patterned silk scarf about her neck, hiding the pink necklace of Murano glass beads beneath, which were always warm against her skin. She pulled on her hat. 'Ruth and Harriet shared a room, so I can ask Ruth questions as I search, if you like?'

'Good idea.'

Lovelace too was shrugging on his thick French-navy Chief Commissioner's woollen overcoat, with its smart golden buttons and gold-burnished epaulettes, which made him look really very handsome. He stood still for a few seconds by the door, then seemed to make up his mind about something.

'Oh, hang it all.'

He returned to the edge of the table once more. His left hand was nervously tapping at the matching navy-and-gold hat he held in the crook of his left arm.

Posie followed his gaze and saw he was looking once again at the sepia photographs of the boy and girl. Eventually he picked up the photograph of the boy and shook the photograph in his hand, his thoughts miles and miles away.

'Go on,' Posie said quietly, as calmly as she could manage. 'Spit it out.'

Lovelace exhaled deeply, his eyes coming to rest on Posie's face at last, as if searching for answers he couldn't ever hope to find there.

'I haven't shared what I'm about to tell you with any of my men yet, Posie. This is *new* information. Top-secret. Gleaned from Whitehall this morning. They gave it to me reluctantly. I've been sworn to absolute secrecy.'

Posie stood very still, waiting. It was quite an art form: this waiting for Richard to convince himself he was acting quite properly. It required patience; no sudden, hurrying movements.

At last he spoke.

'I had it confirmed today that there were *three* British-employed spies working this part of the Kent coast, between 1917 right up to today. Top-drawer agents. The sort that are trusted with big Operations, huge budgets, minimal supervision. I believe now, after what you've told me, that Elsie Moncrieff was one of those three. So, whatever her past, or her nationality, or her accent, she was almost certainly a *British* spy.'

'I say!' Posie whistled under her breath.

Lovelace frowned. 'I was only given this information when I explained that I was coming down here today. They were obliged to give it to me, you see, as a sort of background…'

'And did Whitehall tell you what the three agents were up to here?'

'There were several Operations going on, I think. Certainly, surveillance of the British coast, and looking out for smuggling. Also watching for foreign spies and monitoring anyone who showed abnormal sympathies for foreign regimes. These three agents seem to have crossed over from one Operation to another very well, fluidly. They were close and worked well together. There were three agent call-names. I was told to guard them with my life, and destroy any evidence of them if I came across them.'

'What were the names?'

Lovelace carefully put down the photograph of the boy. He almost whispered:

'One agent was "*the Angel*", one was "*the Jackal*", and the last agent was "*the Flame*". I was given no further information regarding their true identities. The current job was entitled "Operation Firebird", and I was told that of the three assets, at least two were strongly believed to be dead. I don't know if that tally includes Elsie or not. And if it doesn't, then all three are now dead, aren't they?'

'Well, yes. My golly!' Posie's thoughts were jumbled. 'They gave you no information about what this "Operation Firebird" was all about?'

'No.'

Lovelace picked up the tiny scrap of telegram. 'You thought Elsie was German, didn't you?'

Posie stayed silent, nodded.

'I think you were right, darling.'

Lovelace blew out his cheeks, tapped the photograph on the desk again without looking at it. 'By Gad, how these ghosts come back to haunt us, eh?'

'Sorry?'

Lovelace cleared his throat, avoided her gaze: 'Max, Posie. *Your* Max.'

A moment's silence, heavy as an ocean of long-unshed tears hovered over them, binding them to each other, pushing them apart.

Posie's tongue was thick in the roof of her mouth, dry, unable to form the words of protest she should find. *He wasn't mine. Wouldn't ever have been mine. He's gone, anyway. He's dead.*

Isn't he?

Lovelace spoke slowly, carefully. 'Do you remember we met him down here, three years back?'

Lovelace looked grey, his face pinched against his rich pristine navy uniform, like *it* was wearing him, not the other way around. 'Max was convincing. He had that back-story going about how he had a little illegitimate son and a married mistress tucked away down here at St Margaret's Bay. Nothing like a touch of an all-too-human foible in a story, is there? It adds authenticity. *I* believed him.'

'I know you did,' muttered Posie. *Because you are a good man and you trust people. Perhaps because you don't look far enough beneath the surface?*

'This photograph nearly blindsided me when I saw it again. Here. This morning.'

'You mean you've seen it before?' Posie asked, incredulous.

'Oh, yes. *This* was the photograph Max showed me when he was telling me that lie about his illegitimate

221

son. Told me this was the lad himself. Acted very proudly. Made up some guff about that horrible-looking teddy bear in the picture; how he'd bought it for the lad himself.'

Posie grabbed at the picture, almost angrily.

'But darling, how *could* you have believed him? This photograph shows a lad of maybe six years old. If Max had come to England towards the end of the Great War, in 1917, or 1918, then by 1921, when we met him, his illegitimate son would at best only have been a couple of years old. Little more than a baby. Not this great blonde lad here! And the timing isn't right for the clothes, either. I'd wager that this was taken more than thirty-five years back. Have *you* seen any children wearing those big sailor-boat collar blouses recently? Those straw hats?'

Richard Lovelace shook his head. 'No. Although I think *I* was made to wear something similar once. For a photo session with my parents. Before they both died…'

'*Exactly!*' Posie hooted with a sudden conviction that she was absolutely right. 'And Max was pretty much the same age as you, wasn't he? He was probably made to dress up – just like you, around the same time – by his parents, in uncomfortable, fashionable clothes. All Max did was to show you a picture of *himself* as a boy.'

So this *was* Max, then.

At last, proof of a connection.

Posie reached out, picked up the matching picture of the little girl. 'And this was taken at the same time. Wouldn't it make sense that these two were sister and brother? That the blonde girl here was Elsie Moncrieff as a child?'

Lovelace gave a low whistle. 'So Elsie Moncrieff was Max's sister?'

Posie shrugged. After all, there had been that first, uncanny resemblance which had so spooked her. 'Why not? They told you the spies were close. What if Max was one of these three spies, alongside Elsie?'

Max had never mentioned a sister to Posie before, but

there was so much he hadn't mentioned. Hadn't been able to explain. Perhaps even to himself.

'But Max couldn't have been working on this new project, Operation Firebird.' Posie linked her hands, twining her gloved fingers over and over, thinking aloud. 'Because we know that Max left here just after we met him, three years ago. He was involved in other missions, all over the place: Venice, France, London, Newcastle, Edinburgh. Short projects, and longer ones too. He went wherever he was sent. So, either he wasn't a full-time member of this trio, or he helped from afar.'

Lovelace picked up the tiny bit of telegram, flicked at its words: 'Like this, you mean? Perhaps his sister would ask for confirmation of facts? And then Max would call on his contacts, or his own expertise, and send the information back to her. Like here. No code needed, because their original language was enough of a cover in the circumstances.'

Lovelace pointed at the words:

SCHNEIDER.
ABER ROT.
DER ENGEL

'You don't speak German, do you, darling?'

Posie shook her head regretfully. Very basic German words, mostly of a medical nature, had been her limit when she'd worked on the Western Front as an ambulance driver in the Great War: just the bare necessities for shouting out to injured and dying German soldiers as they drove past, or helped to haul them out of shell-holes; a couple of words of reassurance, comfort.

Lovelace seemed to be lost to Posie, years away in time

and location. Was it the Great War he was thinking of, too?

But no.

'*I* speak German, Posie. Not perfectly, but enough. A fine language. I've never told you about how I learnt it, have I? It came about it a funny way. It was helpful, later, in those wretched trenches…well, you don't need *me* to tell you about those, do you, love? You and me will never forget them. But I was a mere nipper when I learnt it. It came to me through music.'

Richard Lovelace had been orphaned early. An only child, he had been taken in by an elderly aunt and uncle who ran a busy boarding-house near Russell Square in London, and they hadn't a clue what to do with a clever, eager-to-learn ten-year-old, whose dreams of being a policeman seemed an all-consuming passion. Out of school-time, he roamed the streets of Camden, looking for amusement, distraction, for playmates. Other boys would have gone to the bad and ended up as petty criminals, part of a gang.

But Richard Lovelace had had the good fortune to hear the local German Band, playing on the Bandstand in Russell Square one Sunday in late summer, all dressed up in their neat red-and-black costumes.

They had been playing a Strauss Waltz. "The Blue Danube." And it had saved him.

'I'd learnt the trumpet from my father. I had a musical streak I suppose; it was in the blood. The local German Band revived it for me. I fair begged them to take me on, although I was a whippersnapper, and bless their souls, they did. I became the youngest member, the only non-German among them. All of them were refugees of sorts, and this little band was the only bit of home they had to cling on to. It became a kind of home for me too. I learnt the lingo fast, to keep up, to understand what was happening. I played with them for near enough seven years in the end. Every

Saturday and Sunday out on a show, with Wednesday night for band practice. Weddings, parties, street-corners: you name it. I got pocket money and a sense of purpose from them. Grand fellas each and every one.'

Posie stared at Lovelace, the bitter-sweet memories being dredged up, a past she had not known about until now. Layers of history which might take years to discover, to uncover. But now was not the time for further digging, and they both knew it.

'Anyhow.' Lovelace cleared his throat and jabbed at the paper.

'"*Der Engel*" is "Angel" in German,' he explained curtly. 'The sender of this telegram was signing his call-name.'

Posie nodded. 'And the other words, Richard?'

'It doesn't make sense. I'll write the translation.'

And he wrote the words hurriedly, and stepped back, looking at them.

TAILOR.
BUT RED.
THE ANGEL.

'A tailor, you say? Like Tony Stone?' asked Posie, glancing at his translation, a thin shimmer of excitement breaking through.

Lovelace shrugged. 'Could be…'

'Oh!' hissed Posie, shaking her head quickly. 'No! It could be the "Taylors" who were paying off Petronella's bank loan. Remember? Maybe Elsie asked the Angel to double-check if that really was the case?'

Lovelace looked at Posie and grinned.

'Atta-girl, darling. I think that's precisely what it meant. *If* we can assume Max was "the Angel", then this is him, from afar, checking and confirming the information Elsie received through her snooping activities.'

'But Max disappeared. He *died*, this July,' said Posie, the elation of their discovery suddenly slipping away. 'Late July. This must have been one of the last times he helped his sister. This telegram must have been sent in the first week or two of July. And then after that Elsie would have been here alone. Running things. With no-one to help her.'

Lovelace shook his head. 'She may not have been alone, love. Remember: there were *three* spies originally down here. Maybe not right here, in this very place, but near enough. Don't forget the clever call-name she used on the hotel telephone.'

Posie scowled. 'What of it? *"Burning Dog?"* What's that all about?'

But then it dawned on her. 'Oh! How clever! A combination of *two* people's call-names!'

A jackal and a flame. A jackal was like a dog, and a flame was a fire. A dog on fire. *A Burning Dog*.

'I say! Elsie was working here with someone, then, wasn't she? The Jackal and the Flame? Together? As one? A pair of them?'

'It makes sense.'

'But who was the other spy? Who was he? Or she?'

Lovelace flicked at his wristwatch. 'Who knows? We don't even know if Elsie was "the Jackal" or if she was "the Flame". And I must go, love.'

Posie gathered Elsie's precious belongings up quickly. She stared a moment too long at the yellow torch still on the desk. Lovelace smiled. 'Is that yours, love? I don't recognise it. Jolly fancy bit of kit.'

Posie paused, then resolved to tell Lovelace what she remembered from her dream. Only she left 'her' Max out of it.

She described the strange intruder, and Rainbird's similar experience in the next room. The now-complete flash-light which spoke as evidence of those visits.

Lovelace stared at Posie a moment too long, then silently, in his gloved hands, reached for the torch. 'I'll get this fingerprinted,' he said calmly but decisively, and Posie saw the unease in his face, the guarded anxious looks he flashed at her.

He took her by the arm and they walked out of the room.

'We'll take the staff stairs and then the covered passageway to the Bay Bungalow.' He dropped his voice even lower. 'And I need to tell you why I'm really here. Because it's about *something else entirely*. A new case which is a national priority right now, which is why Whitehall and MI5 were compelled to speak to me about these three spies.'

Posie looked at her fiancé's profile as they walked side by side down the corridor, ignoring Rainbird's room, making for the back, staff stairs.

'You mean you're not here just to help me?'

'No, darling. Sorry. Far from it. I would have sent you Fox and all the others, of course, but I'm actually here on a completely different case. My men can have no inkling. No-one can. It sounds callous to say it, but Harriet's murder couldn't have happened at a better time for me. It's a crime I can pretend to work on while I'm investigating this other matter. A smokescreen of the best, most authentic kind.'

'What the blazes?' Posie felt angry, let down. 'What can be more important than two dead women, both robbed of their lives while in the prime of youth? What do you need to be sniffing around in, Richard? Tell me.'

But he shook his head urgently:

'Shhh. Let's not speak here. People are coming.'

* * * *

Twenty-Four

Maids were jostling up the staff stairs and giggling in the stairwell, carrying up pitchers of water for guests who didn't have hot and cold running water in their rooms. The arrival of the Scotland Yard team and their hotel requirements had caused a frenzy of out-of-season activity for Mr Potterton and his staff.

Several of the maids stared, eyes boggling at the sight of Lovelace in his shimmery Chief Commissioner's get-up. The need to be silent gave Posie time to think.

And of course, into the busyness of her mind came Max.

Max who had apparently died in late July. Could Max really have been 'the Angel'? Sidney Sherringham had certainly held the very real belief that 'the Angel' was still alive and able to help him. Hadn't Elsie told Sidney that, only a couple of weeks back?

And hadn't Mr Potterton overheard Elsie on Sunday, up in the hotel room, again talking about 'the Angel'?

Elsie had known that 'the Angel' was still alive; had even arranged to meet him on the night she had died.

A *him*.

Had it been Max? Hiding in deep cover all these months? If so, why hadn't he contacted Posie?

Perhaps, if he was still alive, then it *had* been Max last night, in her room. But what had he been doing with that torch? Had it been him who had undone her purse and taken out his old handwritten note? In an effort to get rid of it, perhaps?

Posie thought back to the news of Max's death once more. That walnut-lined office in Whitehall.

Thea.

Thea who had been Max's handler. And if he was one of the three agents, surely that meant Thea must have been the direct handler for the other two agents, also?

The best of the best.

'Oh, Richard!'

They were at the bottom of the stairwell now, in a dim, plain green-painted hallway with cardboard boxes stacked up neatly against all the walls. A sign giving instructions in case of fire had been tacked up on the wall and a dark service passageway ran off to the left. Richard Lovelace turned as Posie scrabbled inside her huge carpet bag, watched as she pulled out the bound-up handkerchief of Elsie's items.

'It was staring me in the face, Richard. Thea Elleridge was the woman to whom Elsie was reporting, wasn't she? Every single week, on a Sunday at two o'clock. *Thea* was actually the handler for all three of them. Look...'

She pulled out the gold wedding band. Pulled out the paper with Max's handwriting on it listing Thea's details.

She pointed excitedly from one to the other. The ring first.

'See?'

To the Fire from the Jackal. WH 8977

'Look at the inscription in the ring!'

She thrust it under Richard's nose. 'The Whitehall number – 8977 – it's the same in both places, on the ring and in the note. It's Thea Elleridge's number. I was a fool to miss this. I don't know what this ring meant to Elsie, whether this was a real wedding band, or whether it was something Thea Elleridge handed out to all her agents as a kind of token. But surely this is proof? This means that Elsie was definitely one of these three agents Whitehall told you about. This was *her* ring. She is described as "the Fire" here. Well, that's almost the same as "Flame", isn't it?'

But before Richard could answer, Posie rushed on.

'And speaking of Thea Elleridge, I believe she came down here to visit Elsie. A woman was seen on the beach with Elsie sometimes. They painted together. I bet the painting was all a handy cover, and she was getting reports from Elsie, and giving more instructions.'

Lovelace nodded, convinced. 'It sounds a good plan, doesn't it? Hardly something to make people suspicious, eh?'

But in all of this, among all of the puzzle pieces coming together, there was something Posie wasn't seeing. It was right in front of her, but refusing to come into focus.

What was it?

Posie closed her eyes. She smelt the sharp sting of bleach in the stairwell, heard the distant laughter from the maids upstairs. She tried to ignore the echoing tap-tap of Richard Lovelace's immaculately-polished black Church's brogue; the slight impatience in him. She felt the shock of the cold wall shake her to her senses.

Suddenly it became clear.

Operation Firebird had been all about the November Drop. Whatever that was. *It had to be*. It might not have started that way, but it had ended up like that. Thea Elleridge had known all about it. The November Drop had happened at the party at White Shaw on Saturday night.

And for whatever reason, perhaps simply because she had had enough, Elsie Moncrieff didn't attend. But the angry man Elsie had met on Sunday afternoon in the hotel – *had it been the Jackal?* – had attended.

Things had gone wrong. And Thea Elleridge was off with flu, uncontactable, and Elsie Moncrieff and the angry man were left floundering, trying to report to Thea about their failure, and to get new instructions.

Yes. That made sense.

But had Elsie died because the November Drop had gone wrong? Or simply because she wanted to leave her job as a spy?

The timing was spot-on, surely?

It seemed likely that one of these two reasons was as much behind the terrible fall from the White Cliffs as anything which Petronella Douglas could have done by way of angry reproach.

But just *what* had Elsie been planning on doing when she left MI5? Spies didn't have lives after spying, did they? Perhaps this was simply something Elsie Moncrieff had failed to grasp.

Posie whispered this all now to Richard, explaining, watching his face grow harder.

'By Gad, this is something,' he agreed. He crossed his arms, quickly checking the stairs again, and the passageway to his left-hand side. Both were empty.

'I don't know what the November Drop is, or was, Posie. But you're right: it sounds like Elsie had messed up. I'll get to the bottom of it if I can. I've left a message for Thea to call me as soon as she can. She's sick at home in Wimbledon.' He stalled for a few seconds, thinking. 'This party…It all happened at the party on Saturday, eh?'

'Yes.'

Posie tried to remember more of what Mr Potterton had heard. 'And then the man in the room – "the Jackal", I'm guessing – talked about something which had vanished. *Vanishing…*'

The effect of this new information was extreme. Lovelace, formerly attentive and concerned, now froze.

'*What* did you just say, Posie?'

Lovelace looked anxious. 'Something vanishing, or *someone*? Could it have been "someone", do you think, Posie?'

'You're asking the wrong person, lovey. Ask Potterton. Is this the top-secret case which you're down here about?'

Lovelace took out his cigarette case and shook out a Turkish. He lit up and took a long drag.

'Have you heard of Jamie Boxwood, darling?'

Posie frowned for a second, not understanding. 'Oh! You mean *Lord* Boxwood? The Inventor chappie?' She remembered Dolly's almost-indiscretion on the telephone call which seemed like weeks ago, but which had only been two nights ago.

'That's right.' Lovelace nodded. 'And, yes: this is the top-secret case I'm here about. It's a matter of National Security. Jamie Boxwood has *vanished*.'

He took another drag of the smoke. 'How I wish I knew the identity of the man who was speaking in that room on Sunday afternoon.'

'But I don't quite see…?'

'This place – White Shaw on Saturday night, the party – was the very last place Boxwood was seen at. There have been no sightings of him since.'

Lovelace recounted in low whispers how Lord Boxwood had been reported missing to Scotland Yard by his wife just yesterday morning. Wednesday morning.

'His *wife*?'

Lovelace looked puzzled. 'Yes. Boxwood is married to a society beauty, no less. Lady Rosaline Clitheroe. And they have two little girls. They all live in a huge white-stuccoed townhouse in Chelsea.'

'But why the blazes did his wife wait that long? Three full days?' asked Posie, trying to form a time-line in her mind. She was vaguely aware of something which Lovelace had just said that was strange, not ringing true. But she couldn't grasp at it, and tried to pay attention as her fiancé raced on.

'Apparently it's not at all unusual for him to go "missing". Boxwood often goes off for days. Part and parcel of him being such a brilliant, barmy, one-in-a-million type of Inventor, apparently. He has an office with a laboratory and a small flat at University College, in Bloomsbury. He apparently holes himself up there for days, very often, so Lady Rosaline wasn't worried this time; just thought he was working, like usual. He specialises in designing submarines, or U-boats. But yesterday, when Lady Rosaline telephoned to the University, they told her Boxwood hadn't been seen there since last week.'

Lovelace explained that Britain was currently ramping up their military resources, just in case. And Jamie Boxwood was part of this project. Since the Great War had ended he had been funded by the government to work on creating vastly superior versions of the U-boats used by both sides in the Great War. It was understood that a breakthrough had been made by Boxwood; plans drawn up.

But as yet, nothing had been delivered to the War Office or the Royal Navy.

'Trouble is, the fella is a drug-user. Cocaine, mostly,' said Lovelace, matter-of-factly. 'Opium, too. His nerves were shot to pieces in the Great War when he was out with the Navy. Boxwood's been volatile lately, out of control. He's lost all his family money and he's whipping through his government salary like water. He's been more and more involved with the wrong crowd, like this Petronella Douglas woman. I think *she's* been supplying Boxwood with his drugs at all these wretched parties. The question is: what did *she* want in return from him? And I've started wondering if Petronella Douglas wanted the almost-complete plans for the new U-boats...'

Posie gasped. 'But what *for*?'

Lovelace ground out his cigarette on the tiled wall, almost laughing. 'Oh, darling, sometimes your innocence actually touches me. But you need to toughen up your views. I expect Petronella wanted the plans for an interested party. A *foreign* party. Commercially these plans must be worth millions.'

'Oh! I say!'

'In fact, if this is true, I expect the interested party has already paid ahead of time. They were sat ready and waiting. The money had already been sent to Petronella…'

'By "Taylors", you mean?'

'Yes. Or "*Schneider*", might make more sense, mightn't it?' Lovelace said grimly. 'Like in that bit of telegram you found? If the interested party are German, which they might be. Perhaps Max meant it literally?'

He shrugged. 'Perhaps Boxwood didn't know about the arrangement to sell the plans in the early stages, only Petronella. Perhaps she was simply being paid a huge amount to facilitate things.'

'But,' and Posie swallowed, nervous, 'that would make Petronella Douglas, and Jamie Boxwood – if he knew about it – *traitors*, wouldn't it?'

'It would,' Lovelace agreed. 'Which is why this is all top-secret. It's also why I need access to Petronella's personal papers. It's massively helpful that we've stuck her in an isolated room, away from her own documents. I'm going to have a good old rummage in her bedroom, and I'll ask that nice honey-trap Mr Sherringham if he knows where things might be kept. I want to see if there's any evidence connecting her to any other countries.'

Posie frowned, concentrating. 'I understand about the need for a smokescreen now. But having heard everything from me, you now think Jamie Boxwood was connected to the November Drop? The Operation which Elsie was tracking?'

'Perhaps he *was* the November Drop.'

'Sorry?'

'The man himself is beyond price. One of a kind. Perhaps the paperwork was what was wanted by our foreign party, or perhaps it was the paperwork *plus* the man? Boxwood may have been needed to turn the machine into a reality. But at present I have no idea if he has disappeared voluntarily, or been kidnapped.'

Posie was gobsmacked. But into her head came a memory of a waxy, plain little face, keen to make money, sell information. Grasping.

'I think it's dangerous, Richard. I told you: Harriet Neame knew about the November Drop. Well, maybe *that* knowledge got her killed and shoved under that wretched bonfire? Maybe Elsie Moncrieff was killed because of it, too? And what about Thea Elleridge herself? She had planned for her spies to monitor this situation over a good long while, and it went wrong. Maybe *she's* been killed, too? I must say I feel dashed nervous about you investigating.'

For a second Lovelace looked very pale beneath his coppery freckles, but he shook off the concerns.

'My remit is to bring Boxwood back alive. I've said I'll do it, and so I'll do it.'

And Posie sighed inwardly as she followed Richard to the Bay Bungalow, to the buzz of a team who were working busily on the 'smokescreen'.

But in all of this Posie tried to keep the name and face of Elsie Moncrieff central to her thoughts, and when, after a few seconds of arriving, she saw a bright, slightly-charred turquoise handbag lying forlornly on the huge table, with an 'EVIDENCE' tag attached, she put on her gloves and drew it to herself.

* * * *

Twenty-Five

She scanned the room first.

The Bay Bungalow was buzzing with energy. It smelt busy. Sweat, and the acrid disinfectant smell which accompanied Dr Poots wherever he went, were mixed up together with the scents of hair oil, and spray starch and tea, with a jarring top note of bleach.

The bungalow had no windows on the side walls, but the entire front was made up of glass windows and doors, leading onto a white-painted wooden veranda, with a direct view of the blustery sea. At the back of the bungalow, where Posie and Richard had entered through the service corridor, was a tiny but well-stocked kitchenette, and three or four small bedrooms, one of which Petronella Douglas was locked inside. The bungalow felt rickety, fragile, and the sudden winds from the beach seemed to rock it precariously every few minutes.

Men from Scotland Yard were everywhere.

Sergeant Fox was occupied at a small rattan table with telephone apparatus, engaged on a call, his long legs crossed. A couple of men were compiling a big chart showing everyone at White Shaw's whereabouts for the time of both Elsie Moncrieff and Harriet Neame's deaths. Nearest the veranda doors another long, thin table had been set up, at which the forensics team were working. Fingerprints had obviously been obtained from everyone at White Shaw and two men were checking and re-checking these. The yellow EVER-READY torch, so recently put together again, had been handed to them by Lovelace himself a couple of minutes earlier, and it was awaiting their expert ministrations.

Lovelace himself was issuing instructions to a Detective even younger than Fox.

'Check on the American, will you, Constable Smallbone? Bruce Douglas arrived last night at the hotel. We think he may have been drugged. Then, I want you to go and talk to *all* of the residents and workers of White Shaw, locked in their rooms. Put the wind up them. Ask them all if they were at the party here on Saturday night and if they saw or heard anything odd.'

'Like *what*, sir?'

Lovelace seemed to be losing patience, clicking his knuckles. 'Oh, *anything*, Smallbone.'

'But we know Miss Moncrieff wasn't even at that party, Chief Commissioner. Surely we're wasting our time?'

The knuckles carried on being clicked. 'Don't come the old acid with me, eh, lad? Just bally well *ask*, please.'

In all of the busyness no-one watched Posie, in her own gloves, examine the turquoise handbag which had recently been used by both of the dead women in the investigation.

It was a beauty, for sure.

The handbag – a plain, square envelope no bigger than a clutch – was made of butter-soft leather, the turquoise dye obviously expertly burnished and the small golden clasp and matching gold chain of the strap were exquisitely crafted. It smelt of leather, of linen, of that undefinable scent in Elsie's room: gardenia, peroxide. It smelt too of fire, although the bonfire had barely touched it.

On opening the bag with a satisfying CLICK, Posie saw that a large, cheap red money-purse had been stuffed inside. Taking it out Posie knew without opening it that it had belonged to Harriet Neame. Within this were a few coins, buttons, a small fold of matches. Nothing interesting.

The rest of the bag was completely empty.

There was a clever zipped side pocket-compartment in the thick cream linen lining. But that too was empty, although a slight acid scent could be detected, and when Posie looked very closely she saw that the pocket-compartment had smudges of dark-blue inkiness at its edges.

Posie suddenly knew what the smell was. What it must have been.

Carbon paper.

The almost-illegible paper copy of an 'Agreement' found in the hot-water bottle in Elsie's flat had been the underneath copy of an original document, hadn't it? And hadn't Posie bemoaned the fact that the original of the mysterious 'Agreement' was missing?

But what if it *had* been kept after all: carefully folded in the safety of Elsie's treasured handbag, its inky underside inconveniently rubbing off against the nice cream lining? Perhaps the bad copy in the hot-water bottle had only been kept in case of a real emergency?

The handbag had, for whatever reason – most likely because of the terrible weather – not been taken by Elsie with her on the night she had died.

The question was, *where was that top copy now?* Had Harriet, when given this bag, thrown its contents away?

Posie frowned. From what she had observed of Harriet Neame, the girl wouldn't have thrown anything away which could potentially have made her money. And there was only one way of finding out what Harriet had done with the contents of this bag.

Posie would need to search Harriet's room, the one she had shared with the cook, Ruth. But Posie would need an official Search Warrant.

She looked about hurriedly for someone to come with her, but Lovelace was already in conference with Dr Poots, both of them studying an orange-coloured pre-post-mortem report.

Lovelace turned as Posie came up, and he put his hand on her arm.

'How did Harriet die, Doctor?' Posie asked, straight-up.

Dr Poots fiddled with his bow-tie, and adjusted his glasses. 'Er, well, she was stabbed, Miss Parker. In the back. A few times. A strange instrument was used; very sharp but jagged. Body's in a dreadful state so I can't be one hundred per cent sure, but it seems to have been a frenzied attack. Poor girl had already turned her back on the assailant; as if she was leaving. That's when he, or she, brought Harriet Neame down.'

'It was unplanned, then?' insisted Posie.

Dr Poots shrugged. 'That is your good fiancé's job, Miss. Not mine.'

Posie was about to ask Lovelace to loan her Sergeant Fox but then the telephone rang again and she saw Fox snatch up the receiver, agree to a diverted call from the main hotel itself.

'London calling? Scotland Yard, you say? Yes, the Chief Commissioner is just here…'

In the doorway of the dark service corridor Posie suddenly saw the forlorn figure of Sergeant Rainbird looming uselessly, regarding the busy room like the Ghost of Christmas Past, sick-looking and out of place. Posie seized the moment as Lovelace took the receiver:

'You and Sergeant Fox are busy here, darling. Can Rainbird accompany me to ask Ruth, the cook, some questions?'

'Yes, darling. *If* he can manage it,' he whispered under his breath, covering the telephone receiver.

'You'd better take one of the Warrants from the table. Remind Rainbird to take his police badge, and not to impersonate a more superior officer this time, eh?'

Ruth Walker was sitting on the edge of her neatly-made single bed, her eyes dry and with no evidence of having shed any tears for the girl she had shared a room with.

A girl who, if she had married Ruth's nephew, Alf, as planned, would have become family.

The woman in her early fifties, almost unrecognisable to Posie out of her white cook's garb, motioned for Posie to sit down opposite her on a shockingly messy bed which must have been Harriet's.

Posie felt a shiver of distaste at the idea of sitting on the murdered girl's bed: the most private, sacred space a person can have; so recently and unexpectedly vacated.

Rainbird hung back, unsure of himself in the obviously female domain. The sparse, large room, identical in almost every way to Elsie's, had none of the comfort or taste.

It was as if a chalk line divided the room: one side, Ruth's, was spotlessly clean, devoid of ornament or colour, a row of hooks holding a single shabby winter coat, black cloche hat and a couple of plain dresses.

The other side, Harriet's, was a mess of tumbled clothes, shoes, penny magazines and Woolworths powder-compacts. Cut-out photographs of the Prince of Wales, and the American actress Clara Bow were tacked haphazardly on the wall above the bed, and a cheap wooden cupboard, doors not closing as it was so full, almost burst with the volume of clothes stuffed inside it.

Ruth followed Posie's gaze about the place, and almost smirked. The effect was unappealing. Ruth had a bad caste to one eye, and this, together with her strange lack of grief was unsettling.

'Squandered it all, the silly beggar,' rasped Ruth, nodding at the cupboard.

'Sorry?' asked Posie, sitting down awkwardly.

'Harriet. She spent the lot. Elsie Moncrieff paid her well – but you know that, dern't ya? – and Harriet spent the lot. Every Monday, come rain or shine, she'd head into Dover on the Number 80 stagecoach. It was her day off. She bought everything: new ribbons; new ready-made dresses; high-class chocolates in Dowling's on Biggin Street. Half of Woolworths, too! Like she was some posh lady! She said she was savin' up for the weddin' to our Alf, but it was a pack of lies!'

'You don't seem unhappy that your nephew's fiancée is dead, Miss Walker?'

A shrug. 'I told her time and again that all her snoopin' would land her a sticky end. And it has, han't it?'

Unsure how much of the details of Harriet's murder had yet been shared with the staff, Posie just nodded, not wanting to put the woman off her stride.

Ruth crossed her arms, no mean feat as her body was as wide and round as a barrel, and her off-duty flannel dress strained at the streams and front buttons. The cook looked about herself with something like disgust.

'I'll be pleased to leave here. I'll leave today, if they let me. Funny old place. Only thing I'll miss is those little boys: I got to thinkin' of them as my own sometimes. Odd, innit? And I've never had, nor wanted children! But they fair touched my heart.'

Posie brought out the turquoise leather bag, and made a show of resting it in her lap.

The effect on the cook was immediate. She kept her one good eye fixed on the bag, her fat fingers drumming nervously.

'I'm not accusing you of anything, Miss Walker,' explained Posie, clearly. 'But I think it was *you* who rescued this handbag from an incinerator which used to burn Elsie Moncrieff's possessions on Monday morning. We know it wasn't Harriet Neame who rescued the bag because, as you told us yourself, she always had her day off on Mondays.'

A silence, a licking of pale, unpainted lips. Ruth Walker was clearly weighing up her options, deciding whether or not to tell the truth, or to keep mum.

Sergeant Rainbird started to fish in the inside of his trench-coat pocket. In actual fact, he was only looking for one of the filched Sullivan Powells he had taken the day before, but Ruth didn't know that and obviously thought he was looking for handcuffs, or worse. She started babbling urgently.

'Yes, it *was* me. I admit it. But rescuing a bag as lovely as this one isn't a crime, is it? It was that great lump Mickey stirring the flames which angered me. All this lovely stuff, and he was just watchin' it burn. Helpin' it on its way! A beautiful pure wool coat Miss Moncrieff had – in a matching turquoise – and I would have grabbed that, only by the time I got to it, it were already half gone. Shame. A cryin' shame.'

'Why did you give the bag to Harriet? You could have kept it for yourself?' Posie paused carefully. 'Or sold it?'

Ruth laughed. 'Can you really see *me* walkin' about the place with somethin' showy like that? And as for sellin' it, how would I do that? No-one down Dover would have bought it; it's too fancy. And as fer sellin' it in London, well: I've never been meself, and I dunno how I'd get it there. The only lad from London is that Sidney Sherringham, and he was half in love with Miss Moncrieff himself. They were right close. He'd never help sell it, would he? He'd think it was wrong.'

'So Harriet took it?'

'Yes. She had some ideas about dyin' the leather black. I never dreamt she'd parade around with it last night. But there always was a touch of vanity to the silly girl.'

'I need to know about what was *inside* the bag, Miss Walker. I'm sure you went through it, didn't you? Both of you.'

A silence which could have been cut with a knife. The

woman on the bed didn't move. She just looked from Posie to Rainbird and back again. Rainbird ground out his smoke in the washbasin, and came over, unfolding the official Search Warrant which he'd had ready all along.

'Shall *I* do the honours, Madam? And start searching?' he asked, surprisingly patient, holding out the paperwork which the cook stared at in fright.

'But it seems a shame when you've got your room so ship-shape, to mess it all up. Or would you like to just show Miss Parker and myself what you found in the bag, originally? And I won't come any closer.'

A nod at last.

A shift of the mighty bulk on the bed and Ruth leant towards her small, cheap bedside cabinet. The drawer was pulled open, and a small open-top workbasket brought out.

'*This* was everything,' muttered the cook. 'I promise.'

Posie saw a beautiful turquoise money-purse, an identical match to the handbag. There was also a French lipstick in a golden case, a small expensive-looking powder-compact with an 'E' engraved on its golden surface, a sachet of peroxide bleach and a new tin of black boot polish.

Posie opened the money-purse, but all she saw inside was loose change, and two scraps of folded paper, one inside the other. The first made her gasp.

Here it was at last. Confirmation of Max's involvement in all this. His *actual* writing.

The usual spot. Come alone.
Half-past eleven tonight.

So Elsie *had* met Max. Max, who, this now proved, was alive. Had he been with Elsie when she had died?

A horrible, sudden and utterly terrible thought entered

243

Posie's mind, just as she was sitting there on the dead girl's bed, staring at the scribbled words.

Could *Max* have been involved in Elsie's death at all? Could he have pushed her? Acting on some higher orders? He'd certainly killed before, that much Posie knew. Would his remit have involved killing his own sister? *If* she was his sister...

But *no*.

Underneath it all, Max had a heart of gold. A human sense of right and wrong.

Posie realised her fingers were shaking, that sick feeling of nausea rising up in her again. She picked up the next folded note quickly. It was a receipt from a jewellery shop called Simpkins in Dover.

SIMPKINS JEWELLERS, EST. 1899. 47, SNARGATE STREET, DOVER.

Client: Moncrieff

Item: Ring ready for collection, 3rd November onwards. To be picked up, as agreed with client.

Price: Already paid.

It didn't seem important. Some trinket of Elsie's which would never now be collected. A date missed forever.

Perhaps Ruth would have gone in to get the thing, pretending to be sent in by Elsie, if Posie and Rainbird hadn't insisted on all of this?

Posie tucked the notes away. She tipped the workbasket contents into Elsie's turquoise bag again. She sat straighter, angrier.

'I wasn't actually looking for lipsticks or money, Miss

Walker. Nor jewellery receipts, lucrative though they can be, I suppose. What I was looking for is not here.'

'What was it, Miss?' But the woman was shifty, avoiding Posie's eye.

'Two things. The first was Harriet's black notebook. Her *current* one. The one with information from Saturday's party. She showed it to me yesterday. Do you know where it is?'

'Aye.' Ruth grinned, satisfied. 'It doesn't exist no more, and that's the God honest truth. When I saw that great gaggle of policemen out there this morning, and saw Alf keening in the corner, I fair ran over here, found it under Harriet's pillow – where she always kept it – and I took it straight to the kitchen and I burnt it on the range. It was trouble. Blessed thing did her no good, did it? It had to go.'

Posie exhaled noisily and heard Rainbird click his tongue in disappointment.

'Thank you for telling me this, Miss Walker. The second thing I needed was a piece of paper. Typed, with an inky backing to it. Anyone who touched it would have come away with inky fingers. Have you seen *that*? It was in the pocket in the lining of the bag.'

The cook seemed to crumple slightly on the bed. When she spoke it was quietly, without her former pride: 'Aye. I know what you mean. It was inky, all right. But I can't tell you what it said, if that's what you're after.' She hung her head slightly. 'I can't read, Miss.'

Posie stretched out a hand. 'That's nothing to be ashamed of, Miss Walker. But Harriet *could* read, and she read it, didn't she? Realised it was important.'

'Aye, Miss. She didn't look at the things from Elsie's bag properly until yesterday, Miss. When you came sniffin' around here, if you'll pardon the expression. I think she thought she might be able to make some money out of you, Miss, with that inky page. That you might have found it interesting?'

'She had it with her when she came to me?'

'Yes.'

Posie remembered the maid's sly look. '*I might also have other information to whet your appetite.*'

Posie could have kicked herself. 'Did she *tell* you what it said? Where is it now?'

Ruth Walker, slightly mollified she wasn't in dire amounts of trouble, shook her head. 'I dunno, Miss. But it was her Death Warrant. That's for sure.'

'Why do you say that?'

'Harriet told me that Elsie had been up to something; that this paper proved it. Elsie was up to funny business with someone else. And Harriet told me she was going to meet this person last night. To see if she could get money out of them.'

'Them?' Posie queried, her thoughts tumbling. Was the Agreement something to do with the spy ring?

'Not *him*? Or *her*?'

'No, Miss.'

Had Harriet discovered who "the Jackal" was?

Or was it something to do with Max, "the Angel"?

It appeared highly likely that Max had been here at St Margaret's Bay last night. Had Harriet actually been meeting Max? Was the death by ragged blade and the depositing of the body under the bonfire *his* handiwork?

But *surely* not…

'What time did Harriet Neame meet this person?' chipped in Rainbird, who had seen Posie's trembling hands, her puzzled, horrified frown.

'At ten o'clock, sir,' replied the cook. 'But I don't know much more. She'd come in from the bonfire about nine o'clock. We had a cup of tea. Then Harriet applied some of that fancy red lipstick of Elsie's which you've got there. It didn't suit her, of course. As she tied on her blue-flowered headscarf – horrible bright thing it was – I asked her if she wanted me to come along for support but Harriet just laughed. Said she wasn't in any sort of danger; she wasn't going far. Well, she was right about that, wasn't she?'

As they left the flat, Sergeant Rainbird walked quietly alongside Posie, letting her think, a quietness and sensitivity she welcomed and appreciated.

Where had Harriet gone and who had she met last night?

And what had been in the Agreement which was so dangerous that a cheap, lowly woman had had to die because of it?

* * * *

Twenty-Six

The Incident Room in the Bay Bungalow was still busy, and Posie was summoned over by an excited, excitable Sergeant Fox. 'I've information for you, Miss!'

Of all the requests she had made the previous night, most of the answers were now trickling through. Posie sat in a rattan chair with her notebook out and her pencil poised.

'I checked on the personal details for all of the staff, and all of them are who they say they are. But Elsie's past, well: I'd say it was all a fiction!'

The fashionable architect, Jolyon Peterson, who had designed White Shaw, had telephoned through first. Fox rolled his eyes theatrically:

'Talk about frightened! As soon as he heard the words "Murder Investigation", he admitted that he'd been paid to provide those oh-so-handy personal references. Elsie had paid him quite a big sum for the introduction. He's famous, but his practice was struggling, even three years back, and he couldn't refuse the money, apparently. He's in financial trouble yet again. Creditors calling, and several clients unhappy with the way their houses are standing up, or not. Which is why he's lying low in the Argentine.'

'I see.' Posie nodded. 'And the priest's hostel that Elsie

ran? The one paid for by the Archbishop of Canterbury? Fictional too?'

Fox shrugged. 'I don't know if it existed or not, Miss. But I do know it *wasn't* paid for by the Archbishop of Canterbury's office. They'd never heard of it. They were livid about it, actually.'

'Anything more on Elsie herself?'

'No. Nothing doing on the marriage certificate, or *any* certificate, come to that. But I *do* have information about Petronella. Companies House told me they'd had a request about three weeks back for all of Douglas & Stone's paperwork. One of the two Directors called for it, asking for all the files to be sent down here to the Bay Hotel. The papers arrived here yesterday. A Mr Bruce Douglas had requested it. Make sense to you?'

'Yes,' Posie confirmed. 'That's the father of Petronella Douglas. He turned up yesterday, but he'd obviously organised things well ahead of his arrival. Worried about the money, I suppose…'

Sergeant Fox raised an eyebrow. 'And talking of money, Miss,…'

But just at that moment Lovelace entered the room, together with a terrified-looking Mr Potterton, scraping his greasy lock of hair back even more than usual. Behind them in the doorway stood Smallbone, looking excited, and Dr Poots, who was filling in another orange paper form, holding it upright against the door-jamb as he ran down a list of tick-points with a sharp pencil.

A hush had come over the room, and Posie saw how Lovelace had stiffened, his face deadly serious, his arms crossed.

No. Not another death…

'I have closed the Bay Hotel to any new guests.'

There was no knuckle cracking, no smoking, no smiles. Posie gasped inwardly.

'There's been another death,' Lovelace announced simply.

The Scotland Yard men were all standing now, alert.

'It's not certain that it's a murder, but its highly likely. We'll get a charge of Manslaughter on this at the very least, lads. Poisoning. It's a drugging.'

Lovelace looked actively away from Posie, as if the sight of her hurt him, before continuing:

'The victim is a Mr Bruce Douglas. An American. He arrived at the hotel last night. He was the father of Miss Petronella Douglas, who, as we all know, is currently residing in custody in this very building, on the suspicion of another possible murder.'

Lovelace cleared his throat. 'I am working on the assumption that we already have our killer; that Petronella Douglas killed her own father. Whether by design or accident, we do not yet know.'

A whistle and an almost-congratulatory cheer went up among the men. Lovelace put his hand up, as if stopping traffic.

'Just a minute, lads. Let's not get ahead of ourselves. Dr Poots here is being kept very busy. He was just about to leave for town with Harriet Neame's body when Mr Douglas' body was discovered. He's confirmed the death was as a result of drugged sherry. He's in the process of testing the strength of the drugs used on Bruce Douglas and whether it differed from the mixtures sent to other, er, *guests*.' Lovelace here made sure not to look at Posie, or Rainbird, who was doing his best to stand ramrod-straight against a wall, but still looking pretty bad.

Lovelace addressed the room again. 'When we have Dr Poots' results in, then we will speak to Petronella Douglas. For now, no-one say anything to her about the death of her father. Understand? You should also all know that I will shortly be handing direct control of this investigation into the deaths of Elsie Moncrieff, Harriet Neame and Bruce Douglas to another Scotland Yard Chief Inspector. He will arrive very soon. I promise you that he's a very capable Detective who will ensure this all goes swimmingly.'

Posie frowned, wondering who this could be, and from the looks of consternation on the faces of the men in the room, this news came as an unwelcome surprise.

But Richard was obviously – unbeknown to his team – shelving the small matters of the three deaths in order to focus on finding his missing Inventor.

Lovelace bounded over to Posie and Fox, and drew up a chair next to them.

'What are you up to, Sergeant?'

Fox swallowed, and opened up his pad in the right place. 'I was about to share some financial information about Petronella Douglas. Miss Parker requested it yesterday.'

'Go on, lad.'

'I heard from Petronella's bank, sir and they confirmed they organised the loan.'

'How much, Constable?'

'A great big sum, sir. Almost twenty thousand pounds. Almost the total value of White Shaw, with its land, if it were to be sold on the open market.'

'I say!' Posie whistled. The sum was simply enormous.

Fox continued, frowning slightly. 'But the loan was paid back very quickly; within a month.'

'*Who* repaid the loan?' Posie was on the edge of her chair, as was Richard.

'Half a jiffy, Miss.' Fox flicked through his notepad, found the place and read out: 'The money came from an undisclosed foreign source. It was from a private bank. Abroad.'

'A bank? Abroad?' pressed Lovelace eagerly. '*Where?*'

Fox shook his head. 'I don't know. Here's the thing: Rutherford's were very cagey. Wouldn't say any more about it'

Lovelace tutted under his breath.

Posie felt a sinking certainty now that Petronella Douglas had acted in complete bad faith; had taken money in an underhand way for underhand services.

But while this information was useful, it didn't prove her treachery.

Lovelace realised this too. He groaned and tore his fingers through his hair. He threw a look of appeal at Fox.

'Jolly good work, lad. Now we need *more*. Find out the name of this foreign bank. Inform the Bank Manager at Rutherford's that you're working directly for me.' He lowered his voice to a virtual whisper. 'Tell him this is a case of National Security, if you must.'

'National…? Right you are, sir.'

Fox's eyes had widened to pools of impossible, disbelieving blue, and he scratched through his straw-blonde cropped hair in near panic.

'Now, Posie, come with me.'

Rising, Posie realised she was still holding Elsie's handbag, which she should never have picked up. There was just so much going on here, *too much*: murders, possible treason, National Security issues. As usual, her mind worked the opposite way, took shelter in small things, in detail. In her mind's eye she saw again the note from Max that tied him to Elsie, to her death. The invitation to a meeting-place.

And the receipt for the jewellery.

Elsie had been planning on leaving. So what was it that she had had repaired, or commissioned, just before she was going to leave this place?

Lovelace was striding towards the French doors, and as Posie turned to follow him, Fox called out to her: 'Oh! Miss! Sorry! Before I forget, a woman called for you. From London. Half an hour back? It came through here, on the trunk-line. She'd called the main hotel. Said you asked her to call. Yesterday?'

Posie's mind flared blankly. Who would call her here? Prudence? Dolly?

Yesterday?

She shook her head, frustrated. 'No clue. What did she sound like, Sergeant?'

'Not like one of your usual friends, Miss, if you don't mind my saying so. A working sort of a gal. Nice, polite. Wouldn't leave her name, though. Seemed nervous.' He stabbed at his notes. 'Yes: she said she'd call you again this afternoon when she finished for the day at her "current house". Whatever that is. A cleaner, Miss?'

Posie frowned. A house? What current house?

Then Posie realised. *A Fashion House!*

The woman must be one of the crew of seamstresses hired by Tony Stone to work on the sample wedding dresses all now packaged up, all waiting uselessly in the van outside. For the show on Saturday.

Probably it had been the woman who had glanced over, eyes nervous beneath her washed-out marigold-coloured cloche hat, as if she had wanted to say something which might – or might not be – important.

Posie felt her heart hammering in real excitement. *At last!* Someone willing to speak. Someone who wanted to break the silence which hung about this place. And she had been right: there *was* something to tell, wasn't there?

'Thank you, Sergeant. Make sure to get me if she calls again. Otherwise please try and get a telephone number. I promise to call the girl back.'

Posie saw that Richard was out on the white-painted balcony now, smoking, waiting for her, leaning against the railing.

She reached the French doors, but saw that a very large open basket full of bright, colourful odds and ends had been shoved in front of the doors, blocking her way. She pushed at it, but it was heavy. A very young, fresh-faced policeman was busy clearing desks and gathering up old cups of tea nearby. He seemed to be some sort of glorified lackey.

'I say! Can you help me? What's this basket doing here? I can't get through!'

The lad flushed beetroot red. 'I just moved it there

for a minute, Miss, sorry.' He started to shove it into the shadows of a corner, pushing and puffing and talking at the same time.

'There's no good place for it, Miss. It came with the bungalow, for the use of their regular guests: it's got games like boules and croquet in it, which is why it's so dashed heavy! We didn't know what to do with it. And there was quite a bit of extra rubbish hanging about in here which we didn't know what to do with this morning, either. From the last guests. There you go!' He stood up, smiling, indicating the clear doorway.

'You'll not believe the things some folks leave behind, Miss. A crying shame!'

'Oh?' Posie's hand was on the door. She grinned. 'Like what?'

'Fishing nets, maps, pairs of shoes! A funny tweed bike saddle, even: a kiddie must have lost that, it's very small. These things were out on the table. So we just tossed everything in that there basket.'

He looked worried for a second, glanced out at Richard. 'We didn't clear it with the Chief Commissioner, though. We were just told to make the room ready quickly. Apart from that the place was good to go: someone had even been here bleaching the floors for us. Stank to high heaven when we first got in this morning. We had to keep all the windows open for at least an hour.'

'I'm sure you did just the right thing. And thank you for your efforts.'

* * * *

Twenty-Seven

Out on the veranda, Posie stood next to Richard, close but not too close, as they were visible to the people in the Incident Room. It was blustery and the sea was still madly rough, white horses everywhere.

'Not much of a private beach today,' said Posie, calmly, sensing Richard's nerves, an edginess about him which was unusual. 'Good job we're not on holiday here, darling. I think we'd feel pretty short-changed.'

Richard Lovelace laughed, and took Posie's hand in his own. He looked out to sea resignedly. 'I'm going to take you somewhere fabulous for our honeymoon, sweetheart. Somewhere warm.'

Italy? Posie was about to say. *Take me to Italy. Tuscany.*

But Richard was going on, urgently now: 'A honeymoon with preferably no killers on the loose. No deaths every few minutes. No drugging. No danger at every bally turn, eh?'

He inhaled deeply. 'Although they do say it's pretty nice down here in summer. You and I have only ever been in the heart of winter, eh? Think of the swimming.'

His face clouded over suddenly. 'You know, Posie, it's the devil of a thing, but I thought I saw someone in swimming a few minutes ago. When I first came out here and lit up.'

He motioned towards the right, towards the cliff known

as Ness Point. Cigarette ash fell all over his navy-and-gold woollen coat and he didn't bother to clean it off. He jabbed again: 'Over *there*.'

Posie squinted her eyes at the grey sea, at the unforgiving crashing waves. 'But that's virtually impossible, darling. Isn't it? The sea is dangerous right now, anyone knows that. Has the Coastguard lifted their ban on boats going out?'

'No. Although I'm told they'll lift the ban by tonight. They say seven-thirty. The sea is calmer than it has been for days now, apparently, although it looks hellish to me. I reckon it would be dashed difficult to swim in this swell.'

'Well, then. You must have imagined it.'

'You're right. I'm pretty tired, love.'

He pulled her towards him and they stood together, quiet. The sky was the widest silvery-grey patchwork of clouds that Posie could remember, the sea below it also a thousand colours of grey. No sails, no liners, no people in sight.

Definitely no swimmers.

'Any progress on Jamie Boxwood?'

Lovelace shook his head wearily. None of those locked up at White Shaw had been forthcoming when asked to remember anything unusual about the party on Saturday night, although Elsie's absence had been noted, time and again.

An accident involving Mickey O'Dowd and some hot coffee had been reported to Constable Smallbone by Sidney Sherringham. It had been an awkward incident, apparently, but not unusual: Mickey was often drunk and had staggered out of the party in disgrace. He admitted as much himself.

But nothing special had been reported about Jamie Boxwood himself by all those in attendance on Saturday night. And neither Tony Stone nor Petronella Douglas had anything to add at all when it came to the man.

'I've been through all of Petronella Douglas' private

papers in that Chinese box which Mr Sherringham showed me and I admit she's been jolly careful: there's no paper trail of evidence linking her to Jamie Boxwood at all. Nor to any foreign banks. Not even to this mysterious "Mr Tell" you mentioned. Nothing! If there *was* anything, I reckon she's burnt it good and proper.'

Posie nodded. 'Seems she was pretty handy at firing up that incinerator in the backyard. Maybe it was a regular occurrence? Prudent, really.'

'Mnnn.' A scowl formed on Lovelace's face. 'I've searched White Shaw, and this wretched hotel, both within an inch of their lives, and Boxwood's definitely not here. I thought I might find him somewhere here, but no such luck. But I'm going to be thorough. Who's to say he's not hiding in one of these other buildings down here, along the beach?'

'But *why?*'

'If the people who paid Petronella a fortune want Boxwood to personally explain how these plans actually work, they probably wanted him and the plans to leave here pronto, on Saturday night. But while time was on their side, the weather conditions certainly weren't.'

'Oh!' exclaimed Posie. 'You mean the plan was for Boxwood to leave here for the Continent by boat, and this was thwarted by the Coastguard's ban? So you think Boxwood and his conspirators may still be sitting here waiting?'

'For calmer seas? Yes. And they'll get calmer seas, tonight apparently.' Lovelace checked his wristwatch. 'It's one o'clock now. Which gives me only a few hours. We need to search the whole village on the beach: those holiday lets; the Adcock Villas; that shut-up tea-room.'

'Then you'll have to tell your team here to help, surely, Richard? Sure as bread is bread you can't possibly do it all alone.'

'It's fine,' he assured Posie. 'I've requested a whole new small team from London, to be headed up by me. They are on their way down here now, with sniffer dogs. It's the Home Office Search Warrant which is holding matters up. I've spoken to the tip-top boss at MI5, Sir Vernon Kell, and he's fine with it all. The Head of Scotland Yard was fine with it too, but the Home Secretary, Joynson-Hicks, stalled. He babbled on about the buildings all being private abodes; that we were overstepping the mark. We've only *just* got his clearance, and the Home Office Warrant won't arrive for two hours. So we have to sit here twiddling our thumbs until then...'

'Well...'

There would be time.

Easily.

It was the jewellery receipt which was troubling her.

It could be something; it could be nothing, but her gut instinct told her she needed to investigate. Two hours, with Richard beside her, would easily be enough time to get to Dover and back again.

'I know I shouldn't have this with me, but still...'

She held aloft the turquoise bag and explained briefly about her meeting with Ruth Walker, her findings. Posie swallowed nervously as she brought out the slips of paper.

'There *was* other stuff in Elsie's handbag. Two things which could be useful.'

She pointed at the first, the note from Max: 'He was *there*. On that cliff.'

Richard Lovelace read the brief note, then looked out to sea again. 'You said there were two things, Posie?' he asked, tightly. 'What was the other?'

'*This.*' She presented him with the jewellery receipt from Simpkins in Dover.

'I have a feeling it's important, that it might throw some valuable new light on the case of Elsie Moncrieff and her death. You said you've got two hours, Richard? I'd love it if you came with me, but I'll go alone if you can't come along.'

She watched Richard Lovelace read the receipt, frowning, before checking his watch again. He put both notes in his inside overcoat pocket. Posie saw how the lines of his whole body had stiffened, as if he was waiting for a mortal blow to fall.

'Richard?'

Slowly he turned to her, and there was pain in his copper-flecked eyes which was almost unbearable to look at.

'I *do* know, darling,' he said, softly.

'About Max, I mean. What he meant to you. That pink necklace you never take off… I do have eyes, you know. We've never spoken of it, have we? I hoped we were out of the woods. He was a dead man. No competition. And then you came to me talking about coming down *here*, where we first met him, and I admit: I felt jealous, and nervous as hell, but I thought you might just be laying ghosts to rest. And I'm not a man who will ever stand in the way of you, or what you want to do. Ever. But I felt real unease. I just feel so dashed protective of you recently, my love: I can't explain it. That's why I…'

'Why you *what*?' Posie stared, not comprehending.

'Oh, nothing. But then we come here, and find out that not only is Max tangled up in all of this wretched business with the dead woman, but actually he's bally well alive and kicking, and…'

'And?'

Lovelace stood looking down at Posie with a resigned, haunted look about his face, a man who has known loss and feels it not only as his personal history but as some kind of expectation.

'Don't get me wrong, I'm only too happy the poor fella isn't dead. What that man has given to this country, and what he's been through, well, he deserves his happiness. He deserves a life; a choice. But what if his choice is *you*, Posie?'

'But it's all over, Richard. This is ridiculous! How can he choose me? I'm engaged to you! I love *you*!'

Posie grabbed at Richard's arm, feeling a surging panic, a wild fright rushing up through her body, as he shook his head.

Laying ghosts to rest.

How well this man knows me, she thought in astonishment as at the same time a horror dawned that she might actually be losing him. Richard Lovelace had become her rock; a reliable and trustworthy friend as much as her all-consuming love.

I love him.

She had never, in all her life, had that before. How could she, or he, be so stupid as to throw that away? Besides, she knew now that they were bound together by more than simply being in love. Their future was spun together, and others – innocent children – depended, or would depend, on them and the strength of their love to stay together.

But Richard was looking at her like he had never seen her before in all his life.

'Every which way I lose here, don't I? Look at me, standing here wearing all this ridiculous glitzy garb! And you couldn't give two hoots! Nothing I can do would ever be good enough, would it? Max is a will-o'-the-wisp; a promise of everything and nothing. Tell me! How can I compete with *him*?'

Lovelace's eyes were angry now, fire burning there in a way Posie hadn't seen before. But she had the horrible feeling that the man before her was close to crying.

She reached up to his face, not caring if anyone was looking at them from inside the bungalow.

'My darling, this isn't fair. You know I haven't sought Max out. Haven't investigated whether or not he was really dead. I just accepted it and drew a line under it. I'm happier than I've ever been, with *you*. And he hasn't contacted me at all. I promise you that.'

Lovelace stepped away. 'You're wrong, Posie.'

'How so?' She felt a sharp fright inside her. Richard was acting oddly. Had he received a message from Max during the months of their engagement and hidden it from her? Heard something from his old acquaintance Thea Elleridge and simply not passed it on?

'That strange letter, Posie. The one you received in late July. When you were about to leave for Tuscany. From Elsie Moncrieff, asking you to come down here and investigate something that was wrong. I didn't pay enough attention, did I? Maybe you didn't, either. What if it was actually a message from Max? The timing fits, doesn't it? Max went missing in mid-July, didn't he? The letter came from Elsie at the end of July. What if he came back here, in deep cover, and stayed here. What if he wanted you? Asked Elsie to write to you to come here? Told her to write in vague terms so no-one could guess?'

'Oh!' Posie gasped. Because actually, that made a sort of sense.

But before she could argue back, the French doors behind them crashed open, and Dr Poots appeared, wearing a Burberry trench-coat and homburg, carrying his doctors' case. His stance was of a man in flight. He was followed by Rainbird, looking eager but apprehensive, as if conscious he had just broken up a lover's tiff. Or something worse.

'It's the American, Lovelace,' said Dr Poots, raising an eyebrow.

'The one who's still alive, I mean. Petronella Douglas. You'd better come quickly.'

* * * *

Twenty-Eight

The young policeman on guard outside Petronella Douglas' small bedroom in the bungalow had become concerned when he'd heard a howling inside, and the sound of something heavy being thrown.

After a few minutes he'd grabbed Dr Poots as being the only relatively senior Scotland Yard man about the place, and Dr Poots had initially stepped outside into the yard behind the bungalow, where there was a window directly into the bedroom.

'She's going berserk in there,' Poots said now, matter-of-factly, as they all trooped through the Incident Room. A maid from the hotel was laying out trays of filled sandwiches on the big table, assisted by the police lackey from earlier, who was carrying through a big soup tureen. Everyone looked longingly at the sandwiches, and Posie heard her stomach growl.

'Petronella's been busy these last few minutes tearing down the curtains, and ripping at the wallpaper,' continued Dr Poots, reaching over and helping himself to a cheese-and-pickle sandwich.

'I think she threw the glass water carafe across the room, so I'm sure it smashed. I hope she's not going to hurt herself. I think we need to intervene. See what's wrong with her. Although I think I know: she's a serious drug addict, and she hasn't had her daily fix. And to compound things, she believes herself innocent. Keeps shouting out, *"I haven't killed anyone!"*

They had reached the door of the bedroom. The policeman waiting there looked relieved to see them.

'Off you go, lad. Get some lunch,' said Lovelace quickly, taking the key from him.

'I can sedate her, if you want?' murmured Dr Poots, chomping on his sandwich. He was impatient to be off, his van loaded up with two bodies.

'But I need to do it quickly. I want to get to Dover town morgue before that wretched fella Oats shows up.'

Posie swung around in disbelief. *'Oats?* Inspector Oats?' She looked incredulously at Richard Lovelace, as if he had personally betrayed her. 'You said to the men here that a very *capable* Detective would be taking control.'

'Chief Inspector Oats now,' Lovelace nodded maddeningly: 'That's right: he's going to come and run the case.'

Rainbird stifled a groan behind them, and Posie wholeheartedly agreed. Oats was a long-term thorn in her side, a man who had thwarted her career as a Private Detective at virtually every turn: a man whose disbelief that a woman could actually do such a job was only matched by his intense hatred for any kind of maverick Private Detective, regardless of their sex. He was old-school, but a man who nevertheless got results.

What was bizarre was that no love was lost between Bill Oats and Richard Lovelace. The two had been junior policemen together, starting out at the same time at Scotland Yard, but Lovelace's meteoric rise to the top of the service compared to Oats' rather more plodding route, had led to Lovelace feeling guilty – good man that he was – and trying to give his old colleague favours and leads when Oats might not otherwise have deserved them.

'Let's get this over with then,' Lovelace muttered, turning the key in the lock. 'You go first, Posie. A woman's touch and all that...We'll be right behind you.'

So Posie entered the small room first, much as you might face an angry lioness. Petronella stopped pacing and stared at them all with a look of intense hatred.

Her red lipstick and black mascara were merged together in an ugly, tear-stained mess and her white silk blouse was smeared. The small, dark bedroom was cold and uninspiring, with just a view of the back wall of the small yard, the service corridor and the bulk of the chalky White Cliffs behind them, into which all the properties of the village on the beach were set.

'Mr Inspector, you let me outta here,' Petronella hissed, with a venomous look at Lovelace. 'You tell me, on what authority are you holdin' me?'

Lovelace sighed and recited various police acts regarding arrest on suspicion of murder, to which no-one, least of all Petronella Douglas, was paying any attention.

'Gee, I sure ain't killed no-one!' she said, shaking her head. 'Least of all my own father. Much though I'd have *liked* to, often enough.'

Lovelace gave a sharp intake of breath. 'How do you know about *that*? Who told you?'

'I heard *you* tellin' everyone, Mr Inspector! Drugged, you said. You didn't have to look far for the suspect, because I was already locked up! Gee, that sure is nice! How convenient for you all!'

Lovelace coloured beetroot-red beneath his smart hat. 'But how…?'

'Call yourself a Detective? The walls are about as thin here as those over at our paper-palace! You can hear everythin'. Well: *almost* everythin'.'

Petronella and Lovelace stared at each other with a kind of mutual hatred.

Posie turned to her fiancé. 'I think it may be helpful if

you leave me with Miss Douglas. Five minutes, maximum, please.'

Lovelace swept the room anxiously with his eyes, relieved to see the water jug and glasses intact, and nothing else dangerous or broken. 'Five minutes, mind. No more. I'll be waiting outside.'

When the door closed, Posie walked to the small desk and pulled out the chair. 'May I?'

The woman in custody nodded, as if all the fight had suddenly gone out of her, and she sank down on the green velveteen coverlet of a single bed.

'Are you upset at your father's death, Miss Douglas?' she asked quietly, politely, after a little bit of calm.

'No.' Petronella had got out a travel-sized perfume vial, and was squirting it about herself. 'Not at all. He was a real bad man. The worst sort of daddy a girl without a mama can have. He was so rich he let me believe I could have the world, and when I reached out for it, he took it all away.'

Posie said nothing, tried to ignore the heavy perfume and the sick-feeling it induced, and she was rewarded by Petronella talking on, staring at the shadows of the bulk of the White Cliffs.

'He liked to think he ran my little Fashion House here, even though he hadn't ever stepped foot in the country before. I always travelled back home, to New York, if we needed to meet. He was always too busy to travel here, apparently. He knew the Fashion House meant – and means – the world to me. But something had changed recently: he'd been asking questions these last few weeks, sending telegrams; asking if all was in order. I wasn't too surprised last night when I saw him arrive, acting like the big boss. He'd threatened to visit: check the books, balance the accounts.'

'But everything was fine between you?'

Petronella harrumphed and tossed her head. 'I sure thought so. *I* went out to greet him, acting like the dutiful daughter. Then I waited for him, down in the bar, with all the others, from seven-fifteen, for at least an hour. I thought he was going to come down and have a drink with me, but he never came. Rude! Always rude! I assumed he was very tired – he had a heart condition, after all – and had fallen asleep after his long journey. After knocking back a load of drink I gave up and went home.'

Posie was digging in her bag. But then she looked up: 'Hang about, you said you were with "others" at the bar in the hotel. Who were *they*?'

Petronella sat, her legs drawn up to her chest, defensive. Her arms and hands were trembling. She scratched her patchily-painted fingernails on the wall and shrugged: 'Oh, well. No-one *that* special. I'd told Sidney at the bonfire that I was heading into the hotel bar for a drink, and he followed on over, half an hour after my father had arrived. Sidney downed several glasses of good red wine with me. He was in a bad mood, very uncharacteristic.'

Posie remembered Sidney's argument with Harriet Neame about the bag. He must have gone straight into the bar after this very argument and hence his bad mood.

'And then Mickey O'Dowd came in, too, just a few minutes later, at about quarter-to eight. He'd been helping on the beach with the fireworks. When he came over and joined us he was stone-cold sober, for once. And then of course my wonderful little husband arrived. That was getting on for eight o'clock. He said he had something to deliver up to *you*. But he had a drink with us first. We were all sitting together cosily for a while. Quite an odd little grouping, wasn't it?'

Posie was trying to make sense of all of this, but she was also pulling out a note from her carpet bag; Petronella's note to her, which had arrived with the sherry the night before.

'Is this *your* writing, Miss Douglas?' she asked firmly. 'Did *you* send me this note?'

Petronella looked over. She looked a little shamefaced.

'Sure. I genuinely wanted to make amends. It seemed a good idea at the time. I was very drunk. I sent a bottle to you, and to that policeman fella you were with, and to Daddy himself. Same sherry, different notes. The Hotel Manager said he'd take them all up.'

'Did you put the same drugs in all of them?' Posie chipped in, quietly.

'Drugs?' Petronella's small eyes opened wide. 'Say! Come hell and high water I swear I haven't been drugging anyone, Lady Detective! Cross my heart!' She swallowed. 'What drugs, anyway? Cocaine? *My* cocaine?'

'Veronal,' Posie replied. 'The sleeping drug. I'm guessing in a big dose it's fatal to anyone with a heart condition?'

Petronella shook her head. 'Say! But that makes no sense. I *do* have a few packets of Veronal, sure. But isn't that drug prescribed to pretty much everyone over here? I keep it in the bathroom at White Shaw; I even leave sachets of the stuff in our guest bedrooms for those guests staying over after the parties, in case they can't sleep. It's pretty commonplace stuff, isn't it? As for myself, I haven't taken Veronal in a good long while, although I do believe Tony tells people I take it, when I've been indulging in harder drugs.' She laughed mockingly. 'It's a slightly more respectable thing to say, huh?'

Petronella had a look of wild abandon in her eyes now, the last resort of the desperate: 'But listen: I asked for three new bottles of Bristol Cream Sherry. If they were new and sealed, how could *anyone* have got drugs into them? Least of all *me*, in my totally drunken state? I fell off my bar stool several times, I remember that...'

Posie shook her head; she didn't know. 'Did you see Mr Potterton take them up?'

'Gee, I sure can't remember. I'd say no. I can't even remember getting on home. Or who took me.'

Posie thought of the person Harriet Neame had gone to meet at ten o'clock the night before. 'Did you meet the maid, Harriet Neame, on your way home at all? By pre-arrangement, or even just in passing? Can you remember that?'

Petronella raised an eyebrow archly. '*That* little minx? The one they've been chatting about all morning: she's dead, isn't she? Murdered? What on earth would I have met *her* for? I told you, I was blind drunk. I expect Sidney tucked me into bed and left. As is his preference these days. *Leaving*. Leaving me… They're all leaving.'

Posie watched as the woman on the bed pulled the coverlet up around herself. Petronella was blue about the mouth now and trembling. A small moan started up in the deep well of her chest cavity. She clawed at her silken blouse.

'I'll get you some tea, Miss Douglas,' said Posie, worried. 'And a hot lunch. It's not warm enough in here.'

'I need more than that, Lady Detective,' muttered the Fashion Designer. 'Can't you get that fat little teddy-bear of a doctor out there to give me a fix? Anything at all?'

'I'll go and speak to him.'

Posie was standing now, uncertain and concerned, disgusted and appalled, all in equal measures.

What kind of a mother had this woman made for those adopted twin boys? What sort of a marriage had Tony Stone put up with, with this woman? How had Sidney Sherringham endured these last few months, even if he had been well paid? And how had Elsie Moncrieff managed to work for Petronella for three years?

And yet there was something terrible about the plight of this woman, too; for all that it was self-inflicted.

Turning at the door, and feeling horrid for pushing the woman when she was at her weakest, lowest point, her most vulnerable, Posie asked anyhow:

'Why did you sack Elsie Moncrieff?'

There was a silence. Posie could hear the low murmur of the conversation Lovelace was having with Dr Poots outside: a muttering about test results, bodies, crime figures.

Then a familiar voice outside broke in, loud and grating, terrible on the ear.

'Hello, hello. What 'ave we here then, lads?'

Lovelace sounding falsely jolly: 'What-ho, Oats!'

'Chief Commissioner Lovelace, I'm reporting for duty to take over this 'ere Incident Room. Anyone goin' to enlighten me on what's been 'appenin? Looks like a bally mare's nest to me.'

'Dashed decent of you to come like this, Bill. I'm appointing Sergeant Rainbird here as your second-in-command. He'll get you up to speed. Bally odd state of affairs, I'm afraid. Nice chance of publicity though. A lot of very famous people involved.'

A harrumph.

'Anyway, I'm off.' Lovelace sounded happy to get away. 'I'll be back within two hours. I'll drive myself, for once. Something urgent has cropped up in a jewellery shop in Dover. Maybe related. I'm taking Miss Parker with me, Oats.'

'*Miss Parker*, Chief?' A cough and an incredulous-sounding swallow of disbelief. 'Er, I didn't know *she* was going to be down here, sir.'

'Oh yes. *She* is. Very much so.'

Posie looked at Petronella curled up on the bed, and she thought she was asleep. So much for asking for the drugs. Or getting her a hot lunch.

But as she placed her hand on the door handle, the American whispered, and Posie struggled to hear: 'Say, Lady Detective. Help me, I don't wanna swing for these deaths. I ain't killed no-one. I promise. Least of all Elsie. She was a good girl.'

'So what did she do then? That angered you so much?'

The woman looked up, and her gaze was crystal clear. 'She stole my dreams from me, Miss Parker. She took them right away.'

* * * *

Twenty-Nine

They travelled in silence almost the whole way to Dover.

Lovelace concentrated on driving the police car, something he did precious little of these days, and Posie focused entirely on eating the sandwiches she had taken from the Incident Room. They were pretty good, as it happened: cheese and pickle, salmon paste, strawberry jam. She was so hungry she almost didn't care what was in them.

Lovelace eyed the sandwiches hungrily out of the corner of his eye but Posie didn't offer any of her own, keeping his separately in a greaseproof-paper-wrapped parcel for when he'd stopped tearing around the sharp corners of the steep roads up to the top of the cliffs.

Max, and their argument – if that was what it had been – from earlier, was not mentioned once.

Ahead of them was a shiny black police van, sealed in on all sides, carrying the baize-covered bodies of Harriet Neame and Bruce Douglas on morgue stretchers, with Dr Poots riding passenger in the front seat. The awful finality of what the van contained seemed to serve as a very constant reminder of the dreadfulness of the case that Posie and Lovelace were both now involved in.

Parting from the van at Dover Police Station, they

drove along the High Street and ended up at the sea-front, on Townwall Street, with the sea and the pebbled beach at their left and a row of tall Regency white townhouses to their right, most of which seemed to be mid-range hotels. Posie, with Lovelace's street map of Dover on her lap, urged him onwards.

'You know something,' said Posie suddenly, with real intrigue in her voice. 'We're heading for 47, Snargate Street, for this jewellery shop. But it's in a dashed odd place for a jewellery shop, isn't it?'

She jabbed at the street on the map in an accusatory manner. 'Right by the Western Docks? Crummy sort of place. Not the centre of town as you'd imagine, with all the shops and customers. Snargate Street. Funny name…but you know, I think I've heard it before.'

Then she grabbed up her notepad, flicking through it urgently.

'Yes: as I thought. Number 35 Snargate Street was the address Elsie Moncrieff had given, or *faked*, I should say, in her references. The supposed boarding-house for clergy who were travelling to or from the Continent. Another lie I suppose. I expect we'll find that number 35 doesn't even exist.'

'Maybe,' said Lovelace softly. 'But maybe not. Keep an open mind, Posie. You know what we both think about coincidences.'

He drove past the new town Pier on the left, the smart harbour for yachts and sailing boats, coloured flags fluttering gaily, then on past the grey huddle of buildings which formed the huge station which was the Western Docks, where the boat train and the Blue Train left for Paris and the Continent every day.

Ahead of them the town was ending, the 'smart' white-painted stucco townhouses all now behind them, another harbour opening up, but this one shabbier and obviously for fishermen and locals. Men were standing around in waders and thick dirty oilcloths, arms crossed, looking mutinous. As long as the Coastguard said that boats were not allowed out, these fishermen had nothing to do, and all the while with hungry mouths to feed at home.

Beyond the harbour the road led away all the way to Folkestone.

'*There!*' Posie said, pointing over sharply to the right. 'Snargate Street!'

And hard against the fisherman's harbour was a straggling line of mis-matched Victorian houses, most with shops on the ground floor, every house painted a different pastel colour. Bright lights like beacons shone out from some of the windows through the November gloom.

Lovelace drove up, and parked as inconspicuously as he could. He sat wordlessly, looking all about him, silently taking the packet of sandwiches Posie passed him and eating quickly, ravenously.

'That's better,' he said, still staring out, brushing off crumbs from his hands. He looked over at Posie and the merest glimmer of a grin flashed over his face.

'You know, love, if Elsie Moncrieff *had* wanted to be based in a place where they could monitor the comings-and-goings of certain people, or groups, this would have been a perfect spot. No: I'd go one better – *the* perfect spot. We've got an almost perfect view of the Western Docks from here, and this little fisherman's harbour, as well as the smart new harbour. I bet you could get a sense of many things going on here – day and night – if you looked hard enough. And we know Elsie and her two pals were good at looking, don't we?'

He was getting more and more excited. 'And if you've got a nice little pretend boarding-house – for priests, wasn't it? – as your cover, well, you can get away with just about anything.'

He laughed. 'I say! I expect this was Thea Elleridge's brainchild, too. She's clever, I'll give her that. I must ask her about this. Have you heard of a funk hole, Posie?'

Posie shook her head.

'It's a place for people to stay in safety,' he explained. 'Usually rich people, in times of war or plague, to hide away. But spies have funk holes, too. Places of safety, where they won't be detected.'

He snapped the door open. 'Number 35, you said?'

They walked along the pavement which was clean apart from a few greasy chip packets blowing about. A fish-and-chip shop loomed on the left, and Posie looked in longingly. It was now one forty-five and the man and woman behind the counter were about to turn off the fat fryer. She could go in…

But Richard was almost marching away in his excitement.

'Here it is! Number 35!'

A cream-painted townhouse was part of the straggle of buildings. It was the sort of place you would walk right past without a second glance. Except that this house, with its faded net curtains in the windows, had a large 'TO LET – HOUSE AS A WHOLE' sign in its bottom front window.

'Look!' Posie hissed. She pointed at the dark-blue shiny door, which was standing ajar. 'Shall we?'

At Lovelace's look of bemusement Posie laughed: 'Haven't you always wanted to run a seedy little guest-house in a port on the coast of England, Richard? Only take your hat and coat off first. Both are much too shiny and full of police symbols. You're almost putting *me* off, let alone anyone we might meet!'

Duly instructed, Lovelace followed Posie inside, coat slung over his arm, hat hidden beneath. Bare, but nicely varnished floorboards creaked beneath their feet. Too late, Posie smelt bleach and the tang of fresh disinfectant.

A woman's head popped around the corner of the very end of the hallway, and she stepped out, revealing herself to be middle-aged, distrustful-looking, with rollers in her grey sparse hair. She was holding a mop in her hand and wielding it like a weapon.

'Can I 'elp you?' she asked suspiciously.

'We saw the sign, "TO LET"?' started Posie, hopefully, but the woman shook her head.

'Can't help you, love. I'm jus' cleanin' the place. I live next door, see? Have done for years. But I do know that the lazy house-agent should take the sign down. You're out of luck, I'm afraid. This place has already been snapped up, by a mother and daughter who want to try their luck as boarding-house keepers. Little goldmine this place is! Good luck to them, I say!'

Posie frowned. This woman had lived here for years, hadn't she? Wasn't it worth Posie *asking*, risking looking foolish? What had she to lose?

She changed tack: 'Well, you know, Mrs…'

The cleaning lady twisted her mouth unattractively. '*Miss* Brown,' she said reluctantly. 'Sally Brown.'

'Well, Miss Brown, I had a good friend who worked here…' Posie tried to remember the dates Elsie had forged in her references. Likely as not fake too, but it was worth a chance, wasn't it?

'She worked here from sometime in 1917. She told me she ran the place as the Housekeeper. Only, I was away in the Great War myself, driving ambulances, and then we lost touch. We happened to be passing, and I wondered if she still worked here? Her name was Elsie.'

At the mention of this name the woman's previously suspicious face split into a beaming countenance. 'Ah, *Elsie*! Why didn't you say so, pet? Ah, but you've missed her by a long mark. More than three years.'

Miss Brown explained that she'd helped to clean the hostel every week. It had often been packed to the rafters with priests.

'Elsie ran this place beautifully. Never any funny business, never any noise or complaints. I suppose you'd expect that with priests, wouldn't you? She was here from the end of 1917 – I remember because it was the same time my only nephew was killed on the Western Front – until about 1921, say. With her husband, of course.'

Both Posie and Lovelace almost drew in their breaths, but managed to smile as if this wasn't gobsmacking news to them.

'Aye. Jack Moncrieff. He worked hard. Kept the place ship-shape, and he seemed to enjoy it, being so near the Pier. He loved fishing, see? Was out all the hours God sends. Day and night. I'd see him with his bike and his fishing rods and his little red bleeping lights. Sometimes he'd take a priest with him. For the experience, I suppose.'

Lovelace and Posie tried their hardest not to exchange looks. Lovelace was looking all about him with interest.

An MI5-funded funk hole. How clever.

Posie smiled. 'What was he like? This Jack Moncrieff? Only, *I* never met him. We were at school, you see, Elsie and me. I lost touch before this marriage.'

'Oh, well. He was lovely. Blonde and wore gold spectacles; he had very bad eyesight, you know? Mebbe that's why he wasn't away fighting in the Great War. He was very posh, but he never made you feel less than worthy. Must have come from a dead good home: I wondered sometimes what his family would think of him if they saw him working in a boarding-house for priests, but it takes all sorts, doesn't it?'

The woman sighed dramatically.

Posie tried not to snap in excitement. The description almost matched perfectly to the man Mr Potterton had seen sitting in Elsie's hotel room with her, more than three years before, in the autumn of 1921, looking at photographs of Petronella Douglas and her clients.

And this man had been called Jack.

'Jack. He must have been *the Jackal?*' she whispered very low, but loud enough for her fiancé to hear.

'Mnnn.'

To the Fire from the Jackal.

Posie had assumed so far that the wedding band was fake. But this eagle-eyed charlady seemed to think the two had actually been married.

'Were they happy here, Miss Brown?'

Posie heard Lovelace give an impatient sigh behind her, but she held her ground. Something in the woman's tone had given her a clue that tragedy had loomed large in the history of this place.

'They *were* happy, Miss. In the beginning. But I reckon things went sour quite quickly. Elsie was expecting a baby when they first arrived here, you know?'

'Oh?'

What? How did that fit in?

The woman nodded, revelling in her part in the telling of the sad tale.

'Yes, I was even busy knitting pram blankets and the like, but Elsie lost it, quite late. Born dead. She must have been near the end of her term; she was that huge she could barely walk. And she came back here after bein' in hospital lookin' like the saddest little soul you've ever met. Fair threw herself into her work. And he – Jack – he didn't handle it very well either. Started drinkin' heavily, along the way here, at the pub. It got worse and worse. They had a friend...'

Lovelace suddenly gave Posie his hand. Squeezed it tight. They both waited. Here was – or was not – the squaring of the circle.

'His name was Father Moriarty. Funny name, isn't it? He was a foreigner, mebbe even German, but he had a parish about the place. He came and took services here now and again – they'd converted the cellar into a chapel downstairs – but more often than not you'd see him walking with Jack late at night. Or even dragging Jack out of the pub. That priest tried to help. I think Elsie was finding it tough, watching the man she loved turn into a drunkard.'

Max.

The woman carried on, swirling her mop on the floor now in a vague pretence of doing some work. 'Funny fellas, these priests. This Father Moriarty, well, he was very easy on the eye, if you don't mind my saying so. What a waste of a good fella!' The woman coloured quickly, changing the subject. Posie, whose hand was still in Lovelace's, breathed slowly, not daring to turn to him.

'And what a waste of a good man, too. Jack Moncrieff. A tragedy.'

'What tragedy?'

'He died. Drowned. Jack fell in the harbour here one night. Must have been drunk as a one-eyed newt, and he was dragged out the next morning. Elsie was beside herself. She was sedated and carried off and I never saw her again. The place closed down just days later. Friends of Elsie's came in the night and cleared the place out. I never saw a thing.'

'When was this, Miss?' asked Lovelace, frowning.

'It were the end of summer, 1921.'

Had the whole thing been staged? Closed for efficiency as one Operation stopped and another started, along the coast at St Margaret's Bay?

But had Jack really died?

Lovelace appeared to be wondering the same thing. He coughed delicately: 'Forgive my impertinence, Miss Brown, but I wonder if you actually saw the body of Mr Moncrieff? When it was got out of the harbour?'

The woman nodded. 'Oh, yes. There was a big crowd of us around the dock as he was pulled out, all tangled up in fishing nets. That poor big fella, no shoes on. Shame. You couldn't have faked *that*. Is that what you're getting at, sir?'

The woman looked at Posie and Lovelace now with something more than a keen interest.

'*Who* did you say you were, again?' she asked suddenly, her manner cooling rapidly.

'We didn't,' said Lovelace, making a show of putting on his hat, and then his coat, buttoning it up slowly. The dim passage light caught all of the embroidered gold and set it a-twinkle.

He fished in his pocket, brought out a half-crown and a shilling.

'That's for you, Miss Brown, for your help and assistance today.'

Out on the street, Posie was thinking of Elsie.

The sadness in her life.

A lost baby behind her, and a dead, alcoholic husband. A brother who had tried to help but had not, ultimately, succeeded. Elsie had had such a dreadful run of luck.

But just then a voice came calling out behind them:

'I say, Miss! You ought to get your story straight next time. You're a rum one and no mistake, for all your fancy ways and big blue doll's eyes! You just said you went to school with Elsie! Only she told me she was Danish, or Finnish, or something Scandinavian. And you sound about as English as the blessed Princess Mary! So what's it to be, hey?'

And on that triumphant note, the charwoman disappeared.

* * * *

Thirty

Simpkins Jewellers was an odd sort of a place.

Lovelace raised his eyebrows at Posie in complete disbelief as they came to a halt outside its greasy, smeary window, the gold flakes of the big gothic lettering on the glass peeling off. A lattice-work of bars criss-crossed the windows, showing nothing more promising than the occasional pair of cheap-looking cufflinks scattered about for a pathetic display.

A dim yellow light shone out from the back of the shop and there was movement within. A grubby handwritten 'OPEN' sign hung on the meshed grille of the glass door.

'Good grief!' muttered Lovelace, lighting a cigarette and taking a deep drag.

'What a bally depressing place! Surely only the down-at-heel come here? Not a girl like Elsie Moncrieff, who was paid well and whose tastes seem to have run to expensive things.'

Posie shrugged petulantly: 'Well, maybe all we're looking at here is a cheap repair of something, from a craftsman that Elsie obviously knew and trusted? Maybe this will turn out to be unimportant for us, but maybe it won't?'

Richard Lovelace checked his watch nervously, anxious

now to return and see if his Home Office Warrant had arrived. 'Let's get this over with then, shall we, darling? Especially if it *is* just a little repair job.'

But it was not.

The tiny, delicate man who had been beavering away at the back of the shop emerged as soon as the shop bell rang. He scampered into action like a small clockwork dormouse. He looked like a kindly, eccentric pixie, his leather apron awry, his shirtsleeves rolled well back. He was in his very late fifties or early sixties, the sort of man you'd overlook, even in his own shop.

'Jeremy Simpkins, at your service. How can I help?'

His jewellers' glasses, perched up on his almost-bald head gave him a faintly comical air, but his look of benevolent welcome disappeared instantly when Lovelace, already an imposing figure, flashed his identity card. Simpkins' small blue eyes grew steely and watchful: 'Oh, I say! Scotland Yard. To what do I owe the pleasure? Is anything the matter?'

And Posie passed over Elsie's receipt.

Mr Simpkins took it in his finely-boned fingers, and read it.

'You'd better come with me,' he said quietly, sombrely, first going up to the grille and turning the sign there to 'CLOSED'.

Offering them seats at the back of the tiny shop, as if they were real customers, he first went behind the protective-glass screen of his workplace, past the workbench where all the tools of his trade were laid out, together with small boxes of precious stones. A small fire burned in a grate in the back wall.

He then disappeared under a baize-curtained open-doorway, and Posie saw, in his absence, that he was working on an intricate diamond-encrusted necklace of a type much more likely to be found in a window of Bond Street than here, on Snargate Street in Dover.

She squeezed Lovelace's arm, and indicated towards the necklace, raising an eyebrow. She noted how Richard had suddenly become more animated, had stopped checking his watch every few seconds. He was looking about with a keen interest.

Simpkins returned a minute later with a large tea-pot of Earl Grey, two cups and saucers and a plate of shortbread biscuits. He poured the tea silently for his guests, which they accepted gratefully. And then Simpkins started looking through a metal cabinet which he had unlocked, his back turned to them, leafing through paper envelopes.

'Here we are,' he said at last, quietly. He came and sat down on a small wooden stool, fingered the envelope uneasily. 'She's dead, isn't she? Elsie. I saw it in the newspaper.'

Posie nodded. 'That's right. Funny old business, her death. I'm a Private Detective. I got Scotland Yard involved when it seemed that Elsie's life *and* death were not altogether straightforward.'

'I see.'

Lovelace sat still, kept looking directly at Jeremy Simpkins. Then he spoke very low: 'I was in touch with Sir Vernon Kell of MI5 this morning, Simpkins. I may not know exactly what you're up to here but I can spy a funk hole when I see it. Two in a row, eh? Novel. And I know about the three agents. But don't worry. I won't mention this to anyone. And you can rely on Posie here to be similarly discreet.'

Simpkins stared at both of them calmly for a few seconds, then nodded. 'That's a relief, then. That you *know*.' It was as if the small man's whole bearing had changed, and a purposeful energy seemed to pulse through him.

'Was this place established at the same time as that priests' boarding-house?' asked Lovelace.

'Roughly.' Simpkins nodded.

Posie swallowed, annoyed at having to keep up. So this

place was an MI5 hideout too? A lucky guess of Richard's? *Very* lucky.

Simpkins played with the small envelope.

'But that's all in the past: I don't work for *them* anymore. Not these last three years. I'm a real jeweller; a Master Jeweller really. A man alone. I'd got myself into a bit of trouble with the creditors in Hatton Garden a few years back; the start of 1918 it was. Next thing I knew I was being asked if I wanted to set up shop here, in this unprepossessing little shabby place, but continuing to work as a Master Craftsman: they promised that the best of the best work would be sent to me, down from Bond Street and Sloane Square, and I'd be paid well, like before.'

He grinned. 'It's worked a treat. Here I am, six years later. Got a three-bedroomed flat above here and it's normally only ever me here. I've always been a solitary type, a loner. I'm known for my expertise and these days the big jewellery names seek *me* out.'

'So what did you do for *them*, then?' asked Posie, genuinely puzzled.

'Oh, well. Not much, as it turned out. Provide a *safer* safe house when the one up the road failed. I knew who I should call if the priests' boarding-house was ever compromised. If ever anything happened to Elsie, or Jack. Or Max…'

Max. This man had known Max! Posie hardly dared breathe.

'Did you know Elsie and Jack well?' she offered instead, hoping for a seam of riches. But the man shook his head.

'I never knew them. As I said, I'm a loner. But I knew *of* them. We looked out for each other, as much as was possible. We weren't supposed to look like the best of friends, after all. But they were a nice pair. I made their wedding rings. They pretended they were married from the start but in actual fact they fell in love on the job, and got married up in London on a quick weekend away.'

The shop owner sighed. 'I'll always remember those rings. I questioned my instructions: I had to melt down this great big medieval ring with a fancy crest on it. Well, I'd never seen purer Welsh gold in all my life, the sort only real royalty or aristocracy would have access to back then, and I asked them if they were sure? It was Jack's ring, and he said it belonged to a past which was well and truly gone. He was quite blunt when he wanted to be.'

The jeweller frowned.

'It all unravelled in the summer of 1921 though, with Jack dying, and Elsie moving on. I thought I'd be pulled out of here, but no: I was told I could take over the rent – which is a song, anyhow – and continue if I liked. On my own terms. Which I do. And that's that, really.'

Only it wasn't as simple as that, Posie knew. As did this canny little man sitting opposite her.

'Elsie stayed in touch, though, obviously?' Posie indicated to the envelope in the man's hands. 'Did you see her often after she left here?'

'I saw her very occasionally, only once or twice over the last three years. She'd changed: started dying her hair this bright blonde, and wearing very fashionable clothes. The Elsie I knew had long red hair and a black buttoned-up dress on all year around.'

'Times changed, perhaps?' Lovelace smiled.

'Perhaps. But she had definitely reinvented herself. She said she was still living locally but I didn't ask more. Didn't ask if she had remarried, or if she was still working for *them*. She would drink a cup of tea with me, like you're sitting here with me now. We never had long. She'd bring me small jobs, odd jobs.'

'Odd jobs?' cut in Lovelace. 'Or *odd* jobs?'

'Yes. The latter. Strange jobs. One time she brought me Jack's wedding ring, asked me to melt it down again and make her a necklace out of it. But it couldn't look fancy: oh no! The cheaper it looked the better. She wanted it to look like she'd picked it up in Woolworths on Biggin Street or something. Very odd. Like I said.'

Posie didn't see too much odd about this instruction. If Elsie had truly loved her dead husband, didn't it make sense for her to remember him by wearing his precious wedding band, made into something eminently more wearable? And posing as a Housekeeper would have meant she couldn't have worn anything ostentatious. Better a Woolworths necklace than a Bond Street one, regardless how old and pure the gold it was made from.

But quite suddenly everything was spinning in the small shop.

Everything was rushing up at Posie.

'Jeepers! Oh, I say!'

The hot, tight, narrow little shop suddenly felt horribly claustrophobic; the fire too close, the artificial light too bright, the questions and answers too much.

She needed air. Great gulps of fresh, pure air.

'Darling?' whispered Lovelace, eyebrows knitted together. 'Are you feeling all right?'

'I'm fine.'

She stood quickly and walked to the window, to the grille, as if she could get that precious air there. It was ridiculous, she knew: the door and windows were closed, locked. There was no air at all.

But standing there, watching the seagulls wheeling around the fishermen's boats outside in the wintery light, she gulped and felt better. She could see a white-painted Victorian pub right opposite them which until now she had taken no notice of.

Lovelace was still sitting, worried, but anxious to preserve a professional front. Mr Simpkins shook his head sadly:

'You remind me of her, Miss, of Elsie. Standing there. You know he drunk himself to death, don't you? Jack Moncrieff? It started slowly, as these things do. But then it became regular: every night, early doors.'

Simpkins pointed towards the pub. 'The Two Kennels isn't a very nice pub; it's really for sailors. But it was close and convenient for Jack. Too close. What a waste! I think Elsie blamed herself somehow. She stood at that grille only a couple of weeks ago and looked out at that pub again, immensely sad.'

Jack. The doomed, dead husband.

The Jackal, who had died in the summer of 1921.

The same man Mr Potterton had seen in the autumn of 1921, plotting the Operation at White Shaw. A dead man.

There was no point chasing for death certificates: Posie knew enough by now to realise that a death certificate would exist even if there had been no death.

Just as a marriage certificate could have been completely eradicated from history, even when there had been a marriage.

This was the reality with which she was dealing.

Posie stared back at Simpkins, over her shoulder. For a couple of seconds he stared back; matched her gaze.

And then he looked away, as if caught off guard. This man was too protective of himself and his nice little position here to tell her the truth. She couldn't simply ask him: '*Is Jack still alive?*'

Because even if he *did* know the truth, he wouldn't give it to her.

'Let's see what Miss Moncrieff gave you, then,' ordered Lovelace. 'What was odd about this order?'

Posie circled back, still standing as the jeweller undid the closed, sealed brown envelope, revealing a red velvet pouch within.

'Elsie told me she was leaving. For good. Told me *this* was the week. She'd be in to pick it up.' Simpkins shook the article out and held it in the palm of his hand. Posie moved closer. It was a ring. Gold. Small.

'This is the third time now that I've melted down the same piece of gold. The necklace was one thing, but this is quite another. Horrible, really! I don't know how she thought she could wear such a thing! I nearly refused. This is the kind of thing my grandfather – God rest his soul – worked on as his bread and butter. But they were morbid people, those early Victorians.'

Lovelace was looking perplexed. 'What kind of a ring is it, exactly? Did she ask you to use those stones? Pearls, are they? Or dull opals? Not much to impress you, is it?'

And Posie leant in, saw the ring with its double stone setting, set together in a fancy scroll of carved gold leaves and flowers.

'Oh! It *is* horrible!' she cried, realisation dawning, as the jeweller confirmed the choice of stone.

'You'd better take it,' he said to her. '*I* don't want it here. It gives me the creeps.'

But it made perfect sense.

The jewellery shop was spinning again, and Posie centred herself, staring out again at the pub.

'We must go, Richard,' said Posie hurriedly. 'But stop at the Western Docks first, please. I need to use the telephone-booth there. I'm going to add to poor Fox's workload. There's a couple of last things I need him to do for me.'

Everything – well, no, *almost* everything – was starting to come together.

* * * *

Thirty-One

They'd arrived back just as a whole cavalcade of motors had shimmied down the steep path to the bay, parking up outside White Shaw in a big flashy show.

'What the deuce? Dash it all! I said I needed a small, *inconspicuous* team!'

Lovelace was having a last cigarette before going on official duty again and he watched in disbelief – his cigarette almost forgotten – from inside their motor as about twenty Metropolitan policemen, all in their smart black frock-coats and hard hats, some with sniffer dogs, were beginning to assemble in neat rows on the tarmac.

Even the brand-new Home Secretary had come, William Joynson-Hicks. All the way from London in one of the police cars, new in his job and only a couple of days into office.

He looked desperate to prove himself; darting about in a ridiculously formal black sateen frock-coat and black top hat, as if he were going out to dinner. The Home Office Search Warrant was probably contained in the smart black leather folder held under his arm like a badge of honour.

'Dash and blast,' Lovelace had whispered at Posie under his breath, grinding out his cigarette angrily on the metal floor of his foot-well, 'I didn't realise *he* would come personally.'

He indicated towards the Home Secretary.

'"Jix", they're calling him. And he's worried as hell. For Lord Jamie Boxwood and these plans to have gone missing on his watch is hardly good news, is it?'

'What's the Home Secretary like?' ventured Posie, genuinely interested.

'They say he's a force to be reckoned with. Hates Communists more than Fascists, apparently. And wants to ban all drugs and drink and nightclubs in London. He wants to bring in a sort of Prohibition.'

'He'll be popular.'

Posie watched this new Home Secretary with interest. If Richard was correct, 'Jix' was going to be up against all of London's Bright Young Things. She watched as the very good-looking, tall, fair man got blown about in the wind off the Channel, holding onto his wildly-unsuitable hat. The three o'clock November light contained no promise of warmth or sun. What Jix needed was a big, warm coat. The man looked fiendishly cold.

And then, a couple of minutes later, a beautiful dark-red Lagonda pulled up.

Lovelace groaned in disbelief. 'Oh no! Sir Vernon Kell, Head of MI5. This is all I need.'

The diminutive Sir Vernon darted out of the motor in a swirling tweed trench-coat. He headed straight for the Home Secretary. Then the two men, both in their early fifties, one tall, the other very short, stood huddled together, a powerhouse of energy and influence.

Lovelace was quietly angry: 'How can we run a discreet search for two hours – which is all we've been allowed – with all these London bobbies? And if nothing is found here, my job will be on the line.'

He put his hand on the door handle and got out, and Posie followed. Immediately he was seen by Jix and Sir Vernon. Lovelace straightened his hat, brushed down his coat, checked his insignia, gritted his teeth.

'Promise me you'll go and sit with Sergeant Fox, darling? Or go somewhere safe? This will all be over by five o'clock.'

'I'll go to my room,' Posie said. 'Come and find me there. And good luck, Richard. Don't forget to search Maypole Manor, will you? That big old empty house would be the perfect spot to hide in; there are "demolition" signs everywhere and it all looks very unsafe and creepy.'

'Mnnn. Hide in, or hide a *body* in, you mean. I don't know if we're looking for Jamie Boxwood alive or dead at present.'

Richard coughed awkwardly: 'And Posie, about earlier? My going on about Max. I'm sorry. It was a stupid schoolboy attack of jealousy. I don't know what came over me. Can you forgive me? Say you will?'

'Of course. There's nothing to be jealous about, darling. And from my side, nothing to forgive.'

* * * *

Back in her lovely room, which was warm and cosy, the fire well banked up, Posie checked there was nothing for her by way of messages, then she laid out her bag and all the bits and pieces to do with the case so far on the table.

She locked the door, and then lay down, fully clothed, on the bed. Posie was still wearing her woollen coat and hat.

She'd only closed her eyes for a second. Hadn't intended to fall sound asleep at all. But she must have nodded off.

Suddenly Posie awoke with a start.

At first she thought she could hear water.

Had she left the bath taps running? She sat up hurriedly, aghast.

The room was still cheerful, brightly lit, but the sky was dark outside now. It must be about four o'clock, or four-thirty.

A curtain moved over by the French doors and Posie realised the door onto the balcony had come unfixed and it was blowing backwards and forwards in the wind from the beach, creaking slightly. You could hear the waves crashing. So *that* was the sound of water she had heard.

In the distance she thought she heard a police tin-whistle; a dog barking; a man shouting, his voice almost lost on the wind in the screeching of a seagull. A cold draft came in.

Posie went to the French doors, about to close them, when she saw someone was standing out on the balcony, watching the proceedings outside.

She recognised the silhouette at once, although he was wearing clothes she'd never seen before, and a hat. She gasped, and her heart thudded uncomfortably hard against her rib-cage.

'*Max?*'

He turned to her and she couldn't see his face in the darkness. But she heard the smile in his voice as he spoke in his soft German accent. A voice she had once longed and longed for:

'*Ach!* Posie! *Mein Gott!* It's been so long. I saw you were sleeping. I sat by your bed for a while. But I'd just decided to leave. I left you a message, actually.'

'Come in, won't you?'

'Only if you turn down the light, please? My head aches.'

She pulled back the curtain firmly, trying not to tremble. Then she stepped back into the room, turned down the electric lamps and watched as he came through.

And she almost gasped again.

Max, always startlingly handsome with his icy blue eyes, deeply-tanned face and his white-blonde cropped hair, looked like he had been through the mill. He'd always had a tendency towards looking tired, but now he looked haggard. Much, *much* older than his real age, which was only about forty, or in his early forties. He had deep grey shadows under his lovely eyes. He was wearing a black sou'wester hat and matching raincoat over a casual linen striped shirt and normal flannel trousers. Black leather shoes.

Posie was unconsciously pulling at the pink Murano glass beads around her neck, a present from Max when they had been in Venice. Cheap, but lovely. The string was stretched to capacity.

'You don't look so good, Max. Are you sick?'

'No. Just tired. I've come a long way to speak to you.' He smiled and put his head on one side, and there was a beautiful luminosity about him which marks only a very, very breathtakingly beautiful man, however tired or ill they are.

'But *you*, Posie Parker: you look quite wonderful. *Ja!* Like a flower in bloom. Better than ever.' He indicated towards one of the green silk-covered chairs by the table. 'Do you mind if I sit?'

'Of course!' Posie pulled it out for him and he sank down into it gratefully. She sat gingerly on the edge of her bed, frowning. 'Don't you want to take your hat off?'

'Best not. Going soon.'

'Shall I call for tea?' She smiled nervously. 'Or something stronger?'

'I don't have much time.'

Looking closer, she thought she saw droplets of water on Max's face. He was shivering slightly. Did he have a fever? This flu which was doing the rounds?

Then she saw that he was wet everywhere. Sopping, actually. His hair, his face, his coat, his shirt. His shoes were leaking water. The silk covering of the green chair beneath him and the back of the chair was already saturated, the colour darkening.

'What's happened, Max?' Posie said urgently. 'Did you fall in the sea?'

He laughed. 'No. I've been in swimming.'

She was about to protest, to ask more questions, when she remembered Lovelace saying he had seen someone swimming in the sea earlier. But that would simply be madness, wouldn't it?

'I thought you were *dead*,' she whispered, folding her arms defensively.

'Almost,' he said simply. He had started to play with the things Posie had laid out on the table, and he had in his hands now the ring Posie had brought back from Simpkins. He held the receipt too, and water dripped on everything.

'I had to lie low, Posie. There were people I didn't trust who found it better, more convenient, that I was dead. So, I let them think that I was.'

'But you never contacted me.' Posie was aware, even to her own ears, that her voice was small, quarrelsome, niggly like a child's. But she had to be careful. She didn't want to push for something she didn't want.

She didn't want Max to think she was about to leave her whole life as it currently stood and run away with him. Because this man, this danger he represented, this vulnerability, was *not* what she wanted.

'*Ach*, Posie. I was *going* to contact you. I adored you. And then, just a couple of months after I had "disappeared", I saw an announcement in *The Times*. About you and that Police Inspector.'

He studied Posie's face, but she stared right back, not ashamed. Resolute in the decision she had made.

Max smiled, but there was a deep sadness there. 'I'm very happy for you, Posie. You deserve so much happiness. I hope your nice policeman knows how lucky he is: he's got what he always wanted, *ja*?'

There was a dreadful pause, as Posie realised to her own horror that hot stinging tears were coursing down her face.

'Don't cry, *mein Schatz*. My sweetheart.' Max shook his head sadly. 'What kind of life could *I* have offered you? Hiding here, hiding there. It's not a way to live; not a way to bring up children, is it? And life is short, and life is for the living, after all.'

He had picked up the old studio photograph of the small, blonde pig-tailed girl. 'I didn't even contact my own sister.' He tapped the picture, but carefully, anxious not to get water on it.

'She was my *twin* sister, you know. We were born on the same day, same hour. We...well, never mind...'

He looked up at Posie, his bright eyes meeting her own. 'You were right about so much, Posie. This is my naughty, wonderful, red-headed twin sister. Elise.'

'*Elise?*' Posie wiped the last of her tears away, determined to hear this out.

'*Ja!* Sounds very German, doesn't it?'

Max laughed. '"Elsie" was better here, we thought. She was a golden girl. She could do everything: languages, mimicking people, singing, making things. She could do anything in the world she set her mind to: once, at school, she wrote and directed a completely new opera. All by herself! Designed and made all the costumes too. She was twelve. A fire-cracker, we called her at home, both for her temperament and her red-hair. A little *brand*. A *fire*, or a flame. It became her call-sign here, working like me, as a spy.'

'But you told me that when the British government took you out of the Great War, basically at gun-point, on pain of death, that you had no ties. That you left no-one important behind?'

The French doors swung open again, but they both ignored the noise. There was shouting on the beach, the noise of a car engine starting up. Flashes of light in the darkness.

Max sighed regretfully, shrugged. 'I told you many things, Posie. My life is all about deep cover.'

'How did Elsie get here?'

'She was always with me, or just a beat behind me. We had this connection. Maybe because we were twins? When I went to Medical School in Berlin, Elise studied nursing there; she was always nearby. Then she followed me out to the field-hospitals of the Great War. Always just one dressing-station or field-hospital behind me.' He paused. Drew a breath, like he was finding it harder and harder to speak.

'Elise found out what had happened to me, when I disappeared from the German Army field-hospital. I still don't know how she did it. She got herself over to England within days, passing herself off as a Belgian nurse on a frigate, needing safe passage.'

Max explained how Elise had presented herself at Whitehall, demanded to be re-united with her twin brother. Threatened to shoot herself if she wasn't employed in a manner similar to him.

'So they took her on. And she became one of the best on their books. We trained on the job, together, that summer of 1917. We were posted down here together, too. In slightly different roles but always working the same Operation. That's how it stayed for the first couple of years. Then I started being sent off around the place, coming and going: a few months here, a few months there. But always returning to the Operation here. I was here a full year once.' He locked onto Posie's gaze and held it. 'When *we* met, actually.'

Posie fought off a sudden irrational urge to reach out her hands to Max and hold on. She clung instead to the narrative being spilled out preciously for her. A dead woman's narrative, being explained by the twin she had loved so much.

'But, I say! Didn't Elsie – *Elise* – mind you coming and going? She had turned her back on her country and her life – even her real name – *all for you.*'

Max shrugged. 'It didn't matter by then. Things had changed. Things always do, don't they? She'd met a man working the same Operation as us, on the South Coast. She fell in love with him. She didn't need me as much.'

'Jack? The Jackal?'

'Yes. He loved Elise more than his life was worth. Looking back, I realise Elise must have been madly in love with him too, to marry him. The whole time she was here it was the only thing she did for her own happiness: anything personal was abandoned.'

Posie leant over. Picked up the ring she had been given by Simpkins. 'You're talking about *this*, Max, aren't you? Abandoning things. But that was brutal. How *could* she?'

Max's face flushed with a red shame. He looked down at the floor, wringing his hands. '*Ja. Ach*, we agreed it was for the best. It was terrible. But there are some things spies just can't do.'

Posie understood the terrible truth now. She opened her mouth to ask more but then came a knocking, a banging at the door.

'Posie? Are you in there?'

Posie stiffened at Lovelace's voice. Both she and Max stared at the door, watched the handle as it rattled urgently from the outside. They both stayed deadly quiet, as if caught doing something inappropriate.

The rattling stopped, footsteps could be heard pounding away down the corridor, a door banging far away. Max rose. 'I was leaving anyway.'

He stood in the doorway to the balcony, fingering the lace curtains, pulling them right back. 'You saw Simpkins?' he whispered, watching Posie as she came closer.

'Simpkins, the jeweller?' she frowned. 'Yes. Why?'

'I was there, you know. Hiding. All summer long. Safest place in the world.'

'Oh!' And the realisation hit Posie like a sharp, dead weight. 'So close! Did Elsie know?'

He shook his head. 'I couldn't risk it. And in fact, she thought *you* could help her find me.'

'*What*?'

'That letter Elise sent you, telling you that something here was "wrong". Have you considered that she thought you could provide her with information about *me*? She'd been told I was dead, but twins have a connection. Elise felt that I was still alive, and tried to explore every avenue she could. The something that was "wrong" was *within her*: for a twin to be separated from their twin for a good long while feels wrong. I'd told her about you, once. I think she thought *you* would know where I was hiding. Maybe that I was being sheltered by you.'

'Oh!' The tears came again now, unbidden.

Max was on the balcony. Posie stepped out and stood beside him. The sea, still out, but on the turn, was calmer. Below them men were carrying something, something long and dark, on what looked like a stretcher.

'Boats will sail again tonight, Posie. Like the Coastguard promised. Seven-thirty. Time is ticking now. For all of us.'

Max reached up, put a hand under his black waterproof hat, felt at his head, grimaced. Looked down at Posie.

'You know, it wasn't the actual spying which killed my sister. It was the *choice* to leave which killed her.'

'I don't understand. You mean spies can never leave?'

He touched her at last, his big, strong, careful, talented hands. Ice-cold, under her chin, gentle and familiar. But the touch burned her and Posie stepped away, scared.

'I can't…'

'*Ach*, use your eyes, sweetheart. Some things are right in front of you. Look around the edges in life. In that lovely room we have just stepped out of. There you will find her ambition. Why Elise had to die.' He gulped. 'I saw it happen. We saw it happen.'

'*We?*'

Max was on the balcony edge now, ready to shimmy

down the cold iron. Behind them, from outside the room, Posie could hear voices in the corridor. A clinking of keys being tried in the lock.

Her fiancé's voice: 'Get a shuffle on, man! She might not be all right. Surely you have the spare key on that fob? Here, half a jiffy. Let me try.'

'Max.' She gripped at his hand, her own palm suddenly feeling searingly hot. 'Tell me: it was you in the room last night, wasn't it? Sitting next to me. You left me that flash-light?'

'*Ja*, I did.'

'But why?'

'It shines a light on something, Posie. It's not just Elise you need to get justice for. Study it. It tells its own story.'

'But…'

He climbed over the rail, and looked up at her in the darkness.

'I'm so glad we met, Posie. It's been wonderful. Look after this new man in your life. He's very important.'

And with that he was gone, and Posie felt as if she was collapsing in on herself, down and down, into some terrible, unfathomable darkness.

* * * *

Thirty-Two

Years later, Posie would ask Lovelace what he had found when they'd at last got inside. And he always said the same thing: Posie had been deeply asleep on the bed, still in her hat and coat and shoes, and he'd had the devil of a job waking her.

There had been nothing untoward in the room at all.

'Darling? You really couldn't hear us? We broke the door down in the end.'

But Posie, staring up at the anxious, wide-eyed face of her fiancé, with Constable Smallbone right behind him, didn't answer. She suddenly saw things with a terrible, certain clarity. She remembered Max's words to her.

A dream, only?

'In that lovely room we have just stepped out of. There you will find her ambition.'

She stood, indicating to the framed paintings of the beach, of the suite itself. 'Richard, you said you'd seen something like these before. *Where* exactly?'

Lovelace frowned. 'Oh, Posie. I don't know. I've seen so much recently. Is it important? Does this have a bearing on Elsie's death? Or the others?'

'Possibly on all three.'

Lovelace swallowed uncomfortably.

'What is it?' asked Posie, suddenly scared. She clutched at his arm.

'Oh! Dash it all. Has someone else died?' She remembered too late just where Richard had been for the last two hours. 'Was it Boxwood? He's dead?'

'No, love. We didn't find him anywhere. We stopped looking when it became completely dark,' assured Lovelace. 'But we *did* find another body. A man. Washed in at the cove beneath Ness Point.'

'Who is he?'

'Haven't a clue, love. It was rather a low point for us all, as it happens. Not least for the poor dead fella himself. Poots is on his way over here. Again.'

Posie moved like she was in a dream. It was just after five o'clock. 'Can you assemble everyone together, darling?'

'*Everyone?*'

'Yes. Soon as possible. I know who you need to arrest. I just need to check a couple of points with Sergeant Fox, but I think we need to include everyone from White Shaw in the catching of this person. You'll need to unlock everyone from their rooms, won't you? And bring that new fancy Home Secretary, Jix. And the MI5 man.'

'But darling, if Elsie was a spy, that's all protected information. I don't think we can reveal state secrets to all and sundry, do you? I don't think Sir Vernon will agree to it in a million years.'

'I think you'll be surprised.'

Lovelace's clever green eyes narrowed. He stared at Posie for several seconds before nodding, turning to Smallbone and ordering that everyone be assembled together in the saloon of the hotel at five-thirty.

When his junior had left, Richard stepped closer to Posie. 'Darling, I hope you've got something good up your sleeve?'

'Mnnn.'

He sighed. 'You don't know *anything* at all about Jamie Boxwood, do you? Even a hunch?'

'No, darling. But this is all linked, isn't it? We've got to work out what happened. And we've got to get a shuffle on.'

Time is ticking for all of us.

Just then the French doors blew in again. Posie walked over, snapped them shut, feeling a cold fist of fear at her throat. She pulled over the lace curtains, noting that her old piece of paper from Max with Thea Elleridge's details on it was on the floor *again*, soaked through. She knelt down, picked it up hastily.

'What it it, Posie?'

'Nothing. Something fell off the table. That's all.'

Hadn't Lovelace picked it up, just this morning, from almost the same place?

He'd said it looked as if it had been tucked inside the door-frame on the inside. Posie looked at the door briefly, at what looked like big criss-cross marks in the condensation of the thin, sheeny glass, as if a child had been playing noughts and crosses there.

But no: surely not. And Lovelace was hurrying her on.

'We'd better go to the Incident Room if you want Fox, eh?'

'Yes. Coming.'

She applied a very red lipstick as they walked, without using a mirror-compact and she sprayed Parma Violet over herself too, although if truth be told, she couldn't smell it: she just seemed to inhale the deep scent of the salty sea at every breath, even inside the building.

In reception, Lovelace gave Mr Potterton orders to make the saloon lounge ready, and Lovelace was about to hurry into the service corridor, when Posie stopped him. She'd seen the headlights of a van turning on the tarmac, and she ran outside.

Dr Poots was getting out of the back of the van. He was holding his doctors' bag and a bulky, brown-paper wrapped package in his arms. He looked perplexed, caught off guard.

'Ah, Miss Parker, and Chief Commissioner...'

Poots motioned towards the van. 'I've had a quick look at that poor drowned fella you called me about. I'll tell you more when I get him back to the Mortuary. Quite a collection we're making here, isn't it? And while I was here I checked in again on our Miss Douglas. But she was quiet as a mouse, sleeping.'

He passed the brown-paper bundle to Lovelace. 'This is the Ever-Ready. Have it back, I took samples. I've checked it myself after my Forensics lads confessed it was too perplexing. It's a nightmare: too many prints to do anything with. Half an hour ago I'd have said it's not much use to you for anything. Except now...'

Lovelace raised an eyebrow. '*Except?*'

'Maybe I've changed my mind. I'll telephone you later.'

'What on earth was all that about?' muttered Lovelace huffily, but Posie's thoughts were elsewhere as they watched the black van turn and head off again. The lights of the van getting smaller and smaller in the darkness.

The van.

'I need to look in Tony Stone's van.'

'What? *Now?* But it's dark! And I've already looked in there and there was nothing.'

'I need less than five minutes.'

And so after some cajoling, Lovelace collected the keys to the navy van, and left Posie to it. She took a torch and searched through everything until she'd found what she needed. She also retrieved the white tissue-wrapped gown bearing the number '40' ticket which she'd tried on the night before.

Who knew where she might get another such dreamy gown from? She'd keep it safe for now.

And if the London show *was* going to go ahead, as it well might, she'd return it to Tony Stone. Of course.

Bounding back to the bungalow, Posie was immediately beckoned over by Sergeant Fox. She hastily deposited the wrapped gown on the hat stand and hurried over.

'Did you get what I asked for when I called from the Western Docks, earlier?' she asked without preamble.

'The thing about Ruth Walker? Yes. You were absolutely right. About the pub, too.'

'And the Orphanage?'

'Yes: they'd had a big donation.'

Posie was noting things down. 'And you checked about the HMT *Aragon*?'

'Yes. You were right about that too. And about Jack Moncrieff, poor devil.'

Fox passed across a sheet of handwritten notes, the fruit of a half-hour's telephone conversation with a friendly archivist back in the book-stacks of New Scotland Yard's cellars.

'And you called London?'

'Yes, you were right. How did you guess?'

'It was *this* place, actually.'

'Oh?'

But then the telephone was ringing again, and Fox was snatching up the receiver, confirming he would take the call on the trunk line.

'Rutherford's Bank, London? Yes. I'll hold.'

It was the Manager.

'Better get the Chief over,' Fox whispered to Posie as he waited for the connection. But evidently the Manager started talking right away, with Fox unable to stop the urgent flow of information.

Fox was making hurried notes when Lovelace grabbed at the receiver.

'The Chief Commissioner here,' he snapped. 'What do you have to tell me, man? And you should bally well know that I have the Home Secretary with me here in the same room, so this had better be useful. Oh, you *do* have information now. What a miracle!'

Much nodding followed.

'Thank you. I see. Yes: that's all.'

And Lovelace rang off.

He turned around, and his eyes were gleaming. 'Petronella Douglas definitely received that twenty thousand from a foreign bank. The reference was "Taylors" but that was just a translation.'

'A translation from *what*, sir?' asked Fox.

'From "*Portnov's*". Apparently, that's Russian for "Taylors." Portnov's Bank are in Leningrad. And they are the bank used by the government of the Soviet Union.'

As if galvanised into action by the mere mention of 'Leningrad', the Home Secretary, holding his black hat, came bolting across the room, almost glaring at Posie.

'You heard that, sir?' Lovelace addressed William Joynson-Hicks triumphantly. 'Very rum goings-on indeed, sir. We have a definite Russian angle to this case now.'

Jix was rubbing his hands together gleefully. 'Fine work, Lovelace. I had no idea the Reds were involved!'

The Reds.

Of course. It had been there all along in that tiny scrap of telegram.

TAILOR.
BUT RED.

Max had known all about this Soviet bank money. The Communist interest. He'd confirmed it to Elsie, from afar.

Jix jammed his hat on his head, and smoothed down his pale-blue silk cravat.

'We can't have the Red Menace getting ahead, stealing our hard-won research, can we? By Jove, how did this happen?'

Fox pushed something across at Posie. It was a page of his handwritten notes. The conversation he'd been having with the Manager at Rutherford's Bank, before Lovelace had taken over the call.

New information. About the American father-in-law.

Posie read the information twice over.

'*Really?*' she gasped.

'Yes! Barely believable, is it?' said Fox, looking incredulous. Behind her she heard Richard inviting the Home Secretary and Sir Vernon Kell to the lounge.

Posie took a deep breath.

Nearly everything was firm in her mind now, although there was scant evidence for her story, she'd be the first to admit.

'Come on, Posie darling. You wanted everyone together. Didn't you?'

She looked around for a last time, noting the very young policeman from earlier, doing something fairly menial over by the door to the veranda.

'Oh!'

She looked beyond him into the dark corners of the bungalow.

It was still there. Hard up against the wall, in the shadows. She dashed towards the basket of swept-up belongings, squatted down and sifted through it.

Yes, here was what Posie was after.

Two items.

Evidence. Of the best possible kind. Things which hadn't made sense at the time, but did now.

She called over to the young policeman. 'Bring this whole basket with you, will you? To the saloon lounge? Sorry it's so dashed heavy.'

But as they finally left the room, the telephone trilled. Fox had gone to get Petronella Douglas, and the equipment blared out, unanswered, ringing out again and again.

Posie snatched it up herself, watching Richard roll his eyes in disbelief. She grinned at him as she gave her name.

'Oh? *I'm* the person the caller wants? Oh, how jolly convenient!'

And after half a minute, Posie found herself talking to the hired seamstress, calling from a London café bar. It was the girl in the marigold-coloured hat.

Her name was really Susan. Susan Phelps. Susan was willing to speak to the police if necessary about something she had seen.

And she gave her evidence down the line, and finally Posie Parker had everything to make her case.

* * * *

Thirty-Three

They were all assembled.

The fire was lit, burning steadily, and a tray bearing a pot of tea and biscuits was set out on a low table.

It all seemed fairly convivial at first glance, until one noted that the door to the saloon lounge was both closed and locked, with Chief Inspector Oats standing sentry in front of it, arms crossed, looking judgemental. Rainbird, Fox and Smallbone were ranged about the walls, and every entrance to the Bay Hotel was guarded by a group of Metropolitan policemen.

The Home Secretary, Jix, was standing next to Oats, nervy and jumpy.

Posie was right in front of the fire-guard, feeling the warmth of the fire at her back, but she was unaccountably cold. The overpowering smell of *Nuit d'Oranges* rose cloyingly into the room: Petronella must have literally doused herself in the stuff before leaving the bedroom. Posie tried to blot it out and listen attentively as Lovelace thanked everyone for complying with the day's lock-down.

'Say, it's not as if we had much choice, is it?' spat Petronella Douglas from right in front of Lovelace. She sat in handcuffs. 'It's all pretty desperate, isn't it, Mr Inspector? Talk about you clutchin' at straws! You've even arrested *me* for a darn murder I didn't commit!'

Oats glanced over at Lovelace questioningly, eyebrow raised, ready to pounce on the woman, but Lovelace shook his head.

Posie looked about her, studying the circle of chairs which formed a ring about the fire. Next to Petronella Douglas, who was still crumpled and tear-stained, right at the centre of the circle, sat her husband, Tony Stone. He was fresh as a daisy, his blue tweed suit beautifully immaculate, a yellow handkerchief and matching lemon cravat the only nods of colour in all the drabness. He was quietly removed from his wife, however, making no move to speak to her or touch her, and occasionally eyeing her handcuffs, nervily sucking his teeth every now and then with something like distaste.

Next to him on his right was Mickey O'Dowd, looking tired and weary, his flannel trousers needing a good press. Mickey was smoking a cigarette and pulling occasionally at the small finger of his right hand. His hands were shaking perceptibly.

Next to him was Sidney Sherringham, who reminded Posie this evening of a friendly cock robin, full of brightness and interest. She wondered briefly and nervously if he was still carrying Elsie's Luger with him, and thought he probably *was*.

On the other side of the circle, on Petronella's left, was Ruth Walker, drab and doughy in her black frock; then came Alf, wide-eyed and nervous. Then came Mr Potterton, whose jittery movements belied the fact that he was secretly enjoying himself a great deal.

Right at the end of the row, nearest Oats and Jix, sat Sir Vernon Kell, pince-nez immaculate, smoking a cigar.

Lovelace made to sit down: 'Miss Parker will now address you all.'

And Posie moved into the space her fiancé had occupied, holding onto her carpet bag for dear life, a flurry of butterflies in her stomach threatening to overwhelm her. *Could* she say this? Had she got it right?

Yes. Yes: she had.

I must go on.

'*It's not just Elise you need to get justice for.*'

'Three people have died here,' Posie began. 'Elsie Moncrieff. Harriet Neame. And Bruce Douglas. And all three of them were murdered by the same person.'

She looked at the faces which stared back at her, variously horrified, surprised, affronted, disbelieving.

'But this case is not usual at all. It's not about love, or lust, or money. It's all about having your dreams snatched away.'

She tried not to look at Petronella Douglas, who had narrowed her eyes in a hate-filled way, and Posie concentrated instead on the bar at the back of the room, where the green glass lights above the mirror twinkled away.

In the mirror she could see the backs of people's heads in the circle, and her own reflected face, its beauty distorted by tiredness, her large blue eyes wide with a wild kind of passion for the truth.

'As nearly all of us here know, this story is not to be repeated.' She shot a look at Mr Potterton, who looked uncomfortable. She saw how Sir Vernon was staring at her, impassively, still smoking.

He nodded just perceptibly.

She had got his consent.

'I need to give you some background first, so we can all understand these murders. It's an odd tale. About how three people came to be working together down here on the South Coast, in Dover. As many of you in this room know, they were employed by our Majesty's Government, on a variety of projects, all of which were top-secret.'

Sidney Sherringham edged over on his seat, his matinee-idol good-looks glaringly out of place here. 'Spies, you mean, Miss Parker? Real-life secret agents?'

Posie shrugged. 'Call them what you will. One of the

three – a man – will concern us less, and won't feature in our story today. He was sent all over the country on missions; returning here only occasionally. The other two ran a permanent safe house in Dover, near the sea-front, acting as a funk hole for spies moving in and out of the country. They ran the place for four years. From 1917 onwards.'

Petronella Douglas squirmed uncomfortably. 'What you talkin' about, Lady Detective? Say, what's this got to do with *us*?'

'Everything and nothing, Miss Douglas.'

Posie pulled out Elsie's gold wedding ring from her bag and held it aloft. 'The two spies I'm talking about who ran the funk hole got married. The woman was a German middle-class girl: an all-rounder. Recruited as an agent by our Majesty's Government in 1917. And her husband... Well: he was definitely a "one-off".'

Posie read aloud from Fox's page of handwritten notes, transcribed from the Scotland Yard archivist.

'He was Lord James Roades, the Earl of Malorney's son. The Roades family had a huge baronial castle in Scotland, and a blood-line going back to the time of William the Conqueror. The family had an impressive military history too, with a man in every generation having fought for King and Country. But the young Lord Roades – let's call him Jack, like he always called himself – he was different. He preferred to run with the lads on his father's estate – the game-keeper's sons – rather than attend school. He got into trouble. He was naughty, good at sports, good at theatre. Jack was blonde and good-looking and he loved girls. He could turn his hand to anything, and he could play the long-game. Later on he would be the perfect match for his wife. *Elise*. Or, as she would come to be known, *Elsie*.'

Gasps went up all around them, but Posie ploughed on.

'Jack wasn't like the rest of his family, as it turned out. He was a pacifist. A *conchie*. He was always having arguments with his father about not wanting to join up when the Great War started, and in early 1917 he simply disappeared. In fact, Lord James Roades became Jack Moncrieff. "Moncrieff" was one of his ancestral family names actually, but a very, very distant one. A name no-one would search for; no-one *has* ever searched for.'

Posie grinned around at her audience. 'Which is why Elsie kept the surname. Sometimes it's easier to hide in plain sight, use what you already have. Indeed Jack Moncrieff has never been seen by any of his family members again.'

'Jack Moncrieff is dead. *That* is why,' called Sir Vernon calmly from his chair, smiling a little.

'I'll come to that in a minute, sir.' Posie nodded politely. She tried not to look down at Lovelace, who was sitting next to her, trying not to pull at his knuckles.

Posie went on: 'So Jack and Elsie got married. They gave everything to the job. They also *gave up* everything.'

'What's that supposed to mean?' asked Mickey O'Dowd, frowning.

Posie looked straight back at Mickey: 'What do most people want when they fall in love?'

Ignoring the ribald chuckle from Chief Inspector Oats, hushed immediately with a censorious look from the Home Secretary, Posie shrugged: 'A baby, of course. Children. Isn't that what everyone wants? Dreams of?'

She heard an indrawn breath beside her from Lovelace, but she carried on, certain now.

'Elsie and Jack were expecting a baby, but it was decided by them and the other man in their unit that spies can't have families. The two don't mix. And so that baby was given away. In about 1918, I suppose it was. Rumours of a stillbirth were put about the place. So far, so good. Although it wasn't good at all. Not for Jack, and not for Elsie. Because Jack couldn't cope with what they'd done. Something in that strong, rebellious man snapped. He started drinking heavily. There was a pub just over the road, and he went there every day. The funk hole was unravelling too; not quite so efficient anymore, not quite as safe as it might once have been. Elsie was miserable, watching the man she loved fall apart. Three years after the birth, she requested a move for them both. But then – and quite suddenly – Jack Moncrieff died.'

She looked over at Sir Vernon Kell, who nodded back sadly.

Posie took in the whole room. 'It was tragic. Jack got drunk and fell into the harbour one night. He was dragged out the next morning, dead as a doornail.'

She looked over at Alf, who had his head in his hands. He was trembling visibly. Posie watched as Ruth Walker patted him slightly on the back, but still Alf didn't look up.

Posie closed her notepad. 'At least, that's the *official* version of this story, anyway.'

Tony Stone was frowning, his small harried face anxious to decipher the story in all its details.

'And so you'se tellin' us that *our* Elsie – Elsie Moncrieff, *our* wee Housekeeper – was this poor wee woman in yer story? She was a sort of spy? And you'se tellin' us that she came tae us, what, straight afterwards? But why? And what about the references from the architect?'

'Faked. He was paid a big fat fee for his lies.' Posie shook her head sadly. 'You and your wife were in a kind of blissful ignorance about the whole thing, Mr Stone.'

'Whadda ya mean?' snarled Petronella, hurtling her body forward towards Posie, trying and failing to stand up. Lovelace put out an arm to protect Posie and Petronella froze, a flush of shame suffusing her face, as if realising her folly.

'Gee, I'm sure sorry, Miss Parker. But why did Elsie come *here*? I just don't understand this story one itty little bit.'

'That's understandable.'

And Posie began again. 'Elsie got the request she had made to move. Not as far as she'd have liked; just up the coast. But she accepted and she moved *here,* changing her appearance, as was necessary. And why *here?* Well, I suppose everything about Douglas & Stone moving to White Shaw seemed too good to be true for the British government. A Fashion House with a reputation for attracting controversial, rich, exciting clients were relocating to one of the most famous smuggling hot-spots of the country! How could they *not* put one of their best spies right inside and watch what happened?'

Tony Stone had almost dropped his cigarette in disbelief. 'Hang about, *we* were being spied on? By *Elsie?* By Elsie, all on her oon?'

His wife was struggling with her handcuffs, white and terrible to look at. The cloying perfume was giving way again to the reek of sweat.

Posie shook her head. 'No, actually. She wasn't alone.'

She threw a look at Sir Vernon, who was no longer smoking. Just sitting, ramrod-straight, an icy veneer glazed over his face. She rushed on. *Oh, I hope this is right. But sure as bread is bread, it must be.*

'They established a small, loyal and well-payed team of observers here, and none of that team ever understood what Elsie was up to. It was very clever.'

Sidney Sherringham looked very put out. He kept looking about the room with dark, furious eyes, as if he personally had been duped. 'So *what* was Elsie doing, then?' he asked, almost spitefully.

'Elsie Moncrieff reported on *everything.* Every Sunday, after the parties, Elsie marched across to *this* hotel and telephoned to Whitehall.'

Mr Potterton was sitting open-mouthed in wonder, and Tony Stone looked paralysed with disbelief.

He ran his fingers through his stringy hair. 'This is crazy! There was nothin' goin' on doon here! Elsie must have been reporting on nothin'!'

'For the most part, yes. But then she and her husband struck gold earlier this year.'

Mickey O'Dowd was shaking his head in sheer disbelief. 'Sorry?' His thick Irish voice was on the verge of anger. 'A "*husband*"?'

Sidney Sherringham sat gawping. He looked bereft, cheated of a truth he had cherished. 'So did Elsie re-marry in that short time, or…'

Posie shook her head decisively.

'No. Jack Moncrieff never died. It was all carefully staged. I couldn't tell you *whose* poor body they dredged from the harbour that day, but what I *do* know is that the government agency who employed Elsie and her husband were dab hands at inventing things: covering things up; erasing information. They would have had many who were willing to help. These assistants were well paid, and MI5 expected absolute loyalty from them.'

She looked directly at Alf, who was still sitting looking at the floor.

'Didn't they, *Alf*?'

* * * *

Thirty-Four

Everyone stared at the motor mechanic, then back at Posie.

'Alf won't speak of it, but he arranged the fake death, I'm sure of it. Because Jack Moncrieff asked him to.'

Posie continued: 'Alf was the Landlord's youngest son at the Two Kennels, the pub near the funk hole, and he adored Jack: would have done anything for him, especially if he was being well paid. As would Ruth here, the Landlord's sister. These two were known to Jack and Elsie over the years, and all it took was a great thwack of money to move them across here, albeit into different roles. Although, conveniently, the arrangement was such that Alf's father was none the wiser: every evening Alf returned home to pull pints in the pub in Dover, explaining his day job away as simply working for a rich man with more money than sense.'

Alf and Ruth didn't say anything, just looked straight ahead.

Petronella Douglas was incandescent with rage, but even *she* was trying to keep up. 'No! Say, you're downright wrong, Miss Lady Detective! Elsie brought the staff details to *me* when we'd just moved here. She told me that the maid, Harriet, had been the contact bringing the others in.'

'No.' Posie shook her head. '*That* was a nice piece of

double-dealing. Even Harriet didn't know she'd been set up: that the nice, normal boy from a pub in Dover whom she'd just met was already working for the woman who would then come and recruit her. Elsie needed a maid who was good at general eavesdropping. Alf had sourced Harriet specially from an advert in an old newspaper and I'd guess he wooed her entirely for this role. But although Harriet was good at the day-to-day snooping of her job, she wasn't that bright. If she was sitting here right now, instead of lying in a morgue in Dover, she'd probably be equally surprised at hearing exactly what Elsie was up to; and the reasons behind how and why she had met Alf, her so-called "sweetheart".'

Posie looked at Ruth, who turned away.

'And Ruth here was trusted by Elsie, very much so. From *years* before Harriet had ever met Alf.'

Posie swallowed, suddenly emotional. 'It was Ruth to whom Elsie had gone after she had given birth. She gave her babies to Ruth to look after and they were raised in a flat at the back of the Two Kennels pub in Dover. When it was decided that the team would move over here, to White Shaw, in 1921, Ruth came too. With the children.'

Lovelace turned in his seat. 'Darling,' he whispered worriedly, 'you're not making much sense.'

Posie looked along the row of people in front of her.

'It all makes perfect sense, doesn't it? Not only was White Shaw the perfect place to spy on, and spy *from*, but in Petronella Douglas and Tony Stone – a rich, childless couple, with Petronella desperate for a baby – Elsie had found the perfect "pretend parents" for her children. Because, you see, Elsie Moncrieff and Jack Moncrieff were parents to twin boys.'

Tony Stone gasped, and looked at his wife as she started howling like a banshee.

'Twins? *My* twins?'

He tried to calm her, but gave up. He frowned. 'Och! Ye

315

cannae mean that, Miss Parker! You're wrong! Those wee laddies came tae us straight from the Orphanage! They had no-one! We adopted them!'

Posie shook her head.

'No. That's not true. Elsie Moncrieff paid a great deal of money to the Orphanage in Dover; bribed them into telephoning Petronella, explaining that the boys were orphans and needed a good home and would she like to apply? I'll bet the first time those boys ever saw the Orphanage was the day you went and collected them there.'

Tony Stone was struggling with this new information. 'Aye, but if we adopted them, three years back, and we've been paying their school fees…well, they're *ours*, aren't they? Petronella's, anyhow?'

Lovelace, who so far had said nothing, shook his head uneasily.

'We will have to check this point, Mr Stone, but as I know myself – for I have been in the process of adopting a baby girl these last few months – the laws surrounding adoption at present are very woolly. There is currently no such thing as "legal adoption". If, as Miss Parker says, Elsie Moncrieff knew what she was doing, then those boys are absolutely nothing to do with you *legally*, Mr Stone. They still belong to the birth parents.'

He cleared his throat. 'Now tell us straight, Posie. You have alleged that Mr Jack Moncrieff, Government Spy, is still alive. Who is he? Or *was* he?'

Posie suddenly, inappropriately, wanted to laugh out loud. *Some things are right in front of you.*

'He is here with us now. In disguise. A disguise Elsie helped him with.'

Posie looked over at Sidney Sherringham. She watched as the artificial electric light played on his face without diminishing the core beauty of the man.

'Those boys are beautiful,' she almost whispered. 'They had a beautiful mother, but their father was pretty handsome too, I'd say.'

Her gaze lingered on Sherringham, and he turned red and looked down, down at his slender, dancer's hands, which he placed together, as if in prayer. Everyone craned their necks to stare at him.

Lovelace moved to the edge of his seat. 'Sherringham? You mean…'

Posie shook her head, smiled teasingly. 'When she sought me out, yesterday, Harriet Neame told me that Elsie often walked on the beach. Occasionally with a woman, but more often with Mickey O'Dowd and the twins.'

Lovelace stared hard. 'You mean O'Dowd?'

'Yes. During these three years there have been snatches of time when Elsie and Jack have played at being a family, although the boys never knew they were their real parents. I think that Jack loved every minute of this, but Elsie was less sure; had already resigned herself to a life without children. She wanted to give it a go, though. And it was a way to spend time with them; these boys they had given away. I *do* think that the boys twigged that Elsie and Jack were a couple, because when I first arrived I was immediately told the truth. Which I should have listened to. The boys said: "*Mickey was Elsie's boyfriend.*" They told me that he'd "*been crying ever since she left*".'

Lovelace was standing, perplexed, and everyone in the room, except for Sir Vernon, Ruth and Alf, had turned in their seats to look at Mickey O'Dowd.

There had been other clues, of course, which had led to this discovery, but Posie kept these to herself for now. The unconscious gesture which Jack had of playing with a ring on his right-hand little finger; a finger on which only an aristocrat would ever wear a signet ring. An ancient ring long gone.

Melted down over the years.

First to make a pair of wedding rings for Elsie and Jack, complete with affectionate call-names. Then, after a few days of starting to work at White Shaw, melted down again to re-make Jack's ring into a cheap-looking St Christopher pendant, to wear instead of the real wedding ring on a chain around his neck, as he had done at the very start of the job. As he had been admonished by his wife for doing: "*Take that thing off, will you? What will people think?*"

The pendant had recently been melted down a third time. To become a double-set tooth ring, inlaid with two front teeth, one from each twin. For Elsie to take away with her. To remind her of the boys. A grisly, creepy, if personal, memento.

There were other clues to Jack's disguise, if you were really looking for them. The tic of touching the nose, as if to push up a pair of thick-glass spectacles which weren't there anymore. Big golden spectacles, quite unnecessary, which had been worn for all those years at the priests' hostel.

And lastly, the hair.

Jack Moncrieff had been naturally blonde. The change of appearance for the move to White Shaw had required hair dye. This was one of the reasons the lovely hotel room was booked every week.

Elsie would dye her own hair first, with half a packet of peroxide, then mix up the other half with a spoon of black boot polish. A horrible concoction, but an effective one nevertheless.

The scent of the vile concoction still hung around Mickey O'Dowd sometimes, even now. If you knew about it.

The man with the broken nose looked at Posie straight up.

'You've got to be joking, lady?' His Irish accent was stronger than ever. 'I'm no spy, Lord bless and keep you. During the time you're talkin' about I was on a boat which was shot to smithereens and the Good Lord saw his way to seeing that I'd survive. I'd never met Miss Moncrieff before I turned up at this house, I swear on my life.'

Lovelace, flustered, looked with wary eyes at Posie.

He thinks I've got this wrong. That I've failed him.

'You fooled me with that one, Mr Moncrieff. I'll admit it. Who can get that terrible image of the HMT *Aragon* out of their heads, once they've been reminded of it? And a real-life war hero! Who can fault that?'

'*POSIE!*' Lovelace hissed in urgent warning. But she wasn't daunted.

She shrugged triumphantly: 'I got Sergeant Fox to check. The Mickey O'Dowd who had served on that ship *did* survive it; he was from Ireland, and he was a poor soul. He got awarded the Victoria Cross and then drunk himself to death in 1918. A terrible tragedy which *you* and MI5 used for your own advantages. The shame of using that poor dead man as a cover!'

She stared briefly at the MI5 boss. 'But I expect you had it sanctioned by those above you, didn't you, Jack?'

'Posie!' hissed Lovelace again.

But she carried on, almost enjoying herself now:

'You had more in common with the dead Mickey O'Dowd than you ever thought possible, didn't you, Jack Moncrieff? Because the beautiful man Elsie Moncrieff had married had already turned into a sour, drunk, ugly, broken-nosed mess by the time she begged MI5 for a move. You both liked to joke, didn't you, about rising like a phoenix? A private joke, as you were working here on "Operation Firebird". But you didn't rise at all! You got worse and worse, and the role of Mickey O'Dowd meant you could just keep on drinking, didn't it? It was part of the cover. Drinks and fights suited that role enormously, and suited *you* down to the ground.'

Posie stared at Jack Moncrieff, sitting calmly in his chair, and he simply stared back.

'You initially met Tony Stone at the Two Kennels, didn't you? A fight night, maybe? A set-up, too. Probably Alf's doing, eh? And according to the plan you and Elsie had hatched, you charmed your way into a job with Tony at White Shaw, quite independently of her. Aren't I right?'

Tony Stone was gaping at his employee: 'Is this true, Mickey? I dinnae think it can be...'

And now Mickey – or Jack – was rising, his height and weight immense, his chin set. He towered above Posie, but she just stared at his grey, beautiful eyes.

The exact same colour as his children's eyes.

'So now we come to the crux of the matter. Elsie was leaving you, Mr Moncrieff, wasn't she?' said Posie, accusingly. 'She was leaving this week. She no longer loved you. She wanted out. Elsie wanted out of being a spy, wanted away from here.'

Posie was aware her words were goading him. Miserable, twisted words, designed to force a reaction.

'You would have done *anything* for her not to leave. Even killed her? Followed her out onto the cliffs and...'

The atmosphere in the room was stretched to breaking point.

And then, all in a burst of sudden silver, in a second's clever movement, a tiny, perfect pistol was trained on Posie Parker.

Another 1906 Parabellum Luger.

These were obviously standard issue guns for MI5 spies at the moment. Not that *that* observation helped Posie right now.

Because here she was, yet again, staring right down the barrel.

****

Thirty-Five

Someone – probably Petronella Douglas – screamed.

Lovelace automatically stood up, covering Posie.

'If you repeat that accusation, Miss Parker, I will shoot you,' rasped Jack Moncrieff. 'I promise you that. Because I swear to goodness that I did not murder Elsie.'

The Irish accent was gone.

Instead, the voice was sonorous and rich with the promise of expensive schooling and landed wealth. The change in voice was eerie. So complete it took your breath away. Tony Stone was staring at his former right-hand man in complete bewilderment.

Gone too were the tremors, the shaking of the hands which had so characterised Mickey O'Dowd, that fake inheritance of disaster he had carried with him so well.

Sir Vernon Kell called out calmly, smoothly: 'All right, Jack, they've twigged you. But now put that nice little gun of ours away. No-one's accusing you of *anything*.'

Posie licked at her lips, the vivid red colour coming off in her mouth, tasting like sickly soap. 'That's right. My apologies. I was just trying to get you to talk. To reveal yourself. It worked too, right? I'm after justice, that's all. Justice for your lovely, clever, talented wife. She was *murdered*. You need to help me here.'

Jack had raised an eyebrow, not quite believing her. 'How?'

She watched as the big man lowered the pistol somewhat. 'Could you tell the room what happened here on Saturday? And Sunday?'

Jack Moncrieff sat down again, although Posie saw how he kept the deadly Luger on his knee. He paused for a moment, then nodded carefully.

'Much of what we were doing here was just waiting. It sounds boring but it was fine: Elsie had her hobby, and I drank a good deal, staying in the role. But in early summer this year we had this big breakthrough, when we realised we had a full-blown traitor on our hands. That Petronella Douglas was happy to trade with the Soviets in order to keep her big glittery house over her head.'

A gasp came from the front row. Petronella Douglas was squirming. '*What?* You're talking nonsense! What on earth?'

Jack stared at Petronella with barely-disguised contempt.

'You arranged for Jamie Boxwood, the Inventor, to come down here fairly often, didn't you? And then you somehow – we couldn't figure out how, unfortunately – cleverly arranged that he would meet a Soviet agent at a party held at White Shaw on the first Saturday in November. We nicknamed this upcoming event the "November Drop". Of course, we knew it was Submarine Plans which would be traded. What else could it have been?'

Petronella was hissing and flailing like a drowning cat: '*I* haven't traded with anyone. Certainly not with the Soviets!'

Tony Stone looked queasy, more ashen-faced than usual, as if he couldn't quite believe what he was hearing.

Lovelace could barely contain himself in his chair. 'You have, though, haven't you, Miss Douglas? You've traded with them to the sweet tune of twenty thousand pounds! And we have the evidence, too.'

Chief Inspector Oats was almost frothing at the mouth in excitement. 'A *traitor*? A traitor in our midst?'

He turned to Jix, beside him. 'Will we be pressing for charges of Treason, Home Secretary? She deserves to hang on a good long rope! Shall I get her in the van right now, sir?'

The slight, dapper Home Secretary was almost skipping from foot to foot.

'Hmmn. I don't know if – being an American – charges of treason *can* be brought against her, unfortunately. But Miss Douglas will certainly be done for conspiracy. We'll get her for something Soviet-related under the '*Incitement to Mutiny Act, 1797*'. She'll be imprisoned for good, that's for sure.'

Oats swallowed and looked pleased, if not completely satisfied.

A rising, keening wail was coming from Petronella now. 'Say, I haven't incited *anyone* to any kind of mutiny!' she protested. 'And I only ever dealt with a middle-man!'

A confession! At last!

Lovelace grinned, and they both watched as Tony Stone suddenly held his head in his hands, emitting a low groaning noise.

'Please do continue, Mr Moncrieff,' said Posie.

Jack Moncrieff splayed his hands apologetically: 'There's not much else to say, Miss Parker. Elsie refused to attend the party on Saturday. Said it wasn't going to be her life anymore. So *I* was left to go in alone. It was a disaster: not only did I lose the Soviet agent and the plans, but Boxwood himself disappeared on Saturday night as if by magic.'

He frowned. 'The next day was no better: we got no instructions. And then...' He took a deep breath. 'Well, you know the rest. Elsie *died*.'

Did Posie imagine it or did the big man wipe away a tear as he looked away, out of the window with its undrawn curtains, into the blackness of the merging sea and sky?

He cleared his throat:

'Since then I've tried to cover our tracks as much as possible: cover *her* tracks, and to destroy any evidence proving she was a spy. Like we're taught to.'

Posie came right up to Jack. She spoke softly now, almost under her breath, hoping only he could hear her. 'You knew Elsie was meeting Max, didn't you?' She felt a jolt of pain twist right up through her. 'Up on that cliff, in the storm?'

'Yes,' Jack said, equally softly. 'But what was the point in stopping her? Those two were like two sides of the same coin. She was in raptures to be in contact with him again. And I know all about you and Max, by the way. As a *couple*, I mean…'

He stared hard at Posie, as if trying to find a defect he had been told might be there, hidden well under the surface. Or else, as if he had been told there was hidden treasure. He blew out his cheeks, as if it had evaded him, either way.

He whispered even lower now: 'Max had spoken of you to Elsie. He loved you like no other, apparently. Because of *that* she wrote to you…'

'Oh…'

Lovelace had turned to look at Posie, frowning, and a moment's awkward silence went on too long, but then Petronella started calling out, becoming rancorous again, desperate to draw attention back to herself.

'Say! Did I imagine it, or did you, Miss Parker, say that Elsie was leaving here? Of her own sweet accord?'

'That's right, Miss Douglas,' smiled Posie 'So actually, there was no need for that horrid little letter sacking her, after all, was there?'

Petronella turned a gratifying red colour. 'But *why* was she leaving?'

'Ah! A jolly good question.' Posie looked at the American

directly. 'I do believe you stumbled upon it on Sunday. So *what* did you see in Elsie's room on the Sunday? Are you going to tell us, Miss Douglas?'

At the sudden silence, Posie turned to Jack again.

'You already told everyone in the room that Elsie had a "hobby". Can you tell us what that was?'

'She had a few hobbies, actually. Elsie was very creative. But the main thing she did was sewing. All the time. And she was pretty good at it, too.'

'Gosh! *That's* a bit of an understatement!' Posie laughed.

Posie thought quickly, kaleidoscope-like, of what had led her to this certainty. A certainty she had woken up with after dreaming of Max.

Elsie's truth.

She thought of the dead girl's fabulous turquoise outfits, and the things which had been cleared out of Elsie's room so quickly on the morning after her death.

These must have included a sewing machine and a dressmaker's dummy.

Not to mention sketches, fabrics. All of these things had been ordered to be destroyed by Petronella Douglas, and burnt by Jack Moncrieff, heartbroken and desolate, believing himself to be covering Elsie's tracks as a spy.

It was in front of me all the time.

Posie thought of Elsie's paintings on the wall in the Bay Hotel, and the very similar sketches and patterns she had found, in the same hand and style, hidden deep in the black portfolios in the navy Douglas & Stone van, packed up ready to go to London.

There, you will find her ambition.

Sketches which wouldn't have meant anything at all to Lovelace, because he hadn't known Elsie's style. But *all* of the sketches hidden in the van in Elsie's hand were detailed studies of gowns.

A particular kind of gown.

And most of all, even now as she addressed the room,

Posie couldn't erase the image of the small pig-tailed girl in the photograph from a German studio, thirty-five years before, clutching at a beautiful doll dressed in an immaculate homemade wedding dress.

A dress so very similar in design and execution to the stunning gown Posie had tried on the night before; the exquisite number '40'. The one she had just retrieved.

Because Elsie Moncrieff had designed and made wedding gowns. A lifetime's passion, first explored in childhood, had culminated here at White Shaw in the achievement of a lifetime.

'When Petronella entered Elsie's flat on Sunday afternoon she came face to face with an unpleasant truth. Evidence that Elsie had been busy creating and making the ladieswear for the Douglas & Stone upcoming show. Petronella came hard up against Elsie's wonderful talent in that room. And it tore her apart.'

Posie looked about the circle, most faces looking puzzled or shocked, then she stared unflinchingly at Petronella. 'You were jealous, weren't you, Miss Douglas? *That* jealousy was the motivation behind sacking Elsie. But you didn't quite realise how wide Elsie's ambition ran, did you?'

Posie explained how Elsie had been secretly thrilled to be posted undercover to White Shaw three years ago, to watch the famously talented Tony Stone at work. But Elsie had been shocked and surprised that Douglas & Stone didn't produce ladieswear. *Talk about missing a trick!*

Elsie had probably bided her time, waited until the right opportunity had arisen. She'd probably waited until spring or summer of 1923, last year, when she herself hadn't been very busy. Elsie must have brought up her plans when she was alone with Tony Stone, probably when they had been checking a fabric order in a cutting-room. Something Tony Stone must have said, or mentioned, must have offered Elsie Moncrieff a way in, an opportunity to bring up her plan…

Posie turned to speak directly to Tony Stone:

'Perhaps you had confided in Elsie about your troubles? You admitted that the Fashion House was losing money; despite the Royal Warrant. You were worried last summer, weren't you, Mr Stone? And you're *still* worried now. So worried, in fact, that you've managed to take out money in loans against the business, in an altogether irregular manner.'

Posie paused for effect and got it, as Petronella turned and glared in disbelief at her husband.

'Say, you did *what*?'

Posie shrugged, ignoring her, locking eyes with the Scot. 'You needed the business to thrive again, didn't you, Mr Stone? For many reasons. In the longer-term, you wanted to get back to having a showroom again in London, at the very heart of things. You couldn't give two hoots about parties, or being down here, by the cold grey sea. You'd left the cold grey sea behind you in Glasgow, hadn't you? And so Elsie suggested her clever, life-changing plan to you, didn't she, Mr Stone? A whole new market for Douglas & Stone. New fame, new praise. More money. A chance to *soar*. Isn't that so?'

The Scot stayed silent as the whole room looked at him.

He sucked his teeth for a bit and then he eventually smiled. 'Och, aye. Yes. It was all a wee bit a fun, that's all.'

'Fun?' Posie almost laughed.

'Well. Yes. I suppose so. In the beginning. The fact is, Elsie offered to produce two small, capsule collections of samples. One of wedding dresses, and the other as a cruise collection for rich women. Simple. It began as a bit of a joke. You – Tony Stone – would simply say *you* had designed the collections. But it was a joke which was to have massive consequences, wasn't it?'

Posie explained how Elsie had done it all alone. In her flat, after a day's work. Solidly, stealthily, Rumpelstiltskin-like, she had produced the capsule collections.

She'd played music loud at all times of the day and night to disguise the whirring sound of her sewing machine, and she never let anyone into the flat itself to see what she was doing.

Even this year, when she had danced on those evenings with Sidney Sherringham, she'd insisted on near-darkness, candlelight, so he couldn't see her machine or her projects.

And then Tony Stone had – without fanfare or announcement, or even explanation to his own wife – added these clothes of Elsie's to his January show of suits, all modelled together at Haresmythe's in Knightsbridge.

To massive acclaim.

The wedding collection in particular had brought about a blazing bolt of fiery praise which managed to catch at the name of Douglas & Stone and burn it in a starry trail through women's fashion magazines and newspapers.

'It went too well, didn't it, Mr Stone? Elsie was *really* talented. The dresses were simple, but a beautiful cut. Just right for now. You had to limit orders, which made the collections even more sought-after. The wedding collection had people talking about your Fashion House like never before. Hounding you for another collection. Which you promised immediately. What a wee bit of fun it was all turning into!'

Suddenly Tony Stone had to hire in a raft of clever London seamstresses, all brought down to St Margaret's Bay to sew up the orders which had flooded in after the January Fashion Show of 1924.

The work had taken two weeks, and Elsie Moncrieff had been at the helm throughout, showing the women her own particular ways of doing things, to make the cruise outfits and wedding dresses exactly the same as the prototypes she had made herself, stitch by stitch. Where needed, she had completed items herself.

Among the seamstresses had been Susan Phelps, with her marigold hat.

She'd been paid an extortionate amount of money to swear never to mention Elsie Moncrieff's name in connection with Douglas & Stone. Ever.

And she'd been promised more work with the next collection.

For there was to be another collection, bigger this time, but just wedding dresses, to be shown at Haresmythe's again. The prototypes to be ready for the first week of November.

'But what about Petronella Douglas?' asked Lovelace, genuinely baffled. '*Surely* she must have realised what her Housekeeper was up to? How could she *not*?'

Posie risked a glance over at the American woman who was now completely white, an explosion of anger gathering up within. Tony Stone looked as if he might be physically sick. He was pulling at his shirt collar as if it were too tight for him, as if he might be strangled at any minute. His face was very red; almost beetroot-colour, actually. Was he about to explode with anger?

'I imagine it was easy to pull the wool over your wife's eyes, wasn't it, Mr Stone? Because of her drug habit?' said Posie. 'And you needed to: because Petronella would have minded, *badly*. It was *her* Fashion House, legally anyway. But more than that, it was her reason for living. Even if she had never sewn a stich in her life.'

Jack Moncrieff shrugged fatefully. 'Oh, it was easily done. Elsie worked along that corridor anyway. She already ordered and paid for Tony's fabrics, and the cutting-rooms were next to her office. If Petronella ever passed by then Elsie could invent an excuse for being in the workroom. *If* Petronella passed by. It rarely happened: she was usually in bed all day, sleeping off a cocaine or drink-fuelled stupor.'

He cleared his throat, and looked slightly apologetic. 'I must say, I didn't realise how bally seriously Elsie was taking it all. At first she told me she was just helping Tony. That she *enjoyed* it.'

Posie smiled. 'I imagine she did. Elsie had rediscovered her true calling. Working on those dresses must have been a thrill. But the problem was that it was an *unpaid* thrill.'

'Darling?' whispered Lovelace. 'This is a lovely story, but let's get back to the spying, the November Drop part of it, shall we? The reason why Elsie, and the others had to die?'

But Posie shook her head.

I was looking at it the wrong way around.

She addressed her fiancé formally, without even a hint of a smile:

'We're jolly well staying right here, Chief Commissioner, on this topic. Because *this*, not the spying, is why Elsie Moncrieff had to die.'

* * * *

Thirty-Six

Lovelace gulped, and from over by the door Posie heard Oats make a snorting sound, with something like '*Mare's nest!*' muttered as audibly as he dared.

Well, for once Posie wholeheartedly agreed with him.

'In Petronella's note sacking Elsie she said, "*You know what you have done.*" But the irony is that Petronella herself didn't know exactly what Elsie had done. I think if she *had* realised, she might very well have murdered Elsie.'

Lovelace scratched his gingery stubble. 'Hang about, Petronella Douglas is *not* our murderer?'

'No. She's many things, but not that. Her alibi holds. I honestly think she had no idea what Elsie was aiming for.'

'And what was that?' asked Jack Moncrieff quietly.

'Oh, you know, Mr Moncrieff. She'd told you often enough what she would do when she left here. You were worried: you feared Elsie might be duped – you even told *me* that Elsie might have misjudged people. She told you on Sunday afternoon that she was leaving for certain, this week. And that was why you went up on the cliffs at Ness Point that night, wasn't it?'

The big man hung his head.

'You wanted to persuade her to stay with you. Aren't I right?'

331

She'd dug out of her bag the blue carbon paper, the underneath copy of the Agreement from the hot-water bottle. She held it aloft to the circle of people.

'*This* is what this case is all about! I told you all that Elsie was unpaid for the work she was doing for Douglas & Stone. But Elsie was also very, very ambitious for herself. And this is the proof. She was no fool, and she wouldn't be taken for a fool. She'd entered into a written Agreement with Tony Stone when the first collection proved to be such a roaring success. Back in January. They typed it up and signed it together in her little study here. This is an unfortunately illegible copy of that Agreement. I imagine Tony kept a copy too, and Elsie had the original, which is now gone.'

Lovelace frowned. 'What did it say?'

Posie shrugged. 'None of us will ever know for sure, will we? Because Harriet Neame had found the original, and now, like her, it's gone.'

Everyone was looking at Tony Stone, who stayed completely still for once.

Posie folded the paper back, noting how blue and inky her hands were. 'I imagine it said that when Tony Stone left White Shaw to start up a brand-new Fashion House, in London, that Elsie Moncrieff would go with him immediately, as his Chief Designer for womenswear. Nothing easier. They'd be in it together, from the off, and although not partners, I believe Elsie wanted nothing less than a financial share in the new business for herself. She'd worked ceaselessly on the new November collection based on the promise in this here Agreement.'

Petronella Douglas was venomous, almost spitting her words out. 'You sure are wrong, Lady Detective! Tony was going *nowhere*! What are you talking about?'

Posie looked quickly – pointedly – at Sidney Sherringham, then back at Petronella.

'Oh, but he *was*, wasn't he? Tony told you so on the

telephone on Sunday afternoon. When he was calling from London. But you didn't believe him, of course, did you, Miss Douglas? I wrote down your actual words. You said: "*You're not going anywhere!*"'

Petronella's face crumpled. 'How can you know this? A bug on the telephone line? Or...' But then she seemed to understand, and shot a piercing, horrified look at her lover. 'No! You mean, all this time, *you*...'

'Yes!' trilled Posie happily. 'Sidney was a spy too. Paid nicely to work his magic.'

For the first time Posie saw Tony Stone's face lighten, the tired lines flattening out and the weak mouth grin widely. Any anger seemed to have left him. 'That'll teach ye,' he muttered at his wife, before swivelling around to Posie.

'Och, this is all a nice wee fairy-tale, Miss Parker, but you're wrong. There was nae any Agreement.'

'That's what you *wished*, I suppose, Mr Stone. That it never existed.'

Because, Posie explained, the Agreement had come to be a burden. Tony Stone was a man in flight, too. Just as Elsie was a spy in flight. And the thing about people in flight is that most just want their freedom.

Tony Stone had been making preparations to leave for ages.

He was fed up of White Shaw, and of being controlled by an overwhelming woman who used his name and talents but wanted nothing more of him.

A woman he knew was probably up to no good, because he'd had recent access to the accounts at Rutherford's Bank.

He was counting the days left at White Shaw.

The prospect of a new Fashion House with Elsie by his side as Chief Designer had been exciting.

'But then reality hit, didn't it?' Posie stared at Tony without any compassion.

'You saw how ruthlessly efficient Elsie could be. How

333

she'd worked tirelessly to get the last pieces of the collection finished. Working all night sometimes; pretending to have a migraine, even, so as to beg off work at a party and so she could finish a particularly tricky item. You saw that you would be swapping Petronella and her strange ways for Elsie, and over time, Elsie might turn out to be even worse. You realised you had to nip it firmly in the bud.'

Posie glanced briefly at the Hotel Manager, who was on the edge of his chair, pasty hands quivering in excitement.

'You were overheard, Mr Stone. In Elsie's room, early on Sunday evening, even though you were apparently in London. And *I* know you've been in that room before, because when you delivered my wedding dress yesterday evening, you knew exactly where to place it, without asking me, without checking. You'd been there before, very recently, hadn't you?'

She carried on: 'You were nervy, trying to get out of the whole arrangement. But Elsie Moncrieff wasn't having it, was she? She steamrolled right over you. You decided to *act*. To seize whatever chance you got, even if that included standing around in the rain, watching Elsie's flat, and seizing any opportunity to follow her which arose. And so Jack Moncrieff *was* right: Elsie had badly misjudged you.'

Tony Stone shook his head, his eyes sad and disappointed: 'Nah. As I said, a wee fairy-tale, Miss Parker. I have an alibi: I was up in London, at the wee club. You can speak to the man if you wannae?'

Sergeant Fox spoke for the first time, his clear voice ringing across the room. 'That won't be necessary, sir. The Oberoy have already confirmed you were nowhere near their premises on Sunday, day or night. They also confirmed that you paid them a considerable sum for a fake alibi.'

He looked over at Lovelace, who frowned. 'They were apologetic, sir. I said we would waive it, this once. *If* they were willing to put it on record.'

'Very well.' Lovelace scowled at Tony Stone for a good

few seconds, who simply stared back. Lovelace turned to Posie.

'So *where* was Mr Stone that Sunday?'

The clues. It had all been there.

Posie smiled. 'It was simple. He was *here*. In the Bay Bungalow. He got Sidney to drop him off in Dover, at the station. Then, a few minutes later, he took a motor-taxi back here, to the back entrance of the Bay Hotel, to that service corridor. All the time he said he was in London he was here, getting some peace: finishing his suits, working steadily, enjoyably. Trying to work out what he would say to Elsie about breaking the Agreement when he met her in the early evening. By using that service corridor...'

Tony Stone laughed in disbelief. "Course I wasnae here! Why would *I* go tae that wee bungalow?'

Because it was close. Because it was comfortable. And it also had that crucial thing. A telephone with a separate line.

'That's what tipped me off,' Posie explained.

'When Sidney reported that Petronella thought she was speaking to Tony on a trunk-line call, that's when I twigged how he could pretend to be in London, while secretly being very close by. Calls were made by the Bay Hotel, but re-routed through the Bay Bungalow. Clever. I think Mr Potterton's more permanent boss, Mr Cluff, was probably in receipt of a fair sum of money from Mr Stone. And Sunday was Mr Cluff's last day of working here before he called in sick. I expect it was Mr Cluff who was responsible for putting the calls through to Petronella, and for taking messages which were coming in from the Oberoy Club, when Petronella was on the warpath. He made it all seem believable.'

Then Posie changed tack. She smiled at Jack Moncrieff, who had been listening intently.

'Please now tell us, Jack. Tell us what happened up there on Ness Point on Sunday night. Because you and Tony were both up there, both in pursuit of Elsie, weren't you? It was a regular little gathering, actually. But who *exactly* pushed her off that cliff?'

* * * *

Thirty-Seven

Jack Moncrieff explained what had happened. And yes, it was true. He'd followed his wife up there, to Ness Point.

Jack Moncrieff had wanted to promise a hundred things and more.

He'd stop drinking. Perhaps they could both be granted their freedom by the Secret Service? Get away. It was unheard of but that didn't mean it was impossible. Maybe start a Fashion House all of her own? If that was what Elsie really wanted. He could always go back to his father in Scotland; reclaim his inheritance. Get the money that way.

They'd take the boys with them. They'd manage it somehow. Their flesh-and-blood boys. Jack wasn't going to leave them all over again. No way.

Above all he wanted to tell Elsie not to leave with Tony Stone. Not to rely on that spineless, snivelling worm who couldn't even stand up to his own wife.

Jack had wanted to speak to Elsie in private, which was virtually impossible at White Shaw. But he also wanted to see Max again. *If* he had come. Which wasn't certain.

It had been a filthy night. The weather had been quite wild. But Jack had been out often enough on nights like this and he wasn't scared.

He'd seen Elsie leave from the window of his own flat, had been waiting for it. He'd given it a couple of minutes, then followed; leaving a good distance. It had been easy enough as Elsie had lugged along that great big yellow flash-light of Tony's, occasionally turning it on but mainly keeping it off.

At points Jack had been convinced that someone else was walking with them, furtively keeping to the shadow of the cliffs. Max, perhaps? But each time he'd stopped, or swung around, there had been no one. It was hard to keep track of things in the darkness, and besides, he'd got his Luger with him anyway. Elsie had had no idea he was behind her. It felt like they'd walked forever, climbing the steep slope, slithering over the wet grass, the wind in their ears and around their necks.

He'd given Elsie a few minutes alone on a bench up there, waiting for her twin. He, Jack, had been sure Max wouldn't turn up.

When Max *did* appear, Jack felt a surge of fizzing happiness.

No matter the dark, roaring rain and the dangerous cliff-edge. He heard them speaking, a low murmur of German, and he was just about to approach them both, these twins he had spent so many years working with, when he saw that they had stood up hurriedly, looking hesitant and scared.

Had they heard him? Was someone else up here too?

Then things went quickly wrong.

There had been a shout. A rolling torch, Elsie screaming. The silhouette of a fairly short person lit up for a second behind Elsie in her black waterproofs. The South Foreland Lighthouse beam, pulsing over and over. An outstretched hand, pushing at Elsie.

Pushing hard…

Jack stood up now.

He came to stand by Posie, who made a space for him

338

by the fire in the saloon, and then he addressed the circle:

'I couldn't find my voice, or my legs. I surged forwards but of course I was too late. And everything was surreal. Max was there, in these strange black waterproofs, but he didn't seem to realise what was happening either, until it was too late. He called her name in German. *Elise*. There was this peculiar scent hanging over everything, a strong scent. It made me feel sick.'

He looked over at Petronella Douglas and frowned. 'I'm no expert on perfumes, but I'm pretty certain it was *that* one. The same perfume. It was strong on the wind and rain. Oranges. A heavy scent, inappropriate. It seemed to suffocate us all.'

'But say, I sure as jeepers wasn't there!'

Jack shrugged and continued, miles away in time and place. 'I saw Max – lit up for a few seconds again, by the beam of the South Foreland Lighthouse – talking to someone further over on the cliff-edge. A woman? They were arguing, I think. Max was crying. But then my attention was grabbed by the figure of someone I knew very well, someone beetling off over the fields behind Ness Point. Someone with blood on their hands. Their mission completed.'

The room was very quiet.

'Who was this woman, Jack?' asked Posie carefully.

He looked away slightly, chin set firmly, grey eyes burning. 'I sure as blazes don't know.'

'Then who was the person who pushed your wife off the cliff, Mr Moncrieff? To her death?'

'It was Tony Stone. No doubt about it. He was the person running away.'

There were a couple of gasps and every single person in the room stared at the Fashion Designer, who sat blankly with his arms crossed.

'Nae! It's all a wee fairy-tale!'

The Fashion Designer shook his head and looked

straight ahead, not at Jack Moncrieff but at a spot far behind him, past the darkness of the window.

To a future out there, but not *here*.

Anywhere but here.

Posie stared at him and his coldness chilled her to the bone. It was as if, rather than fight and defend himself, or even explain, he had retreated somewhere inside himself. As if all the shutters had come down now. Only the eyes were still open.

She had never beheld a killer so calm and removed. *Aren't you sorry?*

Sorry about Elsie at all?

Lovelace sighed deeply, regretfully. 'This is a bally good yarn, Mr Moncrieff, and I *do* believe you. But, as our friend Mr Stone here suggests, it's just a fairy-tale without any evidence. Dash it all! We'll have to let him go. And he knows it. More's the pity.'

But Posie had indicated towards a big basket. It was the odds and ends from the Bay Bungalow. Things swept up from previous guests.

'Oh, but *I* have evidence.' She smiled sweetly. She pulled out two items from the basket and waved them in the air in a proprietorial fashion. One was a fake-silk headscarf, mostly blue, the swirls and flowers on it vivid in all the grassy-greenness of the saloon. The other item looked like a child's bicycle saddle, in a thick tweed.

Posie caught Ruth Walker's eyes, which had widened in a second's instant recognition, and Posie also saw how Alf had narrowed his eyes, suddenly on guard.

'I don't have anything proving that Tony was up on that cliff. He was too clever for that. But he's committed two other murders. And all for the same reason: to protect the future he was running to. His new workrooms in London and his new bedsit. A new Fashion House in its very early stages, but this time *his alone*. His *dreams*.'

Posie waved the blue headscarf.

'I told you that Harriet Neame had managed to obtain a copy of the Agreement. When she read it she must have realised she'd struck gold! So she arranged to meet Tony last night, after the bonfire celebrations had ended, at ten o'clock. She thought she'd try her usual little blackmailing tricks. But Harriet had underestimated Tony Stone.'

'*Where* did she go to meet him last night, Miss Parker?' cut in Ruth, showing more interest than sadness at the girl's death.

'Ah, well: Tony Stone is an old dog who likes to use the same old tricks. The Bay Bungalow was his suggestion. He knew it was deserted. *He'd* used it last, and had even left a few of his sewing bits and pieces there. Like this.' She waved the saddle aloft.

'What is it, Posie?' asked Lovelace, eyebrows knitted together in confusion.

'A tailor's ham!' exclaimed Ruth Walker assuredly. 'Used by those who sew, to press seams. And *I* can confirm that *that* one definitely belongs to Mr Stone. He's got several, but that one's his favourite. Damn his eyes!'

'Yes,' said Posie. 'You'd need to sew to know what this was. It passed me by at first. I don't sew, but I have a good friend who does, and these are littered all over her house. The policemen – no disrespect – who cleared the Bay Bungalow and set up the Incident Room wouldn't have thought anything of it. I suppose it got left behind in the panic after the murder. As did *this*.' She waved the headscarf, folded it and handed it to Alf, who sat blowing out his cheeks, rubbing at his eyes.

'That headscarf was worn by Harriet when she wanted to look jazzy. It must have fallen off in the tussle in the bungalow last night. I imagine Tony sat waiting for Harriet at the bungalow for a few minutes, sewing, keeping calm. He had a sharp knife with him, sharp tailor's scissors, sharp pinking shears and the like.'

Posie suddenly felt sick, not the nausea which had been

creeping up on her over the last two days but a sudden retching feeling of hopelessness at the terrible waste of life in all of this.

'Harriet was stabbed in the back by a strange jagged instrument, wasn't she?' she asked Lovelace, who gently inclined his head.

'I imagine if Dr Poots is able to, given the state of Harriet's body, he'll get a match from one of Tony's precious tools.'

'You rotter!' shouted out Alf suddenly. 'You killed her like an animal! Harriet might not have been worth much to you, to anyone really, not even to me, but no-one deserves to die like that!'

He made as if to stand and lunge at Tony Stone but Rainbird darted forward and held the man back.

Tears were not far off for Posie either, but she forced herself to carry on, keeping an eye on Tony Stone, who had calmly taken out a Sullivan Powell cigarette, was slowly lighting it, shaking the match a few times in the air. Still peculiarly removed.

'I imagine he waited a couple of hours, until everyone at the bonfire had gone home. There must have been blood on the floor of the bungalow, and after Tony came back from unceremoniously dumping Harriet's body under the bonfire he cleaned it all up. I wondered about the smell of bleach in that bungalow today, and I'm certain it was to clean up the blood. Chief Commissioner, you'd better get Poots and his Forensics lads to check it out.'

Sergeant Fox was standing, his arms crossed against his lean chest, his face creased in concentration. He'd done so much for Posie and she now threw him his opportunity, in front of the highest men in government, to shine.

'What Harriet Neame didn't know, when she arrived at her meeting last night, was that she was the *third* person to be murdered by Tony Stone, and the second person to be killed last night. I'm right, aren't I, Sergeant Fox? Please now tell everyone about Bruce Douglas. And why it was necessary for him to be killed.'

Fox swallowed. He tried not to catch Petronella's eye as he stepped up next to Jack Moncrieff, and crumpled his notes as he spoke up nervously:

'The only thing Bruce Douglas, one of the Directors of Douglas & Stone, had to do for the Fashion House every year was to sign the annual accounts which were sent to him at the end of every January. That was pretty much it. *This* January he'd been pleasantly surprised to see that Douglas & Stone were turning a profit at last; they'd had a big chunk of money come in from the sell-out collection. Mr Douglas had signed happily. He couldn't have known that the accounts were just a happy blip. That his daughter was tearing through that hard-earned money already, and would soon be borrowing on White Shaw itself to fund her lavish lifestyle and drug habit. But Mr Douglas would never have found out any of that. It was *Tony's* antics which caused him to travel to St Margaret's Bay last night.'

Lovelace was frowning. 'Go on, lad.' He avoided looking at Rainbird, who was standing at the back, ill-looking and pensive, not having achieved anything like this same level of glory.

'You've done well here, Fox.'

Fox flushed with pride and pleasure. 'Rutherford's Bank told me that Bruce Douglas had made a request for several loans – all in ready cash – from them this summer. Quite separate from Petronella's big loan against the house. These had been manageable chunks of cash. Mr Douglas had asked for them as business loans, and Rutherford's had agreed, saying they would register charges against the Fashion House on the Company's Register, and these would be removed once the loans were repaid. It seemed bally odd to me, and I asked how this arrangement could have been carried out, what with Mr Douglas living in New York! The Manager told me it had all been pre-arranged by telephone, and Mr Douglas himself had come in to the main branch, on the Strand, in the summer to collect the cash.'

Petronella gasped. 'Say, *what*? My father was nowhere near London this summer. He would have been in Florida, Deerfield Beach. Playin' golf!'

'Exactly,' said Posie triumphantly. 'This was all a set-up. What did the Manager say Mr Douglas looked like, Sergeant Fox?'

'He was reported as being tall, broad, handsome. Wore a pince-nez, had thick grey hair and a loud pinstriped-suit. *Very* American. New York accent. Friendly, overly-so. Looked like he had a broken nose.'

'*Oh!*'

Everyone in the room stared at Jack Moncrieff, still up at the fireplace. He half-grinned, looked slightly rueful.

Posie folded her arms, her tale nearly told.

'You were quite some employee, Jack Moncrieff, weren't you? Pretending to be Mr Bruce Douglas. Helping Tony out in this way; getting him the cash he so desperately needed to start planning for his own company, to put down deposits on those London rooms. You, with your wonderful ability at faking accents. In fact, I'm surprised Tony didn't ever suspect you were simply *acting* at being Mickey O'Dowd. What a wonder you are...'

Fox smiled. 'The fake Mr Moncrieff convinced the Manager, and the loans were registered. No-one would have been any the wiser, probably. But, unusually, there was a procedural error. One of the loans didn't have a signature. The papers were duly sent off to New York, first-class post, to get the missing signature. But the real Mr Douglas didn't see them until three weeks ago. As you said, Miss Douglas, your father had been summering in Florida, then he'd been in Texas on business. He only went back to New York – and his office where Rutherford's messages sat waiting – last month. He telephoned to London but couldn't make head nor tail of it. So he decided to come to White Shaw himself. He requested the Company Register in advance, and he had it with him already last night. When he was poisoned. By drinking drugged sherry. A lethal dose.'

The Home Secretary was shaking his head.

'This is terrible! Terrible! A disaster for Anglo-American relations!'

Petronella Douglas had not shown the slightest bit of remorse at her father's death. Not one bit. But now she was shaking her head in disbelief. 'I sure can't understand it! It was *me* who sent up those bottles. And I never drugged them! I saw Potterton putting them on trays! Brand new bottles. Tell everyone, man!'

The Deputy Hotel Manger found several pairs of eyes fixed on him, and his pallid, pasty face suddenly blanched of any bit of colour it had formerly held.

'Er...well. Yes, absolutely.'

'There's more to this than meets the eye. Answer the question, man!' barked Lovelace. But the Deputy Hotel Manager was just staring, frozen, caught out.

'Well...'

Posie sighed. 'It was just money, wasn't it, Potterton? Payment of a bribe. Because Tony Stone was sitting at that bar, too. Along with Jack, and Sidney. A confusion of people. All of you slipping in and out, sharing a few minutes after the bonfire. Drinking heavily. None of you would have noticed if Tony slipped a pound note, or maybe two, over to Potterton in a closed fist. Isn't that so, Mr Potterton? You knew your boss, Mr Cluff, knew and liked Mr Stone. You wouldn't want to lose such a loyal, good customer by denying him anything, if he asked you for help. Would you?'

Potterton, now beetroot-red, hurried to explain:

'Mr Stone said he'd like to read his wife's notes. But not *here*.' Potterton waved behind himself, at the bar area. 'He whispered that I should leave the trays at reception. We were short-staffed last night, so it was easy. I knew no-one would take the trays from reception. They could be left there undisturbed for hours. I dashed out with them, then came back in here to the bar. A couple of minutes later Mr Stone went out, returning five minutes afterwards. I thought nothing more of it, to be honest. Until Mr Douglas was found dead, today.'

Lovelace groaned. 'Why didn't you say something, man? *Something!*'

But the weight of that confession, his part in it all, was too much for such a man. Mr Potterton was trembling violently. He was an observer in life's dramas, not a participant.

Posie tried to calm him.

'*You* didn't actually poison anyone, Mr Potterton. Don't worry. You won't get into trouble. But what you *did* was enable Mr Stone, who always has some sort of sewing kit about him, to sabotage those bottles. To cut the waxed-cloth bottle-top covers with tiny sharp scissors, to add the Veronal he always carries, in differing doses – a massive dose for Mr Douglas, enough to cause death, less for Rainbird and me, just enough to ensure we would both sleep soundly the next morning and not stop him leaving in the van – and then finally, to expertly sew back the waxed-cloth covers. He attached Petronella's notes to each with a piece of string. He had to be careful: it was paramount the right bottle ended up with the correct recipient on account of the different drug levels. He fooled us all. You certainly didn't think those bottles had been tampered with, did you, Mr Potterton, when you went to bring them up to us?'

'Of course not!'

Posie addressed the room again. 'I think it was a shock for Tony Stone, as it was for Petronella, but for different reasons, seeing Bruce Douglas rolling up like that last night. Just as Tony was about to get away and launch this next splendid collection – Elsie's collection – in London, having got rid of Elsie herself, before setting up his new Fashion House, along came trouble of the worst sort. So Tony decided to remove Mr Douglas completely. If Mr Douglas hadn't succumbed to the Veronal, I'm pretty certain he would have been murdered in the same way as poor Harriet Neame.'

In fact, Tony Stone had organised to come back to the hotel later last night, hadn't he? To collect Posie's precious number '40' wedding gown from reception.

It would have been the work of a moment to check on Bruce Douglas and see if he had succumbed to the overdose.

But that would only have been possible if Tony had had the keys to the right bedroom…

'Oh!' Posie gasped, horrified.

'What is it love?'

She turned and faced Mr Potterton straight on. *Not so innocent after all.*

'You gave Mr Stone the keys, didn't you? To Mr Bruce Douglas' room? About nine, or nine-thirty last night? Did he tell you he was concerned; just wanted to 'check' on his father-in-law?'

The Deputy Hotel Manager hung his head, shook it ever so slightly.

Richard Lovelace looked at Potterton incredulously. 'Keys? What were you thinking of, man? I'll have you down the station later, mark my words. *Aiding and abetting.* You've got that, Chief Inspector Oats?'

Oats nodded smartly, rubbed his hands as Potterton started to rock backwards and forwards, moaning slightly on his chair.

Through all of this Tony Stone was still sitting, lethargic, puffing his smoke, staring into the distance. *Was it possible the man was actually unhinged?*

Lovelace, weary now, gave a sign to Chief Inspector Oats. 'Right then, let's be havin' him!'

But just then there was a quick movement. Metal moving like liquid. Bullets.

A scream.

An involuntary howl of pain.

The iron-tang of blood.

* * * *

Thirty-Eight

Jack Moncrieff had the gun out again. But this time he'd already taken careful aim. At Tony Stone.

He'd shot him in the shoulder. And now blood was darkening around the hole where a bullet had ripped through the immaculately-crafted blue Harris tweed. The Fashion Designer was clutching at his shoulder in a dreadful, curled-up whimpering manner, like a dog that can't get up. But still not speaking, or admitting to anything.

'That was for *me*,' said Jack Moncrieff, calmly. 'I hope it hurts. And this next one will be for Elsie. I hope you go to hell, you piece of filth.'

Jack aimed the gun again, ready to fire a second time. More lethally.

'No!'

Sir Vernon Kell, previously so quiet and calm, so utterly composed, was on his feet. The dapper little man stood where he was, but his voice rang out clear and authoritative, although raspy underneath, like he was struggling to breathe.

'Steady, Jack. You've been through a lot. We'll make sure we see you right, eh? Leave this to the regular police chappies now, eh? You'll see: this fashion fella will get his comeuppance. It'll be dragged all over the press if he goes on trial. If you shoot him now, like this, justice won't be done.'

Receiving no reaction, Sir Vernon resorted to desperate measures. 'Think of your boys, lad. We'll see a way to get you to stay together, in real life. If you kill this pathetic little cowlick of a man, you'll end up behind bars. Possibly hang. Come on, Jack, those boys need you. This is all spur of the moment stuff, isn't it?'

No, it's not.

Posie touched Jack on the arm cautiously, felt a fleeting warmth of the strongly-muscled arm which steadied the Luger. Lovelace grabbed at her, held her back.

'This is important,' she hissed.

'So are *you.*'

She spoke as calmly as she could. Addressed Jack clearly as he held onto the gun.

'This is planned, isn't it, Jack? Spies plan, don't they? *That* will never leave you. When I realised earlier this afternoon just who you were, and who had killed Elsie, and *why*, I realised this had put you in a terrible position. You had known since Sunday night that Tony had killed your wife. And yet you said nothing. You didn't help us in any way. Why? It was because you wanted a *private* revenge on Tony Stone, wasn't it? A death which you could witness, keep hold of in your mind's eye. Something to make up for the fact that you had failed to protect Elsie. You would have killed him in the van on the way up to London, too, wouldn't you? If you'd got away this morning…'

For a split-second Jack Moncrieff looked over at Posie, nodded very slightly.

'And when Sidney Sherringham saw you on Monday morning staring silently across the incinerator at Tony Stone, he thought you both believed Petronella had killed Elsie. But you weren't entering a pact of silence with Tony. Your lack of words was because you were waiting, weren't you, Jack? For *now.*'

Posie begged him in the silence: 'Please, sir, put that gun down...*please*. Whatever you are, you are not a killer. Besides, you need to help us now. Again. This is a matter of National Security. I know you can.'

Jack Moncrieff made no visible sign of having heard Posie, just kept his eye on the man bleeding heavily in front of him.

Lovelace had turned, a slight, tearing excitement in his eyes.

'*How* can he help us again, Posie?'

Posie checked her watch. It was half-past six. She walked to the window and opened it fully. It was a clear evening and the tide was still out, but coming in fast.

She marched back to Jack Moncrieff's side. Tamped down the urge to shout at him. 'Come on. We have one hour, Jack. *That's it.*'

Sir Vernon Kell and the Home Secretary shot each other wary looks, laden with meaning.

'Come on, lad. Tell us what you know.' Lovelace spoke cautiously. 'Even if you do finish this wretch off. See if I care! Just speak up!'

But Jack stayed silent.

Posie grabbed at her chair. Sat down. She was ridiculously exhausted. The day had been so long. But she knew the way forward.

Had Max told her? Had she imagined all of that? Or had she come to this conclusion on her own?

The holes which had never knitted together...

'I'll tell everyone, then, shall I? Although I think a couple of people here other than Jack Moncrieff know about it already.'

For there had been another layer behind all of this, this whole story, which had never made sense.

Posie dug in her carpet bag again. Came out with a small, hard, fragment of tortoiseshell.

'Jack Moncrieff is saving one bullet in that pistol for

someone else,' she said calmly to the room. 'For a real traitor.'

And she was rewarded by him lowering the gun, looking over at her in complete surprise.

'You *know*?'

'Oh, yes. All the way through this you've been wronged. And Elsie has been wronged. This *country* has been wronged.'

She watched Sir Vernon turn puce, drawing in and out great wheezy breaths.

'All along I've thought that something was "off" here, that something was out of my reach. It's as if a very important someone, or *something* has been absent. Time and again, almost subconsciously I've felt this absence, recognised it for what it's worth. And it's worth a good deal.'

Posie looked directly at Sir Vernon, then across the room to the immaculate Jix.

'Traitors are important, aren't they, Home Secretary? And Sir Vernon? And you both know, as much as finding the missing Inventor Jamie Boxwood and rescuing those Submarine Plans are important, finding the traitor at the heart of all of this – the *creator* of all of this fiasco – is massively important. It's not something you can blame the Chief Commissioner here for, or anyone else at Scotland Yard.'

She watched as Sir Vernon took off his pince-nez and polished them with a silk pocket-handkerchief. Then looked up at her keenly.

'You'll have a nightmare on your hands, Sir Vernon. A traitor with advanced technical warfare plans, but *so* much more. A traitor who will disappear into the Soviet Union and use the Communist networks already established. A traitor who will base themselves in Leningrad, but keep a firm eye on recruiting more Soviet agents in the United Kingdom. Because this traitor is one of your own, isn't *she*, sirs?'

'Posie?' urged Lovelace. 'What the blazes?'

It was in front of me all the time.

Posie pulled out the slip of paper Max had written on so long ago. It had been stuck onto the door of her room twice now, getting wet. He had tried to tell her on two occasions. Posie spoke the name into the room as if trying to exorcise a very bad ghost.

'Thea Elleridge!'

Jack Moncrieff had put the gun down, and sat down himself. He put his head in his hands, defeated.

Lovelace was hopping from foot to foot. 'What of her, Posie? I was told she would be calling me back this evening. At Whitehall they were hoping for contact.'

Sir Vernon lit an unhurried cigar. 'We've been hoping for contact now for days, Lovelace,' he said calmly. 'We broke into her Wimbledon flat in the early hours of this morning, but no sign of her. A suitcase and money and most of her clothes were gone. A bad situation all round.'

Lovelace stared at the MI5 boss incredulously.

Posie nodded. 'I'll say! From the start all I was hearing was that Thea Elleridge had flu, like many people in the country do. And that she couldn't be contacted. Not even by two of her best agents on Sunday, following the disaster that was the November Drop. I didn't question this. Just accepted it. Thea knew the lie of the land here; she'd been down occasionally, hadn't she? But there was something about the details of the November Drop which didn't ring true. It was something the Chief Commissioner told me, and something that Sidney here told me: the two reports didn't hang together.'

Lovelace had told Posie that Jamie Boxwood's wife had waited three days to inform the police that her husband had gone missing.

And yet Sidney had reported that Jamie Boxwood's wife had actually accompanied him to the party. That, in an unfortunate incident, Jack – or Mickey O'Dowd, as he was – had spilled hot coffee all over the wife's dress. That she'd screamed at him about it. They'd had an altercation.

'Sidney, can you help clarify? You said the wife was "strange". How so? Can you describe her?'

Sidney Sherringham grinned. 'She was plain, plain as you like. Small, but looked like you wouldn't want to cross her in a hurry. Very short black hair in a bob and tortoiseshell glasses on an expensive gold chain. She hung on to Jamie Boxwood like a leech most of the evening, even though, if I'm honest, he didn't seem as keen on it as she was. Maybe it was the scent the woman wore...' Sidney screwed his nose up. 'Although you'd think I'd be used to it by now. It was the exact same perfume Petronella wears.'

Posie smiled. 'Thank you.'

She too remembered the scornful, plain woman in her fancy spectacles in her office at Whitehall, telling her that Max was dead. A strong, expensive perfume – *Nuit d'Oranges* – the kind of stuff no normal girl could ever hope to buy, wafting around the claustrophobic room.

Posie had shelved that memory, the memory of that scent, as being from a time too painful to remember.

A coincidence, yes – a real one this time – that both Thea Elleridge and Petronella Douglas had the same expensive taste in perfume.

'Sidney told me the wife was "strange". And yet the Chief Commissioner had reported that Lord Boxwood is married to a renowned society beauty. And when I realised that there were discrepancies, I wondered who it was who had been standing so close to Jamie Boxwood on Saturday, at that party. I thought perhaps – just perhaps – it had been Thea. Maybe she had stepped in herself to avoid the Soviet agent taking the plans? Hadn't trusted her own agents, perhaps? But then I wondered why there had been an altercation between her and Jack. Because the coffee accident sounded ugly.'

She turned to Jack and asked him straight. 'Because you

realised, didn't you, Jack, that something was very wrong? And you were forced to try and discover what it was by whatever means necessary.'

'That's right, Miss.'

'I should have realised earlier, but I didn't,' Posie explained. '"Mr Tell" was just "T" from "Thea" and the first three letters of her surname, "ELLERIDGE", joined together. Thea had been turned; she of all people was in the ideal position to know all about Jamie Boxwood and his exciting new plans. And from her own agents down here she learnt of the Inventor's frequent visits. So she became the middle-man. A facilitator.'

Jack Moncrieff cut in at last.

'We knew something was strange. We'd always had a fairly unlimited spending budget before, but over the last year that stopped, and it seemed Thea had lost interest in White Shaw and Operation Firebird. But that all changed again when we started reporting on Jamie Boxwood and his attendance at parties down here in spring this year. It was as if Thea suddenly couldn't get enough information from us.'

Sir Vernon coughed over his cigar. 'You should have brought your concerns to *me*, lad.'

Jack almost laughed.

'Oh, you know how it is, sir. If I *had* managed to get to you, I doubt you would have believed me! Besides, it was just a vague hunch, a niggle. Thea backed us in hiring Mr Sherringham, and encouraged us to report on Petronella's activities. She was ever so clever; very interested in "Mr Tell", and all the while it was actually her! Hiding in plain sight. In early July we were excited to report that Petronella had a mysterious financial backer. We thought it must be a German government agency, and Thea encouraged us to think this. It was *Max* who set us right – of course – with his digging around from afar, and his research into Portnov's Bank. Well, when we knew it was the Reds who were after the Submarine Plans, Thea was excited. Said she trusted us to foil the November Drop and get the plans back from the agent sent to collect them.'

He shrugged. 'So imagine my surprise when I see Thea herself, all dolled up, on Jamie's arm at the party on Saturday. What was she *doing*? Jamie Boxwood wasn't in his right mind, seemed drowsy. I had the devil of a job even to get myself near enough to throw coffee on her by "accident". I thought I could force her out of the room into the corridor, or to the bathrooms, to discuss what was happening. But it wasn't possible. She clung to Jamie Boxwood and then, two minutes later, they had both disappeared. I searched and searched, desperate, but they were nowhere to be found at White Shaw. All that work, in tatters.'

'It wasn't your fault, lad,' reassured Sir Vernon. 'We should have *known*. We've had the threat of the Communists infiltrating society all year long. We've discovered letters, alliances, you name it. We've got men on it, now. Telephone wires are being bugged at all levels. But it's too little, too late. Someone got at Thea Elleridge a good long while ago. Made her switch sides. A double agent. The irony was that *she* was the Soviet agent collecting the plans.'

Posie should have known too.

Max had tried to warn her, sticking up the paper with Thea's name on it in a visible place.

And today, that strange marking above it, in the condensation.

'I left you a message, actually.'

Two crosses. A double cross. Placed above Thea's name. *Thea had double-crossed them all.*

Posie held the piece of tortoiseshell up again. 'This is part of Thea's expensive glasses chain. It smashed in some kind of altercation. I found it up on the cliff. You said, didn't you, Jack, that you witnessed Max speaking to a woman on Sunday night. You said you smelt that perfume. *Was* it Thea?'

'Yes.'

But Jack wouldn't look at Posie now, turned his head away as he spoke.

'Max was furious with her. Thea must have intercepted his note to Elsie somehow, and learnt about the rendezvous that way. She was livid with him, too. They began to fight. When the glasses chain broke…'

It was as if he had something else to say, but couldn't find the words.

He just shook his head, again and again.

Lovelace clapped his hands, and looked excited.

'Listen up! This is crucial information from Jack Moncrieff! It means Thea was still in this very locality on Sunday night, a full twenty-four hours after the party. Which means Jamie Boxwood must also have been near. They must have had their plans foiled by the Coastguard's ban. They are probably still here, waiting.' He checked his own wristwatch. 'We don't have much time. The ban will be lifted in half an hour.'

'But where would they be hiding out, Richard?' queried Oats, sensing the urgency of the situation. 'Didn't you do some kind of search earlier? On the sly? Without *us*?'

'Aye,' Lovelace looked rueful. 'It was supposed to be a small, discreet operation. Never mind. We searched everywhere.'

But then Rainbird called out, and what he said made perfect sense.

'Don't you remember, sir? And you, Miss Parker? There were those dreadful chalky tunnels leading all the way from Maypole Manor down to the beach itself. To that little cove right below Ness Point? And Thea Elleridge would have known about them. Max was in them once, and he'd have told her all about it in a report.'

'By Gad, lad, you could well be right! No, half a jiffy, I think you *are* right.'

And with that Lovelace and Posie and Rainbird and Jack Moncrieff were off, tailed uncertainly by Sir Vernon, all bearing storm lanterns found in the hotel.

They left Sergeant Fox and Constable Smallbone behind with the Home Secretary.

Chief Inspector Oats was solemnly guarding the Fashion Designers, whom he took great pleasure in handcuffing to each other. An ambulance had been called for Tony Stone, who had now lost a good deal of blood, but was still conscious, still not talking.

A local doctor was called too, in case Thea Elleridge and Jamie Boxwood were found, and needed medical attention.

Lovelace, with Posie at his side, carried the yellow Ever-Ready torch belonging to Tony Stone, its beam wide and white and bright in the darkness. Jack Moncrieff and Sir Vernon Kell followed on behind, speaking together in a low rumbly murmur, but not loud enough to be heard properly. Rainbird brought up the rear.

They all headed along the gravel road in silence, then down onto the sandy beach, arriving in torchlight to stand in front of the small cove which led up to a sort of stone outcrop, a landing-stage. It had steps carved into it, for when a boat wanted to moor there. The tide was not yet in, but twenty minutes more would see a full, high tide here.

Posie recognised it at once.

'Up there,' she whispered, holding her lantern aloft and heading up the steep steps onto the stone jetty. Above them towered the mass of the White Cliffs, ominous now.

A black hole of a cave yawned sullenly in front of them. Posie blew out the lantern, as did the others. Lovelace turned off the Ever-Ready torch.

'This cave goes well back, do you remember, Rainbird?'

'I remember, Miss. It's a sort of tunnel, rising steeply. In just a minute or so it's completely above the water-line, dry and the sort of place you could – if you were desperate – wait around in. So if they *are* in here, they will be further in.'

And then they pressed on.

* * * *

Thirty-Nine

Posie felt the sand beneath her shoes crackle and crunch. It was very damp in here, and Sir Vernon began to wheeze in the darkness.

'Not much further, sir,' Posie whispered. '*If* they're here.'

But she knew immediately that they were here, or had been here, and everybody knew it, for the scent of damp chalk and sea spray and moulding seaweed was suddenly cut through with something sicklier. The fake scent of oranges.

Ahead, it must be around a curve in the tunnel, a slight light was burning, throwing an orange-amber glow against a chalk wall.

'Stand back, all of you,' growled Sir Vernon, instantly taking control. 'Take cover. *Now*.'

And Posie saw in an instant why this slight, calm man was Head of MI5; why he had been in charge of battle tactics and armies in wars throughout his life.

Immediately Posie and Lovelace and Rainbird slunk back against the cold, wet wall. Jack Moncrieff, too.

And then Sir Vernon surprised her. The man stepped further on in the tunnel, towards the light, and called out, clearly and in a ringing manner. In what sounded like Russian.

'*Vy tam, ledi? Gde vy?*'

'He's clever,' breathed Jack Moncrieff, explaining what had been said. *Are you there, lady? Where are you?*

'He's pretending to be the man who's coming for them, the Soviet agent. Taking a big risk, though. We're just assuming the runner is a Soviet himself.'

Nothing.

A moment's pause which seemed to last forever. Then a parched-sounding voice, answering in a kind of dry relief.

'*Nikolai? Eto vy?* Is that you?'

'*Da, konechno.* Yes. Of course.'

'Oh, thank goodness. You took forever.'

'*More bylo slishkom opasno.* The sea was too dangerous, Miss. No sailing until just now. Did anyone see you here?'

'No. No-one important. But we must leave. I've been here five nights. My supplies are low. He's in a bad way too. The drugs, you know. You have the boat now?'

'*Da.*'

'Nikolai, come here and help me carry him, won't you?'

'Now we move,' said Jack in a low growl. 'We overwhelm her and try and retrieve Boxwood, if possible.' Posie heard the click of his gun as he cocked the trigger, ready.

'You stay at the back, Miss Parker.'

'Fine.'

But Posie followed as Sir Vernon and Jack moved as one, with Lovelace and Rainbird behind. They moved up the tunnel, turned the corner, and then they saw it all.

'Just a second, I'm almost ready.'

In a circle of candlelight, Thea Elleridge had her back to them, and she was strapping on a waterproof, waxed black rucksack. Around her neck was another waterproofed black folder, presumably containing the U-boat plans. She looked dishevelled in a big fisherman's jumper and black waders. A different creature entirely from the woman Posie had met in Whitehall that summer.

On the floor, in a bundle of waxed sheets, was a man covered in a blanket and more tarpaulins.

His head was just visible, blonde-grey thick hair covered in chalk dust, his face grey and haggard, eyes closed. He was shivering uncontrollably, teeth chattering. His whole body was convulsing under the blankets as if he was in the final throes of death.

Open tins of food, cans of potted meat and packets of Jacob's Cream Crackers were all over the sandy floor. A few jugs of water were upturned, empty. Some syringes and empty drug packets lay littered about with old bandages.

'Oh, my!' breathed Posie, and her instincts pushed her forward into the tiny space.

Her brief but effective medical training for the Western Front as part of an ambulance crew kicked in. She had often helped men who were close to death – delirious, dying of hypothermia and lack of sustenance – out of shell-holes where they had been lying for days. She dashed towards the Inventor, flung herself at the ground, ripped off her warm woollen coat in one quick movement.

'Posie! Darling! *NO!*'

'Hands up, all of you!'

For at this very moment Thea Elleridge had turned, and a curious light was burning in her eyes behind her tortoiseshell spectacles, and Posie saw, looking up at her now that one of the lenses was broken, smashed right across.

Thea also had a sharp cut under her eye and over her eyebrow, as if she had been in a bad fight.

Posie noticed that Thea was holding not one, but two, of exactly the same pistol Jack Moncrieff was carrying. She waved the Parabellum Lugers at the men standing in a line with their hands raised.

Posie tried to ignore the guns as she touched Jamie Boxwood's forehead.

He was cold as stone.

She felt for a pulse, pushing back the thin blanket and tarpaulins. She gasped as she saw that the man was bound with thick, tight ropes at his wrists and ankles, all tied with expert knots.

Posie looked around for anything which she could use to cut the ropes away, saw nothing more hopeful than an empty sardine can nearby, its serrated lid hanging off precariously.

She started to hack through the ropes at the man's wrists with this, trying all the while not to cut the Inventor, or herself. It was made even more difficult because he was moving so violently, shivering and whispering all at the same time.

Thea Elleridge laughed. 'Did you think I was a fool, Sir Vernon? So easily tricked? I knew immediately you weren't Nikolai, my Soviet runner. Yes, your Russian's perfect, but you can't disguise the wheeze in your voice, even in another language. You just gave me time enough to make myself ready. To load up.'

Thea Elleridge trained the Lugers suddenly on her boss. 'What a pleasant – if unexpected – little gang. Naturally, led by *you*, Sir Vernon.' She inclined her head at him, then went on to train the pistols on Jack Moncrieff. But she spoke regretfully now, as if they might be meeting for a friendly, final conversation in a bar, two colleagues both leaving a shared place of work:

'Ah, Jack. I'd have expected you to come, of course. After you saw what happened on Sunday.'

'What you *did*, you mean. You devil. He'd done nothing wrong, given *everything*. Then you have to pick up that great big torch and …'

'Shut up. Not a word more from you.'

Thea Elleridge moved the pistols on to Lovelace. She raised her eyebrow.

'Richard? Richard Lovelace. And you're carrying a torch which looks *very* familiar to me: how amusing. You've managed to get yourself mixed up in this bit of flimflam, have you? Shame. You're a smart man, and you deserve to have lived. And who's this? Some lackey behind you?'

'Sergeant Rainbird, Miss,' answered Rainbird bravely, looking distinctly green in the candlelight. 'It's my honour to work with the Chief Commissioner here.' He stood very still, hands raised, and swallowed down his fear.

And then Thea Elleridge trained the guns on Posie.

Sir Vernon coughed demurely, still the very picture of calm. He stepped slightly nearer to Thea Elleridge, put down his hands and took off his pince-nez, polished them, as if he had all the time in the world.

'They're not coming, Thea.'

Posie looked up at Sir Vernon's face. Took strength from his calm. Surely, he *must* be bluffing?

They'd raced here on the assumption that Thea's Communist contact would try and pick her up from this agreed place as soon as the Coastguard stopped their patrols. Surely, they would be here soon? It was now seven-thirty exactly.

'Of course they'll come, Sir Vernon. And what a mess they'll find in here with me. A blood-bath. What a body count, eh?' Thea laughed mirthlessly.

Sir Vernon sounded disappointed, a Headmaster reluctantly chastising a favourite pupil. 'How did it come to this, Thea? All these years, all that service. How *could* you? The worst possible betrayal, too. And with Boxwood?'

Thea Elleridge laughed. 'Oh, Sir Vernon. How clever you are with all your languages and your years of tin-pot manoeuvres! I like you, I really do. But you're so old-fashioned. The world is changing, sir. Fast. The way forward is Communism. It's the *only* way. And first, we've got to build a big power-base, to show the world we're serious about things.'

'And you need U-boats and tip-top weapons for this, do you, Thea?' Sir Vernon was still cool. But Posie could hear an angry tremor behind the wheeze which was getting more pronounced with every word.

'That's right, sir. We do.'

Posie looked up. She'd got the ropes off Boxwood's wrists now, but the welts beneath were raw and looked as if infection had already set in.

'Sir Vernon, sir,' she called up. 'Lord Boxwood here is not in a good way. He's obviously a drug addict, and his supply which Miss Elleridge had brought has run out. He's badly in need of medical attention. He's having bad withdrawal symptoms. I think Miss Elleridge has given him something else, some kind of sedative, maybe? Over several days. Maybe to make him compliant? But it hasn't mixed well with his regular drugs. He's hallucinating, sir. He's got blood poisoning too, by the look of his hands. He's deathly cold. Anyone got any brandy? Something strong to warm him up with?'

'I do.' Jack Moncrieff shoved his way forward, digging in his back pocket for a silver hip-flask which he flicked the lid off in one easy movement.

'Courvoisier,' he said quickly, bending down and helping Posie to pull Boxwood so that he was sitting up a little more.

Posie dribbled a tiny, tiny amount of the strong liquor into the Inventor's mouth. Thea Elleridge watched contemptuously. She hadn't moved her guns off Posie once.

'You'll need him, though, won't you?' said Posie, calmly, now speaking to Thea directly, trying not to tremble. 'He's part of your deal, isn't he? So, you'd better let me fix him up.'

Posie looked up at Sir Vernon, and frowned. 'I think we got this part of the story wrong, sir. I don't think it looks like Jamie Boxwood came here willingly at all.' Posie tried to look past the guns, to Thea's face.

The woman was laughing behind her ridiculous glasses. There was still a length of golden chain hanging down on one side, flapping stupidly, the match to the piece Posie had found on the cliff.

'I think that *you* must have contacted Lord Boxwood

and held yourself out to be a specialist from the British government, maybe with special power to increase his wages. Or power to give him a big one-off payment, maybe? You realised he needed money, just as Petronella Douglas had. You made an appointment to meet with Lord Boxwood at White Shaw, at that party. On condition he bring the U-boat plans, so that you could ostensibly check he was still working on it all. That it was all on track. And you drugged him from the off. So much so that he could hardly walk! He wasn't acting in bad faith.'

Posie wiped away a trickle of brandy from the man's mouth. 'He wasn't – *isn't* – a traitor. But he was going to be used by you, used to show your Communist pals how his fantastic new U-boat worked. And then, probably be got rid of.'

'I say, Miss Parker. I may have underestimated you. Once I thought you were just a snivelling little play-at-being-a-detective girl-about-town, with a dead lover on your hands, and now I think perhaps I should have recruited you when I had the chance.'

Boxwood was murmuring now, nothing which made any sort of sense. But he had stopped shaking so violently, the shivering was ceasing, a slight warmth coming back to his face and hands. 'They say they'll take me home... I still dream of all the noise.'

'What's that he says?' asked Sir Vernon.

'It's nonsense, sir,' explained Posie. 'He's delirious. Thinks he's back in the war.'

'That happens to me too. Even now,' muttered Lovelace. 'All the noise, all the time. Bally war. Poor fella. But at least he's talking, now, eh? *That's* an improvement?'

'I'm not sure he's going to pull through, Richard. I've seen this before. A slight recovery, a sudden warmth, then...'

Posie stroked Boxwood's head, pulled him into her lap, the way she had done for so many men who had come through life into death in the back of her ambulance.

But just then a distinct splashing noise could be heard, not far off.

Then a heavy grinding noise; wood hitting against a wall.

They all stayed very, very still. Then there was a splash, as if someone was jumping from a height into the sea. What sounded like a muttered curse.

Then a light – a torch – flickered on and they could see its brightness coming from around the bend in the tunnel.

Thea Elleridge's eyes had widened.

'Thea?' a man's voice called out. '*My gotovy!*'

'*We're ready!*' translated Sir Vernon quietly, acidly. 'I'll say they are! They got here quickly, the blighters!'

'I'm coming!' shouted Thea. 'Wait a minute. See? I *knew* they would be along. And thank you, Miss Parker. For patching Boxwood up so nicely. We've got a long journey ahead of us.'

'By Gad, he won't make it!' reasoned Lovelace. 'Leave the poor fella here to die, Thea. Whatever else you do. Show some human kindness.'

'A nice idea. But no, thank you, Richard. *You* are the ones who will die here. I hate to do this but I must.'

Thea Elleridge raised her guns a little, keeping them on Posie. 'Miss Parker? You first, unfortunately.'

There was a double click as she cocked the triggers.

And bizarrely, Posie, glancing over at Lovelace with his wide eyes suddenly flickering into a kind of disbelief, felt no fear.

None at all.

Was that it?

She closed her eyes, heard the rasping in and out of the breaths of the dying man in her arms.

'No!' shouted Richard Lovelace, surging forward.

Posie put her head down, but then there was a sudden movement, a terrible darkness blotting out the candlelight, a rushing of air at the same time as a shot rang out, and then another, and what felt like a heavy weight landing on top of her.

A flurry of bullets and a man's wheezy scream; another man's higher-pitched gurgle of pain.

And then a woman's scream.

An ungodly howl.

A pash-pash of water, a boat moving off. Another shot ringing out, but this one from afar.

Another man screaming.

* * * *

They pieced together what happened later.

By the light of the Ever-Ready, Lovelace took in the immediate carnage.

He had jumped to cover Posie, and he'd taken one of the bullets which Thea had fired. In his chest.

He'd have been dead for certain if he hadn't been wearing his ridiculously embroidered and epauleted Chief Commissioner's coat. The bullet had lodged itself in a thick gold tangle of ropes and insignia at his breast, the thick metal badge proclaiming his rank which he detested so much having saved his life.

Rainbird had jumped to cover Sir Vernon Kell, who had been Thea's next target.

Sir Vernon was fine, just breathless and wheezy from having had Rainbird land on him, full-force.

Rainbird was less fine. The bullet intended for the MI5 Chief had ripped through his leg, and he was bleeding heavily.

Posie shuffled across the sand, away from the just-about-still-alive Inventor to try and help Rainbird.

Lovelace rushed over too, holding the Sergeant up,

administering the same flask of brandy, while Posie cut and ripped at the bottom of her dress to make a tourniquet.

As she applied it she tried to reassure Rainbird, over and again, that he would be fine.

But he was coming in and out of consciousness, not making any sense.

'Come on! You've got a wedding to get to, Sergeant,' she chided, tears not very far away, feeling the hopeless weight of blood seeping through the woollen flannel of the tourniquet.

'Prudence will never forgive me for this. You've got to think of *her*, of the wedding. Stay with me, Rainbird, please. We'll get you to a hospital very soon.'

'You've got your Inspectorship to look forward to, my lad,' said Lovelace decisively, 'and maybe more. That was some act of bravery there, Rainbird. The Chief of MI5 is only alive because of you. What a feat. I couldn't have done more myself.'

Rainbird seemed to have something on his mind. His eyelids were fluttering madly.

'I tried, sir. I *tried* to protect her. Like you said, like you sent me here for. I kept my eyes and ears open but I know I messed up. All that business about the Inspectorship. I tried calling you, sir. I did. From Dover Police Station. To try and get your advice. But you weren't available…I'll do better next time.'

'You did just fine, lad. Just fine. Better than that.'

There were more injured bodies to carry out than just Rainbird and Jamie Boxwood.

Thea Elleridge lay, collapsed, unconscious, but still visibly breathing across a stretch of sand. Jack Moncrieff had shot at her – expertly – in the darkness.

And then he'd disappeared around the bend in the tunnel.

There Jack Moncrieff had shot at a man in full waterproofs. Nikolai, waiting on the wet sand near the small boat for Thea Elleridge and the prize which had cost his government so dear.

The Soviet agent had crumpled and collapsed, alive but badly injured.

Jack had not managed to shoot at the other agent, the man driving the boat. And that boat had got away, revving off into the darkness of the sea, lost forever on a mist of suspicion and plots and subterfuge.

Jack Moncrieff had run as fast as he could along the water, back to the Bay Hotel, shouting at Oats to call for more ambulances.

And then he'd brought back with him as many of the London policemen as he could muster, to start carrying the injured from the cave before the tide came in any higher and they were completely cut off.

* * * *

Forty

It was a little later that same evening, and the Bay Hotel's dining-room was busy with policemen eating dinner, the buzz of a case successfully solved crackling in the air.

After all the excitement of Thea Elleridge's shoot-out with the Soviet agent it had been too late for trains to London.

Everyone would leave first thing in the morning.

And then the Bay Hotel would close down for the season. What with everything that had happened, and the flu which had knocked out a good deal of the local population, and the arrest of Mr Potterton, it didn't seem right that it stayed open, nor prudent.

Posie sat with Lovelace at a table, but then he went off to answer a telephone call, so in his absence she finished a plate of roast-chicken sandwiches which were meant for both of them.

Lovelace returned, and by his springy step, Posie knew it was good news.

He was in his off-duty flannels, and looked altogether more himself than in all the gold get-up and finery that his rank now demanded he wear.

'That was Oats. He's still at the hospital.'

He watched as Posie drank a glass of milk. He ran his

hands through his hair. 'They think Rainbird will be fine,' he said, seriously. 'He'll live, and they can save his leg. But he's weak from the flu, and the wedding will certainly have to be postponed. Poor Prudence. But at least she's still got him, eh? He'll be awarded a Police Bravery Award. At least he'll have *that*.'

'And Boxwood?'

'Touch and go,' said Lovelace, grimacing. 'Let's hope the poor fella pulls through. It's touch and go too with that Communist fella, Nikolai. Jack Moncrieff landed him a belter in that cave. But Thea Elleridge and Tony Stone will both definitely live. Although given the confidential nature of the whole thing, *she'll* never see the insides of a Courtroom. But I hope she gets her comeuppance, of some sort. Tony Stone will get his just deserts: probably the long end of a noose. *If* he's not declared incapable of standing trial. There was something about him in the saloon bar that made me wonder if he was quite the ticket, somehow. Too calm by far. And apparently, he just keeps repeating the word "fairy-tale" in his hospital bed, over and over. Still, that's not our lookout, is it?'

Jack Moncrieff had gone off immediately to Dover College, where the twins were at school.

He had been given permission by Sir Vernon Kell to leave active service with MI5 and to explain to his sons that he was really their father; that they would be leaving the South Coast together. To start a new life.

Perhaps they would go back to Scotland. Where Jack's own father, the Earl of Malorney, was currently on his deathbed. Where old grievances could be healed. Lost sons returned. All in the nick of time.

Perhaps.

Posie watched as Sir Vernon and Jix sat at another table, finishing off a bottle of red wine, nodding together seriously, no doubt debating how best to deal with the publicity and fall-out from the affair; how best to deal with

Thea Elleridge, and the Soviet agent called Nikolai who had been shot.

'I doubt any of the true story here will ever see the light of day,' she muttered, waving at Sergeant Fox and Constable Smallbone, just returned from having deposited Petronella Douglas and Mr Potterton in the cells at Dover Police Station.

'Still, for me this was always all about Elsie.'

She watched her husband-to-be as he finished his glass of chilled white wine, poured another from the bottle on the table.

'Was it? Was it *really*?' he asked, eyes half-smiling.

Posie didn't reply. 'So what was that all about, Richard? When Rainbird was first shot in the cave. He said he'd failed you. That you'd *sent* him. To protect something? What was that about?'

Richard Lovelace paused for a moment too long, then shrugged.

'I really have no idea. Poor Rainbird. Didn't know what he was talking about at all, did he?'

Everyone has their own secrets, peculiar to them.

'Ah. Here's Poots. Join us for a drink, Doctor?'

Lovelace was already bounding to the bar, collecting another wine glass. 'It's just me drinking; Posie doesn't feel like it. Will you join us in celebrating the end of this successful case?'

Dr Poots pulled up a chair. He sighed heavily and pulled at his black bow-tie.

'No, Richard. But thank you kindly. I think I'll turn in, ready for our early start back to London tomorrow. Besides, it wasn't successful for everyone was it? I've never had such a high body count in so few hours. Poor duckies. Oh!'

He fiddled with his black leather briefcase, brought out an orange form, the sort Posie recognised by now as a pre-post-mortem report. He passed it to Richard Lovelace who read it quickly.

'You think the fella was killed with *that* particular torch? The Ever-Ready?' Richard sounded incredulous.

'Oh yes. I haven't done the full post-mortem yet but I'd say almost definitely. The mark on the back of the head matches almost exactly the main indentation in the torch. Beats me how the thing was still so complete. I'd have thought with that degree of force – enough to kill the man – the torch would have broken to pieces. Odd. Very odd. There's yellow paint residue in the cut on his head, which perfectly matches the paint on the torch. It's definitely the weapon. So at least we know something about him, poor soul. You're sure, Richard, that you don't know the fella? Only, you looked a little odd when you caught sight of him earlier. Upset, maybe?'

'No. No. He wasn't very recognisable really, was he?'

Dr Poots shook his head, and prepared to go.

'Four days in the water can do that to a man. Awful thing, the sea. I'd say he died on Sunday night…'

Posie frowned as she watched Dr Poots trudging off through the dining-room.

'What was that all about?'

'The body washed onto the beach earlier. When we were searching for Boxwood. Remember? We found the body of a man. At the moment his identity is still unknown.' Lovelace looked briefly away.

'Oh. What a mystery. Someone, somewhere must know who he is. Funny about that torch…'

Posie exhaled deeply and took Richard's hand. She had some news, but she'd save it for a happier evening.

'You know we've been massively indecisive about where and when to get married, Richard darling?'

'I'll say.'

'Well, let's just get married as soon as possible. It doesn't matter where, or how. Let's just get on with it.'

Richard Lovelace's face split with joy.

'We should have asked that jewellery fella earlier if he'd

make us a pair of matching rings. Maybe we can stop by there tomorrow, Posie?'

He grinned. 'Except I'm not Jack Moncrieff with a medieval gold nugget to melt down, and we don't have exciting call-names to include on the inscriptions inside. No Fire and no Jackal here.'

'Thankfully,' said Posie, rolling her eyes. 'I think our lives are quite exciting enough. Besides, I think if we went back to Snargate Street, to Simpkins tomorrow, we'd already find it wasn't there. He'll have disappeared. There would be nothing but an empty window and a banging grate. You've got me a wonderful ring here, darling; I love it to bits. Let's just get our wedding bands at Woolworths. I don't care if they're not fancy.'

Lovelace smiled. 'That's what I love about you, Posie. You're always so unexpected.'

He moved to get up. 'Bed, I think? I'll walk you up to your fancy suite, darling?'

Posie shook her head. 'No. I asked the fella on reception to change my room. I already have the one right next to you. A regular little box room on this floor. No balcony, no window and no view.' She swallowed uneasily. 'I don't think I could stay up there in that suite again. It's too full of memories.'

Lovelace frowned, but then nodded as if he quite understood.

'Right you are. I thought myself that it was a funny sort of place. Damp. Did I tell you that the chair I sat in next to your bed was wet this morning? As if someone had been sitting there for a long time, drenched through.'

Posie stayed calm but a wave of emotion was there below the surface.

'I know,' she said very quietly.

'As if someone had been in swimming.'

****

The next morning was beautiful. Unbelievably clear and bright for a November's day. Not a cloud in the sky and the sea as still and calm as a millpond.

For a moment Posie stood on the empty beach, taking it all in. The endless sea. The sky a wide mass of blue, beneath which boats and cruise liners passed as if they hadn't a care in the world. The shipping lanes were back to normal. The patrols had stopped.

The cliffs in the distance, the guardians of England, seemed so white and striking, like they had been rubbed clean by all the rain and storms. Ness Point looked very high from here, and Posie saw that an old man and his dog were out early, the dog sniffing at the stones on the beaches far, far below.

She could see why people came on holiday here, but she herself would never come back.

Behind her, outside the Bay Hotel, shiny black police cars were turning, important people being ferried off to trains.

Sir Vernon's red Lagonda had already roared off.

The local police force seemed to have recovered a bit, as Posie saw a local bobby with Constable Briggs, back on duty, swing through the gates to White Shaw, where everything was now shut up.

Who knew what they were doing there? Perhaps fetching clothes and overnight things for Petronella Douglas, who would be transferred today to a secure jail up in London, to await trial. Or clothes for Tony Stone, recovering from his bullet wound in Buckland Hospital, here in Dover.

Clothes.

Posie saw with a start that the navy Douglas & Stone van with the Royal Warrant was still parked up in the turning-circle. Still laden with the fruit of all of Elsie Moncrieff's hard work over several months. Hard work which had cost her her life.

What would become of those beautiful dresses? Would they simply be bagged up and taken off as evidence somewhere?

It seemed such a shame.

She, for one, was going to wear the dress Tony Stone had given her, which Elsie had designed and made. Number '40' was already packed up carefully in her bag, and she hadn't mentioned it to anyone.

After all, it would be a crying shame for it to moulder to nothing.

Just then a horn beeped behind her. Lovelace was standing on the running-board of a black motor.

'Come on, darling. Let's be off!'

She had wanted to ask him last night, and again at breakfast, about the man they'd found on the beach.

The man killed on Sunday night. Dead in the water for four days. She had wanted to ask if he had been wearing a black sou'wester hat and a black raincoat. But somehow, she couldn't find the words.

And she *knew* the answer, anyway. Posie had taken all of what she had heard and reassembled it: Thea Elleridge on the cliff; a fight with Max; that torch…

It shines a light on something, Posie.

Justice had now been obtained for Elsie.

But for Max? Perhaps for him – to all extents and purposes a dead man already – it was enough just to have understood what had happened.

To move on, but never to forget him.

Posie turned to trace her steps back over the sand, fingering her pink necklace of Venetian glass beads, wondering if the time had come to take it off.

But just then she thought she saw something – a trick of the light, maybe?

A couple were walking on the cliff-top, small as ants from here. A woman in a streak of turquoise, lit up by the bright sun, and a man, tall beside her in a long black coat, with white-blonde hair.

They were walking fast – practically running – against the light above Ness Point. Joined in space and time and birth and death, and by a hundred other things which Posie might never understand.

By the promise of a future which would never come for them.

When she looked up again, they had gone.

'Darling?'

'Just coming!' she shouted at her fiancé.

They were heading home.

* * * *

EPILOGUE

It was three weeks later.

Posie and Richard Lovelace stood together, looking at the immaculately-painted pink walls of the large nursery in the flat in Museum Chambers.

Posie swallowed. So much pink all in one place was quite something. It called to mind a big pink strawberry blancmange. Or a nightmare version of candy-floss.

Too much candy-floss.

'Do you like it, darling?' Richard Lovelace asked, looking down at his future wife with a raised eyebrow. 'It said "Blush" on the tin. But it's quite vivid, isn't it?'

'I have to say it is absolutely beautifully done. A first-class job.'

'You didn't answer my question.'

Posie bit at her lip. 'Well…'

The rest of the flat looked wonderful, and it was all to her taste, thankfully.

It hadn't really been altered that much at all: all glassware, the drinks cabinet and some precious items had been moved out for safekeeping from the living-room, now painted a pale blue, and some new colourful lithographs brought in to replace the Egyptian hieroglyphs which had formerly been hanging there. A red mask, bought from

Venice, was also now carefully mounted on the wall as you entered the lounge.

Masha the Housekeeper's room next to the nursery was complete too; a small, calm retreat with a brand-new sprigged cotton settee and matching curtains, and whitewashed rattan bed and furniture, with plenty of wall space to hang up her religious paintings.

Posie's bedroom had been changed. It would now be *their* bedroom, and it was decked out in neutral oyster and coffee silks, expensive linen everywhere, a new colonial-style bed the centrepiece of the room.

A single, beautiful slip of a white velvet wedding dress with matching cap and veil hung from a hook by the window.

Elsie's dress.

A partition wall had been erected in the second guest-bedroom, effectively forming two studies, each with one window, overlooking the busy London street below.

Posie had spared no expense in kitting Richard's half out in tastefully masculine dark burgundy and browns. Smart polished leather club chairs and a dark-red settee had been placed in one corner. There was also a drinks' cabinet and a safe. A sumptuous walnut desk complete with a red glass reading lamp had been installed in the other corner, above which hung a framed map of London.

Posie's study was less obviously a place of work, more a place of retreat, and it was painted bright blue and white, with striped seersucker curtains. It had a beachy feel to it. The hieroglyphs had been moved in here, and they hung either side of Posie's window. There was a noticeboard too, above her small white desk. It was currently bare, except for two things.

One was the photograph of Elise as a small child, with her doll in her hands.

The other was a postcard, a cheap throwaway one she had picked up from the reception desk at the Bay Hotel.

It showed Ness Point on a sunny day, overlooking an impossibly-blue and sparkling English Channel.

These were two things she should throw away, she supposed. Just like she should stop wearing this glass necklace.

'Darling? You're shivering.' Richard Lovelace was frowning, concerned, shrugging out of the rough-hewn Harris tweed jacket he usually wore on his days off.

He tucked it around Posie's shoulders. 'Are you all right?'

'I'm fine.' And she meant it. Posie had let go of all the past now. It was gone.

Their wedding was to take place in one week's time. On Saturday, the sixth of December. That was why the flat had been finished so fast, in such a flurry of activity. They'd booked the Swiss Church, one street away from Posie's office on Grape Street. It was a neutral choice, home to neither of them and yet welcoming to both.

'And all this pink?'

Posie stared again at the pink expanse ahead of her. She thought of sturdy little Phyllis, and of fragile little Katie, still in hospital, but hopefully home with them before Christmas, just after the wedding. Both little girls were survivors in their own way. Precious little fighters.

And fighters get on with things well, regardless of the paint colour in their nurseries.

Richard put his arm around her, smiling. 'We'll just get the man to come again on Monday; paint it any shade you like. To be honest, I find it a little garish myself. A lighter shade maybe?'

Posie held him tighter. *What a good man he was*, she thought to herself. So concerned to make everything right. He shouldn't worry.

Things *were* right.

She knew it in her heart of hearts.

And surely this good man who had put up with so very much deserved some good news? News she had had confirmed that afternoon, when she'd trotted off to Harley Street.

'Yes: I think you should telephone the man again, Richard.'

She nodded, certain of her course now. 'Tell him to come on Monday. But don't let's go with the pink, eh? Something neutral, I think. A pale yellow, maybe? And while you're organising things, you'd better call the Army & Navy stores and order some more furniture. Good job this nursery is jolly big.'

Richard Lovelace looked confused. He ran his fingers through his hair.

'*More* furniture? Surely the little girls have everything they need just here: cots, toy-cupboards. What more do you think they might need, darling?'

Posie grinned. It had all made sense to her, finally, on the last evening at St Margaret's Bay. The sickness, the more-than-usual hunger, the emotions going up and down, the dizziness. But she'd waited to be absolutely sure.

'We need another cot. Better buy a neutral colour, but my gut instinct is telling me it should be blue. And you'd better tell Masha when you go home tonight to your house in Clapham that she's going to have her hands *very* full come next summertime.'

Richard Lovelace looked momentarily flabbergasted. 'You mean...? No! But, oh! It was just the once... Oh, I say!'

And as her very soon-to-be-husband's eyes widened in disbelief, and a massive smile broke out all over his entire face, Posie laughed aloud at his joy.

'Yes, a baby.'

A baby boy.

A new man in her life.

And oh, yes: he would be very important to them.

Posie slipped her hand in Richard Lovelace's, and closed her eyes happily.

Life is short, and life is for the living, after all.

Someone very clever had told her that recently, and she, for one, was not going to forget it in a hurry.

* * * *

Historical Note

All of the characters in this book are fictional, unless specifically mentioned below. However, timings, general political events, weather conditions and places (and descriptions of places) are historically accurate to the best of my knowledge, save for the exceptions and details which are listed below.

As in the other Posie Parker books, I refer to the First World War of 1914–1918 as the 'Great War' throughout, which is simpler for the modern reader, although it would not have been referred to in this way in 1924.

I would like to point out that although the glamorous young Prince of Wales (the later King Edward VIII, 1894–1972, famous for his abdication) is mentioned in this novel (we never meet him in the actual story), the storyline which places him as patron of my main characters (a pair of fictional Fashion Designers) is pure invention on my part.

So too are the disagreements between the Prince of Wales and his father, King George V, about his partying with the duo. However, in real-life he did, indeed, famously argue non-stop with his father about the company he kept, the fashions he wore, and the way he lived his life.

As ever, both Posie's work address in London (Grape

Street, Bloomsbury, WC1) and her home address around the corner (Museum Chambers, WC1) are both very real, although you might have to do a bit of imagining to find her there.

1.	(Chapter One) The story about Elsie Moncrieff falling off the cliff at St Margaret's Bay is fictional, and therefore so is the fact that it appears on page two of *The Times* on 4th November 1924. The other news reported in that day's paper (the General Election in Britain and the fascist activities in Italy) is all accurate, taken straight from the pages of newspapers at the time.

2.	(Chapter Two) The Hall I describe where the Coroner is holding Elsie Moncrieff's Inquest is actually the Stone Hall within Dover Town Hall, rather than the main hall itself.

3.	(Chapter Two and throughout the book) The Fashion Designer duo of Petronella Douglas and Tony Stone are fictional, as are the 'competition', the House of Harlow.

4.	(Chapter Two) The perfume worn by Petronella Douglas, *Nuit d'Oranges*, is an invention of my own. But the perfume Posie refers to as being worn by virtually everyone she knows, *Phúl-Nana*, was very real, and was made by Grossmith. It outsold all other fragrances in Britain throughout the 1920s. It can still be purchased today, see: https://www.grossmithlondon.com/phul-nana-1

5.	The flu epidemic which I describe as sweeping through Dover at the time of this novel is fictional.

6. (Chapter Two and later in the book) In the 1920s Traub Manufacturing Company of Detroit became very well-known for their highly-sought-after 'Orange Blossom' line of engagement and wedding rings, such as the one Richard buys for Posie. These rings were mid-range, die-struck and sold in most upmarket American Department Stores.

7. (Chapter Three) Jolyon Peterson, the London architect mentioned by Petronella Douglas (at the Inquest) as the designer of her art-deco home, is fictional.

8. (Throughout) Haresmythe's Department Store in Knightsbridge, London, (where the fashion shows take place) is fictional, but for inspiration as to how such shows took place I was looking at Harrods, Knightsbridge.

9. (Chapter Five) Maypole Manor was the fictional scene-of-crime for the third book in the Posie Parker Mystery Series, *Murder at Maypole Manor*. The real-life site where I imagine Maypole Manor to have been was occupied in the 1920s by a house called The Hermitage.

10. (Chapter Six) Max's history, as re-told here, is fictional.

11. (Throughout) The Green Man pub on the beach at St Margaret's Bay was real in 1924, and still exists, although it is now named The Coastguard.

12. (Chapter Nine) The Oberoy Club on Piccadilly, London (where Tony Stone stays) is fictional.

13. (Chapter Eleven) The story of Harriet Neame is fictional. However, the sorry story of the stealing of silver spoons is inspired by an incident which took place at the tea-rooms at St Margaret's Bay itself, in 1921.

14. (Chapter Twelve) Rutherford's Bank on the Strand is completely fictional. As is (later in the book) Portnov's Bank.

15. (Chapter Fourteen) Mickey O'Dowd is fictional, as is his Victoria Cross. But the attack by U-boat on the HMT *Aragon* on 30 December 1916, as described here, and the subsequent loss of life, on both the *Aragon* and the *Attack* is all true.

16. (Chapter Fourteen and Twenty-Nine) The priests' hostel on Snargate Street in Dover is fictional, although the road and the surrounds are all described accurately. See also note 21.

17. The Bay Hotel (throughout, but particularly in Chapter Seventeen) on the beach-front at St Margaret's Bay really *did* exist and was, together with the Granville Hotel, the very best you could get. (See the Photographs in the next section.) As mentioned in the novel, the early 1920s saw electricity being installed and the Bay Hotel was enjoying something of a boom-time, also with the installation of a full-scale ballroom and outside swimming pool. During the time of this novel it was doing very well, and continued to do so, right through the 1920s and 1930s, when it expanded again considerably. I have followed the correct geographical location of the hotel and its (real-life) bungalow next door (which holiday-goers could also rent out, for which see the Photographs) but I have used my own imagination

in describing Posie's suite, and in the internal layout and furnishing. I have also used artistic licence when 'adding' a service corridor, linking the two properties. For more see the Note on St Margaret's Bay, Kent and Accompanying Photographs in the next section.

18. (Chapter Seventeen) The London Peace Day fireworks of 19th July 1921, as mentioned by Mr Potterton, were indeed splendid and much-talked about for years afterwards. The Peace Day celebrations, including the ringing of church bells across the country, fireworks in most towns, and troops marching on the Cenotaph in London marked the beginning of a 'ritual of remembrance' for those who had fallen in the Great War. Virginia Woolf, contemporary writer of the time, includes her experience of seeing the Peace Day celebrations, including blue fireworks, at Richmond, London, in her diary.

19. (Chapter Twenty-Three) The German Bands to which Richard Lovelace refers were very real and very much a feature of life on the streets of big towns and seaside resorts in the United Kingdom at the end of the nineteenth century. Highly-costumed and well-organised, they played 'Oktoberfest' style music, as well as waltzes and popular dance music from the era. There is an illustration for such a German Band playing in Bloomsbury in the 1902 edition of Macmillan's *Highways and Byways in London* (p.239).

20. (Chapter Twenty-Two and throughout) The history of the formation of MI5 is a complex one, and during the post-Great War period it existed as the respected but poorer younger brother alongside companion but rival intelligence services run by Scotland Yard themselves and another agency, the 'Secret Intelligence Service' (known as the SIS). All of these were streamlined

and reorganised in 1931, with full responsibility for counter-subversion granted to MI5. The agency I have described here, a select and vigorously aggressive offshoot of MI5, run from Whitehall, mainly using foreign assets for work in counter-espionage within the United Kingdom is fictional, although, I believe, not unlikely. The Head of MI5 during this time was Sir Vernon Kell. For more on whom see note 25.

21. (Chapter Twenty-Nine) While I have tried to use the geography of Dover as it would have been in 1924 (the Western Docks, Snargate Street etc) as accurately as possible, I have, however, made one crucial (fictional) change. Snargate Street actually adjoins the Welllington Basin and the Granville Basin, both man-made harbours for yachts. For ease I say in the novel that it adjoins the (simpler but fictional) fisherman's harbour. The view out over the Western Docks and the Pier I describe would have been accurate, apart from the view of the pub, The Two Kennels (which is fictional). The whole harbour complex was redesigned before this novel was set, and re-opened in 1909 by the then-Prince of Wales. It would still have seemed relatively new and smart in 1924.

22. (Chapters Twenty-Nine and Thirty) The funk hole at Snargate Street is fictional, as is Simpkins the Jewellers. Today Snargate Street is mainly a residential street, with some shops catering for fishermen and yachtsmen, as you would expect near any commercial port and harbour. There *was* a Woolworths on Biggin Street in Dover, which opened in 1914 and it was one of the town's most popular shops during the time of this novel.

23. (Chapter Thirty-One) The Home Secretary at the time of this novel was indeed William Joynson-Hicks (later 1st Viscount Brentford), whose dates are 1865–1932. Known popularly as 'Jix', he was a dependable yet controversial Home Secretary in Stanley Baldwin's second government from 1924–1929. He became known for being extremely strict and trying to clamp down on licentiousness, illegal drinking, illegal nightclubs and indecent literature. He was hated by London's 'Bright Young Things'. He also gained a steely reputation for opposing Communism, and helping to lower the voting age for women from thirty years old to twenty-one. I have stretched the boundaries here of what may have been possible, with regard to his visiting White Shaw. While the threat at St Margaret's Bay as described here would have (if real) have been immense, it seems unlikely in a real-life scenario that a brand-new Home Secretary would have come down himself with a Home Office Search Warrant only a couple of days into the job.

24. (Chapter Thirty-Two) Portnov's Bank in Leningrad is entirely fictional, although British worries over Communism (which started in the year of this novel, 1924) in the Soviet Union were very real. The real-life Home Secretary, William Joynson-Hicks, whom I have placed in this novel, was passionately committed to stamping out any sort of Soviet infiltration and influence, and spies and activities were looked for everywhere. See also note 25.

25. (From Chapter Twenty-Seven onwards) The real-life Sir Vernon Kell (1873–1942), was, at this time, and as in this novel, the Head of MI5. A multi-skilled linguist, Kell had been in the army for all of his career by the time he was asked to head up

the Secret Service Bureau (later MI5) focusing on domestic counter-intelligence. His unit successfully masterminded the dismantling of the German spy network in the UK on the outbreak of the Great War. The year this novel is set (1924) saw a massive focus on the likelihood of a Soviet-led Communist threat to the UK, and fears were not relieved by a letter ('the Zinoviev letter') surfacing in the UK in which Grigory Zinoviev of the Soviet Comintern (the main, worldwide Communist Association) and Arthur McManus, British representative on the same committee, discussed how British Communists could promote revolution through acts of sedition.

It is still debated whether or not this letter was faked. Certainly, Sir Vernon thought it was real, and spent many years beyond 1924 focused on this supposed Communist threat. Sir Vernon Kell was famously asthmatic, and I have tried to include a reference to this here.

A Note on St Margaret's Bay, Kent, and Accompanying Photographs

This is a location I return to often, in my writing, in my dreams, in reality. I suppose I have a fascination with the place, as much for its being a kind of frontier, as for the drama and history it has witnessed.

This quiet, tiny, hidden beach near Dover, Kent has proved constant fodder and inspiration for writers. Notably, Noel Coward lived there in the 1940s, later selling his house to Ian Fleming (of James Bond fame), who then lived there in the 1950s, and who based *Moonraker* there. The very steep chalk cliffs which surround the shingle bay are the closest part of England to France (a distance of 20 miles by sea).

Famous throughout history as a focus for smuggling, it is still a hot-spot for the smuggling trade today. In the twentieth century it became a focus for bombing (it was the last place where bombs were dropped at the end of World War One) and as being a fortified stronghold against invasion (World War Two).

Always a popular local seaside destination, the 1920s

were a boom time for St Margaret's Bay, with the Bay Hotel (on the beach itself) and the Granville Hotel (up on the cliff) both flourishing, taking trade from the rich Londoners coming down at the weekends. By the time of this novel it had a growing reputation as being a spot favoured by London's fashionable and famous people *du jour*. Its real heyday came later though, in the 1930s, when film stars, writers and their friends flocked to the beach.

A good online guide I can recommend is: https://www.dovermuseum.co.uk

The cottage Noel Coward owned, named White Cliffs (with its two attendant cottages) can still be viewed far down on the beach in the bay, tucked almost under the cliffs (although please note it is private property). At the time this novel is set, White Cliffs had not yet been built.

What I have added/altered

While the brand-new glass art-deco house belonging to my Fashion Designer couple (known in the story here as White Shaw) is completely fictional, I have borrowed the physical location from Noel Coward's cottage, White Cliffs. It would therefore have been built almost right next to the Bay Bungalow and very near to the Bay Hotel, in an unbroken line with the other properties of 'the village on the beach'. (See **Photograph Number One** and **Photograph Number Two**, below.)

The place where Elsie Moncrieff goes to meet her stranger in the Prologue, at Ness Point, is real enough (see **Photograph Numbers Three** and **Four**) but it was highly unlikely to ever have had a bench placed up there in such a dangerous spot.

Another detail I have invented is the 5th November bonfire set up outside the Bay Hotel, on the gravel road, which to the best of my knowledge never occurred, here or elsewhere in St Margaret's Bay during this period.

Photographs

(**All featured Photographs are the property of the St Margaret's History Society, with whom copyright resides. They are reproduced here by mutual agreement.**)

1. **View of the North End of the Bay, 1920s.** (Shows the full vista of the 'village on the beach', with the Bay Bungalow on the furthest right, with the Bay Hotel and fishermen's cottages immediately next to it.)

164 – Dover Patrol Memorial, St. Margaret's Bay.

2. **A Postcard from 1908 of the 'Bay Bungalow'.** (This was available to rent for holiday makers, and was owned by the Bay Hotel, and the text on the postcard, from an unknown writer reads: *'Dear Molly, I hope you are enjoying yourself. This place is rather horrid and dull. The bays (sic) prawn and bathe but I don't like either prawning or bathing here much. I look through the telescope at every ship that passes. Two battleships have passed as well as several cruisers.'* [Continues on the other side of the postcard.] *'We often see liners. Through the telescope you can see the faces of the people on board quite clearly. This is a photo of our house here. Not a good one I am afraid.'*)

3. A View Towards Ness Point, 1926.

4. The View from Ness Point, 1925.

* * * *

Acknowledgements

I would like to thank Christine Waterman of the St Margaret's History Society for her help in replying to my queries about the history of St Margaret's Bay in the 1920s, and for pointing me towards the extensive treasure-trove that is the St Margaret's History Society archive (see their website: https://www.stmargaretshistory.org.uk). Thank you to them too for agreeing to my use of their photographs (in the previous section).

Needless to say, this is a novel and I have used the historical reality and geography by way of an inspiring *background*. Therefore, there are differences between fiction and the reality. I have tried to point these out in my notes (above). It goes without saying that any historical mistakes are mine and mine alone.

Thank you to Geraldine for her help with the Glaswegian dialect, and to Katia for the Russian.

I am grateful to all members of my family for accompanying me on several trips to St Margaret's Bay, in good weather and in bad, in sunshine and in snow, at high tide, and at low.

And a huge thank you to all my readers, for your lovely words and encouragement. If Posie Parker ever needed champions, she has surely found them in you.

Thank you for joining Posie Parker and her friends.

Enjoyed *Murder on the White Cliffs* (A Posie Parker Mystery #8)? Here's what you can do next.

If you have a tiny moment to spare, I would really appreciate a short review on the page where you bought the book. Your help in spreading the word about the series is invaluable and really appreciated, and reviews make a big difference to helping new readers find the series.

Posie's other cases are available in e-book and paperback formats from Amazon, as well as in Audiobook format. You can find all of the other books, available for purchase, listed here in chronological order:

http://www.amazon.com/L.B.-Hathaway/e/
B00LDXGKE8

and

http://www.amazon.co.uk/L.B.-Hathaway/e/
B00LDXGKE8

You can sign up to be notified of new releases, pre-release specials, free short stories and the chance to win Amazon gift-vouchers here:

http://www.lbhathaway.com/contact/newsletter/

About the Author

Cambridge-educated, British-born L.B. Hathaway writes historical fiction. She worked as a lawyer at Lincoln's Inn in London for almost a decade before becoming a full-time writer. She is a lifelong fan of detective novels set in the Golden Age of Crime, and is an ardent Agatha Christie devotee.

Her other interests, in no particular order, are: very fast downhill skiing, theatre-going, drinking strong tea, Tudor history, exploring castles and generally trying to cram as much into life as possible. She lives in Switzerland with her husband and young family.

The Posie Parker series of cosy crime novels span the 1920s. They each combine a core central mystery, an exploration of the reckless glamour of the age and a feisty protagonist who you would love to have as your best friend.

To find out more and for news of new releases and giveaways, go to:
  http://www.lbhathaway.com

Connect with L.B. Hathaway online:
  (e) mailto:author@lbhathaway.com
  (t) @LbHathaway
  (f) https://www.facebook.com/
  pages/L-B-Hathaway-books/1423516601228019
  (Goodreads) http://www.goodreads.com/author/
  show/8339051.L_B_Hathaway

Made in the USA
Monee, IL
28 December 2021

87410254R00236